THE FIVE IMPOSSIBLE TASKS OF

Eden Smith

by
Tom Llewellyn

HOLIDAY HOUSE   NEW YORK

Library of Congress Cataloging-in-Publication Data is available.

ISBN: 978-0-8234-5312-2 (hardcover)

Dedication TK

CONTENTS

PART I

Hammer

THE GENEALOGY OF EDEN SMITH

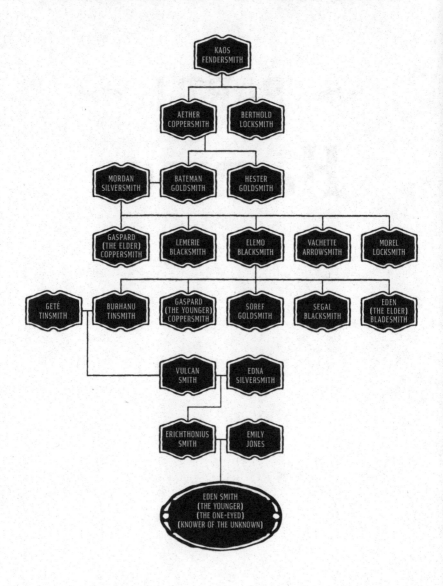

I

The Ancestors

This is the genealogy of Eden Smith.

Kaos Fendersmith, who died performing the Task of Dishes, was the father of Berthold Locksmith, who died from the Task of the Steel Birds, and Aether Coppersmith.

Aether, who died from the Task of the Rats, was the father of Hester Goldsmith and her brother Bateman. Hester, who failed at the Task of Dishes, but survived, only to be banished, was the sister-in-law of Mordan Silversmith.

Mordan, who completed the Task of Dishes but died from the Task of Mrs. Gunsmith's Girdle, was the mother of five children: Elemo Blacksmith; his sister, Lemerie, who caught the rats; his stepbrothers, Gaspard (the Elder) Coppersmith and Vachette Arrowsmith; and his stepsister, Morel Locksmith.

Elemo, who was pecked to death by the steel birds, was the father of Burhanu Tinsmith; his brothers, Gaspard (the Younger) and Soref Goldsmith; and his sisters, Segal Goldsmith and Eden (the Elder) Bladesmith, who stole the girdle.

Burhanu, who nearly captured the birds but then died in the attempt, was the husband of Geté and the father of Vulcan Smith.

Vulcan was the father of Erichthonius, whom everyone called Eric. Eric, who was squashed by a meteor along with his wife, Emily Jones, was the father of Eden Smith, who later generations would call Eden the Younger; Eden the One-Eyed; and Eden, Knower of the Unknown.

Eden Smith attempted all five of the Tasks that had killed so many of her ancestors. She is the hero of this story. Like all great heroes, her family is a train wreck.

II

In Which Eden's Parents Are Squashed and She Enters the Guildhall

The generations from Kaos to Eden were messy from beginning to end. So it's no surprise that Vulcan Smith and Eric Smith—father and son—added to the mess in the form of a nasty fight. They spoke cruel words to each other—the m-word and the f-word— *manufacturer* and *factory*. They swung hammers and blowtorches, anvils and tongs. Eric stomped out of the Guildhall of Smiths and never came back. He started his own foundry and married a woman named Emily Jones—a Jones!—which made Vulcan even angrier. But Eric and Emily were in love. They soon had a daughter and named her Eden.

Exactly seven years later, Eden was waiting at home on her birthday, supervised by a certain Ms. Hathaway, the vice president of Titan Foundry and an early party guest, while her parents drove to the bakery to pick up her favorite kind of cake. Eden's favorite kind was chocolate cake with chocolate frosting. On the way back, Eden's father had a sudden impulse to buy Eden one more present—a live orchid that Eden had spotted at the gift shop in the conservatory at Wright Park, in Tacoma, Washington, U.S.A. Eden's parents were admiring the philodendrons as they exited the shop when a meteorite fell out of the sky and squashed them dead. It also shattered all the windows in the conservatory, ruined most of the cake, and crushed a very nice lemon tree.

Life is hard, but unfair.

When Eden heard a knock on the door, she rushed past Ms. Hathaway to open it. She wanted to see her cake. She wanted to see her presents. She wanted to see her parents.

Instead, a woman with pale white skin and a black mole above her lip stood in the doorway. "Your parents are dead," said the woman. "They've been squashed. I am from The State. The law dictates that you must go live with your nearest relative, if we can find one. Pack your bags."

After a full ten seconds, Eden gasped in enough breath to manage a question. "Where are we going?"

"I said, *pack your bags*." From the corner of her mouth, the woman with the black mole wiped off something that Eden thought looked suspiciously like chocolate frosting.

Ms. Hathaway, who'd followed Eden to the door, proclaimed that Eden would only leave over her dead body, then pulled out her cell phone and began speaking to someone about *company shares* and something called *controlling interest*. While Ms. Hathaway talked, the woman with the black mole tapped her foot as Eden packed. Eden felt panicked. She wanted more time. She wanted to push both these women outside and lock the door. She wanted her mom and dad. Instead, she managed to throw a few random clothes and a framed family photo into one tiny suitcase before she was dragged out of the only home she had ever known and into a car.

Before Eden had her seat belt buckled, the car raced away and squealed around corners, finally screeching to a halt in a strange neighborhood. Eden was hurried into a little house bustling with wide-eyed children of all ages. "A temporary situation, until a relative is located," said the woman with the black mole, already turning toward the door. "Do you know of any relatives? Your mother's parents, perhaps?"

"Mom didn't have any relatives."

"How about your father? Any aunts or uncles?"

"I think he was an only child."

"What about his parents? A grandmother or grandfather, perhaps?"

Eden shrugged, feeling numb. "Dad never talked about his family."

"This is problematic." The woman handed Eden a small, dented cardboard box. "Here. I believe this is for you."

Eden was assigned a cot in a row of cots. She sat on her cot. It squeaked. She hugged the cardboard box to her chest. At first, she couldn't bring herself to open it. When she finally did, she found the orchid plant in a little pot. Its main stem was broken off, just a few inches above the surface of the soil.

There was no funeral. Once a day, the woman with the black mole charged into the tiny house and told Eden no relative had been found, then marched out again.

"What happens," said Eden, "if they don't find any?"

"They never found any of mine," said the wide-eyed girl lying on the cot next to her.

"And how long have you been here?" asked Eden.

"Which time?" asked the girl. "This time, or the other times?"

"I do not like the sound of *that*," said Eden.

One morning, Eden awoke and realized it had been two weeks since her parents had died. She'd already been forced to change schools and leave her friends behind. She'd met with a tired school counselor and had received both pitying and suspicious looks from the parents of her new classmates. She hadn't cried a single tear. She was afraid that if she started, she wouldn't be able to stop.

"Pack your bags again," said the woman with the black mole as she burst into the orphanage that morning. She piled Eden into her car and drove her to a foster home. A purple-haired woman named Sienna ran the home. Eden wondered if Sienna would be her new mother, but two weeks later, she was moved to another foster home in a different school district. This home had three other children in it. Eden was just starting to remember their names when she was moved again, back to the squeaky cot at the orphanage for a week, and then onto another foster home and another new school.

At her fourth home in six months, Ms. Hathaway visited Eden, on a Thursday afternoon. "You'll be relieved to know that Titan Foundry is operating just fine," said Ms. Hathaway with a thin smile. "It's as if your father had never left."

"How long do I have to stay here?" said Eden. "What happens to the foundry now? Could I live there?"

Ms. Hathaway, whose hair reminded Eden of a soldier's helmet and who always dressed in white, pursed her lips, as if she had just bitten into an unripe banana. "Your father had no will. I was surprised, too. But he was a young man. He probably believed he had years to live before he needed to worry about such things. He probably assumed that if he died, his wife would still be around. But, as you know, she is not." Ms. Hathaway patted Eden's hand. "Therefore, company bylaws state that his share of the foundry be distributed to the rest of the stockholders, all neat and tidy. So there's not a thing for you to worry about. Just stay focused on doing well in school and making lots of friends. Oh, and I do need your signature, right here." Ms. Hathaway pointed toward a line on the bottom of a piece of paper filled with words.

"What is it?"

"Just legal mumbo jumbo. Read it if you like."

"I'm seven and a half," said Eden. "I'm pretty sure this is above my reading level."

"Sign, please."

Eden shrugged and scrawled her name. Ms. Hathaway tucked the paper into her purse and walked toward the door, then turned back toward Eden. "I believe this concludes our business." Ms. Hathaway and her white shoes scuttled away and never came back.

School and friends? thought Eden. *How can I focus on school and friends when I change schools and neighborhoods every six weeks?*

Some of the foster homes were nice. One had a hot tub that didn't get very hot. Using a butter knife for a screwdriver, Eden removed the front panel of the hot tub, reconnected a loose wire on the heating element, and put it all back together. It worked perfectly then.

The old woman who ran that home smiled at Eden. "Thank you, Edie."

"It's Eden."

"Well, whatever your name is, you've certainly got a knack for tinkering."

"Does that mean I get to stay here now?" asked Eden. The old woman smiled but didn't answer. Seven days later, the woman with the black mole showed up again.

"Pack your bags," said the woman.

Eden frowned. "I only have one bag, you know. So you should say *bag*. Pack your *bag*."

The woman frowned. "Don't be smart."

Some homes were horrible. One particularly smelly home had nothing to eat but dry toast. The woman who ran it allowed chickens inside the house, but never offered Eden an egg.

After many months, it stopped mattering to Eden if a new home was good or bad. She knew she'd move soon, so she never got too attached to the nice homes or too upset about the bad ones. She never cried. And she learned that she needed to look after herself, because no one else seemed fully invested in taking care of her. She liked things clean, so she learned how to wash her own clothes. She hated being hungry, so she learned how to prepare simple meals, like peanut butter sandwiches and macaroni and cheese, when her caregiver was too busy or forgot. If there were leftovers at dinner, she learned how to sneak the food into her napkin and tuck it into her pocket for later, so she wouldn't get so hungry. She wondered what it would be like to have a real, permanent family again. She wondered what it would be like to have a friend for more than a few weeks.

Each time she moved to a new home, Eden would unpack her suitcase of clothes and set the photo of her parents next to her bed. She'd kiss the tip of her finger and press it on the glass that covered the photo. Next to the photo, she'd put the little pot with the broken orchid plant. The orchid never grew.

One time, when she was back at the orphanage in the little

house, she ran into the wide-eyed girl she'd met there before. The girl asked Eden why she carried around the pot. "It's an orchid," said Eden. "Orchids are the most beautiful flowers in the world. My parents got it for me, just before they died."

"It's not beautiful," said the girl. "It's just dirt."

Eden grimaced. "Do you ever say anything even the least bit cheerful?"

But she had to concede the truth as she stared at the pot of dirt. There was no life in it. Why did she keep it? She stared at her battered suitcase. All it contained were clothes. If they'd told her—if that woman with the black mole had told her that she would never be going home again—she would have packed more than just clothes. She would have taken more things to help her remember her parents, like one of her father's favorite tools or one of her mother's favorite books. Now all she had to remember of her parents was an old photo and a pot of dirt. She longed for more.

Eden sat on her cot. It squeaked. It always squeaked. But this time, the squeak made her so angry that she tore the blankets and mattress off the cot. She looked at the springs underneath, pushing on each one until she found the spring that was making the noise. She noticed that its mounting screws were loose. She looked for a screwdriver, but couldn't find one, so she found a butter knife in the kitchen and used it to tighten the screws. She borrowed a bottle of vegetable oil and rubbed a bit of it on the spring. She pushed the spring again. It was quiet. Eden put the cot back together and stood on it with her arms crossed, still feeling angry, but a bit more satisfied. The wide-eyed girl stared at her without speaking.

As the years went by, dozens more foster homes and new schools went by along with them. Eden watched her classmates join soccer teams and text each other on cell phones and go to sleepovers. She wondered what it would be like to own a cell phone or to sleep at a friend's house. One time she found a broken cell phone on the sidewalk. Using a borrowed butter knife again, she pried off the back and tinkered with the tiny circuits until the phone glowed back to life. It only made her realize she had no one to call. She brought the phone to school the next day to show her classmates, but by then the battery had died and Eden had no way to charge it.

Six months after her thirteenth birthday, on September 21, the first day of autumn, Eden was temporarily moved back to the orphanage. At eleven o'clock the same day, the woman with the black mole rushed in.

"I have news," said the woman. "I finally have news."

"Good news or bad news?" said Eden, her mouth set in a straight line.

"Maybe—just maybe–I can finally close this never-ending case. I've found your grandfather. Your father's father."

Eden's mouth fell open. A grandfather meant family. Family could mean a home. A home could mean belonging somewhere. She felt her heartbeat accelerate.

"A grandfather?" said Eden. "I—I thought all my grandparents were dead. How come I've never even met him?"

"He wasn't easy to locate," said the woman with the black mole. "He wasn't in any of the usual government records. His address was unlisted. He is, I admit, a bit of a mystery. But I found him. I looked and I looked and I finally found him. An actual, honest-to-goodness relative of yours."

"Can I see him?" As Eden said the words, her stomach churned. Her longing for family—she'd pushed it so far down. But here was a chance.

"Yes. Today. His name is Vulcan Smith. Pack your bags. Your *bag*. Hopefully for the last time." The woman with the black mole loaded Eden into her car and raced across the city of Tacoma to a stone building. On the front lawn was a sign that read Guildhall of Smiths Local 292. The woman handed Eden a letter-sized envelope.

"Now what?" said Eden.

"Now you go inside," said the woman, "and live with your grandfather." She nodded at the envelope. "There's a bit of paperwork in there. As soon as your grandpa enrolls you in school, fill out the form and mail it back to me. My card is in there as well. If you need anything, please hesitate to call."

Eden wondered what her grandfather would be like. Would he tell her stories? Would he let her have sleepovers? This building was huge and fancy. Did that mean he was rich? Did he at least have enough money so she could stay with him forever? How old was he? Did he look like her? Did he look like her father?

"Hurry up," said the woman. "I'm late for my other appointments."

Eden took a deep breath and slid out of the car with her suitcase and her broken orchid. The vehicle squealed away.

The Guildhall of Smiths sat on North Eye Street, at the corner of North 10th. It was a circular building of stone and steel that stood four stories tall above ground. It had a green copper roof and a wide porch ringed by green copper columns. Around the building, the manicured lawn was dotted with bronze statues of men and women wielding hammers, swords, and other objects Eden didn't recognize.

Eden held her suitcase tightly against her chest and crossed the porch. Above a black iron door, in silver scrollwork, ran the words Safety First. Eden knocked.

The huge door opened a crack. A man's face peeked out—a wide, rough, reddish face, marked with old scars and wrinkles. He had thin black hair, slicked straight back. "Yeah?"

"My name is Eden. I'm supposed to be moving in here today."

"I don't think so." The door closed.

She knocked again. "I'm Eden. Eden Smith."

"So you're a Smith," said the man. "Congratulations."

"I'm supposed to be—"

"You already told me. You're supposed to be moving in here today. But that ain't gonna happen because this is a place for, you know, old people. An old folks' home. No kids, except during visiting hours between two and four. Come back then."

"No kids? That can't be right. Can't I just wait inside?" Eden tried to peek over the man's shoulder.

"Sorry. It's against the rules to let visitors in before visiting hours." He closed the door.

Eden knocked again. The man yanked the door open. "Listen—"

"Can you at least tell me what time it is now?" said Eden.

The man pulled out a silver pocket watch. "A couple minutes before noon. Come back in two hours." He closed the door.

Eden sat on a wrought-iron bench next to the door. The man at the door had said the building was an old folks' home, but that made no sense. Today, she was going to meet her grandfather for the first time. He was going to fix everything and she was going to stay with him. She set down her orchid, opened her suitcase, and took out the photo of her mother and father. She spoke to the photograph: "I'm mad at you two. Why didn't you ever introduce me to this grandfather before? Is something wrong with him? Is there some horrible reason you never brought me to visit?" Their faces smiled out at her in silence. Eden almost started crying, but bit her lip and willed the tears away, because for the first time in years, she had a glimmer of hope. She just might finally have a home again, if she could ever get inside it.

When she felt enough time had passed, Eden knocked on the front door again. "Now what time is it?"

"One-oh-five," said the man. "You still got almost an hour. Who are you here to see, anyway?"

"My grandpa. I'm moving in with him." Eden ached for her words to be true.

"What's his name?"

Eden pulled out the envelope the woman with the black mole had given her and began to open it.

"You don't know your grandfather's name?" said the man.

"I've never met him."

"Well, what's your dad's name?"

"Eric Smith. He owns—he owned the Titan Foundry."

The man stared, unblinking. "Say that again."

"What part?"

"Who your dad is."

"Eric—Erichthonius Smith."

The man stared again. "And remind me of your name—Edie?"

"Eden. Like the garden. Of *Eden*."

The man stepped outside and eased the front door closed behind him. He wore a brown suit, a yellow tie, and too much cologne. He said, "If your old man is Erichthonius, then your grandfather is Vulcan."

Eden nodded. "That's the name. Vulcan Smith."

"How'd you happen to show up today of all days?"

"A lady from The State dropped me off. She told me I was living here."

"With Vulcan? Where're your mom and dad?"

"Dead."

"Dead? Eric is dead?" The big man pulled a huge yellow handkerchief from his pocket and mopped his face.

"You don't look so good," said Eden.

"I don't feel so good, either. Give me a second....Whew. Okay. I'm Eugene, by the way. Eugene Tinker." He checked his silver pocket watch again. "We'll have to hurry. Come on." He pulled Eden inside the entryway of the Guildhall of Smiths.

III

In Which Eden Sees the Prisoner

Some visitors—emotional types—were known to cry when they first saw Humble Gallery, the entry to the Guildhall of Smiths. Eden did not.

"Stay here," said Eugene. "I'll be right back." He crossed the gallery and slipped through a set of brass double doors.

The inside of the building smelled like iron and sweat. Eden wrinkled her nose and looked around. Every square inch of Humble Gallery shone. A stairway stretched up two full stories, each stair twenty feet wide. The steps were made from a shiny, pinkish metal, the color of a new penny. The handrails were more golden in color, but too bright for gold. The spindles of the railing were a black metal that looked old but strong. The ceiling was covered in pressed silver tiles. The window casings were silver, too. Every surface reflected the blinding lights that came from a silver chandelier the size of a merry-go-round. Eden wanted to touch everything, to see if it all felt as cold as it looked.

On one wall, three mosaics stretched to the ceiling. The images, formed of inlaid gold, silver, and rose-colored metal, looked like they told some sort of story—a hunched, crooked man falling through the air, a woman wearing a crown and trapped in a chair, lots of fire and lots of hammers. The last scene showed the hunched man riding a horse.

In the center of the room stood a twenty-foot-tall black metal column. One side was adorned with metal flowers and vines. The other side was engraved with the following words:

> Blade and ring and lock and wire.
> The work of hammer, forge, and fire.
> Golden mornings, silver songs,
> The iron, the steel, the work of tongs.
> Now this Guild, now this hall,
> Now you stand within these walls.
> Now eleven smiths we bring:
> Precious on the heads of kings,
> Standing 'tween the world and you,
> Holding flame and smoke and flue,
> Sending spark and forming kettle,
> Coating, blending, shining metal,
> Serving supper, setting place,
> Cutting throat and shaving face,
> Best of friend to fight your foe,
> Guarding treasure, causing woe.
> Unsmith, unstill, unbroken, untame.
> Slay the wolf and eat the name.

Just as Eden finished reading, a tall, thin old man in black robes burst from a doorway under the stairs. A silver letter U hung from a chain around his neck. "Eugene, it's time. Eugene? Where is that bumbling fool of a tinker?" He spotted Eden and peered down a long, narrow nose at her. "Who are you and what are you doing here?"

"I'm here to see my grandfather."

"Not today. No visitors today." He stopped and stared closer at Eden. "Who is your grandfather?"

"Vulcan Smith."

The thin man paused. "Did you say Vulcan Smith?"

Eden nodded.

"Does he know you're here? Did he send for you? Of course he did. To play on our sympathies. It won't work."

Eden didn't understand what the man was talking about, but she knew she didn't like him. She felt as if a spider had just crawled onto the back of her hand and she didn't know if it was poisonous or not. Then Eugene appeared through the same door under the stairs. He frowned when he saw the tall, thin man.

"There you are, you bumbling fool," said the tall man. "Did you know about this—this girl coming here?"

Eugene stepped to Eden's side and put a broad hand on her shoulder. "Edie's just a little thing, Mr. Pewtersmith. The State dropped her off. Her parents died and Vulcan's her only living relative."

"Her parents? So her father would be…" His voice trailed off. "And Vulcan doesn't know?"

"I'm sure he doesn't, Mr. Pewtersmith."

Mr. Pewtersmith's lips slowly spread into a smile, but the smile made Eden's mouth go dry. "In that case, Vulcan will be delighted to see her, today of all days. Come along, Eugene. And come along—your name again is?"

"Eden. Not Edie. Eden Smith."

"And when is the last time you've seen your grandfather?"

"Never," she said. "I thought he was dead."

"He's alive enough." He frowned at her. "It's peculiar that you should arrive just at this time."

"Why? What's going on?"

Eugene pulled out his yellow hankie and mopped his face. He squeezed Eden's shoulder. "I ain't had a chance to tell her what's happening, Mr. Pewtersmith."

Mr. Pewtersmith smiled. "Well, my dear, we're having a bit of a ceremony for your grandfather today."

The last thing Eden wanted to do was go to any kind of a ceremony. She just wanted to find this grandfather of hers, go to his apartment, and curl up on a comfortable chair. In the movies she'd seen, grandfathers always had comfortable chairs. She wanted to wrap herself up in a blanket there and forget about everything for an hour or two. But she supposed a ceremony sounded like a good sign—it meant her grandpa must be someone worth celebrating.

Eugene said, "Come on now, sir. There's no need for that. She's just a little girl."

Mr. Pewtersmith's eyes were gray, matching his gray skin, the thick gray hair on his head, and the tiny line of a gray mustache on his lip. He stared down at Eden.

Eden stared back, trying hard to hold his gaze. "I'm thirteen. And a half."

Mr. Pewtersmith sniffed. "At thirteen, I was already working as an apprentice. You'll do what you're told. You'll watch."

"Let me at least explain to her what's going on," Eugene said. "Give her a chance to leave, if she wants."

"There'll be no chances given today," said Mr. Pewtersmith. "Come along." He marched Eden across Humble Gallery. He paused at the set of brass double doors. A small sign above the doors said Main Lodge. Mr. Pewtersmith checked his reflection in the surface of the doors. He fixed one stray hair, then pushed Eden through before she had time to ask Eugene what he meant.

Main Lodge was crowded with elderly men and women. The oldest ones—with wrinkled skin and curving backs—sat hunched over in chairs. The younger ones—who looked to be in their seventies and eighties—stood against the back wall, some standing on their own and others with the support of walkers and canes. Eden remembered that Eugene had called this an *old folks' home*, but surely there were at least a few young people here, weren't there? She couldn't be the only child in here, could she?

A stage stood at the opposite side of the room. On the rear wall of the stage was a metal bas-relief panel depicting a huge black anvil, with a silver hammer striking it. Golden lightning bolts shot out of the spot where the hammer struck. The room buzzed with murmurs. Every eye watched Mr. Pewtersmith as he marched with Eden to the stage in front. He gathered his black robes about his ankles and pointed to the nearest seat in the front row.

"You there, Darcy Arrowsmith, go sit somewhere else."

The woman sitting there whined, "But I've been here since breakfast waiting for the show to begin."

"It's not a show, Darcy Arrowsmith. I need your seat. Move." Darcy grumbled as she tottered away. Mr. Pewtersmith told Eden to sit there, right in front, but Eden remained standing until Darcy Arrowsmith was out of sight. When Eden finally obeyed, Pewtersmith disappeared through a door on the side of the stage.

A few seconds later, Mr. Pewtersmith and eight other elderly people marched onto the stage single file, each carrying or dragging a chair. Eden's eyes darted back and forth as she searched each of them for a family resemblance. But none had her shade of brown skin, her high forehead, or her curly black hair.

The group on stage arranged their chairs. Each chair was made of a different kind of metal. A bearish, bearded man sat in the center. His body scarcely fit in his black metal chair, even though the chair was twice as wide as those on either side. He wore a heavy leather apron. The tanned skin of his forearms was smudged with soot. From his belt hung a short-handled sledgehammer—the head of the hammer the size of a cinder block. The man stood and spoke in a booming voice. "We are here today to consider the status of Vulcan Smith." When she heard the mention of her grandfather's name, Eden scanned the crowd for someone who looked like her—someone who seemed like the guest of honor for this gathering.

The huge man continued. "I, Robert Blacksmith, am chair of this council. I represent iron and steel. And who represents the richness of gold?"

A woman with dark brown skin and black hair streaked with silver rose from a golden stool. She stood with a stoop, as if the gold earrings and chains that hung from her ears and neck weighed her down. She said, "I do. Maureen Goldsmith."

Robert Blacksmith nodded. "And who represents the sharpness of swords?" No one answered. The bearded man repeated the

17

question more loudly. "WHO represents the sharpness of swords?" Still no answer. Maureen leaned over to the tiny woman sitting in a chair made of sword blades. "Helena, it's your turn."

"What?" said the woman.

"It's your turn," said Maureen. "Robert called your name."

"My name? Now?"

"Yes, now."

"Oh!" She stood up. She was so short that she was taller sitting in her chair than she was standing on the floor. Her pale cheeks reddened as she said, "Helena Bladesmith. Present."

Robert Blacksmith sighed, then called for representatives for tin, for copper, for guns, and for silver. Each answered in turn and each stood before his or her chair.

Robert Blacksmith said, "And who represents the unsmiths? The movement of machinists?"

"That would be me," said a bent man in a low metal wheelchair. "Anit Irenya." His wrinkled skin was brown and his hair was wavy and dark. Anit pulled a lever on his armrest and the seat of the chair began to rise until Anit sat above all the other chairs. He smiled and pulled another lever. The chair rolled toward the audience.

"Are you done?" said Robert.

"No," said Anit. He pulled another lever and his chair began to spin. As it spun, silver coins sprayed out and fell tinkling to the stage. The crowd applauded and the chair returned to its original position. "Now I am done."

"This is not the day for such folly, Anit," said Robert Blacksmith. "Who represents the table and the places set?"

Mr. Pewtersmith stood before his chair of dull, silver metal. The back of the chair was made to resemble a fan of peacock feathers. Mr. Pewtersmith scowled at the audience as he touched his necklace and the silver letter U that hung from it. "I do. Uriah Pewtersmith."

Eden didn't care about any of this. She wanted to see her grandfather. If they were here to celebrate him, couldn't they skip the names and get to it?

Robert Blacksmith said, "Council, are you ready to cast sentence?"

The councilmembers nodded.

"Then bring in the prisoner."

Eugene disappeared behind the curtain. A few seconds later, he returned followed by a small man. The small man walked in a jerky fashion, with a step and a clunk. His left leg stopped at the knee. From the knee to the floor was a shiny metal post.

Eden recognized the prisoner instantly. It was her grandfather. It was Vulcan Smith.

IV

The Sentence

For years, Eden's world had felt cracked, as if a fracture separated the time before and the time after her parents' death. Now she felt like her world was shattering into pieces. She'd already lost both her parents. She'd spent years moving from one foster home to another. Now a relative had been found—a grandfather. She was supposed to live with him, but this grandfather seemed to be some sort of criminal. What had he done? What kind of man was he? And if he was a prisoner, what would happen to her? Where would she go? Back to the orphanage? Back to all the foster homes? She didn't think she could bear it.

She stared at Vulcan. He had brown skin and brown eyes like Eden and curly hair like her, although her curls were long, loose, and black and his were short and white. He had a high forehead like hers and just the slightest curve to his nose, like hers. He looked like an older, smaller version of her father. Eden guessed that Vulcan couldn't be much more than five foot five and couldn't have weighed more than one hundred and thirty pounds. He certainly didn't look rich. He wore a faded blue work shirt, worn khaki pants, and an old boot on his one foot. They'd introduced him as *the prisoner.*

Robert Blacksmith said, "Vulcan Smith, you've been convicted of failure to act as a smith and of failure in your daily duties—"

"Don't forget sabotage!" shouted Mr. Pewtersmith.

"—and of sabotaging a fellow smith. Do you have anything to say before we cast sentence?"

"Just that Pewtersmith is a nincompoop. But you already know that." Laughter rippled through the crowd. Even Eden smiled. Maybe this wasn't so serious, after all. Vulcan stood straight and stared Mr. Pewtersmith dead in the eye. "But if you're going to put this fool's interests over mine, then by Saint Dunstan's beard, at least admit that you're dooming me. Admit that you're sentencing me to die. Or worse."

Mr. Pewtersmith sneered. "You did this to yourself. You should have seen this coming."

"I've seen it coming my whole life," muttered Vulcan.

Robert held up a huge hand. "Vulcan, perhaps if you were to apologize. And just start performing some of the simple chores the rest of us do. The basics. How long has it been since you've made your daily dish?"

"No!" spat Mr. Pewtersmith. "We're well past that point. He's had chance after chance. He must be sentenced."

Vulcan squinted at the Council. "Just because I'm not willing to follow some foolish rules, you're condemning the greatest smith who ever lived. All of you know it. Robert, you know it. The councilmembers know it. And you, Pewtersmith, you know it most of all. That's why you've had it in for me your whole life. But you all know what's happening. You know that Pewtersmith is just trying to trick me into doing the Five Tasks—"

Eden heard a gasp from the crowd.

"That's quite enough!" said Mr. Pewtersmith. "We're not here to talk about the You-Know-Whats. We're here to hand down a sentence. Blacksmith, as head of the Council, what's it to be?"

Robert sighed. "Vulcan, my hands are tied."

"Judgment day," whispered Vulcan. "Just do it, Robert."

Robert's huge shoulders sagged. He walked behind Vulcan, then faced the crowd. "Vulcan Smith, you are guilty of the charges. You shall be stripped of your title of Master Smith, Eleventh Level."

Mr. Pewtersmith interrupted. "And, as the rules state, you shall be confined to quarters for the rest of your life." He smiled. "Meaning, you can't leave your room."

"My *rooms*, you mean. Rather stay in my rooms, anyway," said Vulcan. "Least while I'm still alive."

"We'll see how long you stay in them." Mr. Pewtersmith's voice sounded wet. "We'll see how long you manage to remain anywhere in this Guildhall."

"I'm so sorry, Vulcan," said Maureen Goldsmith. "Perhaps death—or worse than death—won't result this time."

Mr. Pewtersmith continued. "Council, as of this moment, the prisoner is officially sentenced. He is to be confined to quarters, immediately, with all the usual terms and conditions."

Vulcan snorted. "*Terms and conditions.* We all know he's talking about the Tasks." At that moment, Vulcan noticed Eden. Their eyes met. He said, "Who's that kid right there?"

Mr. Pewtersmith smiled. "You don't recognize your own granddaughter?"

Eden stared as Vulcan's confused eyes filled with tears, just for half a second, then watched as he blinked the tears back. He cleared his throat. "No one I know. Get on with it."

Eden willed back tears of her own. Mr. Pewtersmith's smile vanished. "The sentence is passed. House arrest with all the usual terms and conditions, for the rest of your life. Eugene, you bumbling fool, escort the prisoner out of the hall."

V

Subbasement Seven, Room K-Minus-One

Eden thought this all had to be some kind of mistake. She kept expecting the woman with the black mole to run in and say, "There's been a terrible misunderstanding. This man isn't your grandfather. Let me take you to your real one."

The woman didn't come. The room was emptying. Eden jumped to her feet and followed Eugene and Vulcan out of the hall, carrying her suitcase and her broken orchid as she followed Vulcan's clunking, uneven gait. They were escorted by two young men in bright blue suit jackets. Before they reached the doors, two tiny old ladies hurried up to the group. The women were no taller than Eden's shoulders. Both wore flowered dresses. Both had pinkish-white skin. One had blonde hair and the other had white. The blonde woman wore thick, oversized glasses and walked with a silver cane etched with birds and flowers. The white-haired woman had cat-eye glasses and carried a blue porcelain teacup in a shaky hand.

"You're the granddaughter," said the blonde woman, as if Eden needed to be told who she was. "Come with us, dearie. And stay close." The blonde woman pointed at Vulcan with her cane. "We'll just accompany you, Vulcan. We'd like to see you properly settled."

"Not necessary, sisters," said Vulcan.

Eugene sighed. "There's no sense in arguing with them, Vulc. They'll just tag along anyway."

Vulcan stared at Eden and muttered a curse word under his breath. Eugene led them all to a set of ornate brass elevator doors. He pushed a button set into a metal plate covered in scrollwork.

The brass elevator doors opened to a pale, young, red-haired man in a tan suit, red bow tie, and red-and-tan pillbox hat. He yanked open an accordion gate and let them in. "What floor, Vulcan?"

"My floor, Buzz."

"Your new one or your old one?"

Vulcan glared at Buzz. "What in Saint Dunstan is that supposed to mean? Just take me to the third floor."

"Third it is." Buzz pulled a brass lever. The elevator hummed upward. Beyond the bars of the elevator cage, Eden could see the walls of the elevator shaft rushing by. She shifted her gaze back to her grandfather.

"What are you looking at?" Vulcan said.

"You."

"Why?"

"Because I've never had a grandfather before. But I imagined you in my mind, my whole life, I think."

"And?"

"You seem kind of, well, worn out. I thought you'd be younger. And more handsome. And I hoped you'd maybe be happy to see me. Or at least be nicer to me, after what I've been through."

Vulcan grunted. "What *you've* been through? Were you paying attention in there?"

"Yes."

"Then you know life is hard for everyone. Not just you."

Eden glared at him. "Are you always like this?"

"Grumpy? Yes. Are you always this blunt?"

"Yes."

"I'm afraid he *is* a bit of a grump, dearie," said the blonde lady.

She tapped her silver cane on the floor of the elevator. "Vulcan is an—oh, what's that word again, Irma?"

"*Iconoclast*," said Irma, taking a sip from her teacup. "He's an iconoclast, Nellie dear."

"I'm a smith," said Vulcan. "It's two o'clock. Time for my lie-down."

The elevator dinged and the doors opened. They stepped onto the third floor. Thick carpet lay underfoot, and etched silver panels covered the walls. Eden followed Vulcan to the end of a hallway, where he stopped in front of a set of silver double doors inlaid with circles of gold. Vulcan pulled a black key from his pocket and tried it in the lock.

Vulcan frowned at the key, tried it again, then cursed.

Nellie leaned toward the doors. "Hush, dearies. I believe I hear someone inside."

"In my rooms?" Vulcan abandoned the key. From his pocket, he pulled a pair of pliers and a length of heavy wire. He bent the end of the wire and put it into the keyhole. He gave it a jerk and the door opened.

A young woman in a blue jacket stood in the doorway, blocking their entry. Behind her was a large apartment furnished in thick carpets, cushiony chairs, and walls paneled in burnished bronze. Oiled tools hung on every wall. Gears, pulleys, nuts, and bolts were stacked around the floor.

Eden thought that if she had to live here, then at least these rooms looked nice. She said, "It's messy, but it *is* beautiful."

"Right on both counts," said Vulcan. "What's this Blue Coat doing in my chambers?"

The Blue Coat said, "Vulcan Smith, your chambers have been confiscated."

"Confiscated? Who in the name of Saint Dunstan would dare such a thing?"

"Order of the Council. You have been reassigned."

"That damn Pewtersmith," said Vulcan. "This is his doing. Where'd that old swindler say I should go instead?"

"Subbasement Seven. Room K-Minus-One."

"Subbasement Seven like hell. The only thing in Subbasement Seven is Kitchens."

Nellie wagged a finger. "Oh, now that's not true, dear. There's more there than just Kitchens."

Irma nodded. "That's right. The janitor closet is there, too."

Vulcan said, "Stand aside then. I at least need to get my things."

"I cannot let you enter," said the Blue Coat. "Your furnishings are now the property of the Guild."

"My *tools* are in there," said Vulcan.

"Your tools are now the property of The Guild."

"Well, what about—"

"—as are your books and your furnishings. All non-Guild property has been moved to your new chambers. Subbasement Seven. Room K-Minus-One."

"I'll K-Minus-One you right in the keister, you blue-jacketed twit."

Eugene pulled Vulcan away and shut the door. "Ain't nothing you do about it, Vulc."

Vulcan stared at the silver doors of his rooms. "I've been bamboozled. Hornswoggled. By a nincompoop. A Pewtersmith. 'Confined to quarters,' he said. I figured that meant *my* quarters, not some underground hovel."

Eden followed the group to the elevator. She felt nauseous and exhausted. She didn't think she could stand any more uncertainty.

When the doors opened, Buzz said, "You want to go to your new floor now, Vulc?"

"What I want is for you to shut your yapper."

"Subbasement Seven it is," said Buzz.

Eden watched Buzz push his lever forward and felt the elevator drop down and down. "How many basement levels are there?"

"Only one *basement level*," said Buzz, "but there are a lot of subbasements."

"How many is a lot?"

"Seven is the farthest down we ever go, dearie," said Nellie. "Below that is Jones-only."

When the elevator stopped, the doors opened to a dimly lit, stone-walled corridor.

"It smells like soup down here," said Eden.

Nellie pointed down the corridor with her cane. "K-Minus-One should be this way. Follow me."

Nellie led them down a series of hallways past a red metal door, behind which they heard a hissing sound. Steam floated out around its edges. "That would be the boiler," said Nellie. A hundred feet later, Eden saw a set of white double doors. "Kitchens is in there," Nellie said. She sniffed. "Yes, Eden. Smells like split pea soup."

"I like chicken noodle." Irma looked into her teacup. "When is chicken noodle?"

"That would be tomorrow, dear sister. K-Minus-One should be just around the corner. Ahh—there it is. Oh my."

"Pewtersmith!" said Vulcan. "That rat bastard gave me a room with a wooden door."

"Doors are easy to fix, dear." Nellie tapped the battered wooden surface with her silver cane. "We'll fix it before you can say—"

"Before you can say *rat bastard!*" Irma nodded. "I want to look inside. I bet it's *awful.*"

Vulcan opened the door. The room was nearly bare. One wall was lined with empty, rusty shelves. A small bed sat against another wall. A single metal chair stood by a rusty table. A metal cabinet stood open in a corner with a few jackets and pants hung inside. A tiny bathroom held a toilet and a sink.

"It's a dump," said Eden, who felt qualified to make that assessment, given the places she'd lived in the last six years. The nauseous feeling in her stomach turned to panic. Was it possible that she'd ended up somewhere even worse than the orphanage? How could she live in this tiny room, with this total grump?

"It's a jail cell," said Vulcan. "By Saint Dunstan's beard, it won't stand."

"It's—it's very uncluttered," said Nellie.

Eden blurted out, "This won't work. This won't work at all."

"Damn right it won't work," said Vulcan. "It won't stand."

"There's only one room. Only one bed," said Eden. "Where am I supposed to sleep?"

"You?" said Vulcan, staring at her. "You can't stay here. This is my room. No room here for a kid—much less a female kid. What the hell are you talking about, anyway?"

"They told me I'm—I'm here. I'm here to live with you."

"With *me*?" Vulcan paced about the room on his mismatched legs. "You can't live with me. This is a Guildhall. It isn't a place for kids. I know your dad isn't a smith anymore, but he is still your dad. Why by Saint Dunstan don't you want to live with him?"

"Because he's dead." She spoke through gritted teeth, trying hard to control her emotions.

"Dead? What are you talking about, dead?"

"He's dead. Mom, too. Six and a half years." The words felt strange to say out loud, as if she had just realized how long they had been gone—how long she had been alone.

"My—my boy? Eric?" Vulcan's whole body sagged until he fell onto the bed.

Nellie looked worriedly at Vulcan, then put a shaky arm around Eden. Eden tried to force out the story of her parents' death, but her voice kept cracking. "There, there, dearie," said Nellie. "Now, what about your mother's family?"

"There is none. That's why I'm here." She nodded toward Vulcan's horizontal form. "He—that man—he's supposed to be my family."

"I'll take care of the girl," said a voice. Eden felt her stomach tighten. She spun around to see Mr. Pewtersmith standing in the doorway. Mr. Pewtersmith smiled at Vulcan. "I see you're getting settled into your new chambers."

Vulcan cursed under his breath.

Nellie glared at Mr. Pewtersmith. "Uriah, this is neither the time nor the place for your gloating. Please leave."

"Fine," he said. He took Eden by the arm, pulled her from the room, and slammed the door.

"Where are you taking her?" shouted Nellie from inside the room.

"Away," whispered Mr. Pewtersmith. He marched Eden to the

elevator as she tried to will her stomach to settle down, but she felt like she might throw up. Her heart beat faster and tears started to overflow her eyes. As Mr. Pewtersmith shoved her into the elevator, she wiped the tears away and took a ragged breath. "You're taking me away? What does that mean?"

Mr. Pewtersmith ignored her. He kept a grip on her arm with one hand. With the other, he picked a bit of lint off the front of his robe. Buzz looked at Eden with apologies in his eyes. They reached the main floor and Mr. Pewtersmith dragged Eden across Humble Gallery to the black iron door. He unlocked the door, yanked it open, and shoved Eden outside. "This is a Guildhall," he said, "for true smiths. There is no place here for brats like you." He slammed the door shut.

Eden heard the door lock. She stood on the porch staring at the door, holding her suitcase in one hand and her orchid in the other. She stood like that for nearly a minute, then turned around and began walking slowly across the porch and down the stairs.

She reached the sidewalk in front of the Guildhall. "Left or right?" she whispered. She wondered which direction might be most likely to lead her somewhere safe. She had no idea.

She heard a noise behind her and turned to see Irma marching through the door with Nellie hurrying after.

"I just think we should discuss it first," hissed Nellie. "Besides, the girl is probably long gone by—oh! Hello, dearie. I didn't see you there."

"Just where are you going?" said Irma, pointing down at Eden with her teacup.

"I—I don't know."

"As I expected. Do we understand correctly that you had come to live with your grandfather? With Vulcan?"

"The State told me I had to come," said Eden. "I didn't choose this. They brought me here."

"*The State?*" said Nellie. "Well, those idiots didn't—"

"—didn't do a thing wrong." said Irma. She bustled down the steps and took one of Eden's hands in her own wrinkled, shaky fingers. "You shall stay with us, Eden. With sister and me."

"Irma!" said Nellie, hurrying after her sister.

"At least for now!" said Irma. "At least until we get Vulcan's rooms settled. She has no other family, Nellie. And neither do we. It will be fun!"

"Will it?" asked Nellie.

"Just us girls," said Irma, taking a sip from her teacup.

Nellie took a deep breath and nodded. "Just us girls. Of course. After all, your grandmother Edna was like a sister to us, may she rest in peace. We shall have to find a spare bed and have it brought to our rooms. A dresser, too, I suppose. And clear out a bit of closet space to hang your dresses. Now let's go back inside. It's chilly out here and I don't have my sweater."

The rooms of Nellie and Irma Silversmith were on the second floor above ground level, in the East Wing. They had two bedrooms, a small office, a parlor, and a bathroom. A silver door on the back wall of the parlor led to their workshop. The walls were silver as well and hung with even more silver decorations—mostly flowers and birds. Every table and shelf held silver sparrows, silver daffodils, silver hummingbirds, and silver daisies.

"I take it you like silver," said Eden. She pointed to a single, tiny bare space on the wall. "You missed a spot."

Nellie smiled at her. "We'll let that comment pass, as you are our guest."

With Eugene's help, the sisters managed to clear enough space in the office to fit a dresser and a small bed for Eden. Nellie promised they would fix it up more properly, but that it was time for "a bit of a lie-down. And after that, we'll have tea. But at this moment, I can barely keep my eyes open. Eugene, you'll join us for tea after nap time? Eden, you do take naps, don't you?"

Eden hadn't taken a nap in years, but she realized how tired she felt. "A nap sounds nice right now."

Irma yawned. "A nap sounds nice all the time. When I'm sleeping, I dream about naps."

Eugene left. The sisters returned to their bedrooms and Eden lay on the bed in the cluttered office and stared at the silver flowers and birds on her walls. A small window looked out on the grounds below. Eden spotted one of the statues she'd seen earlier—a woman brandishing a short sword over her head. The statue was facing away from the window, toward the street. From her second-story view, Eden could see the rest of the neighborhood stretching out from her to the south. The little houses looked so small in comparison to the Guildhall. Eden wondered about the families that lived inside them, and whether they were happy.

On one wall, amidst all the silver decorations, was a framed letter. Eden could just make out the words from where she lay: "His Majesty, Harald V, King of Norway, wishes to send his sincere appreciation for the exquisite craftsmanship demonstrated in the making of his royal silverware." The letter was signed in a curly script and stamped with a large gold seal. On another wall was a black-and-white photograph of what looked like younger versions of Nellie and Irma, surrounded by football players. A man in a suit was holding up a large silver trophy with a life-sized silver football on the top.

On the bedside table next to her was a jar labeled Mrs. Gunsmith's Beauty Cream. The jar was decorated with a picture of a stunning, round-faced woman with flawless skin. The woman in the picture stared out at Eden, as if to say, *Who are you and what are you doing here?* Eden dug through her luggage and found the photo of her mom and dad. She leaned it against the jar of beauty cream. She set her little pot of dirt with the shriveled orchid stem next to it, where it could collect sunlight from the little window.

How could she ever sleep in this strange place, surrounded by all these strange metal things and strange people?

She looked at the photo of her parents. It didn't seem possible that they had already been gone for so long. Lately, it had been getting harder to remember them in detail. Harder to remember what it was like to sit down to dinner with them. Or how it felt to get in trouble for hiding her peas in her milk glass. Or to get driven to school by her mom. She remembered getting carried to her room by her dad after falling asleep on the couch, but the words he said to her, the smell of him—that was mostly gone.

Without thinking, she kissed the tip of her finger, then pressed it against the faces of her mother and father in the photograph. "I miss you. I could really use a little help today," she said. "But you're not here."

She tried to imagine what her mother would have said to her: *Eden, don't hold it in. Have yourself a really good cry. Just let it all out.*

Instead, she bit her lip to keep the tears inside. She lay just that way, gripping her lip between her teeth, until she yawned in spite of herself. The silver flowers and birds went out of focus. She closed her eyes and slept.

An hour later, Nellie woke Eden and led her into the parlor. Eugene was there. Eden heard a knock on the door and Nellie let in a woman with a silver tea trolley. Nellie said, "Cucumber sandwiches for four, with no crusts, and a pot of chamomile, also for four. Thank you, dear Miss Clara."

Miss Clara was a short, pudgy woman wearing a pink pantsuit that was too tight and a pink beret on her head. "For four, is it? I see you have company today."

"Perhaps we do, but it isn't any business of yours, Clara Jones. Just the tea and sandwiches, thank you."

"No need to get snippy with me, Nellie Silversmith," said Miss Clara, as she loaded a tray with cups, a teapot, and plates of food while she stared at Eden. "You haven't introduced me to your young friend."

"Just the tea and sandwiches," Nellie repeated. She took the offered tray from Miss Clara and pushed the woman and the trolley out the door. She handed the tray to Eden. "Your presence here is sure to cause quite a stir. Breathe a word to that one and she'll recite it to everyone in the Guildhall by dinnertime. No need for that. Now then, tea."

Eden set the silver tray with the silver teapot on a low table. The four of them—Nellie, Irma, Eugene, and Eden—sat on couches around the table. With shaky hands, Irma poured tea into three small silver cups for Eugene, Eden, and Nellie, then poured some into her own blue teacup. She took a silver bottle from her purse and poured a splash of its contents into her cup, then added two sugar cubes. "Sugar for you, Eden?"

"Yes. Four cubes, please."

"A sweet tooth! Four it is."

Eden was hungry, but she eyed the food with a frown. "What kind of sandwiches are those?"

"Cucumber, dearie."

"Cucumber? Sandwiches? That's a thing?" Eden picked up one of the triangles of bread. She took a bite. She was surprised how good it tasted. She was even more surprised how the act of sitting quietly and sharing food with these people made her feel so much better. "So...is everything in this place made of metal?" she asked.

"Don't be silly," said Irma, as she replaced the stopper on her silver bottle. "These couch cushions are not. The bedding is not. We're smiths. Not fanatics."

"I'm a Smith, too," said Eden.

"By birth, maybe," said Eugene. "But the sisters are talking about something else."

"But—but I am a Smith. My father was a Smith. My grandfather—well, you know he's a Smith, too. So what does it matter if I'm not a member of your club?"

"Careful now, kid," said Eugene. "The Guildhall ain't a club. It's—well—it's a lot more than that. It's kinda hard to explain to someone who ain't a smith—"

"I *am* a Smith," said Eden.

"A name is one thing," said Nellie.

"But you must do the work," said Irma, raising a spoon like a baton. "The work of hammer, of forge, of fire!"

"Come on now, ladies," Eugene said. "Settle down."

Irma sang out, "*Blade and ring and lock and wire! The work of hammer, forge, and fire!*"

"*Golden mornings!*" sang Nellie. "*Silver songs! The iron, the steel, the work of tongs!*"

"Are there any more cucumber sandwiches?" said Irma.

VI

In Which Eden Meets the Little Nat
While a Door Is Transformed

Eden waited for the sisters to take dainty bites of their sandwiches before she turned to Eugene.

The silver teacup he held looked tiny in his huge hands. Eden noticed that he wore a gold ring on his left pinky. "You were saying?" she asked. "About the Guildhall?"

"Ah. Right." Eugene smiled. "Eden, to be a member of the Guildhall is about the greatest thing a smith can achieve. The smiths who belong are among the grand masters of metalworkers."

"Too true." Nellie adjusted a pillow behind her back. "Right now, sister and I are working on a tea set, like this one, but much more distinguished, for the Queen Consort of England. She is paying us a pretty penny for it. It is a delightful commission."

"And a rare one, these days," said Irma, tapping the rim of her teacup. "Not as much call for silver tea sets as there used to be."

Eugene nodded. "Metalwork of this quality is a dying art. And this Guildhall here, right here in Tacoma—well, it's one of the last of its kind. The members are among the few remaining great ones. So great that their customers include the likes of the Queen Consort of England. She's a lady who knows superior quality and can afford it.

Commissions like these—that's how members keep this Guildhall open and pay the staff and the taxes and the costs of such a place. Well, that and their precious metal reserves—gold, silver, platinum, that sort of thing. Anyway, the greatest of all these metalworkers, some of us would say the greatest that's ever been, was—is—Vulcan Smith."

"*He* would certainly say so," said Nellie.

Eden imagined her grumpy little grandfather, lying in his cell of a room. "He's really that good?"

Eugene nodded. "Vulc is the only smith to ever hold the title of Eleventh-Level Master. And now the very Guildhall that gave him the title has stripped it from him and locked him up."

"I still don't understand why," said Eden. "What did he do?"

"Oh, just little things, mostly," said Nellie.

"But *so* many of them," said Irma. "And for *so* long."

Nellie said, "Vulcan is prickly. He can't bear to indulge anything he thinks is stupid. That goes for rules *and* people. First he refused to go to Guildhall meetings. Not that I can blame him—boring things. But attendance is a requirement for membership. Then he stopped eating in Supperdinner Hall with the rest of us. Said he preferred his own company and that of Eugene. Fine, but the rules are: all meals are *supposed* to be eaten in Supperdinner Hall, unless you've taken ill. And finally, he quit making his daily dish." Nellie looked at Eden pointedly. "*Everyone* makes a daily dish."

"Vulcan hasn't made one in more than a year," said Irma.

"What's a *daily dish*?" said Eden.

Nellie ignored her question. "I suppose he might have gotten away with all of those things. We all knew of them and did nothing. But Uriah Pewtersmith—"

"I do not like him," interrupted Eden. "He scares me."

"He scares all of us, dearie. But as I was saying, Uriah kept meticulous notes of every infraction. He's always had it in for Vulcan."

"He has?"

"Eden, your family line and the Pewtersmiths have never gotten along," said Irma. "They've been feuding for ten generations."

"Feuding why?" Eden was twisting the teaspoon in her fingers.

Nellie said, "No one knows for sure. I suspect it is because Vulcan and his family are so naturally talented and the Pewtersmiths are so naturally bitter. Some people fail to celebrate superior talent and feel the need to try to tear it down. Insecurities and such. If there's more to it than that, I don't know. But, as I was saying, after all those small infractions, Vulcan then doomed himself. On Uriah's birthday. The cake."

"I prefer pudding," said Irma, "but even so, I would have liked to have had a piece of that cake—before it exploded."

Eugene set down his silver teacup. "This all came to a head just last week, Eden. It was Pewtersmith's eightieth birthday. Pewtersmith made a big fuss over the whole thing. Reserved Main Lodge. Decorated it with his family crest. Brought in caterers from outside. Hired an actual choir. Vulcan couldn't resist. I mean, can you blame him? People turn eighty all the time around here. Pewtersmith's the only one who saw fit to treat it like a coronation."

Irma took a sip from her teacup. "Your grandfather's never been very good at resisting temptation."

Eugene nodded. "So Vulc—he snuck the cake back to his rooms, hollowed it out, and filled the center with acetylene gas. Replaced one of the candles with a fuse. At the end of the party, Pewtersmith's snooty sister, Morgana, lit the candles. Right as Pewtersmith bent over to blow it out—"

"*Kaboom!*" said Irma. "Right in his face."

"Singed his eyebrows off," said Nellie. "The poor dear. And that was the straw that broke the camel's back. Uriah brought charges, along with all his notes of Vulcan's countless past infractions. And the rules—well, the rules are very clear. Uriah was in his rights."

"He may have been within his rights," said Irma, "but he's still a horrid man."

Eden kept twisting her teaspoon. "But my grandfather's only confined to his room. That's not a death sentence."

"You're bending the spoon, dearie," said Nellie.

"What?"

"The spoon. In your hands. Be careful with it. That's solid sterling."

"Sorry," said Eden, "but I want to know why he—why my grandpa kept saying he was doomed."

Irma opened her mouth to speak, but Nellie shushed her.

"Can you please just tell me," said Eden.

"It doesn't matter," said Eugene. "Nothing we can do. You heard Pewtersmith. Vulc's sentence is for life."

"With all the usual terms and conditions," said Irma.

"What does that *mean*?" asked Eden. "What terms? And what conditions?"

Irma said, "It means the Five Tasks are his only hope for release. And because they're the hope, the Tasks are the death sentence, too."

"Hush now, sister," said Nellie.

"The *what*?" said Eden, dropping the spoon. "What are you talking about?"

Irma smiled. "The Tasks. The same ones that killed so many of your ancestors. Gave them just enough hope to kill them dead as doornails. That's what Vulcan meant. He knows. Everyone knows. Hope is a dangerous thing."

"Irma!" said Nellie. "You've said far too much."

"Oh, but I disagree," said Irma. "Eden deserves the truth."

"No!" Nellie stomped her silver cane down on the floor like an exclamation point. "We will not speak on this any further. Eden, it just means there's nothing we can do about it. Carry that tea tray back into the hall, dearie. Time to get to work."

Eugene left. Nellie and Irma slung their large purses over their arms and followed Eden into the hallway.

Eden frowned. Why wouldn't Nellie explain what the Tasks were? What was so bad about them? She said, "Where are we going?"

"To fix that door for poor Vulcan," said Nellie. "Perhaps we can't overturn his sentence—"

"—but at least we can cover up that shameful wooden surface," said Irma.

"What floor, ladies?" said Buzz, as they entered the elevator.

"Subbasement Seven, Buzz," said Nellie. "I'm afraid we'll be spending a great deal of time on that dreadful floor."

Buzz pushed his lever and then looked at Eden. "It's after four o'clock. Past visiting hours."

"Of course it is," said Nellie. "There are no visitors here. Only residents."

Buzz frowned. "What's your name, miss?"

"Eden." She felt her face grow hot. Was she a resident here now? Would she actually be staying here? For how long?

"Last name?"

"Her last name is Smith, Buzz." Nellie tapped her cane on the floor. "What is yours?"

"Just doing my job, ma'am. You gotta admit, it's a bit irregular."

"It didn't used to be," said Nellie, as the elevator dinged. "Goodbye, Buzz." They stepped off into the dim light of Subbasement Seven and made their way to Vulcan's room.

Outside his door, Nellie set down her purse with a clunk, then lay her silver cane next to it. She reached into the purse and pulled out a steel hammer with a short wooden handle. Then she upended the purse and out dropped a miniature anvil. Eden was amazed that such a heavy object had been inside Nellie's purse. She thought the anvil must have weighed ten pounds or more. Nellie set it upright and placed the hammer on top of it. "Now then," she said, "we'll need a bit of heat."

"Coming right up, sister." Irma set her teacup shakily on the floor. From her purse, she pulled out a canister marked with the words Acetylene Gas. A hose ran from the top of the canister to a small torch. Irma turned a nozzle on the gas and clicked a spark next to the end of the torch. A yellow jet of flame shot out.

Eden jumped back. "I don't think you should be doing that. It looks really dangerous."

"You're quite right, dearie," said Irma. From her purse, she extracted three pairs of white leather gloves embroidered with silver flowers and distributed them to the group. Then she handed Eden a pair of silver-rimmed cat-eye glasses. "Put these on, dearie. Safety first. That's what I always say." Irma adjusted a nozzle on the jet until the yellow flame turned a translucent blue and hissed like a teakettle. She pulled out a series of small tools from her bag—tongs, pincers, pliers, and calipers. She motioned at Eden, waving the flaming torch around as she did so. "Dearie, perhaps you could go gather us some spare metal?"

Eden dodged the flame. "Some what?"

"Just some scrap silver, dear. Whatever you can find." Irma waved at her with the torch. "Are you sure you're a Smith? Try a closet. Or Kitchens. Anywhere. But hurry along."

Eden backed away from Irma and her torch, then walked around the corner to the double doors of Kitchens. She heard pots and pans banging as she pushed them open. She collided with a boy, knocking a stack of stainless-steel pans out of his hands.

A tall, thin woman stepped into view, with a handful of cooks peeking out from behind her. "What now, Nathaniel? Did you break something again?" The woman wore cook's whites, with pale, pinned-back blonde hair. The fair skin of her forehead had a thin sheen of sweat on it. She held a wooden spoon in her right hand. "Who is this girl? Where did you wander in from? Visiting your grandma?"

"My grandfather, actually," said Eden.

"You're a long way from the visiting room," said the woman. "Come, Nathaniel. Pick up the pans and say hello."

"Hi." Nathaniel began restacking the pans.

Eden bent down to help. "Sorry about that."

"It's fine," said Nathaniel. "But who are you?"

"I'm—I'm Eden. Eden Smith."

"Got it. You're a smith. But what are you doing down here in Kitchens?"

Nathaniel couldn't have been more than a year older than her, if that. He was blond, like the woman, with similar coloring, and he was tall like her, but fleshier. His hair was cut short, but still managed to stick up in all directions. He wore a white chef's coat and black-and-white checkered pants. He smiled.

"I live here," Eden said. "I mean, not in Kitchens, but I live in the building."

"Here? You live here? Since when?" said the woman.

"Since today, I guess. My grandfather lives in the room next door to you."

"Your grandfather is Vulcan Smith?" said Nathaniel.

"I heard about Vulcan having a granddaughter on the premises," said the woman. She turned to her staff and clapped her wooden spoon against a palm. "Everyone back to work now. We've got dinner to prepare and a schedule to keep. Now then, Eden. Did you say you live in the Guildhall?"

"Yes. I was—I mean. Yes."

"You don't sound very sure."

"I'm not. I'm staying with the sisters and—oh! I should be getting back to them. They sent me to find some spare metal so they could fix Vulcan's door."

The woman frowned. "They did, did they? Sent a poor girl like you in here to steal my best copper kettles. Well, they can't have them. Nathaniel, set down those pans—you'll have to wash them again anyway—and fetch Eden the drawer of mismatched silverware. The sisters made it in the first place, so I suppose they can have it back." She clapped with her wooden spoon once more. "Hurry up about it, Nathaniel!"

Nathaniel rushed away without a word. The woman clucked her tongue after him. "Someday, he'll become worth all the effort. Now then, young lady, I don't like funny business this close to mealtime. My name is Lillian Jones. Mrs. Jones to you. I am the head cook. Nathaniel is my son. And you say you live here, but that's impossible. There hasn't been a smith your age living in this place since, well, since *I* was your age. So tell me the truth."

Eden's face grew hot again. She said, "I *do* live here, at least for now. Come and ask the sisters if you don't believe me. They can probably explain it better than I can."

"Nellie and Irma Silversmith are not exactly known for their clarity," said Lillian. "How old are you?"

"Thirteen."

"And you go to school?"

"Yes. I'm in the eighth grade."

"And will you continue in your current school, now that you live here at least for now?"

Eden stared at her. She didn't know the answer to that question. Would she change schools again, like she'd done so many times before? Would she have to introduce herself as the new girl again? If she wasn't going to stay very long, what was the point? "Won't I?"

"I'm asking you."

Before Eden could answer, Nathaniel rushed around a refrigerator, carrying a wooden drawer full of silver knives, forks, and spoons.

"About time," said Lillian. She nodded curtly at Eden. "Seems like you still have some things to figure out, young lady. You'd best get figuring. Don't be all day, Nathaniel. You're needed back here."

The silverware clattered as they walked. "She's a bit much sometimes," said Nathaniel.

"She's a lot," said Eden. She wondered if Nathaniel could hear the jealousy in her voice.

They turned the corner to see Nellie and Irma, with their anvil, torch, and tools laid out in front of them. "Ahh," said Nellie, "you've returned successful from your hunt. Oh, and you've brought the little Nat with you." Nellie looked into the drawer. "This will do fine. Now then, Nat, be a good boy and fetch us a bucket of cold water."

"Yes, ma'am," said Nathaniel. He set down the drawer and turned back toward Kitchens.

Nellie selected a large silver serving spoon from the drawer. "How about this old thing, sister?"

"That will do nicely for starters," said Irma. She clamped the spoon in a set of tongs and held it against the anvil, then picked up her torch and began blasting the spoon with the flame. The spoon began glowing red. "Now then, let's start with something simple. How about a nice bouquet of flowers—but what kind of flowers?"

"Daffodils are always lovely," said Nellie. "I do believe Vulcan favors them." Nellie picked up the hammer.

Irma said, "Say when, sister." When the spoon glowed nearly white hot, Nellie nodded and took the tongs from her sister. She began hammering the spoon against the anvil. The hallway rang with the loud, bright sounds.

"If this doesn't wake him up, then nothing will," said Eden.

"That little bit of pounding?" said Irma. "Your grandfather is a famously heavy sleeper. And even if he were awake, the sound of hammers is a lullaby for a smith, that's what I always say." Irma kept blasting the spoon with the torch.

Nellie traded the hammer for pliers and snips. She began pinching and twisting the glowing metal. "Where is that nitwit boy with the water?" she shouted above the din. "We need water. Go check on him, would you dear?" Eden ran toward Kitchens, but Nathaniel was already walking back, carrying a bucket and sloshing at every step. He set the bucket down next to the sisters.

Before Eden could get a clear look at the progress, Nellie plunged her sculpture into the water. A huge cloud of steam billowed upward with a loud hiss. Irma shut off the torch. When the hissing and boiling stopped, Nellie pulled the tongs from the water. Two silver daffodils were held in the end of her tongs, formed from the old spoon. The perfect stems were long and slim, with delicate, scalloped leaves curling from them. The flowers at the top had intricate cup shapes, with thin, pointed petals bending outward.

Other than being made of silver, Eden thought they looked real enough to fool a bee. "How—how did you—how did you do that?"

"Hammer, tongs, and fire, my dear. Hammer, tongs, and fire."

Irma said, "Oh, they're quite lovely, sister. What do you think, Eden?"

She reached out and touched the petals of the silver daffodils with the tips of her fingers. The petals were so delicate, they almost felt real. "I—I think they're—they're beautiful. It's like magic, what you did."

"Magic? No! We do not like that word. Smithing is not magic. There is no trick to it, other than commitment to the craft. Because smithing is craft. It only looks like magic to those who don't understand the meaning of hard work. Although, in the days of Saint Patrick, smithing was considered to be among the black arts. Witches, smiths, and wizards—Saint Patrick lumped them all together."

"I want to make one." Eden picked a silver spoon out of the

drawer and squeezed it in her hands, trying to imagine what it would take to transform it.

"Me, too," said Nathaniel. "I'd give my right arm to be able to do that."

"You?" said Irma, wrinkling her nose. "You're a Jones. This is not for you. Now Eden, dearie, you're a smith, so fetch your pliers and have a turn."

"I don't have any pliers." The word sounded familiar to her. She was fairly sure it was a tool of some kind and was almost as sure that her dad had owned at least one pair.

"No pliers?" said Nellie. "How old are you?"

"I'm thirteen—and a half."

"Then you must have pliers. Did you lose them?"

"Lose them? I never got any."

"What are pliers?" said Nathaniel.

"Son of a cook!" Nellie nodded toward Eden. "Eden, tell him what pliers are."

Eden gripped the spoon in her hand. "A tool, I think. But I'm not sure."

Irma put her gloved hands to her mouth. "How can that be?"

"It was that father of hers—the *manufacturer!*"

"The *factory owner!*"

"The *presser of metal!*"

Eden's face flushed hot. "Don't you ever say mean things about my father!"

Nellie smoothed down the front of her dress. "Quite right, dearie. You are quite right. By the way, you are bending another spoon. Irma, we should be ashamed of ourselves. We were not acting ladylike. And we did love him, before. Now affix these daffodils and heat another spoon for me. Eden, you're tall. You can help manage the top of the door."

Eden and Irma pounded the daffodils onto Vulcan's wooden door. With hammer, torch, and tongs, the sisters transformed the drawer of silverware into a garden scene on the door: Irma attached silver grasses and ferns along the bottom and silver daffodils, daisies, and columbines across the middle, and had Eden nail huge silver sunflowers blooming across the top. Nellie hammered tiny silver forget-me-nots to fill in all the spaces in between. Irma made a garter snake coiled at the bottom of the largest daisy. "Vulcan is a boy, after all," she said. "Well, an old man, but all men are boys, deep down. And boys like snakes, that's what I always say."

"Girls can like snakes, too, you know," said Eden.

"Of course they can, dear," said Nellie. "Anything is possible, if you set your mind to it." Nellie turned off the torch and placed her hammer back inside her purse. She handed the empty drawer to Nathaniel. "Run along back to Kitchens, now, little Nat."

He didn't move.

"I said run along."

Nathaniel pulled at the collar of his chef's coat. "Are you sure you don't need any more silverware?"

"Oh, run along with you!" said Nellie. "Keep your Jones nose out of smithing work. Scat now." She turned to the door, which no longer showed even a square inch of wood. "Quite presentable, if I do say so myself. Shall we show it to Vulcan?" Nellie tapped on the door with the head of her cane.

"Go away!" came a shout from inside. "You just ruined my nap!"

"It's us, dear," Nellie said. "We're here with your granddaughter and have something to show you."

"I'm sleeping!"

"You're not, dear. You're talking to us. Come out and look."

"Saint Dunstan's hammer!" muttered Vulcan from inside. Eden heard his clunking steps, and a few seconds later, the door opened.

Eden was shocked by how different her grandfather looked, compared to when she had seen him on trial, earlier that day. Then he had stood straight and defiant, with a fiery anger in his eyes. Now it looked like there was less of him. And what was left seemed bent over. His eyes looked dull. She wondered how much had to do with his sentencing and how much had to do with learning of his son's—her father's—death.

Vulcan muttered, "What's so sainted important—oh. Well now, look at that." He scanned the door from top to bottom, running his fingers absently along the metalwork. "That's not horrible."

"Do you like it?" asked Nellie.

"I don't hate it. I don't hate that thing down there, especially. The, uhh…"

"The *snake*. That was mine, dear," said Irma. "I said, 'Vulcan is a boy and boys like snakes.'"

"The kid do any of it?"

"I don't have any tools," said Eden. She wanted her grandfather to know she would have helped, if she could have.

"Not even a pair of pliers," said Nellie.

"She's still here though, I see." Vulcan's voice trailed off. "I'm going back to bed." He spun around on his metal prosthetic, slouched back inside his room, and closed the door.

"That's it?" said Eden. "He doesn't even say hi to me. Doesn't even look at me." She wondered how much it would have helped if she had done more of the work. Would he have liked her better?

The sisters gathered their tools. "Don't be too hard on him, dearie," said Irma, as she snapped her large purse closed. "I think he is just a bit sad—a bit heartbroken."

Nellie picked up her silver cane and hefted her own purse. "Of course he is sad, sister. Think about the day he has had. Somehow, we have got to free him from that dreadful room. It is not good for him."

"It will probably kill him," said Irma. "Oh well."

"He could have at least invited me in—us in—for a few minutes," said Eden.

Nellie patted her arm. "Give it time, dearie." A bell clanged far away. "Oh! And speaking of time, that is the bell for dinner. Come along. We'll take you to Supperdinner Hall. But we must hurry."

"Can we do that?" said Irma. "It is after visiting hours."

"We can do it, sister. Eden is not a visitor. She is a smith. She lives here. With us."

"I do?"

"Still some details to work out. Now hurry along. We don't want to be late. Oh, your presence is going to cause quite a stir. Quite a stir, indeed. The first new smith in—well, it must be thirty years, if it is a day!"

VII

In Which Eden Visits Supperdinner Hall and Makes a Decision

A bell sounded again as Nellie, Irma, and Eden waited for the elevator to take them to Supperdinner Hall.

"That'll be the second bell," said Irma. Her fingers clasped a silver beetle pendant that hung from her neck on a silver chain. Irma clicked open its wings, revealing a small watch inside. "I've never been late for dinner before. Buzz better get here soon."

The elevator opened. Buzz pulled his lever. As they rode up, Nellie frowned at Eden's sneakers and jeans. "Is this what young female smiths wear these days?"

Eden rolled her eyes. "It's what *I* wear."

"And it's normal, this clothing? I don't suppose you packed anything prettier, dearie? A nice dress, perhaps?"

Eden could feel her face growing hot. For years, she'd felt self-conscious about her clothes. The woman with the black mole had always provided her with hand-me-downs. None of them had been what Eden would describe as *nice*. And the clothes she had—what *would* happen once she started growing out of them? "I, umm, haven't exactly had a lot of pretty things in my wardrobe lately. Dresses or otherwise."

"Oh, of course dear. I completely understand. You should, though. Sister and I will work to address this. But I reckon what you have on will do for now. We're late already. You are naturally attractive, like your grandfather, so that will help."

The elevator dinged. Buzz said, "Here we are, ladies. You'd better hurry. Doors close in thirty seconds. Good luck, Eden."

"I need luck?"

"Hurry now, dearie," said Nellie, toddling along with her silver cane as fast as her short legs would go.

The hallway they rushed down was empty. They turned a corner just as another bell rang. "Third bell," said Nellie. "Hold those doors! You there! Blue Coats! Hold those doors!" She shouted to the two young men in blue jackets who were closing an ornate set of golden double doors. From the other side came the sounds of rattling glasses and dishes and the chatter of many people. The Blue Coats paused. Nellie forced her cane into the gap and pried the doors back open. "Thank you."

One of the Blue Coats held up a hand. "You're both welcome here, ladies. But we cannot let the girl inside. No visitors are allowed on any of the premises at this time of day. And visitors are never allowed in Supperdinner Hall."

"She is not a visitor," said Nellie. "She lives here."

"She is a smith," smiled Irma. "Isn't it exciting?"

"It is very irregular, ma'am. Both ma'ams. She is a child."

"I'm thirteen and a half," said Eden. "So I'm officially a teenager."

"Did you hear that?" said Nellie. "She is thirteen."

"And a half!" said Irma.

Nellie shook her cane. "I was twelve when I first ate in this hall. Long before you were born, young man. Now kindly move aside."

The men looked at each other. "I'm afraid—"

"Let her through," said a rough voice behind them. Eden turned around. Eugene stood there. He nodded to the two Blue Coats.

Nellie said, "Oh, thank you, Eugene." Eden and the sisters stepped through the doorway.

"Aren't you coming, too?" asked Eden.

Eugene smiled, although Eden thought his eyes still looked sad. "I'll be right out here," he said.

Supperdinner Hall was a large, round room, with three concentric rings of circular tables. The outer ring—where the most everyone sat—was made up of eighteen round bronze and copper tables, with each table seating about eight people. The middle ring was made of six round silver tables. At the center of the room was a single golden table. Eden recognized the nine people who sat there—the Council that had sentenced her grandfather—including Robert Blacksmith with his thick, white beard and Mr. Pewtersmith, tall, thin, and smiling. When he saw Eden, Mr. Pewtersmith's smile fell into a frown. Even from across the room, he scared her.

Eden distracted herself from Mr. Pewtersmith by examining the room. In the center of each table stood vases of flowers, but both flowers and vases were crafted of metal—silver, brass, bronze, copper, and steel. The golden table in the middle held a huge gold vase of gold flowers. Eden wanted to examine each bloom. How could something made of metal look so alive? She wondered if the silver centerpieces had been made by Nellie and Irma.

The hum of the room grew quiet. "Why are they all looking at me?" Eden whispered, nodding at the diners.

"Just smile and wave," whispered Irma. "Pretend you're marching in a parade." She held her blue teacup like a baton and led the way to a table in the silver circle, greeting people as she went. "How is the soup, Johann? I see you've got some nice color in your cheeks this evening. Hello, Helena! What a lovely hat."

The entire room watched their progress. They reached their table, but there was no seat for her. She stood awkwardly, as she watched Robert Blacksmith rise to his feet. He lifted the pewter dish in front of him and tapped it twice with a spoon. Every diner in the hall did the same, filling the room for a moment with the *ping ping* of spoons on bowls. Nellie grabbed one of the Blue Coats—a woman—and asked her to fetch another chair and a spare dish.

"There are no spare dishes," said the Blue Coat, "because there are no visitors allowed in this room."

"I have always found you Blue Coats to be both resourceful and trustworthy, so I'm sure you can find one spare dish somewhere in this building. And to be clear, Eden is not a visitor," said Nellie. Every head seemed to lean her direction.

"What did she say?" said Helena Bladesmith, seated at the center table.

"What?" said the man next to her.

Someone shouted, "No visitors allowed in Supperdinner Hall!"

"She is *not* a visitor." Nellie spoke loud enough for the whole room to hear. "This is Eden Smith, granddaughter of Vulcan Smith."

At the center table, Mr. Pewtersmith polished his soup spoon on a gray handkerchief, then smiled at his reflection in it. "It doesn't matter whose granddaughter she is. I thought I made it clear that she does not belong in this Guildhall. She certainly does not belong here, where we eat." He sniffed. "Supperdinner Hall is for smiths only."

Eden felt her face grow hot. She couldn't stand to be where so many people did not want her. Her eyes darted toward the doors. She felt like sprinting through them and leaving the entire Guildhall behind. But where could she go?

Nellie put her hand on Eden's shoulder. Eden could feel the old hand shaking. "Eden is *not* here as a visitor, Uriah Pewtersmith. She is here as a smith. I formally sponsor her for membership to this Guildhall."

A gasp spread across the room.

Mr. Pewtersmith shook his head. "Nellie Silversmith, I know you struggle with senility. She's a child."

"I am not senile, Uriah. I sponsor her. How old were you when you first came here?"

"Not the same thing at all," said Mr. Pewtersmith. "I didn't just wander in off the street. I came here to serve as an apprentice."

"Well then," said Nellie, "so does she. Don't you, dearie?"

Eden looked at Nellie. Nellie's eyebrows raised, as if waiting for her answer.

"Don't I what?" said Eden.

"Don't you want to stay here—as an apprentice smith? Once apprenticed, you could live here forever."

Forever?

Her eyes scanned the room. There were no other kids. There weren't even adults the age of her late parents. The entire room, other than the men and women in blue jackets, were as old as grandparents and great-grandparents. And her own grandfather didn't seem to want anything to do with her. Nellie and Irma did. And maybe Eugene. Was that enough?

Canes leaned against tables. Both the canes and the tables were made with such care. Every object in the room was an object of craft and beauty. The room smelled musty, but everything in it seemed like something that could be relied upon.

The head of the man closest to her waggled gently back and forth. He smiled at her with watery eyes. These people had been here—in this same building—for years and years. Eden hadn't stayed in the same place for more than a month since she was seven years old. Did she really want to stay here forever? She took a deep breath and immediately knew the answer.

Eden said, "Could you repeat the question?"

"I was just informing Mr. Pewtersmith that you want to live here as an apprentice," said Nellie. "Isn't that right?"

Eden stood straight and nodded. "Yes."

"Who cares what she wants?" Spit flew from Mr. Pewtersmith's mouth. "The brat's opinion doesn't factor into this. And what kind of apprentice? Modern children know nothing about fires and forges. What kind of smithing could she even do?"

Nellie stood, cane in hand. "Let's not get ahead of ourselves, Uriah. If I recall correctly, she does not have to declare that for some time."

"Ten weeks," said Irma. "She is allowed ten weeks to decide."

"Thank you, sister. Right now, I sponsor her membership. I need someone to second my sponsorship."

"I second it!" shouted Irma.

Nellie bowed toward Irma. "Thank you again, sister. Council, it is to you."

"The answer is obviously no," said Mr. Pewtersmith, rising to his feet. "The whole thing is preposterous. We haven't had a new member of this Guildhall for twenty-five years."

"*Thirty* years," said Nellie. "Perhaps even thirty-five. But my goodness, Uriah, isn't that a sign that it's high time that we *did*? Council? Again, I put it to you."

"I said *no*," said Mr. Pewtersmith. "And I represent the Council."

Nellie Silversmith pursed her lips. "You sit *on* the Council, Uriah. You do not represent its other members. What say the rest of you?"

"She's too young!" said Mr. Pewtersmith. "Robert Blacksmith, you surely agree."

The huge man at the center table squinted at Eden. "The girl is but a child, Nellie. It's like Pewtersmith said, we've had none her age for thirty years—"

"Thirty-five," said Irma.

"So again, it's about time," said Nellie. "Or do you, Robert Blacksmith, want us to die out? Do you really want us to be the last of the smiths? Don't you want to pass on your skills to the younger generation?"

"I do. Many of us do. But to a wee one like her? Look at her puny arms."

Mr. Pewtersmith nodded. "There. You see. The Council—"

"That's only two of you," said Nellie. "And I am both ashamed of and surprised by you, Robert. Maureen, surely you'd like to have a young lady join us here."

Maureen Goldsmith leaned forward, her neck heavy with gold jewelry. "Is she sweet?"

"Not particularly," said Irma.

"Hush, sister!" said Nellie, stomping the floor with her cane. "She may not be sweet. But only because her will is strong. And she is a Smith. Her grandfather is none other than Vulcan Smith."

"We all know who her grandfather is," said Mr. Pewtersmith. "A criminal. And her father, the *manufacturer*, was a blight upon us all. And now you want to bring another leaf of that shameful family tree here. Well, I'll not have it."

Listening to these words, Eden felt confused and mad at the

same time. Why did these people call her father a *manufacturer*, like it was some sort of dirty word? And how dare Pewtersmith say her family was shameful! She wanted to hit him across his face.

"Well, I will." Maureen Goldsmith nodded. "I say yes. We need some young smiths, plain and simple. How can we take any pleasure in resting on our laurels if our legacy dies with us? I've always been annoyed by sweet children. And besides, puny arms can be deceiving."

"Thank you, dear," said Nellie. "That's one for our side. And what about the rest of you? Who else agrees to let her stay?"

Three other hands slowly raised—two men and one woman. Eden recognized one of the men as Anit Irenya. The voters smiled toward Eden. Those smiles nearly made her cry. She smiled back.

"That's not enough," said Mr. Pewtersmith. "Four yes votes get you a loss. Now then, who thinks the traitor's brat should leave?"

Robert Blacksmith, Mr. Pewtersmith, and two others raised their hands—one large, handsome man and one rawboned woman. Nellie counted slowly, mouthing the numbers. "You only have four as well. Who didn't vote? Helena? It's up to you."

"What is?" said Helena.

"The vote. We are voting."

"Boating? I don't like boats. Dry land for me."

"Not boating," said Nellie patiently. "We are *voting*. To see if this child can join the Guild as an apprentice."

"Oh! Then I suppose I should vote, too! Why didn't anyone tell me?" Helena Bladesmith climbed down from her chair and tottered over to Eden. She leaned in close. "So you're Vulcan's granddaughter? What is your name again?"

"Eden."

"Say it again, dear," said Helena. "I hear very little."

"And understand even less," said Irma.

"My name is Eden Smith."

"Eden! A most auspicious name. Long ago, another had that name, you know. Your ancestor, I believe." She leaned close to Eden and sniffed. "Hmm...you've got the scent of a smith about you. A bit of smoke. Real smiths always smell like a fire is nearby. The original Eden was a bladesmith, like me. It was said that she smelled like the fires of Hades. And Vulcan—well. What do you think of him?"

"He's grumpy," said Eden.

"Speak up, dear."

"Grumpy! He's grumpy!"

"He certainly is," said Helena. "And they say he's a criminal. Do you think he's a criminal?"

"No!" said Eden, and she longed to be right.

Helena shrugged. "He might be. But he's such a good-looking man. I vote yes."

"What did she say?" said a voice from across the room.

"Please speak up," said another.

"Helena voted yes!" shouted Nellie. "Four plus one makes five. We win. She's in. Eden is the newest member of the Guildhall of Smiths!"

"Hip hip!" shouted Maureen. "Hip hip—oh, what's the next word?"

"Hooray," said Irma.

"Hip hip hooray!" shouted Maureen.

A cheer went up around the room, from everyone except Mr. Pewtersmith and the other councilmembers who had voted no.

"Come, Uriah," said Nellie. "Let's not be a sore loser. Now where is that Blue Coat with the extra chair?"

"If you see her," said Irma, lifting her teacup, "ask her to bring some whiskey and ice as well. We need to celebrate. And tell her to hold the ice."

"This isn't over," said Mr. Pewtersmith. He dropped onto his chair and turned away.

"What exactly just happened?" said Eden.

"You were just voted in," said Nellie. "You, Eden Smith, are the newest member of this Guildhall. You are a smith. Well, an apprentice smith."

"Does that mean I get to stay?"

"Yes, yes, you get to stay."

VIII

The Pillar of Saint Dunstan

Nellie and Irma finished their soup before the Blue Coat returned with a chair, silverware, and a dish made of a dull, silvery metal. Eden didn't mind waiting. She didn't much like soup, and her stomach was flip-flopping from watching this room of strangers decide her fate. Platters of fish came out next—whole fish with whiskers on the sides of their faces.

"Catfish!" said the man sitting next to her. His name was Kerlin Arrowsmith and he spoke with a heavy Southern accent. "I'd better put in my choppers." Kerlin pulled a set of false teeth from his jacket pocket and fitted them into his mouth. He made a few practice bites. Eden wanted to scream. "Dear lady," Kerlin said to Nellie, "would you please pass the mahguj."

"Of course, dear," said Nellie. She picked up a jar of brown goo and handed it to Eden. Eden looked at it, then handed it to Kerlin, who smeared it on his fish.

Eden frowned. "What is that stuff?"

"This?" said Kerlin, his mouth full. "Why, this is only the most delicious thing you've ever tasted."

"Okay...but what is it?"

"It's mahguj, of course. Made right here at the Guildhall, and nowhere else in the world. That's why we also call it Guild jelly."

"I've never heard of it. What's it made out of?"

"I don't rightly know," said Kerlin.

"Neither do I," said Nellie, "but Kerlin is right. It is quite delicious."

Eden dipped the tip of her spoon into the jar and took a tiny bite. "Oh my goodness," she said. The jelly was savory and sweet all at the same time, like raspberry jam mixed with bacon and soy sauce. She dipped out a big spoonful and ate it, then did it again. She hadn't realized how hungry she was. She skipped the catfish altogether and ate more mahguj. She wondered if she should try to wrap the half-full jar in her napkin and sneak it away for later. Before she could, a Blue Coat whisked the jar away from her, along with all the dishes on the table.

After the fish came a course of creamed ham and creamed spinach—Eden ate a little of that, just to fill her stomach. That was followed by vanilla pudding, served with coffee and tea.

"Pudding! Finally," said Irma. "I wait all day for pudding."

"Is it always pudding?" asked Eden. "For dessert, I mean."

"Always! Isn't that delightful?"

"Pudding's good," said Eden, "but do you ever have cake? Like chocolate cake? With chocolate frosting?"

"Cake? Instead of pudding? Don't be ridiculous. Eden, pour a little coffee into this teacup, dearie. Not too much. Just a bit to flavor my whiskey." Irma took a sip. "Now then, you have a decision to make and we had best get on with it."

"Oh, now don't rush her, sister." Nellie wiped the corners of her mouth with a cloth napkin. "She has ten weeks to decide."

"Decide what?" said Eden. She picked up her pudding spoon and began bending it in her fingers.

"Well, what kind of smith you will be, of course," said Nellie.

"Can't I just be the same as you?"

"A silversmith? Oh, that would be lovely, dearie. The pieces we make are the most beautiful. Like that lovely silver pudding spoon you are destroying right now."

"Sorry," said Eden, setting down the bent spoon. "Your last name is Silversmith, isn't it? Does your name decide the kind of work you do?"

Irma shook her head. "Quite the opposite. The work you do determines your last name. You must be a Smith by name of course, to begin with. Then the work you choose—well, it should be chosen carefully, because it should be *true to you*. Take sister and me, for example. We are aesthetically oriented by nature, so naturally, we specialize in the decorative arts."

"Like the flowers on Grandpa's door," said Eden. "What other kinds of smiths are there? I mean, what are my choices?"

Nellie said, "That's the right question, dearie. There are many kinds—goldsmiths and silversmiths—"

"A bit of crossover there," said Irma. "Both work in fine metals, but goldsmiths must have a luxurious inner life, as they do mostly jewelry."

"And there are blacksmiths, who work in iron and steel."

"I think I've seen a blacksmith. At the fair. They make horseshoes."

A cup slammed down at the Council table next to them. Robert Blacksmith stood and stomped over to Eden. "Horseshoes! Why is it always horseshoes? Do you really think that's all we blacksmiths make? If it is iron or steel, then it comes from me and mine. Blacksmithing *is* smithing." He lifted the short-handled sledgehammer that hung from his belt and held it in the air. "None of those puny little hammers for us. Or tongs the size of tweezers! Come to my forge and you'll see some real power. Steel and iron. Iron and steel."

Nellie stood. Her head didn't even reach Robert's armpit. "Robert Blacksmith, you old eavesdropper! You just voted against the girl, and now you're asking her to come to your forge?"

"Oh, and I suppose you'd rather I continue to shun her. Is she staying? Then she may as well learn the craft properly. She should begin at black metal, as they say, and be a real smith." He hung the sledgehammer back on his belt. "And the realest of smiths are we blacksmiths."

"Hmmphh!" said Irma. "Real *arrogant*, you must mean. Sit down, you old Scot." Robert sat. Irma turned to Eden. "But you see, dearie, how Robert just illustrated the point. He is fiery and strong. Just like his work."

"What did he mean, 'begin at black metal'?" asked Eden, still staring at Robert Blacksmith's huge arms and chest.

"He's quoting an old saying," said Nellie, retaking her seat. "'Begin at black metal and read me a riddle.' The idea is that apprentices should start as blacksmiths, who love riddles, I suppose. But that's old-fashioned hogwash. You may begin with any kind of smithing that you like. I suggest you stay away from Robert for a while, until you've dipped your toe in with someone a bit, well, calmer."

"If I may, my dear, I would ask you to consider arrowsmithing." It was Kerlin Arrowsmith, the Southern gentleman who sat next to Eden. He bowed slightly in her direction. "We arrowsmiths would be proud to welcome an apprentice such as yourself to our humble shop."

"That's very sweet, Kerlin," said Nellie.

Irma said, "Even though no one uses arrows anymore, except at summer camp."

"Dear lady, perhaps you haven't seen the quality of *my* arrows—"

"Oh, we've all seen them. As if we could stop you from showing them off," said Irma. "Eden, perhaps you should begin with the machinists, like Vulcan."

"Now sister," said Nellie, "we all appreciate the machinists, but they've always been off-limits for a brand-new apprentice, as you well know. No one starts as a machinist. Besides, just look at them." Nellie pointed to a far table where shiny metal machines sat next to each diner, automatically cutting the food and feeding the people sitting there. Another machine that looked like a robotic fountain kept refilling their glasses with little spurts of water and wine. A metal vase of metal flowers sat in the middle of the table, just like at all the other tables, but these flowers raised and lowered on their own as if they were pistons on a machine. A metal bee circled around them on a wire.

Eden recognized Anit Irenya, the machinist from the Council.

He had left the Council table and was now visiting with his fellow machinists at their table. Anit saw Eden and nodded in her direction. He pulled a leaf on the center bouquet and a steel daisy began to spin. The flower raised into the air like a helicopter and sailed across the room, right to Eden's hand. She caught it and smiled.

"They look kind of amazing," said Eden, not sure if she was talking about the flowers or the machinists themselves. She smelled the flower, expecting a floral scent. It smelled like machine oil. "But yeah. Maybe a bit much for a starting place. So goldsmiths, silversmiths, blacksmiths, arrowsmiths, machinists, and—"

"—and bladesmiths!" said Helena, turning from the Council table. "Come to my workshop, young lady. My family has been making the finest blades since the days of King Boleslaw. In Poland, my family name was Miecznik. It means *swordfish*, the traditional name for the sword maker to the king. My grandfather changed Miecznik to Bladesmith when he came to America. I wish he hadn't, but we can't escape the decisions of our ancestors, can we? So, do I make swords? Yes, certainly, but also axes. And kitchen knives that will cut a slice of bread so thin you can see through it. Razors so sharp you can shave the whiskers from a housefly. You really can. I've done it."

Eden almost spit the water out when little Helena yanked a dagger out from the front of her dress and slammed the point down into a cube of cheddar cheese.

Helena kept talking as if she had done nothing unusual. "The first Eden Smith—your own ancestor—was a bladesmith. The swords she made had names. You should know the names of those swords."

Nellie patted the corners of her mouth with a napkin, then stood. "Helena is a sweetheart and a dear friend of ours. She is worth consideration. But I just had an idea, Irma. Let's you and I show her the song. 'The Song of Smiths.' Eden, you've been to Humble Gallery? Oh, of course you have. Have you seen the song? On the Pillar of Saint Dunstan? He was the founder of our Guild, more than one thousand years ago. The beginning of all of us. He once used his tongs to grab the devil by the nose. The pillar is in honor of him, but in honor of all other smiths, too."

Eden remembered the pillar with the words on it in the entry-way. While the rest of the diners in the room kept eating, Eden followed the sisters out of Supperdinner Hall.

They stopped in front of the black pillar, and Nellie used her silver cane to point to the engraved words.

"*Blade and ring and lock and wire. The work of hammer, forge, and fire. Golden mornings, silver songs, the iron, the steel, the work of tongs. Now this Guild, now this hall, now you stand within these walls. Now eleven smiths we bring—*"

Nellie paused and rested on her cane. "That part is a kind of introduction. An overview, I suppose you might say. From here on, though, each line of the song is about the different kinds of smiths—the main kinds, not silly nonsense like arrowsmithing, you understand?"

"I think so," said Eden.

"Now, *Precious on the heads of kings*—that's goldsmiths, you see? Crowns and jewelry and such. Still very busy. They get jewelry orders from all over the world. The next line says, *Standing 'tween the world and you*. That's locksmiths, because locks keep the world out, I suppose. Also very busy. *Holding flame and smoke and flue*. Fendersmiths, the poor dears. They make metal fireplaces. Not much call for their work, anymore. Dear old Constance Fendersmith, she's a bit lost these days. Lacks purpose. *Sending spark and forming kettle*. That would be coppersmiths—copper pots for cooking, obviously. These days, most copper is used for making copper wire for electricity, but we don't do that here. That happens in one of those other places."

"What places?" asked Eden.

"You know. The f-word." Nellie leaned close and whispered, "*Factory*." She stood straight again. "Where was I? *Coating, blending, shining metal*. That line is about tinsmiths. You would think tinsmiths would have faded into the past, but Fred Tinsmith—one of Vulcan's oldest friends, well, he and the others have found whole new industries to work in. You will meet him soon, I am sure. Then comes pewtersmiths—*serving supper, setting place*. Pewter, you see, is used for bowls and plates, including our daily dish. You ate off one just now."

59

"I've never heard of pewter before coming here," said Eden.

"Doesn't surprise me. A bit outdated. Perhaps that's why Uriah is so angry all the time. Now where was I?"

"Bladesmiths is next," said Irma. *"Cutting throat and shaving face."*

"That's right," said Nellie. "Swords and razors and such, as Helena mentioned just minutes ago. *Best of friend to fight your foe.* That would be blacksmithing. Steel, you know, used for armor and all sorts of things, including horseshoes, no matter what Robert says. Then comes gunsmiths—*Guarding treasure, causing woe.* True words, those. Gunsmiths are much busier these days than I would like, but their business does keep the Guildhall from dipping too deeply into our precious-metal reserves, as they often remind us. Then machinists—*Unsmith, unstill, unbroken, untame.*"

"Unsmith?" said Eden."

"Because they are the only metalsmiths without *smith* in their title. They are *unstill*, because they both use and make machines that move, as you've seen. They are *unbroken*, because they fix things. And you've met your grandfather, a machinist himself, so you already know why they are *untame*. A wild bunch and always busy with orders. And their names are their own."

"I kind of like that," said Eden. *"Their names are their own.* I don't know what it means, but I like it."

Nellie said, "Eden, to become a machinist is no easy thing. Those who succeed get to choose their own last names. Like Irenya. Or plain old Smith, like your grandfather. And finally comes silversmiths. That's sister and me, dearie. *Slay the wolf and eat the name.* Silver bullets for werewolves. And we make knives, forks, and spoons. To eat with."

"I never liked our line," said Irma. *"Eat the name.* It makes no sense. We don't eat our name. Too strange. I wish we had a nice line, like the goldsmiths."

"Does this pillar have something to do with those Tasks you mentioned? The Five Tasks?"

Nellie's hand flew to Eden's mouth. "Hush! As I said before, we will not speak of such things. Nothing good has ever come from them. Now then, time for bed, I think."

IX

In Which Eden Eats Breakfast and Gains a Companion

Eden lay awake for hours that night. She still felt like a stranger in the Guildhall. She still didn't know what it meant to be an apprentice. And she wondered why Nellie wouldn't let anyone tell her about the Five Tasks. If it would help her grandfather, then she needed to know about it.

She tried to push the Tasks out of her mind by focusing on one word: *forever*. The thought of having a forever home—even one without many other kids—calmed her spinning brain. She whispered the word out loud: "Forever." Then she fell asleep.

When she awoke in the morning, she could already hear the sisters puttering around in their rooms. She dressed, then checked on her little orchid. She'd been watering it carefully since her arrival at the Guildhall and making sure it had the right amount of sunlight from her window, but the orchid still looked as dead as ever. She picked up the photo of her parents, then kissed her fingertip and pressed it onto the picture. She began speaking to the photo. "I miss—" But then she stopped, because she realized Nellie and Irma seemed to be talking about her. She set down the photo and put her ear to the door.

"…breaks my heart for the poor little thing," said Nellie. "No mother or father."

"Not that her father was much of a loss," said Irma. "He started so well and ended so shamefully."

"Now, sister, don't speak ill of the dead. Perhaps it wasn't completely his fault. After all, it couldn't have been easy, having Vulcan as a parent."

"But it could have been wonderful, too," said Irma.

"Of course, wonderful. But in a hard way. It was no great surprise to any of us when—oh sister, do you remember that day?"

Eden could picture Irma nodding. She pushed her ear tighter against the door.

"Such a fight!" said Nellie. "I thought they were going to come to blows!"

"You can't blame Vulcan," said Irma. "The brashness of that young man to even suggest such a thing. And he did far more than just suggest it. He actually did it."

"What was that phrase he kept shouting?"

"*Mass-produced.*"

The words caught Eden by surprise. She'd heard her father, Erichthonius Smith, use those words many times to describe his work at Titan Foundry. "All of our products are mass-produced to the highest standards" is what it had said on the sign above the company gate. So why would those two words—*mass-produced*—cause a fight?

"Where is that girl?" said Nellie. "Perhaps I'll wake her." Eden heard the tap of Nellie's cane on her door. She jumped back just as the door opened and Nellie said, "Eden—oh, good morning, dearie. You seem about ready to go. Is that what you're wearing today?"

Eden looked down at her hoodie, jeans, and sneakers. "Yes."

Nellie used her cane like a shepherd's staff and guided Eden out of her room. "Very well, dearie, but something a little prettier every now and then wouldn't kill you. A nice dress, perhaps? Don't you have a nice dress?"

"I—"

Nellie's hand flew to her mouth. "Oh, forgive me, dear. You

already told me you're in need of some nicer things. I am so forgetful these days. *A dress for Eden. A dress for Eden. Don't forget, Nellie Silversmith.* Now then, we were just going to have a bit of breakfast, then take a bite to your grandfather—see if he's up for a little visit. After that, we'll find you a spot for the day."

"A spot?"

"Yes, dear. It's been a long time since we've had an apprentice here, but the way it basically works is that you have ten weeks to choose your specific trade—the kind of smith you will be. Between now and then, you'll be farming yourself out, so to speak, to the various kinds of smiths. Maybe a week with each—or perhaps a little less or a little more. Think of it as a bit of a world tour before you settle on just one."

Eden looked back and forth between the faces of the two old women. "What about school? Will I still go to school?"

"What do you mean, dearie?"

"I mean *school*. I'm pretty sure it's the law that I go to school."

"Laws?" said Nellie. "We don't worry a great deal about such things. We tend to keep to ourselves, other than serving our customers. We try not to bother the outside world and hope the outside world does not bother us. It mostly works."

Eden had worked hard at school, to the surprise of her teachers, who always seemed to expect less of foster children. "But I don't want to fall behind. Shouldn't I be taking classes in math and reading and writing and science and history—"

"Oh! All sorts of history, of course!" said Nellie. "All the way back to Tubal-Cain and Hephaestus and all the way up to Humble Blacksmith, who oversaw the construction of this Guildhall and named the entryway after himself. The bladesmiths will teach you about Masamune, Japan's greatest swordsmith. The locksmiths may teach you about Bessie Smith, because she opened so many doors. And if Robert Blacksmith convinces you to come to his forge, he'll blather on and on about Seppo Ilmarinen, the Eternal Hammerer. Robert loves to hammer."

"And I'm afraid there's no escaping math," said Irma. "Angles and equations all day long. But instead of learning at a desk, which seems rather pointless, you'll learn math the proper way, at a workbench, then put your answers straight to work, with hammer and tongs."

"And science," said Nellie. "Smithing is science. Chemistry, geology, metallurgy—even economics. But here, we take science out of textbooks. We set things on fire. What's the point of science without a little smoke?"

"What about reading and writing?" said Eden.

Irma shrugged. "Never seen the value."

"Oh, sister," Nellie said. "Don't forget about Records. Eden, think of Records as a lovely kind of library, but a library guarded by a huge—"

"But I will go back to regular school, won't I?" interrupted Eden. "I mean, eventually?"

Nellie frowned. "Is that what you want, dearie? To go back?"

Eden shrugged. "I just thought—I mean—I don't know."

"Don't you like it here?"

"I love it here." The words came out without hesitation, so much so that they surprised Eden. "I mean, I'm supposed to live with my grandfather, and it's pretty obvious he doesn't want me, so that's... not great. But the rest of it...well, I love the rest of it."

Nellie patted her hand. "Vulcan has always been difficult."

The talk of school reminded Eden of the envelope the woman with the black mole had given her. "Oh, I think I have a form that needs to be filled out." She ran back into her room and found the now-crumpled envelope. She pulled out the form, which had Eden's name and the address of the Guildhall at the top. A section had been highlighted in yellow, where the name of Eden's new school was supposed to be recorded. Eden showed the form to Nellie.

"The name of your school? Hmm. We learn on the job here. We don't have a school with a name. How about I list it as, let me see... ah! I have it." In a shaky, cursive script, Nellie wrote Guildhall Academy. "That should do it. Just leave the rest of it with me, dearie, and I will have a Blue Coat mail the form for you. Now then, let's have some breakfast, shall we? Here is your blank of pewter to make your dish."

"My what?"

"Your daily dish. You must make a bowl. Every day before breakfast. You must prove you made it by tapping it—at dinner." Eden remembered how Robert had led all those at Supperdinner Hall in pinging their bowls with their spoons.

Nellie handed Eden a flat disk of a dull, gray metal, around the size of a dinner plate, and walked across the room to where a machine sat on a workbench. "Ever worked a lathe, dearie?" said Nellie. Eden shook her head no. Nellie handed her a pair of the silver-rimmed, safety cat-eye glasses. "Safety first. Watch me, then."

The lathe consisted of an electric motor with a shaft sticking out one end. On the end of that shaft was a round piece of steel shaped like a solid cereal bowl. Nellie placed the metal disk against the bottom of the bowl shape, then turned a dial until another shaft pinned the disk tightly in place. She turned on the motor. The shaft, bowl shape, and metal disk began to spin. Then, for the next few minutes, Nellie pushed against the spinning disk with a short wooden stick—about as big around as a broom handle. As she pushed, the spinning disk was molded against the curved shape until it took on the form of a bowl. In less than three minutes, she removed a flawless metal bowl from the lathe.

"That's cool," said Eden. "Is that how all bowls are made?"

"It is how pewter bowls are made," said Nellie. "It is called *spinning pewter*. Quite a basic skill. Now then, you've never done this before, so let me walk you through it."

"I've got it," said Eden.

"I'll show you, dearie. I don't mind."

"I've got it."

Nellie sighed. "You truly are Vulcan's grandchild."

"At least *you* think so," said Eden. She copied Nellie's example—placing the disk, centering it, and, once it began to spin, shaping it into a bowl. In three minutes, her bowl was done and looked identical to Nellie's.

"My dear!" said Nellie. "You are a natural. You've never done this before?"

"No, but I think my dad had lathes at his factory—"

"Hush!" said Nellie. "*Factory* is not a word we use in here. Don't ever say it. However, you did a superb job. I wish your grandfather had seen that. You have a knack—"

"—for mechanical things?"

"I was going to say *metallurgical things*, but close enough."

"You don't really do this every day, do you?"

"We do," said Nellie. "A smith must smith, every day. This little morning ritual ensures that we do so."

"If you did this every day, you'd have hundreds of bowls."

"More like thousands," said Nellie, "or tens of thousands."

Eden frowned. "What do you do with them all?"

"I believe we store them. I seem to recall a room somewhere. But, to the point, every single smith does this every day. Well, except for Vulcan. But look what happened there."

A knock sounded on the door just then. Miss Clara Jones, again dressed in pink, stood outside the room with her tea trolley. As Nellie picked out their breakfast foods, Miss Clara stared Eden up and down.

"Get a good look, Clara Jones," said Nellie, "so that you can describe her accurately."

"I have no idea what you're talking about, Nellie Silversmith." Miss Clara slammed the door and left. Eden stifled a laugh. She might have felt a little sorry for Miss Clara Jones, but she'd never enjoyed being the new kid. Or the stares that came with it. It felt good to have Nellie speak up in her defense.

Irma poured the tea. "Four sugar cubes for you, dear?"

Eden nodded. She liked that Irma had remembered.

As they ate, Nellie said, "Now then, about your first apprentice experience: We've decided to start you on an easy one. You'll be working with our dear friend, Helena Bladesmith, who is usually as gentle and soft as a pressed rose petal. But be careful. She may be small, but she can be dangerous. She has a sharp edge if you anger her. Avoid doing that and she will ease you into the smithing process."

"I have to do it alone? Can't one of you come with me?"

"I wish we could, dearie, but we have our own work to do. The Queen Consort of England won't wait forever for her new silver tea service. Now where did my pillow go?"

Eden picked a pillow up off the floor. "I really don't want to go by myself." She'd only known the sisters for a day, but the thought of leaving them gave Eden a sudden urge to panic. She took a deep breath.

"My dear girl," said Nellie. "Just look at you! Your hands are shaking worse than mine. Here, put that pillow behind my back and have another cup of tea. Sister and I will be right here, waiting for you. Irma and I apprenticed at your age and we survived just fine. Although I suppose we did have others around who were our age, which was so much fun. If there *was* another child here, we wouldn't hesitate to allow them to accompany you. But there's not." She picked up a spare bowl of oatmeal and a spoon. "Now let's go see that grandfather of yours and tell him your news."

"What news is that?"

"That you're on your way to becoming a smith. That you are officially an apprentice. It's the biggest development in this place in the last twenty years. It is sure to cheer him up."

<hr>

Vulcan looked even worse than the day before. His whole body slumped. Instead of saying hello to Eden, he complained that the sisters had woken him. When Nellie told him the news—that Eden was the first new apprentice in thirty-five years—Vulcan only grunted.

Nellie stomped her cane on the floor of Vulcan's room. "That is all you have to say? Even if this were some random child, this would be a monumental announcement, Vulcan. But Eden is your own flesh and blood."

"It's fine," said Eden. "He's not interested in me. He doesn't need to be. I'm not interested in him, either."

"Now see what you've done, you old fool." Nellie glared at Vulcan. "You're turning your own kin against you. Again."

Vulcan turned an eye toward Eden but said nothing. He

reluctantly agreed to eat some breakfast, but when Nellie handed him the bowl of oatmeal, he mumbled that there wasn't enough sugar on it.

"For an old man, you are such an infant," said Nellie. "I suppose I will have to run to Kitchens and get some sugar."

"I'll go," said Eden. She mostly wanted the distraction, but she reasoned that little actions such as this just might make her grandfather like her. She jogged around the corner to the white double doors of Kitchens. Inside, she found Nathaniel sitting at a stainless-steel table with what looked like a Spanish lesson book spread out in front of him. He was dressed the same as the day before, in checkered pants and his white chef's jacket. His short hair stuck up in even more directions.

"Don't shirk on your language studies," said Lillian, as she came into view, wooden spoon in hand. "I'll be giving you a test tomorrow."

"So you've told me," said Nathaniel.

"Don't get sassy with me, Nathaniel Jones. Oh, Eden, I didn't see you there. What can I do for you?"

"I need some sugar, please. For my grandfather's breakfast."

"Sugar? Well, I suppose Vulcan deserves a small vice right now. Anything else?"

A sudden idea sprang into Eden's head. She blurted, "I need Nathaniel, too! I need him to come with me today. To my apprenticeship."

"You need what?" said Lillian. Nathaniel stared at Eden, his eyes wide and his mouth hanging open.

"I need Nathaniel! Oh please, Mrs. Jones, I don't want to go by myself with all these strangers. Can Nathaniel please come with me. Just for this first day?"

"It seems very improper. Nathaniel is not a smith. Thank goodness."

"The sisters—Nellie—she said if there were another young person here I could—well, Nathaniel is young. He and I are the only kids."

"He has his schoolwork to do."

Nathaniel pulled at the collar of his chef's jacket. "Aw, come on, Mom. Just this once?"

"Please?" begged Eden.

Mrs. Jones smoothed down the front of her chef's uniform and looked hard at her son. Finally, she spoke. "It must be difficult for both of you, being the only children in this place, with nothing but adults to keep you company. I suppose you can go for a few hours, Nathaniel. But Eden, if anyone complains—any smith, that is—you must make it clear that Nathaniel is there at *your* request, and not on his own."

Nathaniel stared at his mother. "I can actually go?"

"Not until I fix your hair." Lillian licked her fingers and tried to slick down Nathaniel's unruly hair, but as far as Eden could tell, it didn't help one bit. "I guess that will have to do," said Lillian. "Now you'd better leave quickly, before I change my mind. And you'll have to catch up on your schoolwork before bed."

Eden ran from Kitchens with a cup of sugar, dragging Nathaniel by the arm. "Keep running," he shouted, "just in case."

It took some pleading with the sisters to convince them to allow Nathaniel to accompany Eden. "He is not a smith, you know," said Nellie, drumming the tip of her cane on the floor. "He's a Jones. Little Nat Jones."

"I know. He's just my guest. Just there as my—as my companion. And you basically promised! You said if there was a way for me to have one—a companion—"

"Don't throw my own words back at me, Eden. It is not ladylike. Very well. I will personally allow it. But Helena Bladesmith may have her own opinion. And keep in mind that you are only an apprentice here. You are in no position to make demands."

"But—" Eden bit her lip. "I mean, thank you."

Nellie smiled. "You're welcome, dearie. Now then, here is a pair of pliers you can use. My spare set. Go to the elevator and tell Buzz you're going to Helena's shop. Now go! Go go go!"

X

In Which Eden First Learns of the Five Tasks

They hurried along the dim corridors through the basement. Nathaniel said, "Are we going...up? To one of the upper floors?"

"I guess so," said Eden. "Why?"

"It's just that I've never been higher than the first floor."

"Never? Why not? Is it against the rules?"

"I'm not sure what the rules are," said Nathaniel. "The Blue Coats are Joneses and they're allowed up there. But the kitchen staff—we stick to the main floor and the basement levels."

"That's—that's terrible."

Nathaniel said nothing.

"Don't you think it's terrible?" asked Eden.

"I'm not supposed to talk about it. And you don't know. I like it down here. We've got all the food. And it's nice and cool. Nicer than you realize."

Eden stopped. "Wait. Do you *live* here? Do all the Joneses live here—in the Guildhall, I mean?"

"A lot do. Some live in Tacoma and commute, but most of us live here. Including me. I'm the only Jones kid who lives here, though.

We have our own levels. I'd show you, but only Joneses are allowed on those floors. Why?"

"I just thought—well, here's the elevator." She pushed the button.

When the elevator arrived, Buzz smiled at Eden and frowned at Nathaniel. Eden told Buzz they were going to meet Helena.

"Helena Bladesmith?" Buzz said. "But that's on the Council floor."

"Is it?" said Eden. "All I know is that it's been arranged by the sisters."

"Seems highly improper. Can't remember ever taking kitchen help to the Council floor. Ever."

Buzz took a key from his pocket and opened a small gold cover on the elevator wall. A gold button was under the cover. Buzz straightened his bow tie, adjusted his hat, then pushed the button.

Nathaniel let out a low whistle as they stepped off the elevator. A thick green carpet lay under their feet. The walls were decorated in intricate bas-relief scenes of silver and gold. The first scene depicted a blacksmith nailing a horseshoe onto the hoof of a horse. The blacksmith had a halo over his head. The second scene showed the same blacksmith a nailing horseshoe onto the hoof of the devil. In the final scene, the devil was dancing away with the horseshoes on his hooves and a pained look on his face.

"Wow," whispered Nathaniel. "This floor is fancy."

"All the ones I've been on are pretty nice," said Eden. "Are the Joneses floors like this?"

Nathaniel frowned but said nothing.

They found Helena Bladesmith's door. Its steel surface was bent and scored by several gouges that cut all the way through, as if someone had tried to hack their way out from inside. Eden knocked. No answer. She knocked again, louder. Still nothing. Eden pounded on the door with her fist.

"Coming!" said a high, shaky voice from inside. A few seconds later, the door opened. Helena stood there smiling, out of breath. "Hello hello hello! Such an exciting day!" Helena was even shorter than Nellie and Irma, with the top of her head only reaching Eden's armpit. She wore round goggles that covered her eyes and a dark leather apron that covered her torso. Her smile disappeared when she saw Nathaniel. "What is *he* doing here?"

"This is my, umm, companion," said Eden. "The sisters said I could bring him along. For company. His name is—"

"I know who he is. The little Nat. He's a *Jones*. You know that, don't you?"

"I know his name is Nathaniel Jones, if that's what you mean."

"It means he is not a smith. He's the scullery boy from the basement. I'll have a talk with the sisters about this. In the meantime, I suppose the Nat can join you, as long as he doesn't touch anything."

They walked through Helena's apartment. On a nearby wall hung rows of sabers, rapiers, cutlasses, broadswords, and katana swords. Another wall was covered in knives—throwing knives, daggers, dirks, hunting knives, and pocketknives of all sizes. A third wall held nothing but axes—small hatchets, hefty woodsman axes, and huge, curved battle-axes.

Helena handed Eden a brand-new leather apron, heavy leather gloves, and round safety goggles. She found an old, patched set of the same for Nathaniel. "I'll allow you to use these," she said to him, "but you had better take good care of them. Or else."

The center of the apartment was cleared and empty except for a large pillar of wood. The pillar was so scarred it looked like someone had spent years trying to chop it down. At the back of the room was a metal door. Helena pulled the door open with a grunt.

A blast of heat met them, along with a steady roaring sound, like a strong wind. "I should probably turn off that furnace!" shouted Helena. She crossed her workshop to a black furnace about four feet square. A black pipe rose from the top. A door on the front of the box hung open and the fire that burned inside was so bright that Eden had to shield her eyes. Helena shut the door with a gloved hand. "Won't be using it much this morning, but I do like my workshop to be hot. We'll be putting the finishing touches on a sword today, which means grinding and polishing. Give it an edge and a shine. It's a ceremonial piece for the reigning prince of Liechtenstein."

The shop was ringed in scarred, wooden workbenches. On top of the workbenches lay hammers, tongs, and bars of rusty steel. Grinding and polishing wheels, connected by belts to bulbous electric motors, stood silent. Helena picked up a roughly shaped sword blade from a workbench. The sword was longer than Helena was tall. She held it in her gloved hands. Where the handle should be was just a thin rod of steel. She powered on a huge grinding wheel and pushed the edge of the sword against the wheel, emitting a shower of sparks that bounced off her leather apron.

Eden and Nathaniel jumped out of the way. "Careful!" shouted Eden.

"I am being careful," said Helena. "Safety first." She pushed the sword harder against the grinding wheel and even more sparks shot out.

"Do you want me to help you with that?" said Eden, inching toward the sparks. She wanted to work. She wanted to impress her grandfather.

"I don't want your help right now. Just your attention." Helena handed the blade to Eden. It was lighter than Eden expected. Helena showed Eden how she sharpened the blade. After an hour, she gave Eden a turn. While Nathaniel watched, Eden went from one grinding wheel to another, and then began using a series of polishing wheels as the blade slowly took on a mirrorlike shine.

"Let's see how close we are." Helena picked up a small hammer and hit the sword with it. *Ping!* It rang like a bell.

Eden jumped. "Oh!"

Helena smiled. "You feel that, eh? Good steel struck hard? There is no sound sweeter to a true smith. That was a perfect F-sharp. Just the note I was going for. I find that if you can achieve an F-sharp, these two-handed swords tend to keep a better edge. Now a saber—all sabers should be tuned half a note higher, to the key of G. If you get a saber in an F-sharp, it will be nothing but trouble. Come now, let's go try it on the tree trunk."

Helena led them out of the workshop back into her apartment and stopped in front of the scarred pillar of wood. She handed the sword to Eden. "Hold it correctly, please. For a longsword like this, that means both hands. Now go ahead and give it a few good whacks."

Eden held the sword and tapped the blade against the pillar. "Like that?"

"No. Swing the bloody thing."

Eden swung harder and a small chip of the wooden pillar broke loose. "Sorry."

Helena grabbed the sword from her. "Do you know what one of these is for? For chopping your enemy into bits." She swung the sword with a grunt. It thunked into the wood and stuck there. "I just imagined I was chopping off Uriah Pewtersmith's left leg." She smiled and handed the sword back to Eden. "Now you chop off his right one."

Eden gripped the sword in both hands. She pictured Mr. Pewtersmith, standing on the stage at the sentencing of her grandfather. She swung the sword at the pillar until her hands stung and bits of wood went flying. "How does it feel, Eden?" asked Helena. "Good? I knew it would. That's enough now."

Eden breathed heavily. She smiled.

Nathaniel said politely, "Would it be all right if I were to try it?"

"You?" said Helena. "Hold one of my swords? No."

"Why not?" said Eden. "I'm sure Nathaniel's got enemies he'd like to chop."

"I said no." Helena sighed. "Smiths do smithing, as their nature dictates. Joneses do Jones work, because that work is true to their nature as well. Better that way."

"I dunno." Eden chopped the sword into the pillar again. "Right now it sounds better for smiths, but worse for Joneses."

Helena took the sword from Eden. "I said, that's enough now." Eden wasn't sure if Helena was talking about chopping or talking. Helena smiled and continued, "Now, about that Vulcan Smith. I still can't get over the fact that Mr. Eleventh-Level Master has a granddaughter."

"What does that mean, exactly?"

"It means he's the only smith ever to have achieved master status in eleven arts. Goldsmithing, silversmithing, fendersmithing, coppersmithing, blacksmithing, locksmithing, tinsmithing, pewtersmithing, gunsmithing, machining, hmm…how many was that? I've only achieved master status in one, and it took most of my life. Many smiths in this very building have never achieved even one. He achieved *eleven*." Helena rested on the sword as if it were a cane. "If there were ever a smith who had any chance of completing the Five, well, it would be him."

"You mean the Five Impossible Tasks?" said Eden. "Irma mentioned them, but Nellie wouldn't let her tell me about them."

"I see," said Helena. "Well, if Nellie doesn't want you to know of them, then I shouldn't say anything." She raised an eyebrow. "Unless, that is, you really, really, really want me to."

"I do."

Helena's eyes sparkled. "I was hoping you would. Now then, when a smith is stripped of his or her title or banished from the Guild, there is only one way they can ever get their status back. And that is to complete the Five Impossible Tasks."

Eden wrinkled her eyebrows. "So if my grandfather could complete these Tasks, he'd get his old rooms back?"

Helena swung the sword at the wooden pillar. "His rooms, his title, and all his rights. Oh, he'd get it all back and more. Any smith that could complete the Tasks would be the most famous smith of all times. More celebrated than Saint Dunstan himself."

"Then why hasn't he started on them?"

"Come again?"

Eden shouted, "Why hasn't Vulcan started on them? On the Tasks?"

"Started on them? Let's hope to heaven he *hasn't* started on them. Because they're not meant to be completed, you see."

"But you said so yourself—if anyone could do it—"

"—it would be Vulcan. It's just a way of giving a compliment. I didn't mean he *should* do it. Because he can't. Not actually. No one can." She swung the sword again. This time she missed the wooden pillar completely. Eden had to duck to keep from getting her head chopped off.

Eden said, "But what if Vulcan were to try it?"

Helena's eyes sparkled again. "He'd *die*." She stretched out that tiny sentence as if she were performing on a stage. "And if you're his helper, he'd kill you in the attempt. Or worse! But enough about that. Time to get back to work. It's your turn to make something."

"A sword? Can I make a sword?"

"Let's start with something small"—Helena smiled—"like a butter knife."

"Oh, good," said Eden. "I like butter knives. I've got a little experience with them. They make pretty good screwdrivers."

XI

A Knife for a Grandfather

It took Eden two hours to make the butter knife and engrave decorations on the handle. Whenever Nathaniel tried to step in and help, Helena scolded him away. After the knife was complete, Helena turned it over and over in her wrinkled fingers.

"Is something wrong with it?" asked Eden.

"Where did you learn to do this?"

"Do what?"

"This—this level of work. You've obviously trained somewhere before coming to me."

Eden shrugged. "Nellie told me I have a knack. But you're my first teacher."

"I'm your first," whispered Helena, handing back the knife. "I didn't realize just how good of a teacher I was. We shall continue tomorrow at the same time."

Eden and Nathaniel walked back to the elevator. "So what did you think?" said Eden, butter knife in hand.

Nathaniel shrugged. "I didn't get to do any smithing."

Eden said, "Yeah, I noticed. Why wouldn't Helena Bladesmith let you?"

"Because I'm a Jones. Not a Smith."

"So?"

"In the Guildhall, Smiths are the only ones who can work in metal."

"She said that Joneses do Jones work. What kind of work do Joneses do?"

"Cooking. And guarding. We have a Jones doctor and some nurses here that are Joneses. The gardeners and plumbers are all Joneses. Mailroom. A records-keeper. And we do some cleaning. Like washing dishes. Oh, and there's an astrophysicist. I'm gonna be late. Mom's gonna be mad."

"Wait, don't go yet. You're all paid by the smiths? And what about the Blue Jackets? What are they?"

"Blue *Coats*, not Blue *Jackets*. All Blue Coats are Joneses. They're guards, wait staff, first aid—all sorts of things."

"And why are you all named Jones? Are you all related?"

"All I know is that Jones is my name and we're all bound by the same oath."

"There's an oath? What oath?"

"I'm not allowed to tell you. And you ask way too many questions," said Nathaniel.

"And you keep way too many secrets. The Jones jobs don't sound too bad. They seem pretty…normal."

"They're not smithing."

"And you want to smith?" asked Eden.

"I want the right to try it. No one likes to be told they can't do something."

"Then go be a smith somewhere else. Tacoma's a big city. I even know of a foundry around here."

"I'm a little tied down, don't you think?"

"Are you a prisoner?"

Nathaniel stopped in front of the elevator. "What? No. Nobody's a prisoner. Except maybe your grandfather."

"What do you mean, *maybe*?"

"I'm just saying I don't know what his deal is." Nathaniel pressed the elevator call button. "What I do know is that the Guildhall is where my mom is, and our home is, and it also happens to be the place where the best smiths in the world live. This is the best place to learn." He frowned. "They just won't teach *me*."

"I'm gonna talk to the sisters about this," said Eden.

"Good luck," said Nathaniel. "It's always been this way."

"Times change."

They rode the elevator down to the basement with Buzz. When they stepped off and the doors had closed, Nathaniel said, "Buzz is a Jones, too. So I guess we also operate elevators."

"Hmmph," said Eden.

They hurried along the basement hallway until they reached the doors of Kitchens. Eden could hear Mrs. Jones complaining about the time. Nathaniel balled up his fists and took a deep breath. "Here I go," he said. He pushed through the doors and was gone.

Instead of returning to the sisters, Eden walked to her grandfather's room. She'd made a decision. She was going to offer the butter knife to Vulcan as a gift. Maybe it would make some small difference in his feelings toward her. She knocked.

"Go away," came Vulcan's voice from inside.

"It's me. Eden. Your granddaughter."

"Saint Dunstan's hairy white beard! I know you're my blasted granddaughter. You don't have to explain that to me every time."

"I brought you a present," said Eden. "Something I made for you. Something I, umm, smithed."

Eden heard her grandfather's clunking steps. The door opened. Vulcan held out his calloused hand.

Eden passed him the butter knife. Vulcan grunted. He turned the knife one way, then the other. He flicked the edge with his thumb then balanced the knife on a finger. "Who helped you?"

"Helena Bladesmith."

"How much did she do?"

"I watched her make a sword, then I made this. She told me what to do, but I did it all. Well, almost all."

"And this is your—"

"—first time? Yes. Is it all right?"

"It's lousy," said Vulcan. "An amateur piece. Out of balance. Something a level-three would make."

Eden felt her eyes filling with tears. She gritted her teeth and willed the tears back.

Vulcan held the knife up in the light. "But if it's really your first piece—"

"It is."

"—then it's not horrible. It takes most of these smiths a couple of years to get to level three. And you—just a kid who's never held a bar of steel in her hand—you do this? On your first try?"

Eden sniffed. "So it's okay?"

Vulcan grunted. "What's this design on the handle?" Vulcan pointed to the engraving Eden had done on the knife—a tree inside a circle.

"I know it's pretty simple."

"Nothing wrong with simple. What's it mean?"

"It's meant to be the tree from the Garden of Eden. My name is Eden. So it's kind of a symbol for me, I guess."

Vulcan frowned at her. "Your skills aren't bad. Better than I expected." He pulled the knife inside and shut the door.

Eden sat down on the hallway floor, outside Vulcan's room, staring into her empty hands.

⁓

Eugene Tinker found her there, half an hour later. He was carrying a box and breathing heavily.

"Didn't expect to see you here, Eden. How's the old man?"

Eden shrugged.

"Vulc has been through a lot lately. And I think it's kinda hard for him, your seeing him like this."

"You think *I'm* making it hard on *him*? You've gotta be kidding."

Eugene set his box down on the floor of the hallway and mopped his face with his yellow hankie. The box was full of oily gears, pulleys, and wire. "That's not what I said. It's not something you're doing. Just your being here. I think you may remind him of everything he's lost. His son, his status, even his old rooms."

"Like he's the only one who's lost things? Or people?" A mental list began forming in Eden's brain, but she shook it away. "Why can't I at least be something he's *gained*?"

Eugene twisted the yellow hankie in his hands. "I think it's gonna take some time is all."

"Do you know about the Five Tasks, Eugene?"

Eugene stared down at her in silence.

"Helena said that the only way a dishonored smith can regain their status is to complete the Five Impossible Tasks."

Eugene scrunched up his face. "'Course I know about them."

"Then tell me. Please."

"I'm pretty sure I ain't supposed to talk about 'em, With you, I mean. No sense worrying you," said Eugene. "Those things can get a smith killed. Or worse."

"Worse? What could be worse than being killed?"

Eugene said nothing.

"It doesn't matter. If my grandfather were to do the Tasks, he's too good of a smith to fail, isn't he? If he completed them, and regained his status—and his rooms—maybe he'd, well, feel better about things. Like me. So maybe he could tell me what to do and I could—you know—do it. I could be his helper."

Eugene sat his heavy body next to her on the floor, with the box of parts between him and and Eden. "His helper, eh? Did Helena use that word, *helper*? Did she happen to tell you what happens to helpers?"

"So there *are* helpers? Tell me, Eugene. Start with the Five Tasks—tell me what they are."

"What do you think this is? Story time?"

"Would that be so bad?"

Eugene laughed. "I guess not. Get comfortable. This might take a while."

XII

The Five Impossible Tasks

As she settled herself against the wall, Eden ran her finger over an oily gear in the box that Eugene had set down next to her. "What's all this stuff for?"

"For Vulc. Give him something to work on. Keep his skills sharp." He took the gear from her and put it back in the box. "Now, the story of the Five Tasks—I'll start by saying it ain't my story to tell," said Eugene. "Do you know what Nellie will do if she finds out I told you?"

"I won't say a word," said Eden, picking up the gear again. "And the main thing about stories isn't who tells them. It's that they get told."

"If you say so." Eugene sucked in a deep breath, then slowly let it out between clenched teeth. "It all started during the days of your ancestor, Kaos Fendersmith. Back in 1881. Ten years before this building was built. Now Kaos, he was a troublemaker. Talented, but reckless. He liked fire. He wanted to build the hottest furnace ever. The Council wouldn't let him, but Kaos built it anyway. He figured that once he had it done and they realized how good it was, that they'd thank him for it. So he built it in his own rooms and fired it up. And he was right. It *was* better. It burned so hot that the hardest piece of iron would have turned to liquid in the blink of an eye."

"Would have?" asked Eden.

Eugene took the oily gear back from her again. "It was never tried—not with metal, anyway. As soon as Kaos lit it, the furnace burned so hot that it caught his rooms on fire. Then the furnace burned through the floor and fell to the floor below and caught that on fire, too. It burned all the way to the bottom and burned the whole Guildhall to the ground. Three people died in the fire. Not one of the three was really a decent smith, mind you. None of them over a level four. But people get upset about death, and the Council gets upset about stupidity, and everyone wanted to punish Kaos in a way that fit the crime. Wanted to execute him."

"But it was an accident! They weren't serious, were they? About killing him?" Eden swallowed hard.

Eugene nodded. "They were. But they couldn't do that, of course. He was a master smith—a fendersmith. And even though we keep to ourselves in here, I suppose there are at least a few laws we need to follow. Even way back then."

"Like...not going around executing each other?" Eden said.

"Like that. So after they rebuilt the hall, they—well—they imprisoned him in his rooms for the rest of his life. Said if he wanted to stay in the Guildhall, it'd be from the confines of his own rooms. Kaos appealed. Said he was a master smith, but they said that didn't matter. One year later, he appealed again. But the Council ignored him again. The next year, when Humble Blacksmith chaired the Council and this here building was still shiny and new, Kaos appealed one more time. Finally, the Council said they'd give him a chance to redeem himself."

"They were probably tired of hearing him complain," said Eden, picking up a coil of wire.

"You may be right," said Eugene. "One member of the Council, Malachi Pewtersmith—"

"Figures it was a Pewtersmith," said Eden. "Was he related to *our* Mr. Pewtersmith?"

Eugene twisted the ring on his left pinkie. "Yes. Malachi was *his* great-great-great-great-something. The Pewtersmiths have had it in for the Smith-smiths *that* long. Old Malachi, he calls all the smiths into Main Lodge. He gets up in front and says how merciful he is. That he's been thinking on it long and hard, and it's his idea to give Kaos a chance to prove his worth, regain his status, and free himself from his imprisonment—if he's talented enough. And then he sets forth the Five. The Tasks." Eugene mopped his face with his hankie again. "Surprisingly hot down here in the subbasements. You'd think it would be cooler. Anyway, as soon as old Malachi announces them, everyone realizes the Tasks are impossible. And deadly. But Kaos—Vulcan's bloodline, you know—"

"Mine, too," said Eden. "Don't leave me out of it." Hearing stories of her ancestors—even these tragic ones—fed a hunger Eden hadn't known existed.

"Yes, your bloodline, too," said Eugene. "Anyway, Kaos, he's still got a lot of pride and fury, so he gathers up his courage and jumps right in. Gets a machinist to help him and starts on his first Task the next day."

"What happened?"

Eugene shrugged. "Dead by lunchtime."

Eden gasped. "Dead? You mean he died from the very first Task? I thought you said he was a master smith!"

Eugene nodded. "He was. Yet he died in a pile of dirty dishes."

Eden twisted the wire between her fingers. "But the Task was just to wash the dishes? That doesn't sound very hard. In most of my foster homes, I had to do the dishes after dinner practically every night."

"Foster homes?" said Eugene. "Before you found this place, eh?"

Eden nodded.

"Eden, sorry if it seems like I don't care what you've been through." He jutted his chin toward Vulcan's door. "I've been so focused on my old friend's struggles that I've been ignoring yours. It couldn't have been easy, these past years."

"It wasn't." Eden's eyes felt suddenly watery. She felt the sudden need to clear her throat. "But—but tell me about the dishes."

"Right. Well, here, there are a *lot* of dishes. And the Task says you have to wash all of them. In one day."

Eden frowned. "How many dishes can there be? I mean, how many people live here?"

"Two hundred and ten," said Eugene. "Well, two-eleven now with you, Eden."

"So two hundred and eleven. That's how many you have to wash?"

"No," said Eugene. "That's how many we *make*, every day."

"You mean the daily dish?" said Eden. "I made one this morning."

"It's pretty silly," muttered Eugene. "Vulc calls it the dumbest rule in the history of this Guildhall. But it is a rule. Two hundred and ten new dishes have been stacking up, dirty, every single day for decades and decades. So about two hundred dishes times three sixty-five—for each day of the year—times years and years. *That's* how many you have to wash. In a day. Kaos tried. It killed him."

"I'm afraid to ask about the other Tasks," said Eden.

Eugene nodded. "There are harder ones." He looked at Vulcan's door and his voice dropped to a whisper. "Like the birds. Steel birds. Mechanical. Like wind-up toys, but bigger and smarter. Not sure *smarter* is the right word. They were crafted by one of Vulcan's heroes, the great machinist, Thợ Tiện, and Thợ may have made them too well. He built the birds to chase some pigeons out of the attic, back in 1894. Problem was, Thợ Tiện's mechanical birds were so realistically made that they acted like real birds. They turned the attic into their nesting ground and then, just like real birds, they protected it. Tried to kill anyone who came in. And they kept winding each other up on their own. They're still doing it. They've never run down. No one's been able to go in the attic since then." Eugene leaned in close and whispered, even lower. "Some people say they've even had babies."

"Mechanical birds can't wind themselves up," said Eden, "and they can't have babies."

"Thợ Tiện was a very good machinist, Eden," said Eugene.

"I'm *not* buying the babies thing, Eugene. Still, it doesn't sound that bad," said Eden. "You just have to catch the birds. Jeez, this floor is hard. I think my butt's gone numb." She stood up and marched in place a few times before leaning against the wall of the corridor.

"Don't you think that someone would have gotten rid of the birds by now if it was easy?" said Eugene. "They've been up there, keeping everyone out of the attic for more than a hundred years. Your ancestor—Berthold Arrowsmith. No. Berthold *Locksmith*. Whatever his name was, he died trying that Task when *he* was imprisoned. You gotta be at the top of your game to beat even one Task. If you're not..."

Eugene adjusted his bulky body. "My butt might be numb, too, now that you mention it. Anyway, Berthold's first assigned Task was the birds. He and an assistant went into the attic. Everyone outside heard what sounded like a scream. And that was it. Old Berthold and his helper must have been pecked to death."

"*Must have been*? You mean you don't know? How can you not know?"

"No one's ever gone back in and checked." Eugene was quiet for a moment, then said, "The birds got Vulcan's dad, too. Your great grandfather Burhanu."

"Wait a minute," said Eden. "Was it always just *my* ancestors who did this? Didn't anyone else in this place try to do these Tasks?"

Eugene shrugged. "A few did. A tinsmith here, a locksmith there. But it takes a pretty serious accusation to get a smith in this kind of trouble—in enough trouble to get imprisoned. Or banished. Those accusations almost always came from Pewtersmiths. And the Pewtersmiths—well, they seem to have it in for your family, Eden."

"I really don't like those guys."

"Me neither. Anyway, the birds took your great-grandfather Burhanu from us when *he* tried the Task." Then Eugene pointed with his thick thumb toward Vulcan's room. "The birds also got Vulc's leg. That's why he walks with that prosthetic thingamajig now. He lost his real leg to the Birds. He was there. Not helping. Just watching."

"What did they do? I mean, what was Burhanu's strategy?"

Eugene shrugged. "I don't know. But Vulc should—him being there and all. Can't imagine he would forget that day. But whatever they tried, it must not have worked."

Eden stared at the floor. "Okay, okay. So maybe it *is* hard," she whispered. "What's the next one?"

"That would be the rats," said Eugene. "For this Task, you have to get all the rats out of the Guildhall."

Eden shivered. "Ugh. I don't want any part of that one. Rats are disgusting. Naked tails. Long teeth. Just thinking about them gives me the creeps."

"I've always thought that this Task doesn't seem so bad," said Eugene. "Of course, your ancestor, Aether Coppersmith—he thought it would be easy, too."

"Please don't tell me he died from the rats."

"Haven't you figured it out yet?" came a voice from inside Vulcan's room. The door flung open and Vulcan leaned into the corridor. "Don't you get it?"

"I thought you were locked in your room," Eden said.

"I may be under arrest," growled Vulcan, "and I may not have a title anymore, but I'm still a master locksmith. Not that it does any good. I'm still doomed."

Eugene said, "Eden, whenever your ancestors tried the Tasks, they all failed. And died. Or worse."

"It's our fate," groaned Vulcan. "Inescapable. Except for Eric. He got out in time, but even then.... We all know what the outside world does to us smiths."

"What does it do?"

Vulcan shrunk back into his room, as if there were some horrible presence in the hallway. "It withers us away. It makes us lesser. It unsmiths us." Vulcan let out a moan.

Eugene struggled to his feet. "It's okay, Vulc. No one's making you go out there."

"Not yet," wailed Vulcan, "but they will. You and I both know how this is going to end."

Eden wanted to tell her grandfather that it wasn't that bad in the outside world. She wanted to tell him that there were green parks, ice-cream parlors, and kind people. She'd seen little of these things herself, but she still recognized they existed. And yet, in the short time she'd spent in the Guildhall, she had already developed an attachment to the place. She knew this because the thought of leaving it made her stomach churn. She realized that this smith in front of her felt a much deeper attachment to the Guildhall—and a much deeper dread of the outside world.

Eden looked at her grandfather from the doorway. "That's what you mean, isn't it? When you say *or worse*, you mean that you'd rather die than live out there, don't you."

Vulcan stared back at her, then nodded once.

Eugene mopped his forehead again. "Eden, for a smith, banishment is worse than dying. Far worse. Death kills the body. Banishment—especially for a smith like Vulc—kills the soul. It takes them from the only thing they love doing. And the only place they feel at home."

"Then we'd better not fail," said Eden. "So, dishes, birds, and rats. What are the last two?"

Eugene smiled. "Can't forget about Mrs. Gunsmith's girdle. Ain't that right, Vulc?"

Vulcan stomped his steel leg on the floor. "You're out here telling her all this like it's some kind of a bedtime story. It's dangerous. She shouldn't know."

Eden's face grew even hotter. "You act like I'm not part of this. But I'm living here now. And I'm your granddaughter. We're supposed to be family. So what's this next one? And what's a girdle?"

No one spoke. Finally, Vulcan said, "To hell with it. Tell her. Won't change anything."

"Normally, a girdle is thought of as a kind of old-fashioned ladies' undergarment," said Eugene. His voice sounded thin, as if his mouth was dry. "Used 'em more back in the day to make themselves look skinnier, if such a thing was desired."

"So...you have to make this lady some underwear?"

"Make it? No. It's already made. You have to steal it."

"*What?* That just sounds wrong. Stealing someone's underwear."

"You misunderstand me, Eden. I said *normally*. The Gunsmiths ain't normal. This here girdle ain't undies. It's an antique belt—a gun belt, I guess you'd call it. Made of titanium, so it's practically bullet-proof. It's got fancy pearl-handled revolvers on each side and bullets all the way around. Like something a cowboy or cowgirl might have worn back in the day." Eugene frowned. "I personally got no patience for guns and what they do, but the gunsmiths are still smiths. And that gun belt—the original Mrs. Gunsmith's girdle—it's been a prized possession of theirs since the first frontier days of this Guild-hall. There's even a song about it."

"There's a song?"

Eugene cleared his throat. "Remember it, Vulc? Want to sing it with me? Eh? Don't make me sing it by myself." When Vulcan failed to join him, Eugene began to sing what sounded like a sad, old coun-try song, in a squeaky, tuneless voice:

Oh the beauty! O the legend!
Mrs. Gunsmith was her name!
If you ever saw her visage,
you would understand her fame!
Just as famous as the woman
was the girdle 'round her buns.
Underwear? No! Outerwear!
Only there to hold her guns.
Held off bandits! Height of fashion!
With her girdle, she was dressed.
It could even stop a bullet
in the Wild Guildhall West!
If you ever steal that girdle,
don't forget these words I've said!
If Mister Gunsmith catches you
then you're as good as dead.

"Maybe don't quit your day job, Eugene," said Eden. "Mrs. Gunsmith—I know that name from somewhere." She remembered the jar that sat on her bedside table, next to her pot of dirt holding the orchid stump, behind the photograph of her parents. "Is that the same gunsmith lady who makes beauty cream?"

"Not the same one," said Eugene. "That beauty cream is a more recent development. The Mrs. Gunsmith who makes that stuff is probably the great-great-great-great-granddaughter of the one who originally owned the belt—the girdle—whatever you call it," said Eugene. "The gun belt used to be worn by the senior female gunsmith 'til the Guildhall got more civilized. Nowadays, I hear that Mrs. Gunsmith's girdle hangs on the wall in the private quarters of the senior member of the gunsmiths. Currently, that would be *Mr. Gunsmith.*" Eugene mopped his face with his hankie. "All the Gunsmiths are a tough lot, especially when it comes to defending the honor of the first Mrs. Gunsmith. Who can blame them, eh Vulc?"

"What's that supposed to mean?" said Eden.

"Oh, she was supposedly the most beautiful of creatures, Mrs. Gunsmith. No surprise there. If you ask me, the Gunsmith ladies tend to be a sight for sore eyes. Gents too, for that matter, I suppose."

"Oh come on. This all sounds completely backward. And ridiculous."

"I guess it is." Eugene sighed. "But it's also deadly serious. Right now, their senior member—Mr. Gunsmith? He's terrifying. Mean as a rusty nail and tough as they come. Stealing that girdle from his bedroom? Well, it ain't gonna be easy."

Eden nodded. "So that's four. What's Task number five?"

Eugene picked up a tiny washer and dropped it into his other hand. "No one knows. No one's ever gotten that far. Number five is the Unknown Task."

Eden crossed her arms. "Okay. So they're dangerous. But what's the harm in trying? I mean, we can always stop."

"Wrong. Once you start, you can't stop." Vulcan spun on his leg and stared down at Eden. "If you stop—"

Approaching footsteps and voices interrupted him. Nellie and Irma came around the corner of the corridor. Nellie said, "Oh, there you are, Eden. We haven't seen you all day. You're having a little visit? Out here in the hallway?"

"We're making plans." Eden's voice sounded hard and sharp. Her eyes were narrow and she held her mouth in a straight line.

"Plans for what?" said Nellie, catching her breath. "Why don't we go inside and sit down?"

"Plans to restore Grandpa to his rightful position—by completing the Five Impossible Tasks. Isn't that right, *Grandpa*?" The last word had a bitter edge to it.

Nellie's face turned pale. "Tell me you two are not speaking to this poor girl of such horrible things."

"Wasn't me," said Vulcan.

"She had a right to know," muttered Eugene.

Nellie swung her cane through the air. "Eugene, I ought to beat you about the head and shoulders."

"Don't worry," said Vulcan. "We're not doing it."

"Thank heavens for that," said Nellie.

"We *are* going to do it," said Eden. "Everyone keeps saying this cranky man is the greatest smith who has ever lived. That if anyone can do the Tasks, it's him."

Vulcan squinted. "That's what Pewtersmith wants. Wants me to try them. But only fools would take on such a foolish challenge. I should know. The one task I witnessed, I barely survived."

"Only fools?" said Nellie, staring at Vulcan. "That is not very comforting. Especially if Pewtersmith really does expect you to take on the Tasks. He must think Eden is the helper Vulcan was waiting for."

"Oh, right!" said Eden. "Eugene, you were going to tell me about helpers."

"Ah," said Eugene. "Well, seems every smith who has tried the Tasks has had a helper—"

"Eugene!" scolded Nellie. "That's enough. Now let's go visit with Vulcan and talk about something else. Perhaps over a cup of tea."

"No! Tell me," said Eden.

Nellie said, "What I'll tell you is this. Just because Vulcan is imprisoned—and just because you are here—does *not* make you his helper."

"Why do you care so much if I'm a helper or not?"

Irma leaned forward. "Because you're going to die, of course. If you try the Tasks. In almost all the times a master smith tried to complete the Tasks, they've perished."

"I know that," said Eden, "but I'm not a master smith."

"The helpers die, too." Irma sipped again from her cup. "Ooh, this tea is strong. Just the way I like it."

XIII

In Which a Companion Becomes an Apprentice

The visit with Vulcan didn't last long. When Eden returned with the sisters to their rooms she asked, "Do you think it's true? That it's my grandfather's fate to die from the Tasks?"

Nellie sat down heavily on a couch. "It is hard to argue with the proof of history, but I don't want to discuss this anymore." She yawned. "Only a few minutes left for my nap. But before I lie down, Eden, you must tell us about your day with dear Helena Bladesmith. Did you enjoy the work?"

"I did," said Eden. "I think I'm good at it. I made a knife and gave it to Vulcan."

"To your grandfather? How sweet of you. Did he love it?"

Eden smirked at her.

"Well, give him time."

"That's all anyone ever says. *Give him time. He'll come around.* I'll probably be an old lady by then. No offense. But I did like the work. And it was nice to have Nathaniel there."

"Helena didn't mind?"

"Oh, she minded. She was mean to him and she wouldn't let

him touch anything. I don't understand why. What difference does it make what his last name is?"

Nellie's eyes scanned the room. "But it does make a difference. Where is that blasted pillow?"

"Smiths only come from smiths," said Irma. "That's what I always say."

Eden found the pillow and tucked it behind Nellie. Nellie sighed. "Thank you, dearie. That feels much better. As sister was saying, smiths only come from Smiths. And Joneses—well, they've never been artisans, dearie. They're sheepherders and gardeners and poets, as well as doctors and accountants. Oh, and astrophysicists."

Irma nodded. "Quite right, sister. Simpler folk, you know. Trustworthy and resourceful. But simple."

"Um, I'm not sure any of those things are exactly *simple*," Eden said.

Irma sipped her tea in reply.

"Are you saying that all the smiths in all the world are descended from Smiths?" Eden asked.

"That's right. Or from Schmidts, Zmeds, Irenyas, and such. But still Smiths in their native tongues. Hand me that blanket, dear. I think I might just take a nap right here on this couch."

"How far back?"

"How far back what?"

"How far back did all Smiths come from other Smiths?"

"Well, *all* the way back dearie. Goodness, if you're going to continue with this line of talk, then perhaps I will go to my room for my nap, after all."

"Then where did the first Smith come from?" said Eden. She stepped into Nellie's path and crossed her arms.

"You had better watch your tone, young lady," said Nellie. "That's enough history for today. It's nap time. Please step aside."

"This is all just a way for you to exclude people."

"I said to watch your tone!" said Nellie. "It is a way for us to ensure our young apprentices are of the highest quality."

"What apprentices? And my mom was a Jones, you know," said Eden. "I'm half Jones."

"Oh, we know, dearie. Believe me, we'll never forget that."

"Neither will I," said Eden.

"I wonder what's for dinner," said Irma. "Smells like meat loaf."

"I'm not hungry," said Eden. "I'll just stay here. That's what we *simpler folk* do."

"Oh, of course you're hungry," said Nellie. She wrapped a knitted shawl around Eden's shoulders. "Come along to dinner. I've completely missed my chance to nap. But we'll just set this nasty subject aside and talk about more pleasant things."

"I'm not setting anything aside," said Eden.

Nellie frowned as she picked up her cane. Eden followed behind them silently as they walked to the elevator.

Buzz held the doors open for them. "Good evening, sisters. Good evening, Eden."

"Good evening, Buzz," said Nellie and Irma.

"Hey, Buzz," said Eden. "Did you know my mom was a Jones?"

Buzz's mouth dropped opened, but he said nothing. Nellie frowned at Eden. Eden frowned right back.

When they reached Supperdinner Hall, they found their table and sat down. Robert Blacksmith repeated his tradition of pinging his spoon on his pewter dish. All the other diners copied him in unison.

Helena Bladesmith nodded at Eden from the neighboring Council table. "Here she is! My young apprentice. Her first day today, and by the end of it, I already had her forging her own blade. Just a butter knife, but a very pretty one. The girl shows some natural talent, of course, but I like to believe that my overwhelming skill as a teacher was the real trick. Are you ready for me to push you even further tomorrow, Eden?"

Eden said nothing. She was thinking about her mother, Emily Jones. *A Jones.* Eden's mother had been a college professor, teaching English literature, but she wouldn't have been welcomed into this dining room, except as a server. How would her mom have dealt with that?

Her dad, Eric Smith, had been loud, like Vulcan, but her mom,

Emily Jones, had been calm. Still, Eden couldn't remember a time when her mom didn't get her way, with her father or anyone else. She may have been quiet, but she could be a little bit cunning, too. "I am not sneaky," her mom used to say. "I am wise as a serpent and gentle as a dove."

Thinking about her mother gave Eden an idea.

"Eden," called Helena. "Did you hear me? Are you excited for tomorrow?"

Eden looked up and smiled her sweetest smile. "Oh, of course, Ms. Bladesmith. I was amazed, too. By how much you taught me. Maybe tomorrow we can make something to bring here—to bring to dinner and show the Council."

Helena beamed. "An excellent idea, Eden." She turned back to the Council. "Did you hear that? Tomorrow, you will see what a determined teacher can wring out of a student in just a few days."

Irma leaned close to Eden and whispered, "You're up to something."

"I don't know what you're talking about," said Eden.

"Neither do I," said Irma, "except that I know you're up to something."

Eden smiled. She knew her mom would have been proud. "Could you please pass the mashed peas?"

The next morning, after making her daily pewter bowl and eating breakfast, Eden stopped by Kitchens to collect Nathaniel. Smoke was pouring out between the double doors. Eden opened one door and stepped inside. Lillian was waving the smoke away with a baking sheet and yelling at her staff. "Just throw the burnt ones in the sink and start on new dough. And I said to turn the fan on *high!*" She spotted Eden. "Not now, child."

Eden covered her nose and mouth with her shirt collar. "But I'm here for Nathaniel."

"Nathaniel? He's the one who burnt tonight's dinner rolls. And he's still catching up on his schoolwork from yesterday. We are not smiths, you know. Nathaniel doesn't have the luxury to just skip work whenever he wants. One day he may be out there on his own and he needs to be prepared."

"Out? Out where?"

"Where do you think? Out *there*, in the world, outside of this Guildhall. You were there not so long ago yourself. You know what it's like."

"But—doing what?"

"Whatever he darn well pleases, obviously." She waved the cookie sheet a few more times. "Certainly not cooking for *smiths*. I may be a culinary wizard—and I *am*—and I may get paid accordingly—and I *do*—but my Nathaniel? Well, he tries. But he is a burner of rolls. No true sophistication to his palate whatsoever. Or even the slightest interest in boiling so much as an egg. So I must prepare him for other great things. Starting with the Spanish conjugations he didn't do yesterday."

"But I need him to come with me," said Eden, "today especially."

"Sorry. Nathaniel can't be spared. As I understand it, he wasn't permitted to try his hand at anything in Helena Bladesmith's work-shop anyway."

"But maybe today—"

"And you should be focusing on studies of your own, too—reading, writing, and such. Not metalworking. There are plenty of talented metallurgists out there in foundries and factories all over who you can learn from one day, if you wish. But for now, I'd advise a more general curriculum, and not one taught by a bunch of obstinate snobs with their heads buried in the sand. Please don't repeat that. They are, after all, my employers. Now off you go." Lillian pushed Eden out the doors of Kitchens. Eden stared at the closed doors for a moment, then marched toward the elevator with the word *factories* buzzing in her ears.

Helena answered her door at the first knock. "There she is! Ohh, and I see you're alone. We'll get so much more done without—well, without a Jones. We shall work on fencing blades today—foils and rapiers. Imagine the looks on the faces of the Council when we show up with a fencing foil, made by you, on just the second day—"

"No." Eden crossed her arms.

"Excuse me?"

"I said no."

"Well, perhaps you're right," said Helena. "Let's stick with something a bit simpler. Perhaps a nice battle-axe."

"No," repeated Eden.

"You're starting to confuse me, dear. What would you like to work on? Another butter knife?"

"Nothing."

"But what about the Council? We can't turn up at dinner empty-handed."

"Nothing. Unless Nathaniel can work with me. And not just watch," said Eden. "He gets to work. He gets to make something."

Helena Bladesmith's hands flew to her mouth. "You mean smithing? No no no. That could never be. Smithing cannot be done by a Jones."

"Yes, it can." Eden stomped her foot.

"It is simply not done!"

"Why not? I smithed yesterday, didn't I?"

"You did! But you are a smith and therefore naturally talented."

"I'm only half smith. My mother was a Jones. Did you know that?"

Helena coughed. "That father of yours—leaving this place. Marrying a—well, I don't pretend to understand, but smithing is only for Smiths. Joneses—but you say—hmmm. Oh, I am so confused." She covered her face in her hands, then looked out through her fingers. "Wasn't yesterday nice?"

"Not for Nathaniel. Either he gets to learn, too, or I'm not going to make anything."

"No. It simply can't be. It's never been done."

Eden took a few steps back. "Then I guess I'll go find someone else to take me on as their apprentice. And *they* can be the ones to show off my work at dinner."

Helena glared at her. "You are a devious child. But you know that, don't you?"

Eden shrugged. "I'm not devious. I'm wise as a serpent and gentle as a dove."

"Gentle? You? Go get the boy, then. But not a word of this to anyone."

"Yes!" Eden raced down the hall. She waited impatiently for the elevator, then tapped her feet the whole ride to the subbasement. She ran to Kitchens and pounded on the door.

Lillian answered, still holding her cookie-sheet fan. "What? What is the emergency? Oh! You again. I thought I made it clear that Nathaniel must stay here today."

"It's not me asking for him," said Eden between breaths. "It's Helena Bladesmith. She sent me to get him."

"Helena Bladesmith?" Lillian stared down her nose at Eden. "If I go up there and ask her, she'll confirm this?"

"Ask away," said Eden. "Can you please get Nathaniel? Or I can."

"I'll get him," said Lillian, "but I know you're behind this, Eden. You talked Helena into asking, putting me in an awkward situation." Lillian clapped her hand against the cookie sheet. "Nathaniel! Come!" Nathaniel looked confused when he stepped through the smoke, but before his mother could explain anything, Eden grabbed him and pulled him down the hallway.

Nathaniel stopped. "If we're going back to Helena Bladesmith's, then I don't really want to go."

"You want to stay in Kitchens?"

"I don't want to just sit and watch you work," said Nathaniel.

"Good," said Eden, smiling.

Nathaniel stopped walking. "What—what do you mean?"

"Nathaniel Jones, today you will smith."

"Me? I'll actually be making stuff?"

Eden nodded.

"Well then what are we standing around for?" said Nathaniel. "Hurry!" He grabbed Eden's sleeve and ran toward the elevator.

When they reached Helena's rooms, Helena looked up and down the hallway before she pulled them inside and slammed her door. "Little Nat, not a word about this to anyone, or—well, I don't know what I will do, but it won't be particularly nice. And butter knives it is then, I suppose." Helena sniffed the air. Then she leaned in toward Nathaniel and sniffed again. "Hmmm."

"What's wrong?" said Nathaniel.

"Nothing. It's just that, well, I could swear you smell like smoke. Smiths tend to smell like smoke. But never a Jones. Very strange."

Nathaniel shrugged. "Oh, that's because—"

"—because he's meant to be a smith!" said Eden, interrupting. "Nathaniel's a natural!"

Helena sniffed again. "We'll see."

They set to work. Eden turned a blank of steel into a round-tipped blade and set to work engraving another tree into the side.

Nathaniel's hands shook as he did the same work. He managed to make a butter knife, but then kept cutting the tips of his fingers on the blade. By the end of the day, nearly all his fingers were covered in bandages. The handle of his knife was short and lumpy, but Nathaniel's face beamed as he held it.

"It's nothing like yours," he said to Eden, "but it looks like a knife. I mean, if you showed it to someone and asked what it was, they would say that it was a knife, right? And I made it."

"I bet you can't wait to show your mom," said Eden.

Nathaniel gulped. "Maybe not today. I'd better get going, too. If I fall behind on my schoolwork, she'll never let me go again." He handed the knife to Eden. "Here, you hold this for me."

"But don't you want to take it with you?"

"You hold it." He walked quickly toward the door.

"What about tomorrow?" said Eden. "Can I pick you up tomorrow?"

Nathaniel squinted at his creation in Eden's hand. "It really does look like a knife. See you in the morning."

XIV

In Which Eden Learns There Is No Going Back

Eden helped Helena clean up her shop and nodded when Helena asked if she would bring her engraved knife to Supperdinner Hall that night. Helena said, "And not a word about that Jones boy being here."

At dinner that evening, Eden walked in with the sisters, feeling grateful for how the day had turned out. She had held her ground. Nathaniel—a Jones—had done smithing work today. She felt as if her mother's presence was right there with her. Now if she could just help her grandfather.

Eden tried to be courteous, even when it turned out the dinner was meat loaf again. Nellie and Irma beamed at her when Helena presented her knife to the Council.

"She made this today, under my tutelage," said Helena. "You can see my influence there, in the shape of the handle and the floral engravings. Not the work of a typical apprentice, I can tell you that!"

"Let me see," said Mr. Pewtersmith. He snatched the knife from Helena and looked at his reflection in the blade. "Hmm, very pretty. And this was on just your second day?"

"Yes." Eden hated having to talk directly to Mr. Pewtersmith.

"Remarkable. The brat has talent. It's been many years since we've had a young person here," he said, "but even back in my day, I'd bet not one in a thousand could have done this work while still under an apprenticeship. And on the second day—not one in a million. Truly remarkable."

Helena beamed. "Oh, so kind of you to say so, Uriah. Of course, I can only take most of the credit. The girl does show some raw talent, too."

"She certainly does," said Mr. Pewtersmith. "But it is—remarkable—that a child with such talent shows up on the same day that her grandfather is found guilty. She shows up, just when her grandfather needs help the most."

Nellie's cane was leaning against the table. Nellie picked it up. "I know what you're getting at, Uriah. Just keep it to yourself."

"Even you see it? Then it *must* be obvious." He stood behind Eden's chair. "Fate brought her here, to help the poor man. We are all heartbroken with how his life has turned out. Heartbroken that one of ours—a loutish oaf, but with some unrefined skill—should end his days in a subbasement cell."

Nellie gripped the head of her cane tighter. "Because you put him there, Uriah."

"Fate! Fate put him there!" said Mr. Pewtersmith, stroking the silver letter U that hung from the chain around his neck. "But fate also brought Eden to us. To help Vulcan Smith. To be his helper." He smiled at Nellie and Irma. "Surely you've told her of the Five Tasks by now."

"Someone did," said Nellie.

Helena waved. "It was me! The Five *Impossible* Tasks! I told her!" She smiled. "I have my hearing aid in tonight. I can hear practically everything."

"Good for you, Helena," said Nellie.

"What?" said Helena.

Mr. Pewtersmith nodded. "Surely I'm not the only one who sees that she has arrived to help Vulcan regain his freedom. The Tasks have never been completed without a helper."

"They've never been completed at all," said Nellie.

Mr. Pewtersmith smiled. "Some of them have, but never without assistance. And there Vulcan sits, in his cell."

"In his *room*," said Eden. She snatched her butter knife out of Mr. Pewtersmith's hand.

"Of course. *In his room*. Unable to start without assistance. Without a helper. And here is that helper." Mr. Pewtersmith rested a hand lightly on top of Eden's head. "Bless you, my child. Bless you for coming."

"I didn't come because of fate," said Eden, pulling her head away. "I came because the State brought me here after my parents died."

"And how did they die?"

"Uriah Pewtersmith," said Nellie, stomping her cane against the floor, "this is neither the time nor the place."

Helena Bladesmith interrupted. "The time? I'm sorry, but I don't wear a watch. Irma, what time is it?"

"I'm ignoring you," said Irma.

Uriah barked at Eden: "Your parents—how did they die?"

"They were hit by a meteor," hissed Eden.

"A meteor!" shouted Mr. Pewtersmith. "Deus ex machina! The machine of the gods! If that is not the hand of the fates, reaching down from the heavens to put a plan into motion—well then."

"It doesn't matter what you say, Uriah," said Nellie. "Vulcan would never agree to let Eden help. He'd stay there forever before he put his precious granddaughter in danger."

"He'd stay there out of cowardice." Mr. Pewtersmith placed his hands on Eden's shoulders. "Would you like to hear something interesting, Eden? Just today, I was in Records, reading the rules of the Five Tasks. Do you know what I discovered?"

Eden tried to squirm away from Mr. Pewtersmith's touch, but he squeezed tighter. He said, "I've found out that the Five can be completed by a proxy."

"Let me go," said Eden.

Mr. Pewtersmith tightened his grip even more. "Do you know what that word means? *Proxy*? It means a *substitute*. In other words, little Smith, if your grandfather is too much of a coward to do the Tasks, you can do them. You can complete the Tasks in his stead. And when you are done, your grandfather will still go free. All you have to do is say so. You do the work and the coward benefits."

"He's not a coward!" Eden's fingers strained against the butter knife. "You're not half the smith he is!" Her words surprised her. Vulcan had practically shunned her, yet here she was defending him.

"He's a prisoner," smiled Mr. Pewtersmith. "I'm not."

"Uriah is trying to goad you," said Nellie through pursed lips. "You must ignore him, dearie."

"And whatever you do, don't say you'll do the Five," said Irma. "Because once you say it, there's no going back."

Mr. Pewtersmith squeezed tighter. "Irma Silversmith is correct. It is a serious commitment. There is no going back. But if you choose not to do them, then you are Vulcan's jailer."

"I'm not!" said Eden. The blade of the butter knife began to bend from the pressure of her fingers. "He's locked in his room because of you. You're the reason he won't—"

"Won't what? Embrace you? Welcome you into his quarters? Into his life? Into the bosom of *family*?" Mr. Pewtersmith waved a hand, as if he were brushing away a fly. "It's not me causing this. It's you. You can choose to do the Tasks. You have that option. Complete them and Vulcan goes free and goes back to rooms big enough for the both of you. Therefore, if you don't do them, then you are choosing not to help and, by extension, it is you who is imprisoning your grandfather."

Nellie pointed her cane at Mr. Pewtersmith. "Be quiet, Uriah!"

"If you don't do them," continued Mr. Pewtersmith, "then both you and your grandfather are cowards."

"Quiet, I said!" Nellie stood.

Mr. Pewtersmith spun Eden's chair around and faced her. "You, your grandfather, and your own dead father! All crushed by the weight of their own egos! All traitors! And all cowards!"

Eden pushed up out of her seat. "Shut up, you horrible man! I will do them! And I'll show you! I'll do the Five Impossible Tasks! Then Grandpa will be free!"

"Then you agree?" said Mr. Pewtersmith. "You choose?"

Nellie yelled, "No, Eden! Say nothing! You don't realize what's at stake!"

Eden's mouth was set in a hard line. Her eyes blazed. "I choose."

A gasp went up from all who heard. "Oh, Eden!" shouted Nellie. "Oh my dear, take it back!"

"I won't! I'm doing the Tasks."

"There is no taking it back!" said Mr. Pewtersmith, smiling. "You heard her! So did I. So did all of us. She is an apprentice smith. And she is committed."

As a ripple of whispers spread out across Supperdinner Hall, the shaky hands of women held hankies and dabbed at crying eyes, while men blew their noses as they stared at Eden.

"Oh my dear," said Nellie. "Oh, what have you said? What have you done?"

Eden tossed the bent butter knife onto the table. "I want to go see my grandpa."

"What about pudding?" said Irma.

Every eye followed Eden and the sisters as they left Supperdinner Hall. The three of them were silent as Buzz took them down to Subbasement Seven and silent as they walked to Vulcan's room. Vulcan opened the door and grunted at them. On the floor of the room was the beginning of a strange-looking chair, made from spare parts, with gears and chains attached to the uneven legs and crooked back.

"A terrible thing has happened!" cried Nellie, sitting heavily on Vulcan's bed.

Vulcan twisted a bit of wire on the chair with a pair of pliers. "What are you yammering about?"

"The girl. She's done it. The poor little thing. Oh, Vulcan! I am so sorry."

Vulcan gave the wires another twist. "Done what?"

Nellie blew her nose into her handkerchief. "It was Uriah

Pewtersmith, really. He wouldn't let up! I should have kicked him in his bony shins."

Vulcan turned to Eden. "What in Saint Dunstan's furnace is she talking about?"

"I said yes. About the Tasks. The Five. I don't want to wait. If this is all going to happen, then let's pick a Task and get started."

"Can't do it," said Vulcan. "If it was just me—"

Nellie cried. "You don't understand, Vulcan. Eden said yes. She chose. Vulcan, she chose on your behalf."

Vulcan dropped the pliers. "She said we'd do the Five? Who heard her?"

"She said *she* would. *For you.* We all heard it. Uriah Pewtersmith, the Council—all of Supperdinner Hall heard it."

The words stuck in Eden's brain. Had she actually done it for Vulcan? Or for herself? Had she said yes to shut up Mr. Pewtersmith? Or had she said yes for her grandfather—for her longing for a family?

"They can't let her do it!" said Vulcan. "She doesn't know how dangerous they are. She's just a dumb kid."

"She's a member of this Guildhall," said Nellie. "That's all that is required."

"I'm not dumb. I'm glad I said it," said Eden. "Besides, you're supposed to be the greatest smith who has ever lived. You can prove it. You can help me."

"The only thing I'll be helping with is getting you the hell out of your commitment. I won't have you risking your life for me. I won't lose another member of my family."

"No!" Eden shouted, so loud that the adults in the room stiffened. A feeling of fear was spreading across her stomach. "I'm doing the Tasks. With you. We can do this. I know it because you can do anything. Everyone says so!"

"Wrong! Locked in this room, I can't even seem to remember how to build something as simple as a chair. Now you've sealed both our fates. Pewtersmith has won."

Eden shrugged. "You and I both know we were going to try it eventually. We're Smiths."

Vulcan said nothing.

"I'm staying. I'm doing the Tasks. So let's get it started," said Eden. "Let's get it over with. Which Task is it going to be first?"

"You really committed?"

"I did."

Vulcan said, "Then I suppose I need to help keep you alive. And keep you here."

"I suppose you do," said Eden, her eyes shining. "So where do we start?"

Vulcan scratched his belly. "Well, I guess we might as well start by doing the dishes."

He tightened one more bolt, then sat down in his new chair. It squeaked once, then crashed to the floor.

PART II
Tongs

XV

Dishes and Records of Dishes

A few mornings later, Eden and the sisters were gathered in their parlor, waiting for breakfast. A knock came on the door and Miss Clara entered with her silver tea trolley. Nellie ordered breakfast and said goodbye to Miss Clara, but the woman stood there, smiling.

Nellie sighed. "Clara Jones, I said *thank you*. You may go."

"I have more, for young Eden." Miss Clara's smile grew wider as she held out a simple can opener. Eden took it. Then Miss Clara handed her a plain, unlabeled tin can—it reminded Eden of a can that would contain tomato soup.

"What is this?" said Nellie.

Miss Clara beamed. "It's the first one! And I've been chosen to deliver each of them. Can you believe it? Me!"

Nellie sucked in her breath, then pushed Miss Clara and her cart into the hallway and shut the door. She turned to Eden. "Oh my dear. It's begun. I suppose you should open it."

Eden shook the can. Something rattled inside. She knew without asking what it was. Without speaking, she removed the top with the can opener. Inside was a curl of tin with words stamped upon it:

**WITHIN ONE DAY, DEFINED AS SUNRISE TO
SUNSET, EVERY SINGLE DISH MUST BE RENDERED
FREE OF DIRT, FOOD, AND OTHER IMPURITIES,
AND CLEANED TO A HIGH SHINE. IF THE REQUIRE-
MENTS ARE NOT MET, OR IF THIS OR ANY OTHER
TASK IS ABANDONED, THEN THE SMITH AND THE
DESIGNATED HELPER WILL BE BANISHED FROM
ALL GUILDHALLS FOREVER.**

Eden's stomach tightened as she read it. "Banished? That's in the rules?"

"Nellie nodded. "I'm afraid so, dearie. You and your designated helper—that would be Vulcan—would have to leave and never come back. Now then, stand up straight. Take a deep breath. There's nothing to be done other than begin." Nellie pushed her toward the doorway. "So let's begin."

Fifteen minutes later, Eugene, Eden, and the sisters were in a corridor of Subbasement Five on their way to inspect Dishes. "To be a member of the Guild of Smiths," said Eugene, "requires a person to be a working smith, every day. But some kinds of smithing are, you know, easier than others. One lazy smith figured this out—Horatio Locksmith. Old Horatio realized that the simplest thing he knew how to make was a pewter bowl. It's one of the first things every apprentice learns."

"Just like me," said Eden, remembering turning her first dish in the sisters' room.

"Right," said Eugene. "And just like you, Horatio Locksmith could spin that blank of pewter into a bowl in just a few minutes. He began doing this every morning before breakfast, to meet his daily requirement of smithing. And then he spent the rest of the day lazing around in Records. Guess he liked reading more than doing something useful."

Eugene stopped. "I gotta rest for a minute." He mopped sweat off his face with his hankie. "It wasn't too long before others began to notice Horatio's strategy. Within a couple of weeks, a dozen smiths were spinning new pewter bowls every morning, too, to meet their daily requirements. Within a month, half the Guildhall was doing it. And within three months, the other half joined in. And finally, it became a rule."

"I forgot that story—that it happened that way," said Nellie.

"Lots of people forgot." Eugene started walking again. "The rule is reinforced at dinner every night when Robert Blacksmith makes everyone tap their daily dishes. But Eden, the main point here is that a lot of bowls are made every day. Decades and decades ago, pewter bowls began stacking up in a storeroom. So another storeroom was added, then another. Soon, a huge basement storeroom, called Dishes, was added onto this level of the Guildhall. Finally, when the Five Tasks were created, old Malachi Pewtersmith thought it'd make a good Task—the Task of washing all those dishes. In a day. Because it's, well, impossible."

They reached a door made of heavy steel.

"Why does this door warp outward?" Eden asked.

Eugene frowned, looking at it, "I don't know. Never noticed that before."

Nellie rapped on it with the head of her cane. "I nearly forgot about this room, too. Ugly door, but seems solid enough." They opened the door and a wave of stench poured out. Eden slapped a hand over her nose and mouth, then stepped into a huge room, with ceilings at least twenty feet high. Eden thought it was bigger than one of her middle-school gymnasiums. Nearly the entire room was full of bowls in all shapes and sizes, stacked all the way to the ceiling. Every bowl was dirty. Every bowl smelled from the leftover food that had dried on them. Flies flitted around the stacks. All the bowls were made of pewter. The gray floor appeared to be made of pewter, too.

"Phew," said Eden. "It really stinks in here. Why hasn't anyone washed these before?"

"What's the point?" said Nellie, holding a silver-embroidered handkerchief to her nose. "There's no reason to wash today's dish if you have to make a new one tomorrow."

"Seems like you should at least recycle them," said Eden, through her fingers. "There's so many. If one of these stacks were to fall on you, you'd be squished."

"That's just what happened to Kaos Fendersmith, your great-great-great-great-grandfather," said Nellie. "Buried alive under a pile of dirty pewter bowls."

"I wonder why the floor is pewter." Eden tapped it with her sneaker.

"I was wondering the same thing, dearie," said Nellie.

The stacks of dishes towered over Eden. She strained her neck to see them all. "It would take a million years to wash these." She thought of the curl of stamped tin in her pocket. "But I don't have a million years. The rule of the Task says I have to do it in a day."

"Now then," said Nellie, "let's continue reviewing our history. Eugene, remind us what has happened in the past in this room."

Eugene cleared his throat. "This Task has been attempted three times. Kaos Fendersmith died in the collapse. Hester Goldsmith washed a small portion of the dishes then...she gave up."

"The saddest tale of all," said Irma.

Nellie nodded. "Hester the Sorrowful, we call her. I don't like to speak of her."

"Why?"

Nellie dabbed at her eyes with her lace handkerchief. "Because she quit the Tasks and faced the consequences. A fate worse than death."

"She was banished?" asked Eden.

"Yes. Hester and her helper were cast out of this and all Guildhalls."

"What happened to her? Where did she go?"

"No one knows," said Nellie. "It's said that they just wandered the earth, going from one Guildhall to another, but none would let them in."

Eden gulped, and that fearful feeling lodged in her stomach all over again. They couldn't quit. If they stopped halfway through—even if they stopped now, she and her grandpa would be banished forever from all guildhalls, including this one—from this place she now called home. And, just like Hester, they would have no place to go.

Eugene continued. "Mordan Silversmith finally completed the Task successfully."

"A silversmith succeeded? How?"

"Not sure," he said. "All records of success are sealed. The public records include a few tiny clues, but that's it."

"Such as?"

"All we know is how much Mordan complained about the room itself. About its shoddy construction and ugly walls."

"I can see why she complained." Irma waved at the walls with her blue teacup. "It is indeed very ugly."

"I don't think you get it," said Eugene. "This room, the way it is now, is what it looked like *after* Mordan Silversmith redesigned it. She wanted it to look like this." Eden looked around at the rusty steel panels that lined the walls and ceiling.

"She may have been good at washing dishes, but she was a horrible decorator," said Nellie. "As a silversmith, I am embarrassed for her. Where is the silver decor? Where is the sense of style? At any rate, there must be some record of her success, Eugene. Some story of it."

"If there is, it's in Sealed Records," he said. "All I know is what's public."

"You still know a lot, Eugene," Eden said.

Eugene smiled. "Tinkers are keepers of history. And I've been doing even more reading since Vulc's sentencing."

Eden had an idea. "We should get Nathaniel and his mom to help with this Task. If anyone knows about washing dishes, it would be them."

"Absolutely not," said Nellie. "They are *not* smiths. They cannot help."

"Because of the rules?" said Eden.

"Because it wouldn't be proper," said Nellie. "And I'm sure Eden can figure this out. It's a lot of washing up, but it is still just washing up." She walked over to a stack of dishes and ran her finger along the edge of a bowl. The tower of dishes swayed at her touch. Nellie reached out to steady it, but the dishes above began to tip farther. She held her silver cane tightly in her hands, closed her eyes, and stood very still. The twenty-foot tower of dishes crashed all around her, with metal bowls bouncing and clanging off the pewter floor.

"Sister!" cried Irma. "Oh my dear!"

The crashing of dishes stopped. Nellie, eyes still closed and hankie still held to her nose, stood in the middle of the pile. Eden ran and hugged her. "Are you okay?"

"I am unharmed," said Nellie. "Not a single dish touched me, but that was rather terrifying. I believe we have seen enough for one day. It is time for bed. Eden, if we want to leave this room, you will have to stop hugging me and let me go."

That night, Eden lay awake, picturing the room of dirty dishes and trying to imagine a washing station that would handle all those stacks in a single day. She kissed the tip of her finger, then pressed it on the faces of her mom and dad in the photo on her bedside table. "Since you two left me, I've had to do the dishes hundreds of times," she whispered. "Couldn't you help me with them just once?"

The next morning, Eden awoke early, while the sisters were still sleeping. She made her way down to Subbasement Seven and walked along the corridor until she stood outside Vulcan's door. She wanted to knock, but she was afraid her grandfather would not invite her in. She took a deep breath. Just before her knuckles rapped on the silver door, it opened and Eugene slipped out, closing the door behind him.

"I wouldn't bother him now," he whispered. "He's had a bit of a rough night. He dreamt about the birds."

"Good or bad?"

"Said he dreamt they had babies and the babies came for him. They came for his other leg." Eugene led Eden away from Vulcan's room. "Any new thoughts about that first Task?"

"Huge stacks of dishes in a huge ugly room. What's there to think about?"

"It *is* ugly, isn't it? I always thought someone should redo those nasty wall panels and get rid of that stupid pewter floor."

Eden pulled the curl of stamped tin from her pocket and read it again. *Within one day, defined as sunrise to sunset, every single dish must be rendered free of dirt, food, and other impurities, and cleaned to a high shine.*"

"Within one day," said Eugene. "By sunset. It sounds, well, you know."

"I know," sighed Eden. "Impossible."

After breakfast, Eden swung by Kitchens and picked up Nathaniel, who was dressed as usual in his checkered pants and chef's coat. Lillian tried to smooth down her son's hair. "Be sure to pay attention to what Helena says. And no sass. You represent your family name, so represent us well."

At her door, Helena smiled at Eden and frowned at Nathaniel. She led them into her shop and picked up a long-handled axe from a workbench. "This is what we are making today. Woodsman axes. Humble tools, but blades nonetheless, and more complicated than they seem. The back side of the blade must be hard enough to work as a hammer. The front side must take an edge as sharp as a razor. So then, first we go to the crucible."

Helena kept talking about the intricacies of axes. Eden tried to pay attention, but her mind was on Dishes and the Impossible Task that needed to happen there.

Helena opened the door of her furnace, casting the workshop in a fiery light. In seconds, the temperature of the room rose. "How hot do we need to make it?" asked Nathaniel.

"For steel, the crucible must be twenty-six hundred degrees Fahrenheit."

"Do you ever make axes out of other metals?" asked Nathaniel.

Helena sighed. "I am a bladesmith, you foolish little Nat. Bladesmiths work in steel."

"I thought blacksmiths worked in steel," said Eden.

"They do," said Helena, "but they mostly make horseshoes and fireplace pokers and other lowly things. We bladesmiths take steel to its ultimate level."

"What if you made an axe out of gold?" said Nathaniel. "How hot would the furnace need to be?"

"A smith should know the answer to that," said Helena. "And since you asked, this will be homework for the both of you this afternoon. After my class, go to Records and look up the melting point of all the typical metals."

"I can't do that today," said Eden, thinking about Dishes. "I have something else I need to work on."

"Did an apprentice just refuse the directive of a master smith?" Helena ran her thumb over the edge of her ax.

Eden's eyes widened. She remembered the words of Nellie, warning her not to anger Helena. *She may be small,* Nellie had said, *but she can be dangerous.* Eden shook her head no.

Helena smiled. "Good. Gold, iron, steel, copper, aluminum, tin, pewter—find their melting points. Bring the answers back to me tomorrow. Now no more questions. Especially not from a Jones!"

After their session with Helena, both Eden and Nathaniel looked at their axes with pride. Eden's was close to flawless. Nathaniel's was lopsided and bent to one side. "If you blur your eyes, it actually looks like an axe," he said with a smile.

"Just keep blurring your eyes, then," said Eden. "Let's go to the records place and get our stupid homework done so I can get back to saving Grandpa."

Neither of them had any idea where to find it, so, carrying their axes, they went to the elevator and asked Buzz to take them there.

"It's not *the* records," said Buzz, pushing his lever. "It's just Records. That'd be Subbasement Two." He nodded at Nathaniel's axe. "Planning on chopping some wood later?"

Nathaniel beamed. "You *can* tell it's an axe, can't you? I made it."

"You made it?" said Buzz. "What do you mean, you made it?"

"I—I smithed it."

The elevator kept zooming downward. "But you're little Nat! The kitchen boy! You're one of us! Under the same oath! You're a Jones, and—"

"Buzz?" Eden interrupted. "What's the deal with this oath, exactly?"

Buzz was lost in his own thoughts. He just kept mumbling, "A Jones…made an ax? A Jones…made an ax?"

"That's right," said Nathaniel, "I may be under the oath, but I'm learning how to smith. I'm not supposed to tell anyone, but—well—just look at it!"

Buzz's mumbles continued as he stared at his panel of lights. Then, in a daze, he pulled his lever to the stop position and opened the doors.

Eden gasped. She stared out at what looked like a sunlit park, with rolling green grass where the floor should be and bright yellow light above. Flowering trees and manicured shrubs dotted the scene, along with bubbling fountains and what appeared to be streams or small canals. Blue-jacketed Joneses lounged on picnic blankets and benches, or strolled along flower-lined paths. Birds flew by. Eden was pretty sure she even saw a few fluffy, white sheep.

"Buzz!" shouted Nathaniel. "Wrong floor!"

Buzz shook his head clear and slammed the doors back shut before anyone on the floor noticed them. "Sorry." His face was bright red and he seemed to have forgotten how to operate the elevator. He finally pulled the lever back and they began moving upward. Buzz mopped his sweaty face with his sleeve. "Golly. It really was the wrong floor, wasn't it? Haven't made a mistake like that in twenty years. Eden..." His voice trailed off.

"What *was* that?" Eden demanded.

"Eden, I need to ask you to, umm, forget what you just—would you? Would you pretend?"

"That I didn't see it? You want me to forget that I saw—that?"

"Eden, if you were to tell anyone that I took you there—well, first I'd lose my job. But second, it's, well, it's more complicated than that."

Nathaniel held his axe as if he were trying to crush the wooden handle in his fists. "You're not supposed to go there. That was a Jones-only floor. No smith has ever seen it before."

"No smith ever? Why not? It's so beautiful."

Nathaniel said, "It's like everyone keeps telling you, Eden. The smiths stay to themselves, you know. They stick to their smithing. We Joneses—well, except for me, I guess—we stay to our own things, too. Like gardening and sheepherding and astrophysics. We just happen to do it down here. And since the smiths have their thing—smithing—that they don't share, then I guess we don't want to share this."

"If you can do all that, then why do you care about smithing?"

"Because," said Buzz. "Because smithing really is like magic. And because we've been told—for a thousand years—that we can't do it. Eden, I love my job here. And the order of things in this place—it matters. It's mattered for hundreds and hundreds of years. Can I get your promise to not tell?"

"Fine. I promise. But I still don't get it."

Buzz sighed and adjusted his hat. "Thank you. Here's your actual floor."

Eden and Nathaniel left Buzz at Subbasement Two. "That's a lot to ask," said Eden. "Asking me to forget what I saw down there. Are all the Jones floors like that?"

"I'm really not supposed to talk about it," said Nathaniel.

"Do you think I could go visit sometime?"

"No! Not a chance. Never."

"This place is so weird. You're all so weird. So much weirder than the outside world. You know that, don't you?"

"I know we're different, if that's what you mean. But we're okay, aren't we? I mean, compared to the, umm, outside world, it's not so bad here, is it?"

"Not so bad?" Eden laughed. "It's amazing. It's the most amazing place I've ever been."

After the glowing green landscape she'd seen below, Subbasement Two seemed particularly bleak. Eden and Nathaniel walked along a hallway past a series of oiled metal doors. The doors had the scene of a bloody battle etched into the metal, with cannons firing, soldiers charging, and dead bodies lying on the ground.

Eden felt a shiver go down her spine. "I wonder what's in there."

"I don't want to know," said Nathaniel.

They finally came to a green door labeled Records. A sign said "Please knock for access," then listed the hours Records was open. Eden knocked.

While they waited for someone to come, they looked at a map on the wall outside the door. It showed the different sections of Records in alphabetical order: Ancestry, Criminal, Fiction, Historical, Purchasing, Speeches, Weights and Measures, and dozens more.

"Holy soap," said Nathaniel. "This place must be huge."

"Do you see anything about melting points? Or temperatures?"

"That would be weights and measures," said a voice. Both

children jumped. A tall, thin woman stood at the opened green door. She had short, straight gray hair. She wore a purple scarf around her neck, a matching purple fez on her head, and a pair of tiny eyeglasses on the tip of her nose, connected to a thin chain. A huge black dog stood at her side, growling low. The dog looked half like a Saint Bernard and half like a wolf, with a head as big as a bear's. On all fours, the dog stood as high as the woman's chest. The muscles of his bulging neck strained so hard against a silver-colored collar that Eden kept expecting the collar to burst. It didn't.

"I know you," the woman said to Nathaniel. "Lillian's boy. What are you doing so far from Kitchens?"

Neither of the children said a word. They stared at the giant dog and his bared teeth, which were dripping with drool.

"Did you hear me?" said the woman.

Eden gulped. "Does—does he bite?"

"Of course he bites," said the woman. "One cannot eat a person without biting them. Now then, what do you want?"

"I—I'm Eden Smith. Vulcan Smith's granddaughter."

The woman looked Eden up and down. "I did not ask who you are. Everyone knows who you are, Eden Smith. But what do you want?"

Without taking her eyes off the huge dog, Eden explained the assignment that Helena had given them.

The woman squinted at her. "I've heard that you are a troublemaker. Are you? A maker of trouble?"

"I don't think so," said Eden.

"Mm. What I hear of you involving Nathaniel in your smithing lessons indicates otherwise."

Nathaniel started to object. "But I want—"

"*Trouble*," the woman went on, "is not welcome at Records. You want information? Then you will follow the rules. I am Sylvia Jones. And this beast is Bones. Bones Jones. He is the forty-second of his line and his name. He and his canine ancestors have protected Records for more than one hundred and fifty years. And prior to that, his pedigree can be traced all the way back to Saint Dunstan's time, where dogs like Bones protected Welsh sheep from hungry

121

English wolves. Bones ensures the Records rules are followed. He takes his job seriously. If you agree to follow the rules—and to avoid any sudden movements—then you may come with me."

They stepped inside of Records, where straight rows of gray-green metal cabinets stretched on for what seemed like miles.

"Wow," whispered Eden. "How big is this place?"

"Not big enough. More records are added every month." Sylvia and Bones led the children through the cabinets. Sylvia walked like an arthritic duchess, with her back perfectly straight, her elbows in, and her hands out. As they followed, they passed a large black-and-white photograph hanging on a wall. Eden recognized the metal mosaics and the black pillar—it was a photo of Humble Gallery, full of people. But the people were of all ages—old, middle-aged, and young. The young people were lined across the front of the crowd. Eden stopped. "Sylvia, what's this picture?"

Sylvia said, "Apprentices, just about to begin their training."

Eden said. "Is my grandfather in that picture?"

"He's in the next one." Sylvia walked them a dozen more feet and stopped in front of a similar photo. "Front row, second from the left."

Eden immediately spotted her grandfather because he looked so much like her. He was grinning, as if he'd been caught in a laugh. In the photo, young fair-haired girls—about Eden's age now—stood on either side of Vulcan, laughing, too. The girls wore flowered dresses. *Those must be the sisters*, Eden thought. Eden touched her grandfather's face with her fingertip. "So many young people. Must be at least a dozen apprentices there."

"There are eleven," said Sylvia as she walked.

"But how come there are no young people here now?" asked Eden.

"They grew old. Or they left," said Sylvia. "You should know that better than anyone, Eden Smith. Your father is the most famous leaver of them all."

They came to a large table that held stacks of charts. With her long fingers, Sylvia felt her way down the stack, then pulled out a chart labeled Melting Points of Metals and Alloys. "Yours is a bit of a trick assignment," said Sylvia. "Typical of Helena."

"What do you mean?"

"The pure metals are easy. Steel, gold, silver—they all have a single melting point. But pewter is an alloy—a blend of tin, antimony, silver, and copper—so it has a melting *range*."

Eden said, "It says here on the chart that the melting range for pewter is four hundred and thirty-seven to four hundred and sixty-four."

"Fahrenheit," added Sylvia.

"Hey, I found steel!" shouted Nathaniel.

Bones lunged at Nathaniel, pinning him against the table. "Down Bones!" hissed Sylvia. "Nathaniel, one must always be quiet in Records. It is one of the primary rules. Bones does not like loud noises."

Nathaniel gulped as Bones licked his arm.

Sylvia frowned. "Did he just lick you? Either he likes you, or he wishes to eat you. Probably because you smell like Kitchens. Like food."

"I smell like…like food?"

"Bones loves to eat. Anything. And almost *anyone*. So you, young Mister Jones, had better be especially quiet."

Nathaniel gulped again and tried to pull his arm away, but Bones growled and kept licking. Nathaniel whispered. "Sorry. I was just excited. I saw that steel has a melting point of two thousand five hundred degrees, umm, Fahrenheit. We melted steel today when I made this axe."

"*You* made an axe? But you're—"

"—a Jones. I know."

Sylvia sighed. "I would like to make an axe. Or I would have, when I was younger and my joints did not ache all day. I was never allowed. None of us were. I am smarter than almost any smith who comes here. I bet I have read more books about smithing than all the smiths put together. But was I ever allowed to actually smith?" Sylvia smiled. "And now my body has grown older than my mind. I have inflamed joints. Everything hurts, except a hot bath. Ohh, how I love a hot bath."

Eden set down her pencil. "Sylvia, do you know everything there is in Records?"

"Oh, heavens no. Look at the size of this place. But when it comes to finding stories, one does not need to know all the answers. One just needs to know where to look."

"So, let's say I wanted to look up information about the past. Like history stuff."

Sylvia frowned. "History of the Five Impossible Tasks, perhaps?"

"How'd you guess?"

"Everybody knows, Eden. From the moment Pewtersmith accused Vulcan, everybody knew how this would play out. Then you arrived as his helper."

"He's my helper now," said Eden. "I'm the one doing the Tasks."

"You? But you are just a child." Sylvia's hand went to her heart. "You do not stand a chance."

"So I've heard. I'm just trying to get some hints—from my ancestors. I know that Mordan Silversmith is the only one who managed to clean all the dishes in a single day. But I don't know how she did it."

Sylvia rolled up the chart. "And you never will. All official accounts of past attempts are sealed. It is my job to keep them sealed, in order to preserve the integrity of the Five Tasks. No hints or sneak peeks or unfair advantages. Try to find those records and Bones will have at you." Bones growled at the sound of his name. "You do not want that, do you?"

"N-n-no, we don't," said Nathaniel. "Nice Bones. Sit."

Sylvia's stern face softened. "I heard a rumor. Is it true that you are half Jones?"

Eden nodded. "My mom was a Jones. Emily Jones."

"Emily, eh? I don't believe I ever met her. She certainly never worked at this Guildhall. If she had, I would know."

"She was a teacher. A college teacher. A professor."

"Where did she come from?"

Eden shrugged. "Where? From ... out there."

"Yes, but where *precisely*?"

"I don't know *precisely*."

"Very inconvenient. You shall have to find out someday. Still, a Jones is a Jones, all the way back to the days of old Saint D. And if your mother was one, then I have no desire to see you die. Now, if you want to see what clues for the Five Tasks *are* publicly available, I can show you what little we do have. Those files are in the Criminal section."

"Criminal?" said Eden. "That's where they keep my ancestors?"

"Not all of them," said Sylvia, raising one eyebrow. "Just the famous ones." Sylvia pulled Bones away from Nathaniel and led them through Records until they came to another long row of gray-green metal cabinets. "Now let me see," said Sylvia. "Ahhh, here is the file. Yes, as I feared, there is not much in it." She pulled out a thin folder and handed it to Eden. "Use that table there. Bones will guard you to make sure you follow the rules. First rule is: Do not pull any other files without me."

Sylvia walked stiffly away while Bones followed the two children to the table and sat on the ground, licking his chops and staring at Nathaniel. "Nice doggy," he said, his voice cracking. "Eden, hurry up and read whatever it is you need to so we can get out of here."

Eden felt a now-familiar hunger as she opened the folder that contained pieces of her family story. "Okay." She pulled out a single sheet of paper. "It says Mordan Silversmith was charged with theft, for stealing the idea for a kerosene-powered mantle clock from Zechariah Pewtersmith. I don't see how a Pewtersmith could design a clock. That's not exactly their specialty. Then it says there was a trial and that Mordan's guilt was proven. If a Pewtersmith was involved, the whole thing was probably a scam. Then it lists out Mordan's sentence, which sounds just like what they did to Grandpa. Then—oh, maybe this is it. Says that she announced her decision to—let's see, *to reestablish herself into the good graces of the Guild of Smiths, by completing the Five Impossible Tasks.*"

"Just skip all that and see how she got past dishes," hissed Nathaniel. "Bones is drooling on me."

"I'm going as fast as I can. Here, it lists her helper as Madeline Goldsmith. Says that she received the assignment of *dishes* as her first Task. And then it says that before beginning the Task, Mordan demanded that Madeline be allowed to remodel the room *by installing heavy steel panels on the walls and ceiling.* There was a fireplace in the room. They left that intact."

"Then what?" said Nathaniel.

"Then it says, they successfully completed the Task."

"How?"

"Doesn't say. Just says that their next assigned Task was Mrs. Gunsmith's girdle and that they both died in the attempt."

"Died?" screeched Nathaniel. Bones leaped to his feet and rushed at Nathaniel, growling and baring his teeth. The huge dog's black face was eye-level, and Nathaniel could feel Bones' hot breath. "Sorry, Bones!" whispered Nathaniel. "I'm being quiet! See? Nice doggy!"

Bones edged close to Nathaniel, growling low. "I—I don't understand," whispered Nathaniel. "How could Mordan perform the Tasks if she was locked in her room?"

"Grandpa said they let you out, but just on the day of the Task. Like a hall pass from prison. Now be quiet and listen." She read:

> *Before beginning the Task of Dishes, Mordan Silversmith demanded that the room be remodeled. She stated, "We cannot work in such a room. If I am to prove worthy of the reinstatement of my title as a smith, we must be able to work in an environment fit for a smith. I demand that I be allowed to remodel it." Her demand was agreed to, and her helper, Madeline, lined the ceiling and walls with heavy steel panels. When the installation was complete, Mordan was satisfied. She went on record as saying, "I am about to be tested as I never have before, so it is fitting that I do so in a room like a crucible."*

Eden closed the book. "That's it."

"There's *got* to be something more," said Nathaniel, a bit too loudly. Bones snapped at him and caught Nathaniel's sleeve in his mouth. With a growl, Bones tore half the sleeve off.

Sylvia rushed back into the room. "No more today. That is Bones' way of saying it is time for you to go."

XVI

Machinist Bingo

"Tonight, you must wear a dress," said Nellie.

"Why?" said Eden. "What's tonight?" It was two days since she and Nathaniel had visited Records. Eden and the sisters were sitting on the couches in their parlor, having afternoon tea.

"Haven't we told you?" said Nellie.

"No. But—" Eden felt a familiar knot forming in her stomach. "But I still don't have a dress."

"Oh, but you do, dear. *A dress for Eden*, I kept telling myself, and so I remembered. I guessed your size, but I have a good eye for such things. Now, tonight. If you feel the need for youthful company, I suppose you may bring your friend, the little Nat. But tell him to at least wear a collared shirt not stained from washing pots and pans."

"But what *is* tonight?"

"It's bingo night. Now, four sugar cubes for you, Eden?" She handed Eden a cup of steaming tea.

Irma took a sip from her own teacup. "Bingo is like puberty for old people. Once you pass seventy-five, it just happens."

"Oh. Do I have to go?" said Eden. "I already know how to play bingo. We used to play it at some of the schools I went to. Back when

I went to school." Eden had been planning to work on solving the Task of Dishes with Nathaniel that evening. She couldn't do that if she was stuck at a bingo game.

"This is different," said Nellie. "This is Machinist Bingo. I think you'll enjoy it. Bring your friend."

"Fine," said Eden. "But right now, can I ask you a question? It's kind of stupid." She picked up a silver teaspoon and squeezed it in her fingers.

Nellie said, "There are no stupid questions, dearie."

"Of course there are," said Irma. "Hundreds of them."

Eden frowned. "Well, I never know what to call the two of you. It feels funny to call you by your first names—Nellie and Irma. I mean, they're nice names. But—"

"But we're so much older than you?" said Nellie.

"I suppose that's part of it," said Eden. "It would also be weird to call either of you Ms. Silversmith, because—because we're starting to know each other so well." She picked a pillow off the floor and tucked it behind Nellie's back.

"I agree," said Nellie, leaning into the pillow with a sigh. "We are practically family, I think. And we were very close to Vulcan's wife. To Edna."

"She would have been my grandmother," said Eden. "Grandma Edna. I wished I'd met her."

"I believe she died before you were born. If she'd lived longer, she would have sought you out. Nothing would have stopped her. She loved your father—even after he betrayed us. Not that we need to talk about that, other than to say that Edna loved him all the way to the end." Nellie smiled, her eyes watery. "Edna was our best friend. Thick as thieves, the three of us were. Like sisters."

"Then we should be your aunties," said Irma, waving her teacup. "Your great-aunties, if you want to get technical."

"So I could call you Aunty Nellie?" said Eden. "And Aunty Irma? That's what I was hoping for."

"Oh, Eden," said Nellie. "I would love that. Would you call me Aunty?"

"Yes ... Aunty Nellie." Just saying those words—family words—sent a little thrill through Eden. She sighed.

"Then come give your aunty a hug," said Nellie.

"I want one as well," said Irma, leaning back against the couch, "but not right now. I'm too comfortable to stand up."

At six thirty, Nellie and Irma knocked on the door of Eden's room. A cream-colored dress was draped over Nellie's arm. Swirls of intricate silver embroidery covered the surface of the cloth. Silver buttons shaped like moons and stars adorned the collar and sleeves. Silver crescent moons formed a scalloped hem at the bottom. Eden thought it was the most beautiful dress she had ever seen. She stared at it without speaking.

Nellie laughed. "Well, try it on, dearie. There is not much time before we have to leave."

Eden changed into the dress and looked at her reflection in a silver tray that hung from a wall. The dress was indeed beautiful. Eden smiled at her reflection. Maybe—and this was an overwhelming feeling she had—maybe what all this meant, these aunties and this room and this gift, maybe what it meant was that she was on someone's mind. Maybe she was thought of. Maybe she was even well cared for. It had been so long since she had felt this way—to have others looking after her needs—her food, her clothing, her education, even giving her lovely things now and then. Was this how it felt to be loved?

She stepped out of her room. Irma kissed her on the cheek. "Oh, dearie, you look so becoming. See? You *can* look ladylike when you want to."

Nellie said, "Even if I bought all of Mrs. Gunsmith's Beauty Cream, I'd never be as comely. Your mother must have been very beautiful. And speaking of beauty, I almost forgot." Nellie dug inside her huge purse. "Now, where are they? I know I put them in here somewhere. Ahh!" She pulled out two small silver boxes and handed them to Eden. "Presents, from sister and me."

Eden opened the first box and found a silver bracelet in the shape of a snake biting its own tail.

Irma took a sip from her teacup. "That one's from me, dearie. Girls can like snakes, too, you know."

"It's amazing." Eden smiled as she slipped the bracelet onto her wrist.

"Now mine," said Nellie, tapping her cane on the floor. "Don't keep me waiting."

Eden opened the other silver box. Inside was a silver chain. Each link in the chain was a tiny silver daffodil. "Your grandfather's favorite flower," said Nellie. "I hope it is not presumptuous to assume that you might like them as well."

Eden touched the tiny flowers with her fingertip. "Aunty, help me put it on."

With shaky fingers, Nellie clasped the chain of flowers on Eden's neck. "Oh my," Nellie said. "Such a vision. Such a lovely. Silver goes well on you, dearie." She took out a lace hankie and dabbed at her eyes.

At seven o'clock, they gathered in Humble Gallery, right outside the doors of Main Lodge. Nellie said, "It's time to find our seats. Where is the little Nat? You did ring down to invite him, yes? Oh, here he comes now, looking surprisingly presentable, except for that hair. He looks as if a blond hedgehog is sitting on his head."

Instead of his checkered pants and chef's jacket, Nathaniel wore green slacks, a white shirt, and a red tie. As usual, Lillian had tried to slick her son's hair down, but the bits that still stuck up somehow made it look even more unruly.

Eden laughed.

"What are you laughing at?" Nathaniel's face turned red.

"Nothing. Just never seen you dressed up before. You look nice."

"S-so do you," said Nathaniel. "I-I like your dress. I mean, you're dressed up, too. I mean, you look nice. Too."

"Please shut up, little Nat," said Nellie. "Are we all here? Then let's go. Come, sister."

Main Lodge was completely full, buzzing with the chatter of the old smiths. "No one dares to miss bingo," said Irma. Nellie had reserved four seats for them in advance, just three rows from the front. The curtain opened. Council members sat in their custom chairs on the sides of the stage.

Robert Blacksmith stood up in front of his iron chair. He wore a short black jacket and a green and blue kilt. His blacksmith's hammer hung from a broad leather belt. A bingo cage—a hollow wire wheel full of numbered balls—sat on a small table in front of him. "Good evening, smiths. Welcome to another episode of Machinist Bingo. Before we bring out our contestants, I do have a few announcements. The first is a bit of good news / bad news. The bad news is that poor old Ethel Fendersmith has passed away. Memorial details will be circulated in the coming days." A round of sympathetic murmurs filled Main Lodge. "The good news, however, is that her lovely rooms on the third floor are now available. If you're interested, please see Eugene Tinker. Also, the kitchen staff asked me to mention that Kerlin Arrowsmith left his false teeth in his water glass at dinner again. Kerlin, the kitchen staff will send them up to your rooms by morning, in time for your breakfast." Robert tapped his fingers on the head of his hammer. "And now, on to our main event. Standard rules apply tonight. First to win three times is the champion. So then, let's choose our first two contestants." Robert spun the bingo cage until two numbered balls rolled out. Robert picked up the balls and shouted, "B nine and G forty-four!"

Two machinists entered from offstage, each rolling out contraptions hidden under cloths.

"Don't we get cards?" said Eden.

"In Machinist Bingo, there are no cards."

"If we don't get cards, why do you even call it bingo?"

"It's always been called bingo. *Build Ingenious eNgines that Gobble up Others.* B-I-N-G-O. Bingo! Now hush up and watch."

"Welcome back, Francis," said Robert Blacksmith to one of the contestants, a hunched-over man wearing a stocking cap. "What did you bring this month?"

"Same as every month," croaked Francis. "My Tinker Toy Trebuchet. But I've made a few adjustments." Francis pulled off the cloth, revealing a model of an old catapult. It was covered in rust and Eden could see it had been repaired many times, with its broken sections held together by bits of wire.

"That man should be ashamed to call himself a smith," whispered Irma.

"You know how these machinists are, sister," said Nellie, pointing with the head of her silver cane. "Just look at his competition—Sadie Plainly, that ninny. No one wants to see your floppy arms, old girl."

"Aunty!" said Eden.

"Quite right, Eden. I should not comment on the ninny's appearance. Forgive me."

Eden tried hard not to roll her eyes.

On the opposite side of the stage stood a woman in a short sleeveless dress, with hair dyed red and wearing bright red lipstick. She pushed her own contraption next to Francis' trebuchet, then removed the cloth to reveal an ornate gold box inlaid with various metals. A winding key stuck out of one side.

"Wow," Eden said. "Is that a music box? That's really beautiful. She definitely wins."

"Don't be too quick to judge," said Nellie. "This is not a beauty contest."

"Then what is it?"

"War."

Irma sipped from her teacup. "They're going to destroy each other."

"Oldest goes first," shouted Robert. "That's you, Francis."

"Excellent," said Francis. With shaky hands, he turned a crank on his catapult. The catapult arm bent farther back with each turn. When it was done, Francis loaded a steel ball. "Ready?" said Francis. He pushed a button. The catapult arm sprung forward. The steel ball shot through the air, ripped a hole through the music box, ricocheted off a wall, flew across the room, and shattered a pitcher of water on the table at the back of Main Lodge. A cheer went up from the crowd.

Robert shouted, "Not bad, Francis. You *have* made some adjustments. Much better than last time." Francis smiled and patted his catapult. Robert said, "What do you say, Sadie Plainly? Do you admit defeat?"

"Not on your life, blacksmith." Sadie pushed her box right up against Francis' catapult. She used both hands to wind the key on the side of the box. Then she opened the lid.

A tinkling music-box tune began to play. A silver ballerina about a foot tall unfolded and began to turn gracefully to the music.

"Oh, that is very pretty," said Irma. "I've always pretended to love the ballet."

The silver ballerina held a classic pose, up on one toe, with her other leg bent. She wore a frilly pink tutu. One arm was held out gracefully. The other hung broken in half, shot off by the catapult ball. As the ballerina rotated, Sadie hummed and turned to the tinkling music. Her saggy bare arms swayed as she danced.

The music clicked to a stop. Eden heard a whirring noise, like the sound an old clock makes right before it chimes. Suddenly, the silver leg of the ballerina kicked out, right into the center of the catapult. Metal parts flew in every direction. The ballerina returned to her graceful pose. The catapult was destroyed. The crowd cheered.

"The ballerina stays!" shouted Robert Blacksmith.

"That was amazing!" said Eden, gripping the arms of her chair. "I want to do this. I want to play."

"Me, too," said Nathaniel. "How do we get a turn?"

"You don't," said Nellie. "At least no time soon. You must be a master machinist. And that takes years. So just watch."

Robert rotated the bingo cage again, then called out, "O sixty-three." A tiny woman walked onto the stage. She was so wrinkled that her face looked like a dried apple.

"Yuriko Kajiya," said Nellie. "You're lucky to see her. She holds the record for the most wins—even more than your grandfather."

"Yuriko," said Robert, "where is your machine?"

"Here!" shouted Yuriko. Her voice was loud and sharp. From her sleeve, she pulled out a metal sphere, no bigger than one of the numbered bingo balls. She held it in her palm.

"Very interesting," said Robert. "As the challenger, you go first."

Yuriko nodded and dropped the ball. It landed heavily on the stage. It began to hum, then the top of the ball opened. A shaft rose, and a propeller unfolded from the shaft and began to spin. The humming grew louder. Like a helicopter, the ball began to hover above the stage. It tilted toward the silver ballerina, edging closer, inch by inch. As Eden watched, the propeller zipped forward and sliced the ballerina in two. The propeller slipped back inside the ball. The ball fell intact to the floor. The crowd cheered.

"Very impressive, Yuriko," said Robert. "Sadie, do you have a response?"

"Not a polite one," said Sadie. She picked up the broken pieces of her ballerina and moped off the stage.

"The ball stays!" Robert read another number. "N thirty-six!" A machinist named Dirk Burns came out from behind the curtain. From under a cloth, he revealed a small steel robot holding a giant hammer. The robot had a face painted on it that made it look like a smiling young boy. Dirk set the robot down next to Yuriko's tiny ball and pushed a button on the robot's head. Lights in the robot's eyes flashed red. Steam shot out of his ears. The robot lifted its hammering arm with a series of beeps. The propeller again rose out of the ball and began to spin. It flew toward the robot and cut the arm off. Then the propeller cut the robot in two. The ball rolled away unhurt. The crowd cheered again.

"That was a quick death," frowned Eden. "Kind of a letdown."

"Yeah, that robot was awesome," said Nathaniel. "What a waste."

"That's two wins for Yuriko!" shouted Robert Blacksmith. "One more and she is the new champion."

Robert announced a fifteen-minute intermission, during which Clara Jones, dressed in pink, rolled her tea trolley around Main Lodge. Eden asked for a cucumber sandwich. While she was eating it, she felt a tap on her shoulder. She turned and nearly screamed when she saw a robotic hand there, at the end of a long, telescoping pole.

The other end of the pole was held by Anit Irenya, the machinist from the Council who was sitting in his wheelchair in the next row over. As the pole retracted, the finger on the robotic hand motioned for Eden to follow it back to its owner. She did.

"I was hoping to see you here," he said. "Bingo night provides a glimpse into the inventiveness of we machinists."

"It's amazing," said Eden. "I'd like to play some time."

"Of course you would," said Anit. "Your grandfather is one of us, you know—a machinist. Perhaps he may even be the best of us. I hope that someday you can see him compete here, on this stage."

"I hope so, too," said Eden, but she remembered Vulcan splayed out on the floor of his room, on top of the remains of his failed chair. She wondered if he'd ever be great again.

"Years from now, it is possible you could play as well," said Anit, "but becoming a machinist is a long and difficult road. Few complete it."

"Do you think I might?" said Eden.

"That's your story," said Anit. "I never tell another person's story." He placed a wrinkled, brown hand on Eden's arm. "And first you must survive the Tasks. I hear your first assignment is dishes. A deadly place to start. I have some advice for you."

"Yes?" Eden was desperate for any help she could get.

Anit smiled. "Stop thinking like a dishwasher. Start thinking like a smith."

Eden returned to her seat, wondering what it meant to *think like a smith*. She sat down just as Robert Blacksmith read the next contestant's number: G fifty.

The new contestant was a short man with huge eyebrows. His name was Gwyneth Goff. Gwyneth pulled a red cloth off his machine. It was a metal dragon, painted the same red as the cloth.

"Oh, what a lovely dragon," said Irma. "Gwyneth is from the country of Wales—a land that loves its dragons. *Goff* is Welsh for *smith*. My, that one's a lovely piece of work. And hopefully, a dragon means fire."

On Robert's command, Gwyneth pushed a button on a remote control. The metal dragon beat its wings as it marched across the stage to Yuriko's ball. It tilted its head toward the floor, then released a huge burst of flames that seemed to fill the entire stage. Eden could feel the heat on her face.

Nellie and Irma cheered. "A classic strategy," said Nellie.

"Every true smith loves a good fire," said Irma. "That's what I always say."

The ball smoked, but otherwise seemed unhurt. The propeller spun out of its top again. It zoomed toward the metal dragon, but the dragon blasted it with a massive eruption of fire. The propeller tried to fight through the inferno without success, then fell to the stage. The dragon blasted it again. The propeller withdrew inside the ball and the ball rolled away. The dragon marched after it. The ball rolled away again. Then a tiny green string spun out of the ball and lay on the floor. The dragon marched up to it and blasted the string with another jet of fire.

The string erupted with sparks.

"It's a fuse!" shouted Eden.

She was right. In a second, the sparks ran along the fuse to the ball. The ball exploded, shaking the lights of Main Lodge, destroying the dragon, and tearing a three-foot hole in the stage.

No one ran for the exits. Instead, to Eden's surprise, the crowd cheered. She joined in. "It appears we have a tie!" shouted Robert. He stepped over the hole and lifted the hands of Gwyneth and Yuriko into the air. "I declare them both to be winners!"

"Machinist Bingo nearly always ends this way," said Nellie, as she clapped.

"Total annihilation," said Irma, taking a sip from her teacup. "Just the way we like it."

XVII

Five Hundred Degrees

Three days later, on Saturday morning, Eugene led Nathaniel and Eden into Vulcan's room.

Vulcan was working on his guest chair again. "About time. I need a test subject."

"Hello to you, too," said Eden, wishing that even once he'd show her even the smallest kindness. Vulcan grunted at her.

"Test subject for what?" asked Nathaniel.

Vulcan frowned. "Since we're doing the Tasks, I've been trying to get my skills back into shape by working on this thing. I know it seemed a little rough last time, but I've made some adjustments." He nodded at Nathaniel. "Come on, what's-your-name, take a seat."

Nathaniel looked at the chair. It was a simple metal frame, but with gears and pulleys and other pieces of metal attached. "What about *safety first*?"

"It's just a chair," said Vulcan. "What do you think is going to happen? Sit down."

Nathaniel gulped. "Ummm...I think I'll pass."

Vulcan fumed. "Pass? Saint Dunstan! You don't get to pass! Sit!"

Nathaniel sat. The chair held his weight. He let out a nervous sigh and settled in. "Not bad," Nathaniel said. "Surprisingly comfortable."

"Of course it's comfortable. Now, if you'd like to recline, just push this lever here," said Vulcan. He pushed a lever and the chair leaned back.

"Hey, that's nice," said Nathaniel. "If only I could put my feet up." Vulcan grunted and pushed another lever. A footrest came up under Nathaniel's feet. Nathaniel said, "Say, Mr. Smith, this is comfy! Maybe you're not in as bad of shape as everyone says."

"Is that what they're saying? Then tell them about this chair, because it also works as a step ladder. Watch this." He pulled another lever and the chair began to fold and bend with Nathaniel trapped inside.

"Hey!" shouted Nathaniel. "That hurts! Let me out!"

"Hold on, little Nat. Just a slight miscalculation." Vulcan pushed the lever the other way and the ladder began bending and folding again while Nathaniel squawked in pain.

"Ouch! Oooh! Ohh...wait! No, not that way! Ohhh...my poor body."

With one final lurch, the chair dumped Nathaniel out on the floor and then fell to pieces on top of him.

"Hmm," said Vulcan. "I was sure I had it right that time."

Eden said, "Instead of wasting your time making chairs, shouldn't you be trying to help me solve the Task of Dishes?"

Nathaniel picked himself up off the floor with a groan. "The worst part is that at the end of every day, I add another cartful of dishes to the room. I feel like I'm making the Task harder. Maybe I could just stash the dishes somewhere else and take some away instead."

"Oh, no you don't, Nat," said Vulcan. "You'll get us caught for cheating."

As they left, Eden said, "You're welcome."

"For what?" said Vulcan.

"You needed a test subject. We came."

"Oh." Vulcan squinted at her. "Well, thank you then, I guess."

Eden pulled back. "Did you just say *thank you?* Maybe there's hope for you, after all."

⁓

Eden spent the rest of the day in Records, searching for anything else she could discover about Mordan Silversmith.

She found nothing.

The next day was Sunday. Eden woke up to find herself staring at the photo of her parents. Whether it was because of her strained relationship with Vulcan or some other unknown reason, she had a sudden, surprising feeling of homesickness. But for what home, she wasn't sure. She was looking out the small window when the answer hit her. She raised the idea over breakfast.

"Aunty," said Eden to Nellie. "I'd like to go out. Is that something you ever do?"

Nellie was polishing the silver sugar bowl with a napkin. "Go out? To the garden?"

"I was thinking a little farther. Like maybe somewhere in the city."

Nellie looked up. "You mean off the grounds of the Guildhall? Why on earth would we do that?"

"Well, because it's kind of weird, just being here all the time. I mean, don't you ever miss the world out there?"

"Miss what, exactly?" said Irma.

"Like, miss seeing what the rest of the world is up to. Miss doing what—what other, you know, what other kids are doing."

Irma took a sip from her teacup. "What are they doing? Do they do something fascinating?"

"No," said Eden with a sigh. "I mean, don't you ever want to just go hang out somewhere?"

"*Hang out?*" said Nellie. "Hang out of what? A window?"

"No! I mean, like, go to an ice-cream place or a coffee shop and just, you know, *hang out.*"

"A coffee shop?" said Irma. "Would they also serve tea there?"

"Yes!" said Eden. "I mean, I think they would. And hot chocolate, I bet."

Irma sniffed her tea. "I wonder if the tea they serve outside of the Guildhall is perhaps better than the tea that Miss Clara serves. I've always been a bit suspicious of her selection."

"I must think about this for a moment," said Nellie, returning to her polishing. "Where would such a shop be located?"

Eden had heard her classmates often talk about the coffee shops they frequented. She had been to a few over the years, but had never been allowed to stay very long. She had to admit that she didn't know where one was. "I'm not sure, exactly. We might have to drive around a bit until we find one."

"Drive around?" said Nellie.

"Oh!" shouted Irma. "Sister, I have the most excellent idea. We could take Barney Oldfield out for a spin."

"Who is Barney Oldfield?" said Eden.

Nellie set down the sugar bowl. "A fascinating idea, sister. Eden, Barney Oldfield is not a who. He is a what. Go and get a jacket."

"Where are we going?"

"Where?" said Nellie. "We are going *out*."

Eden quickly found a jacket—she hadn't worn one since she'd arrived at the Guildhall—then waited for nearly half an hour for the sisters to change their clothes. When they stepped back into the parlor, Nellie and Irma were both wearing old black leather jackets, black leather pants, and black boots. They had white motorcycle helmets on their heads, with goggles perched on the helmets.

Irma handed Eden a black helmet. "This should fit you, dearie. Safety first."

Eden laughed. "Why are you dressed like that?"

"This is our riding gear, of course," said Nellie, tightening a buckle on her jacket. "A bit snugger than I remember, but it still fits."

"Why do you need it?"

"All shall be revealed. Follow us."

Eden followed the sisters to the elevator. She assumed the other smiths would think their outfits hilarious, but no one seemed to notice. Buzz may have widened his eyes a bit, but he delivered them to the main floor without commenting.

In Humble Gallery, Nellie led them through a doorway and down a long hall. At the end of the hall, they went through another door that opened into a garage. It was full of cars covered with cloths and its walls were lined with long tool benches. A garage door opened to a wide driveway. A few Joneses wore coveralls and tinkered around. One of the Joneses, an older man with a thick moustache, looked up when the door opened.

"Got your message, Ms. Silversmith. He's ready for you."

"Thank you, dear," said Nellie. "Am I to assume he is still in good working order?"

"He is, ma'am," said the Jones. "I look after him myself. You'll have no problem. But..."

"But what, young man?"

"But, I have to ask, ma'am, do you have a driver's license? A current one, I mean?"

"A lady never answers questions about her documentation," said Nellie. "You let me worry about that. Bring him out, please."

The mechanic nodded, then disappeared into the shadows of the garage. A few seconds later, Eden heard the roar of an engine. She saw an old, shiny silver motorcycle, complete with sidecar, roll into view. The Jones mechanic pushed down the kickstand and hopped off the cycle. "Here you go, ma'am."

"Eden," said Nellie, pulling her goggles down over her eyes, "let me introduce you to Barney Oldfield. He belongs to sister and me."

"We're going on that?" said Eden. She gulped, then pulled on her own goggles.

Irma positioned herself in the sidecar while Nellie climbed onto the seat. Nellie grabbed the swept-back handlebars and gunned the throttle. The engine roared.

"What are you waiting for, Eden?" shouted Nellie over the noise.

Eden climbed on the seat behind Nellie and wrapped her arms around Nellie's waist. "When's the last time you rode this?"

Nellie gunned the throttle again and released the clutch. The motorcycle bucked forward, roared across the driveway and into the street. "What?"

"I said, how long has it been since you've ridden this?"

"How long? Why, it must be fifty years, at least!"

As the motorcycle tore around a corner, Eden held tighter to Nellie's soft middle. She looked down at Irma, who was smiling and sipping from her teacup, as if she were sitting on a sofa in a quiet room instead of screeching down Tacoma's streets in a motorcycle sidecar.

Eden heard Nellie shouting something to her, but she couldn't make out the words over the noise of the engine. She leaned her head forward. "What?"

"I said, remind me which side of the street I am supposed to drive on!"

Eden screamed as Nellie barreled right toward an oncoming bus. They swerved out of the way at the last second.

"Never mind," said Nellie. "I remember now."

The motorcycle careened around cars, drove onto sidewalks, and ran through what Eden was certain were at least six red lights. At first, Eden was too busy fearing for her life to notice her surroundings, but then she started to see familiar sites. They roared past Lowell Elementary School, which she'd attended two different times. They went by Franklin Elementary and Hilltop Heritage Middle School—she'd gone to both of those as well. As they drove through someone's front yard, Eden was pretty sure she spotted the house of Sienna, the purple-haired foster mom she'd stayed with years ago.

Eden noticed a park ahead of them. She recognized it as Wright Park, the same one that housed the conservatory where her parents had died. It was a beautiful park, full of huge old trees, grassy hills, and a large duck pond. Nellie must have mistaken one of its paths for a road, because the next thing Eden knew, they were right in the middle of the park, thundering toward the bridge over the pond. The bridge was occupied by a group of girls looking down at the ducks. When the girls spotted the motorcycle barreling toward them, they screamed and dove into the water. Eden begged Nellie to stop, but Nellie couldn't seem to hear her. Irma was still happily sipping her tea. Eden just held on tighter and prayed they would survive.

The motorcycle roared out of the park and crossed a busy

intersection, diagonally. Cars squealed their brakes and honked their horns. Nellie bounced the motorcycle over a curb and screeched it to a halt. She shut off the motor.

Eden let out a shaky breath. Then she noticed that they were parked next to a sandwich-board sign that read Cosmonaut Coffee. Nellie said, "Will this do?"

~

The tables of the small shop were mostly occupied by people staring at their laptops. Nellie frowned at them, muttering something under her breath, then approached the counter where a young man in a baseball cap was working.

"Is this where we place our orders?" asked Nellie.

The man nodded.

"Then I would like cucumber sandwiches for three."

"Sorry, we don't serve sandwiches here. We have scones."

"Very well. Scones for three then. With butter and marmalade, please."

"We have vegan butter and vegan honey. Will that do?"

"Fine. And a pot of English breakfast tea with milk, please."

"What kind of milk?"

"There are kinds?"

"We've got oat milk, almond milk, rice milk, soy milk, and coconut milk."

"Oh, this is very confusing. I was hoping for the traditional kind. The milk that comes from a cow."

Eden ordered a vanilla latte. She'd had one years before and liked it.

"That'll be fourteen dollars even," said the barista.

Nellie pulled out a small coin purse and handed the man a gold coin.

"What's this?" said the barista.

"I believe it is a twenty-dollar gold piece," said Nellie. "You may keep a dollar for yourself."

The barista examined the coin, turning it over and over, then

143

handed Nellie a five-dollar bill in change. Nellie examined the bill with equal curiosity, while Eden shepherded them to a table.

In a corner of the small room, a half dozen kids about Eden's age gathered around their phones, whispering and laughing with each other. Irma spotted them. "Oh, Eden, there you go! A group of youngsters. Introduce yourself."

Eden hissed. "Shhh! What? No!"

"But I thought you wanted to … what was that term you used? Hang out? Isn't that what they are doing?"

"Please keep your voice down. I don't know them."

Irma smiled. "That is why you introduce yourself."

"Would you please whisper?" Eden felt suddenly sick to her stomach. "I wouldn't even know what to say to them."

Nellie chuckled. "Not know what to say? Why Eden, you are an apprentice at a Guildhall! What could be more fascinating to a young person than that? Talk to them about melting points. Tell them about that lovely butter knife you made."

Irma nodded. "Any child not interested in cutlery is not a child worth knowing. That's what I always say. Now go on." Irma gave Eden a firm push.

Eden took a deep breath and walked toward the teenagers. With each step, the sick feeling in her stomach grew. Why was she doing this? She looked once toward Nellie and Irma, their faces nodding at her under their helmets. She turned back to the teenagers.

One of the girls looked up from her phone. "Hey. You need something?"

Eden felt her face growing hot as she thought about the question. Did she need something from these people? They were her age. This was the group she was supposed to be part of, not the smiths back at the Guildhall. She was supposed to be texting and shopping and uploading and, well, hanging out. Wasn't she?

The girl who had spoken was looking up at her. The others continued staring at their phones as they chatted. The girl waited a moment for Eden to speak. When she didn't, the girl's gaze went back to her own phone.

When Eden found her voice a split-second later, she also discovered that she was smiling. "No," she told the girl. "I'm good. Sorry to interrupt."

Eden returned to the sisters. "I'm ready to go back now."

"So am I," said Irma. "The tea is too hot and these scones are too dry. Although this vegan butter is not half bad. I may suggest it to Miss Clara."

Eden barely noticed the terrifying ride back. When they had parked Barney Oldfield and returned to Humble Gallery, she spotted Eugene, standing inside by the front door. A sudden urge overtook her and she ran and hugged him.

"Hey now! What's this all about?" Eugene said, as he hugged her back.

"Nothing." Eden hugged him harder. "It's just good to be home."

The next morning, and in the following days, Eden and Nathaniel went to Helena's rooms to continue their apprentice training in bladesmithing. Nathaniel's work was still lumpy, but improving. Eden kept astounding her teacher with her progress.

On the tenth day, just as Eden finished the final touches on a ceremonial cutlass, the sisters stopped in to check on her progress. They saw the sword sitting on Helena's scarred wooden table.

"My, this is a beautiful thing," said Nellie to Helena. "May I touch it?"

"Of course, of course," said Helena. "I am personally quite proud. It is remarkable, isn't it?"

"It is more than remarkable," said Nellie picking up the sword and staring down its length. "Look at its balance and clean lines. And such an edge. I cannot see a single flaw. It's the best work you've ever done, Helena."

Helena reddened. "It's good, but certainly not the best work I've ever done."

"Oh, I think it is," Nellie said. "When have you made better?"

Helena snatched a huge battle-axe off the wall near her. "I make better every day. Take this axe, for instance."

"It's a fine axe," said Nellie, running her fingers over the sword hilt, "but this sword is miraculous."

Helena swung the axe against the stone floor, sending out sparks and bits of stone. She exploded. "Put it down, you old twit! Out of my shop! And take the girl and the Jones boy with you!"

Nellie jumped back. "Oh come now, Helena! What did I say?"

"Sister, *she* didn't make it," said Irma, backing toward the door. "Eden did."

"What? That can't be true. Oh, Helena, I am sorry."

"Save your apologies!" Helena shouted. She stomped toward Nellie, swinging the battle-axe above her head. "Find the girl another master smith! Out of my shop, I say! Out, out, out!"

Nellie grabbed the beautiful sword. Pushing the others in front of her, she slipped outside, just as Helena slammed the axe into the door. Its blade cut all the way through.

Eden stared at the protruding axe blade. "What just happened? Did I do something wrong?"

"The problem," said Nellie between breaths, "is that you did *nothing* wrong. Your work is too good for dear Helena's fragile ego. You have such a large measure of Vulcan in you and are just too talented. Your work in bladesmithing has reached master levels in less than two weeks. Astonishing! Remarkable!"

Eden said, "So you're not mad at me?"

"Mad?" Nellie ran her fingers along the flat of the sword. "Why would we be mad? Dear one, we couldn't be prouder of you. Look at this workmanship. Astonishing!"

"You must name it," said Irma.

"Why would I name a sword?"

Nellie said, "All the best swords have names, dearie. Don't think about it too much. What comes into your mind? There are no wrong answers."

Eden stared at the sword in Nellie's hand. "How about *Task Slayer*?"

"Oh, I don't think so," said Nellie.

"*Task Slayer*?" Irma shook her head. "I don't like that at all."

Eden laughed. "Okay then. Well, how about *Grandfather Healer*?"

"Awful." Nellie closed her eyes.

"Even worse than the first one," said Irma.

"I thought you said there are no wrong answers," said Eden.

"*She* said that," said Irma. "Not me."

"Fine." Eden looked back and forth between the sisters as they stared at her impatiently. "How about *Sister Silversmith.*"

Nellie poked the tip of the sword against the floor. "*Sister Silversmith.* That's it. Just right. Now let's go and show it to Vulcan."

In his room, Vulcan handled the sword for a long time without speaking. He turned it every way, running his fingers along the edge.

"Oh, you old fool," said Nellie, pounding the floor with her cane. "You know it's good work. Say something nice to the girl."

"I remember when I used to be this good." Vulcan wrapped *Sister Silversmith* in an old cloth and set it on his table. "She should work with Fred next."

"Fred Tinsmith? After displaying talent like this?" said Nellie. "Oh, Vulcan, tin is such a poor metal. Don't you think she'd be better off with a gold or silversmith? So she can work with something worthy of her skills? Even a blacksmith would be better than a—a tinman."

"Nonsense. Fred will teach her how to work. Really work. And not just make showpieces."

"Vulcan—"

"I'll admit that the sword is remarkable—"

"And amazing!" said Irma.

"—but it's not the typical work-a-day labor that a real smith needs to do. Besides…"

"I'll do it," said Eden.

"Now, Eden. Don't agree just yet," said Nellie.

Eden folded her arms. "I'll do it. I'll work with Fred Tinsmith. As long as Nathaniel can work with me."

Nellie's eyes grew wide. Irma smiled. Vulcan barked out a short single laugh. "She's an agitator, this one."

"She's your granddaughter," said Nellie, "so that goes without saying."

The next morning, Eden and Nathaniel rode the elevator to the second floor. Eden pictured the sunny green floor she'd accidentally spotted before. She smiled, wide-eyed at Buzz. He frowned back at her, then spoke directly to Nathaniel. "You, uhh, you doing more smithing today, Jones?"

"I am, actually."

Buzz nodded. "Must be nice. Crossing boundaries. Breaking through. Deciding for yourself what you can and can't do."

Nathaniel shrugged. "I guess so."

Buzz let go of his lever and grabbed Nathaniel by the collar. "Don't just guess! You've got to do it! Whenever you can. And you've got to not stink it up. If you stink it up, then what chance will I ever have to be a smith? To—to make a sword?"

Nathaniel gulped and nodded at Buzz. Eden's eyes swung to Nathaniel, with his skinny arms and messy hair. Was he carrying more responsibility than she had realized?

They left the elevator and walked to the far end of the second floor, as Vulcan had instructed them. The hallway grew dimmer and the ornate metal gave way to scarred walls and floors. They found Fred Tinsmith's worn and dented tin door and knocked.

A tall, rawboned man opened the door. He wore an old baseball cap perched crookedly on top of his head and a pair of tattered canvas overalls with leather patches on the knees. "You're Vulcan's granddaughter," he said to Eden. He turned to Nathaniel. "But who are you?"

"I'm Nat Jones."

Fred nodded. "Thought you were a Jones. Why are you here?"

"To learn tinsmithing," said Nathaniel.

Fred lifted his hat and scratched the tuft of white hair on his head. "Well, come on then."

"You don't care that I'm a Jones?" said Nathaniel.

Fred grunted. "I care about three things: showing up on time, working hard, and keeping your yapper shut. Lots of thing I don't care about. Names is one."

They followed Fred inside his shop. The walls and workbenches were covered in pots, pans, ladles, cans, and what Eden assumed was junk—old scraps of metal piled high. At one end of the shop was a fireplace with a black pot hanging over it and a large anvil in front. Hammers of all shapes and sizes lay around the anvil.

Fred said. "Jonesy, go fetch some more wood for the fire. Six doors down the hall is wood storage. Keep the pieces small and fill that box there." He pointed to a large box by the fireplace. Nathaniel set off down the hall. Fred scratched his shoulder. "Eden, you can start cleaning."

"Cleaning?" Eden wrinkled her nose. "What's that got to do with—"

"Broom's in the corner."

"I thought we were going to learn about tinsmithing."

"You're an apprentice, ain't you?" said Fred. "Then you do what you're told."

"But I already *know* how to clean. I'm the granddaughter of Vulcan Smith! I'm here to learn *smithing*!" said Eden.

Nathaniel came in with his first armload of wood. He piled it into the wood box and headed out for another load.

"You're a Smith. He's a Jones," said Fred. "While you're yapping, he's working."

Eden huffed, but she found the broom and began to sweep the shop. Before she was half done, Nathaniel had finished building a neat stack of firewood and asked Fred for his next Task. Fred put him to work sorting tools—hanging the scattered hammers and snips in their racks above the workbench. Nathaniel finished that, then began sorting the scraps of metal. Eden kept sweeping while Fred talked to Nathaniel. "Put the steel in that bin there at the end. The copper can go in the next one over. Those bars of lead are mighty heavy, but we don't need much of it. Pile them on the workbench so I don't need to bend over to pick them up."

"If you're a tinsmith, then why do you have all these other metals?" asked Nathaniel.

"I still make a few things out of just tin—a few pots, a few spoons, maybe a Revere lantern, which is a pretty thing—but mostly tin is used for alloys. Bronze, pewter, bell metal. Or as a coating for steel, because tin doesn't rust and it's easy to work with. Low melting point. Melt it right over a fire."

"Pewter is mostly tin, right?" said Nathaniel.

"It is," said Fred. "Ninety-four percent, the way I make it. You're a bright boy." Eden glared at Nathaniel from across the room. He shrugged back at her.

Fred scratched his scruffy cheek. "I'll tell you what, Jonesy. You get this place cleaned up, we'll mix a batch of pewter." Fred nodded toward Eden. "Make sure she does her share of the work." Eden glared again, sweeping the floor hard enough to kick up clouds of dust.

It took another three hours to get the room clean to Fred's satisfaction. For lunch, Fred gave them each a thick slice of bread spread with butter, a thick piece of cheese on top, and an apple on the side. They ate, then Fred led them to the pot that hung over the fire. "Not much to making pewter," he said. "We mix it in this old steel crucible, because steel has a much higher melting point." He showed them how to weigh out the tin and add it to the pot. They measured in some antimony—a bright silver metal—and then a tiny amount of copper. "The fire is probably hot enough already," said Fred, "as it only has to get to about five hundred degrees."

"And it won't hurt the steel pot?" asked Eden

Fred scratched his chin. "Not a pot. A *crucible*. Want to answer that one, boy?"

"It won't hurt the steel crucible," said Nathaniel, "because steel has a much higher melting point."

"*Crucible*," repeated Eden. "Not a pot. A crucible." Eden took a big bite of bread and cheese. With her mouth still full, she said, "What if you had a whole room of pewter? How hot would it have to get to melt it? In the crucible?"

"Doesn't matter how much you have," said Fred. "If you get pewter to five hundred degrees, it melts."

"Every time?"

"Of course every time." Fred frowned. "Vulcan told me you were smart. Maybe he's just biased 'cause you're his kin."

"He sure doesn't act biased," said Eden, taking another bite. "Never says anything nice to me. But maybe he will now, because I think I just figured out how to solve the first Impossible Task."

XVIII

Outside the Door of Dishes

They gathered that evening in Vulcan's cramped room: Eden, Nathaniel, Vulcan, the sisters, and Eugene Tinker. Vulcan leaned against the table. The rest sat along the edge of the bed. No one sat in the guest chair.

Eden explained what she had learned. "It's kind of obvious, when you think about it. My ancestor, Mordan Silversmith, had the Dishes room lined with steel plates."

"We know that, dearie," said Nellie. "We've all seen the room."

"I know," said Eden. "But when Nathaniel and I read about it in Records, Mordan said that if she was going to be tested, she wanted the room to be her *crucible*."

"That's a metaphor." Nellie leaned forward on her silver cane. "If one finds oneself in a crucible, metaphorically speaking, it means they are in for some very tough times. Tested by fire and such."

"What if she meant it *literally*?" said Eden.

"In what way, dearie?"

"What if she meant for the room—the steel-lined room full of pewter dishes—to serve as a crucible, as a literal crucible?"

"I don't know what you mean."

"Oh, I do!" said Irma, taking a sip from her blue teacup. "It's so obvious, I'm ashamed I've never figured it out before this."

"Figured what out?" said Nellie.

Eden stood up and began pacing. "It's a steel room, with a good stone fireplace and chimney. No windows. One heavy steel door. Steel has a melting point of twenty-five hundred degrees. Pewter melts at five hundred. So we heat up the whole room. Turn the whole place into a giant crucible, like it said in the file. The fireplace and its chimney provide ventilation. The steel-plated walls protect the room itself. In one day, we get the room hot enough to melt all the dishes at once."

"A whole room?" said Nellie. "How would you get it hot enough? Besides, the Task is to clean the dishes, not melt them."

"Is it?" said Eden. She pulled the curl of stamped tin from her pocket. It had been in there so long that the curl had flattened. She unfolded it and read, "*Within one day, defined as sunrise to sunset, every single dish must be rendered free of dirt, food, and other impurities, and cleaned to a high shine.* There!" shouted Eden. "It doesn't say they still have to be dishes, just that they must be cleaned to a high shine. If the pewter was freshly melted, wouldn't it be shiny?"

"It would," said Vulcan. "Like liquid silver. Even I know that."

Eden thought she saw the faintest sparkle in her grandfather's eyes. She said, "Now all we have to do is heat up the room. And we have to heat it hot enough to burn the food and grime away completely. Fred Tinsmith said five hundred degrees would do it."

"Heat it up to five hundred degrees?" Nellie thumped the floor of Vulcan's room with her cane. "How in the world are you going to do that?"

"I can help," said Vulcan. "Maybe I can't smith. Maybe I shouldn't be trusted to even build a chair, but by Saint Dunstan's hammer, I'm the helper, and I can help. I'll call in a couple of favors. You five just be ready. A few days from now, we just might be one Impossible Task closer to the end."

Two days later, right after breakfast, Eden and Nathaniel stood outside the door of a smith named Arnau Herrero, a small, thin man with skin like brown leather, thick glasses, and wisps of white hair on his head. "Hola, niños."

Nathaniel waved. "Hola Señor Herrero. Es bueno verte. ¿Te despertamos?"

"No, no, no, te estaba esperando."

"What are you saying?" said Eden, feeling a little jealous of Nathaniel's language skills.

Nathaniel turned to Eden. "We're just saying hello."

Arnau smiled. "You're here for the fuel? For Vulcan?"

"That's right," said Eden. "My grandfather sent us."

"The fuel I have for you is heavy and very unstable," said Arnau. "I call it Herrero's Hot Sauce—a little thermite, *un poco de magnesio*, and a few special touches my mama taught me. I come from a long line of good cooks. Different from the sort in your family, though." He winked at Nathaniel. "Here. I put it in this wooden box with a handle for each of you. Whatever you do, do not drop it, or you might blow us all to kingdom come."

"Thank you, Señor Herrero," said Eden.

Arnau nodded. Then he took a heavy padlock from his pocket, closed it over the clasp of the box, and handed the key to Nathaniel. "Never know what prying eyes might want to look inside." He smiled. "This I do as a favor for Vulcan. A good man? Maybe not. But a good friend? Always. Me, I mostly work in tungsten. For the sciences. If you ever choose to work in tungsten, come and see me. For tungsten, we make the hottest fires. Vulcan came to the right man, that's for sure."

Eden and Nathaniel each took a handle of the box and lifted it. It was much heavier than Eden had expected, and she stumbled with her end. "*¡Ten cuidado!*" said Arnau. "Remember, drop that box of Herrero's Hot Sauce and *kaboom!*"

Eden and Nathaniel walked as carefully as they could toward the elevator. Every thirty feet or so, they had to set the heavy box down and rest their arms. As they turned a corner, they saw a tall figure approaching from the far end of the corridor.

"Pewtersmith!" said Eden. "Just what we need."

Mr. Pewtersmith met them halfway down the corridor. "Ah, the young apprentice brat and her friend, the Jones scullery boy. What do you have there?"

"Not sure," lied Eden. "My grandfather asked us to pick it up."

"From whom? From that old fool, Herrero? Show me what's inside."

"I would, but we're in a hurry," said Eden. "My grandfather said he needed it right away."

Mr. Pewtersmith's eyes darkened. "I'm not asking your permission. I'm telling you to set it down and open it. This is not up for discussion."

Eden nodded to Nathaniel and they set the box down as gently as they could. Mr. Pewtersmith noticed the padlock. "Give me the key."

"I don't have it," said Eden. "Like I said, we're just delivering it to my grandfather."

Mr. Pewtersmith narrowed his eyes at her. He grunted as he lifted the box from the ground. "What's in here? Lead bricks?" He gave the box a shake.

"Don't shake it!" hissed Eden.

Mr. Pewtersmith stopped and stared at her. "Why not?"

"Because it's—my grandfather said it's fragile."

"Fragile, eh?" said Mr. Pewtersmith. He lowered the box toward the ground, and then dropped it. It hit the floor with a loud thud. Eden and Nathaniel grimaced, waiting for the *kaboom*. Nothing happened. Mr. Pewtersmith eyed them up and down with a sneer, then left.

Eden's breath came out in a rush. "That was close. Let's get this out of here."

When they reached Vulcan's room, he opened the box and inspected the contents as they told him what happened. Inside were canisters of a rust-colored goo.

"Herrero's Hot Sauce? Remind me what this is for," said Vulcan.

Eden stared at him. "You're the one who sent us for it. It's from Arnau Herrero. For the dishes."

"Right," said Vulcan. "For the dishes. But why would Herrero give you so much of it? This stuff is dangerous. You should get it out of here before someone gets hurt."

Eden sucked in her breath. She motioned toward Nathaniel and the two of them left.

"He's just having a bad day," said Nathaniel. "My great grandpa used to talk like that, when he was near the end."

"Near the end?" hissed Eden. "Nathaniel, maybe keep your family stories to yourself from now on."

They walked the box to Dishes without any more interruptions, where they met Eugene and the sisters. The space outside the door was littered with carts and equipment. They eased the box down in front of the stone fireplace inside the room.

"Okay," said Eden. "Let's do this."

Nathaniel left to search for stray dishes while Eden and Eugene set to work removing the doorknob on the old steel door and fitting a long, hollow steel pipe into the hole. The pipe was about four feet long. Eden fitted it in place until two feet of pipe were inside the room and two feet were outside. "A nice snug fit," said Eugene, out of breath.

Nellie opened the wooden box. "So this is Herrero's famous Hot Sauce. I've heard of it, but never seen it work. It is supposed to put out some amazing heat. Eden, dearie, be careful as you set these canisters around the room." Using both hands, Eden set the first one next to the fireplace, then, one by one, set the remaining canisters among the huge piles of pewter dishes. Nellie said, "Be careful, but hurry, dearie. We have to have all the dishes done by sunset. Who knows if that is enough time to get this room hot enough."

Nathaniel came back with his cart, which had exactly a dozen more dishes on it. "This is all of them. I checked with the Blue Coats in Supperdinner Hall. They said every last dish was accounted for."

Nellie inspected the room, pointing with her cane as she counted the canisters of Herrero's Hot Sauce among the towering piles of pewter. "So many dishes," she said. "I hope all this effort is enough."

They moved to the hallway. Eden watched Nellie examine a large metal tank. It looked like a large version of a tank a scuba diver would wear on his back. She looked at a handful of small rockets on the ground nearby. "Are you sure these will light?" Nellie said.

"They'll light," said Eden. "Eugene and I have practiced, but I brought extras, just to be sure."

"And what about this door?" said Nellie. "Will it hold?"

"Not so sure about that," said Eugene. "It's solid steel, but it's old. And by the looks of it, it's been through this once before."

Nellie said, "That's further proof that Eden's theory is correct. Mordan Silversmith did light this room up and the door held then. It's been tested. And what about the fan?" She looked toward the metal box with a circular hole in the back, a pipe on the front, and a heavy electrical cord.

"Triple-checked," said Eugene. "If the power goes out, we brought a battery pack."

Eden felt nauseous. She was the one who had thought of heating up the room. But if it didn't work, she and her grandfather would be banished. Eden couldn't bear the thought of leaving the Guildhall behind and going back into foster care. And what would become of Vulcan?

"Are we ready?" said Nellie. "Eugene, fetch the Council. Tell them we are prepared to begin the first Task."

"No!" said Eden. "Don't bring them here! Mr. Pewtersmith will come with them!"

"Uriah Pewtersmith must be here. They all must be here to witness the event," said Nellie. "Eugene, please go quickly. And Eden, can you please remind me how this all works?"

Eden took a deep breath. "First, we'll close this door and lock it." She touched the warped metal with her fingers. "Please be a good door. Please be a strong door." She turned to the metal tank. "Then, using this tank, I'll pump the room full of acetylene gas. Fill it up like a balloon. I'll then light a rocket and fire it through the pipe into the room, igniting the gas."

"There will be quite a boom when that happens," said Nellie, tapping her cane. "Hopefully the door will hold. It will hold! I'm sure it will. Acetylene burns very hot and the temperature inside will rise quickly."

"Right," said Eden. "We have to get the whole room to five hundred degrees. If we do, the pewter will slowly begin to melt. But there's so much of it, we don't want to take chances. When we hit five hundred, the canisters of Herrero's Hot Sauce will ignite, just as a guarantee. Grandpa said that stuff burns hot enough even to melt steel, but in such a big room, hopefully the heat will dissipate before the Hot Sauce melts through the steel floor."

"The floor!" said Nellie. "But dearie, the floor isn't steel. It's pewter!"

Eden nodded. "Let's hope there's steel underneath, Auntie. Let's hope that pewter down there now is the pewter that melted when Mordan performed the Task." She paused. "But just in case, what if there's no steel underneath?"

"Then we burn the whole Guildhall down"—Irma smiled—"and we all die."

Nellie frowned. "Now sister, I feel reasonably confident there's steel beneath that pewter. And if Eden's plan works, she will melt even the most stubborn dish."

"That's the idea," Eden said, trying to keep the worry from her voice. "Once the hot sauce is lit, we keep blowing in air with a fan to keep it all burning, because fire needs air. Then we let it all burn until the fire goes out."

"And once it cools, we open the doors and take a look!" said Nellie.

"Yes," said Eden. "So...do you think it'll work?"

Irma took a sip from her teacup. "Death is the only certainty."

"Sister, dear," said Nellie, "stop being negative."

"I'm not being negative, sister. I'm stating a truth. And no matter what happens, it will be quite a show."

A few minutes later, all of the Council except Mr. Pewtersmith gathered around outside the door of Dishes. Helena Bladesmith carefully inspected the closed door, the pipe, the tank of acetylene, and the rockets. Other members of the Council whispered among themselves.

"Where is Mr. Pewtersmith?" said Eden.

"He's coming, dearie. Eugene also had to fetch your grandfather. All must be present."

After what felt to Eden like hours, but was really only about fifteen minutes, Mr. Pewtersmith marched down the hall, dressed in the same robe he wore when he judged Vulcan. Vulcan bumped along behind him with uneven steps, wearing his work clothes. *Grandpa looks more worn down than ever*, Eden thought.

"What do we have here, then, Vulcan?" said Mr. Pewtersmith. "You and your little mob are wasting no time. Only one other smith has ever managed to complete this Task, you know."

Eden glared at him. "You think we don't know our own family history?"

"I think you don't know how to speak to your betters," said Mr. Pewtersmith. "And I also think you're about to find out that you never should have risked your life on some harebrained idea of your grandfather's."

Vulcan spoke up. "It's not my idea. It's Eden's."

A wave of murmurs came from the members of the Council. Eden felt her face growing hot, but she wasn't sure if it was the attention from all the people present or the particular attention of her grandfather. Mr. Pewtersmith said, "You mean to say, Vulcan, that you're betting your future on an idea that comes from an *apprentice*. A child. Untested. Fine with me. Let's go inside and watch the failure commence."

"We won't be going inside," said Eden. "Not until we're done." She gulped. She was speaking as if she knew what she was doing, but what if she was mistaken? What if they failed this very first Task and were banished from the Guildhall? What if something went wrong? What if someone died? What if they *all* died?

Eugene took a deep breath and began connecting the tank of acetylene to the pipe that went through the door.

"You're going to wash the dishes with acetylene?" said Mr. Pewtersmith. "That's a new one."

Before she could stop herself, Eden blurted, "We're not going to wash them. We're going to melt them."

158

"Stop!" Mr. Pewtersmith held up a hand. "This is a cheat! The Task is to wash the dishes!"

"The Task," said Eden, reading from her slip of stamped tin, "is this: *Within one day, defined as sunrise to sunset, every single dish must be rendered free of dirt, food, and other impurities, and cleaned to a high shine.* That is what we will do, by sunset today."

Shouts broke out among the Council. Irma joined in, until Nellie reminded her to stay quiet. Mr. Pewtersmith shouted the loudest, demanding disqualification. Helena Bladesmith and Maureen Goldsmith shouted in favor of proceeding. Eden was relieved that Helena still seemed to be on her side. Robert Blacksmith took the slip of tin from Eden, holding it in his huge fingers and moving his lips as he read the words over and over again. Finally, he turned to the crowd.

"Silence!" he roared. The hallway outside Dishes grew quiet. "I've read these words ten times over and can see no reason why Eden can't proceed. If she can actually melt them all by sunset—all the dishes—then every single dish will be clean. We all know it."

"Nonsense! What if the brat burns down the entire Guildhall?" shouted Mr. Pewtersmith.

"I won't," said Eden, turning toward her grandfather. "Will I?"

Vulcan shrugged. "Beats me."

"Besides," said Robert. "Every true smith loves a good fire. Isn't that even right for you, Pewtersmith? You're a true smith, ain't you?"

Mr. Pewtersmith frowned but said nothing.

"A vote then," said Robert Blacksmith. "All in favor?"

Nearly the whole Council said, "Aye."

"All opposed?"

Only Mr. Pewtersmith said, "Nay."

Robert Blacksmith nodded.

Eden set to work.

XIX

In Which Eden Hears a Steady Roar

It took five minutes for the acetylene tank to empty into the huge storage room. Eugene capped off the pipe, while Eden began preparing a rocket.

Nellie gripped the head of her cane with both hands. "Pray for the door. Pray that it will hold."

Eugene moved the Council and everyone far away from the door and the end of the pipe. Eden lit the fuse of a rocket and held it in her shaky hands until the fuse was almost burnt away. As the small rocket began to spit flames, Eden thrust it into the pipe. The rocket shot inside.

BOOM! The building shook so hard that Eden feared it might fall down. A crash of falling metal dishes followed. A jet of flames shot out of the pipe halfway across the hallway. The door strained on its hinges and bowed outward. But it held firm.

"So far so good," said Nellie.

"No one's died," said Irma, smiling.

"No one's died *yet*," muttered Mr. Pewtersmith.

A steady roar began inside the room. Eugene mopped his forehead, then removed his jacket. Eden connected the fan to the end of the flaming pipe. She turned on the fan. It whirred loudly and began pumping air into the room.

"Is it working?" said Irma. She fanned her face with her hand.

"It's a big room," said Nellie. "It will take more than one tank of acetylene to heat the whole thing up enough. Just wait and listen."

A series of loud *whoops* began to sound off inside, muffled by the steel and stone walls. "Herrero's Hot Sauce," said Nellie. "Now we have really got a fire."

"We should have brought marshmallows," said Irma. "It's been years since I've had a roasted marshmallow."

"Now what?" said Eden.

"Now we wait, dearie. Now we wait."

They didn't wait long. In just a few minutes, the edges of the steel door began to grow pink. A few minutes more and the entire door was so hot that it glowed cherry red. It began to bend outward, ever so slightly. As it did, a stream of silvery liquid oozed out from beneath the door and left a smoky trail on the stones of the corridor.

"Watch your feet," said Eugene.

"You fools are going to catch the building on fire!" shouted Mr. Pewtersmith.

Robert Blacksmith ignored him and nodded at the liquid. "Molten pewter," he said. "Very clean."

It took two more hours until it was all over. The fire inside burned itself out. The door cooled from red to black again, but was still too hot to touch. Eugene sprayed it with cold water, then tried to open it, but the heat inside had welded the door shut. He brought out two huge crowbars. Eugene took one and Robert Blacksmith took the other. They pried on the door. Finally, the seal broke with a loud *crack*.

"Now that we can open it, I'm not sure that we should," said Eugene. "It's still awful hot in there."

"Oh, stand aside!" said Mr, Pewtersmith. "I want to be the first to see the failure!" He grabbed the door and yanked it open. A blast of hot air knocked Mr. Pewtersmith onto the floor, scorching his robe and his eyebrows.

"Poor Uriah," said Irma. "Those eyebrows had just about grown back in after his birthday explosion."

Eden looked inside Dishes. The room that had once been so full now seemed mostly empty. The towers of dirty dishes were gone. In their place was a shiny new layer of smoking silver metal, which had cooled to a solid mass and covered the floor nearly two feet deep. Not a speck of ash remained. It was as if someone had laid a thick new floor of pure pewter.

"It's so shiny," said Nathaniel.

"And so clean," said Eden.

Nellie smiled. "Cleaned to a high shine!" "Rendered free of dirt, food, and other impurities. What say you, Council?"

Robert Blacksmith tugged at his beard. "I'm satisfied. The first Impossible Task is complete."

Nearly all present cheered. Mr. Pewtersmith grunted and stomped down the hallway, his smoking robes billowing behind him.

Irma pointed after Pewtersmith with her teacup. "I do love seeing him angry."

"It *was* a good idea, dearie," said Nellie. "Wasn't it, Vulcan?"

"Wasn't bad," he said, "but we still have four to go."

✤

Later that night, the mood in Vulcan's chambers was electric, though not the mood of Vulcan himself. A knock came on the door and Miss Clara entered with her tea trolley. Nellie lifted a cup of tea off the trolley in a toast. "Thank you for coming at my request, Miss Clara. We have need of your services, for we have joined the ranks of history. Eden is now one of only a few Smiths to have overcome an Impossible Task."

"This calls for a celebration!" said Irma. She hummed as she poured whiskey into her own teacup, then took a bite from a cucumber sandwich.

"I only had the idea," said Eden, raising her cup to the room. "It was all your help that made it happen."

"That calls for a celebration, too!" said Irma, pouring another dollop of whiskey into her teacup. "Did you see the look on old

Pewtersmith's face? Looked like he was sucking a lemon. And no one died! Not a single person! Not even you, little Nat! This calls for another celebration!"

Eden was glowing. She felt lightheaded. Perhaps it could happen. Perhaps they could complete the Five Impossible Tasks. Perhaps they were possible after all. And perhaps, finally, her grandfather might want her around.

But Vulcan was silent. He lay on his bed looking up at the ceiling.

"Aren't you encouraged now, Grandpa?" asked Eden.

Vulcan grunted. "That was only one. And who knows what comes next."

Miss Clara interrupted, smiling. "Perhaps I can help with that." She reached into the lower levels of her tea trolley and pulled out a tin can, identical to the one that had held the first Task. The room went silent.

Nellie's hand went to her mouth. "Oh, Miss Clara, really? You had to deliver that tonight? Can't we have a single evening for, well, for celebrating?"

"I'm only the messenger," said Clara, "but would you mind if I stayed and watched you open it?"

Nellie pushed Clara out of the room. Eden gave the tin can a shake. The rattle inside sounded identical to the one the can made that held the first Task. Eden fetched her can opener, took a breath, and opened the can.

"It's what I think it is, isn't it?" said Vulcan, his eyes closed.

Eden nodded. "Steel birds." She read from the second coil of stamped tin.

> WITHIN ONE DAY, THE STEEL BIRDS THAT RESIDE IN THE GUILDHALL ATTIC MUST BE CAPTURED AND HELD IN CAPTIVITY UNTIL SUNSET. IF THE REQUIREMENTS ARE NOT MET, OR IF THIS OR ANY OTHER TASK IS ABANDONED, THEN THE SMITH AND THE DESIGNATED HELPER WILL BE BANISHED FROM ALL GUILDHALLS FOREVER.

"I truly hate these Tasks," said Nellie. "Those birds sound quite difficult to capture. Perhaps it would be better to try the rats."

Eden dropped sugar cubes into her tea. "The rats? Uggh! But if that would be better, *could* we do the rats next?"

"We must take the Tasks in the order given," said Vulcan. "The birds next. There's no escaping them." He looked at the ceiling, "The birds took my father. They're coming for me. The rest of me."

"Tell me about them again, Eugene," Eden said.

Eugene sighed. "The birds were made by Thợ Tiện, the famous machinist, back in 1902. Made six mechanical birds to keep the pigeons out of the attic. No pigeons come near the place now, but no one's been able to go into the attic since. The steel birds have made themselves at home up there. They're wind-up birds. And Thợ Tiện made them so realistic that they act like real birds—ones that got out of control. Remember what they did to Elemo Blacksmith."

Eden was afraid to ask. "What happened?"

"We don't know much," said Eugene. "Records are sealed for all the histories of the Tasks. But the unofficial story is that Elemo made what he thought was a tough suit of armor. Used tungsten and titanium from head to toe."

"Sounds like a good idea," said Eden, "especially for a blacksmith."

"That's what I thought," said Eugene, "but I guess the steel birds tore the armor right off him. And there's the other thing I told you, Eden, remember?" Eugene took a slow swallow of tea. "Legend has it that the birds have been having babies. That there's more than six up there now."

"I still say that's ridiculous," said Eden, gripping her teaspoon. "They're mechanical, aren't they? Then they can't have babies. And if they're so fierce, how come they haven't escaped the attic?

Eugene said, "I don't know if they're fierce, exactly, or just working how they were built to work. Like real birds defending their home. For these birds, their home's the attic. They ain't never been outside."

Eden had a sudden idea. "Grandpa, you were there when your dad tried it, right?"

Vulcan grunted.

"What did your dad try? What was his approach with the birds?"

"Lost my leg," muttered Vulcan.

"Yes, Grandpa. I know you lost your leg and I'm sorry. But what was your dad's plan?"

Vulcan stared up at the ceiling. "He...we...it was..." His voice trailed off. "Take a look. Yes. First thing we should do is take a look," said Vulcan. "Someone should go up to the attic and peek inside."

Nellie nodded. "Or course, we'll take a look, Vulcan. But what did your father try?"

"We should get a picture of the place. Take a look."

Nellie shook her head. "I'm afraid he doesn't remember, dearie. So perhaps we should go look. But the entrance to the attic is on the top floor. The Council floor. I believe Uriah Pewtersmith's rooms are closest to the attic stairs. A pity."

"What's wrong with that?" asked Eden.

"Oh, nothing, really. I'd just hate to have that man spying on our doings."

Eden bent her teaspoon into a U. "How can we look inside the attic without getting pecked to death?"

"No more spoons for you, Eden," said Nellie, snatching the bent spoon from her. "You're destroying the silverware faster than we can replace it."

"I've got something that could help with the birds," said Eugene. The tinker pulled a small silver tube out of his pocket. "Just an old thing I kept from my travels. Called a peephole. Nothing to it. There are peepholes like this on front doors of houses and apartments all over the country. Has a fisheye lens on one end, so you can get a wide view. We just need a titanium drill to make a hole in the door. Then we slip this in the hole and take a look. There's a chance the birds might peck the glass, but the hole will be too small for them to reach you through the door."

"Nathaniel and I will do it," said Eden. "Won't we, Nathaniel?"

Nathaniel had been sitting silently on the edge of the room. "We will?"

Eden nodded. "Yes. Tomorrow morning. It's Sunday, so we don't have our apprenticeship."

"We'll go with them," said Nellie. "And Eugene can come, too. It's far too dangerous for these children to go by themselves."

"Dangerous?" said Vulcan. With a twist of a hand, he disconnected his prosthetic leg and held it like a club. "You don't have to tell me it's dangerous. I've got this to remind me, every day. It's all dangerous. She'll be lucky to survive any of this. That's precisely why they should do this small thing themselves. You want the girl to survive these Tasks? Then quit babying her and let her and what's-his-name try this on their own."

Nellie frowned, but said nothing.

"But what about Mr. Pewtersmith?" said Nathaniel.

"What about him?" said Eden, sounding more courageous than she felt. "The old coot can gawk all he wants."

The next morning, a special breakfast was held in Supperdinner Hall. Smith after smith came up to Eden and congratulated her for her role in the first Task. "My dear, I could feel the heat from my workshop," said Kerlin Arrowsmith. "That must have been some kind of fire. That was bold thinking, young lady. What I would have given to see the look on old Pewtersmith's face when you melted all those dishes. In one day!"

The machinist Anit Irenya called her over to his wheelchair. "I see you are beginning to think like a smith," he said. "When will you get your next Task assigned?"

"I already got it," she said. "The birds."

Anit sucked in his breath. "I was there, you know."

"Where?"

"When Vulcan's father—when Burhanu died in the attempt. I was just an apprentice—before I had become a machinist. The birds are the reason I'm in this wheelchair." He patted his thin knee. "Vulcan and I were there as observers. I lost the use of both my legs. And Vulcan lost one, too, so I suppose three legs were lost that day. A bad day for legs and fathers."

"Can you tell me? What Burhanu tried?"

Anit shook his head. "It is forbidden, even for a machinist. But if Vulcan is your helper, then surely he can tell you."

"He can't remember."

"Vulcan can't? He's that bad off?"

"Either he can't remember or he's blocked it out. Either way, I can't get any information out of him. But if you could—"

"I would if I could. But no. And Eden, remember—not all the smiths who live in this Guildhall are on your side. Watch out for saboteurs."

"You mean Pewtersmith?" asked Eden.

"Yes. But others will take his side."

After breakfast, Eden and Nathaniel boarded the elevator. Eden carried the metal toolbox with the drill and peephole inside.

"Where to, lady and gent?" said Buzz.

"Top floor," said Eden.

"Council floor again?" asked Buzz. "I thought you'd already finished working with Helena Bladesmith. You sure you're supposed to go up there?"

"I'm sure," said Eden.

Buzz nodded. "Council floor it is, Ms. Smith. And Mr. Jones." Buzz tightened his bow tie and adjusted his hat. He took the key from his pocket and opened the small gold cover on the wall. He pushed the small gold button under the cover.

When they reached the Council floor, the two children stepped into the hallway. Every twenty feet or so, they passed the door of a Councilmember's living quarters: Robert Blacksmith, Helena Bladesmith, Maureen Goldsmith...

"Look," said Eden. "That last door on the left—that's Pewtersmith's door." She pointed farther down the hallway. "And those are the stairs up to the attic. And there at the top of the stairs, that steel door must be the way in."

Eden carried the toolbox up the stairs and took out the titanium drill. The drill had a battery pack set into the handle. "I just make a hole, right?" said Eden.

"Pretty sure," said Nathaniel.

"Safety first," said Eden. She and Nathaniel each put on a pair of goggles. Eden pushed the drill against the center of the attic door and pulled the trigger. A loud whirring noise sounded and tiny metal shavings dropped from the door as the drill cut into the metal.

Mr. Pewtersmith stepped out of his door and stared at them. "So it's the birds next, is it?"

Eden's stomach sank at the sound of the voice. "You probably already knew that."

Mr. Pewtersmith shrugged.

"Can we help you with something?" said Eden.

"*You* help *me*? I think not." He kept watching.

Eden tried to hide her nerves as she shrugged at Nathaniel, then picked up the drill and returned to work. It took nearly ten minutes, but the drill finally broke through the other side. Light came out, and Eden and Nathaniel could see movement inside, but not much else.

Nathaniel took the peephole from the box and slid it into place. He put his eye to it.

"Oh my," Nathaniel said. "Oh my lord."

"What? What do you see?" said Eden. "Let me look."

Nathaniel moved aside. Eden put her eye to the peephole. The fisheye lens gave a distorted view, but she could still see dozens of the strangest birds flying and hopping around the room.

"They had babies," Eden said. "Lots of babies."

XX

The Alpha Birds

Back in Vulcan's rooms at lunchtime, Eden tried to describe the scene inside the attic.

"It's kind of hard to see through that peephole," she said, "and Pewtersmith kept pushing us off so he could look for himself. But it's terrifying in there. There must be at least thirty birds. Some are big. Some are little. A few of them are beautifully made, with lovely, crafted steel feathers and perfectly shaped beaks."

Nathaniel interrupted. "We think maybe those are the original ones Thợ Tiện made. But the other ones—definitely *not* beautiful."

"It looks like they took the room apart," said Eden, "and everything in it. They tore up the walls and the floor and everything else that was stored up there. Whatever was in that attic, they used it all to make their—I guess you'd call them their babies."

"They made more of themselves," said Vulcan, his voice thick, "just like I've seen in my dreams."

Eden gritted her teeth. "They did. Out of junk. Rusty bits of metal. Old nails. Splinters of wood. Wire. Hinges from old boxes. Old photographs shaped into feathers. All stuck together in the form of birds. Moving, flying, pecking birds.

"Amazing."

Eden nodded. "That's just what Pewtersmith said. He pushed us out of the way and looked through the peephole. He seemed pretty happy about the whole thing. He said, *You and your runt of a grandfather are not going to survive this one.*"

"He said that to you?" said Nellie, gripping her cane like a club. "That horrible man. What a cruel, cruel thing to say to a little girl."

Irma nodded. "He's probably right. They'll probably both die."

"Now sister, that's what you said about the last Task, and look, here we all are, fit as fiddles."

Irma nodded, smiling. "And ready to walk into the attic to get pecked to death."

"Like old Berthold," said Eden "He's still in there. His skeleton is, at least."

"You saw him?" asked Vulcan.

"We saw two skeletons. We figured one was Berthold and one was his—his helper."

"Oh, now this is just too much," said Nellie. "Those birds are clearly killers."

"We watched them all morning," said Nathaniel. "The original birds seemed to be—what would you call them? The leaders?"

"I suppose they would be the alpha birds," said Nellie.

Nathaniel nodded. "Yeah. *The alpha birds.* With their own junk babies. Mr. Smith, don't you remember what your father did when he tried this Task?"

Vulcan didn't answer.

Eugene twisted the ring on his pinkie. "Elemo Blacksmith—we already talked about how he died while attempting this Task. But his son, Burhanu Tinsmith—Vulcan's dad—he took some other route." Eugene glanced at Vulcan. "Vulcan was there. He should know what it was." Eugene paused, waiting for Vulcan to speak, then continued. "Late at night, over a few tankards of beer, I used to hear a few of the old timers say that Burhanu would have succeeded in capturing the steel birds, except—"

"Except what?"

"Except he was sabotaged."

"Sabotaged? How? By who?" said Eden.

"By a Pewtersmith, of course." Vulcan slammed his fist on the table. "He didn't deserve to die. I may be a troublemaker, but Dad was a peacemaker. He wanted everyone to get along and feel welcome. He never understood why the Guildhall needed to be exclusive. That's probably why they convicted him in the first place."

Eden held her breath, hoping Vulcan would continue and tell them more about Burhanu, but he grew quiet.

Eugene pulled out his hankie, considered it, then put it back in his pocket. "I don't think you're gonna get any more out of him, Eden. I wish there was more I knew, but like all the other records of the Impossible Tasks, this record is sealed."

Irma piped up, "Now how come we don't put more effort toward that? Nearly all of the Tasks—well, your ancestors have solved them—or nearly solved them already. So why kill yourselves trying to come up with new ideas, when others have already figured them out?"

Nellie folded and unfolded a napkin in her lap. "Sister, I know you mean well, but the records are sealed. No one can access the sealed section of Records except the Council chair. We would have to get past that terrifying beast of a dog. And that dog has eaten three smiths already."

"Four," said Irma, draining her teacup. "You've forgotten dear Gladys."

"Oh! You're right, sister. Gladys *was* a bit of a loud talker, and Bones didn't like that. But all of the other three were eaten for—well—for trying to access parts of the Records that were sealed. That's what *sealed* means. It means that Bones will eat you."

Nathaniel gulped but said nothing.

Eden held her head high the next morning as she and Nathaniel walked into Fred Tinsmith's workshop. She had completed the first Task. She was the talk of the Guildhall.

Fred looked up from an old frying pan he was mending. "About time you got here. Plenty to do today. You can start by cleaning the soot out of my furnace."

"Cleaning out soot?" said Eden. "Didn't you hear about what happened? About how we completed the Impossible Task?"

Fred spit in the frying pan then gave it a rub with a rag. "Uh-huh. You're still apprentices, ain't you? Then shut your yappers and get busy. You ain't afraid of hard work, are you?"

She took a deep breath. "I've been working hard my whole life. No, I am not afraid of hard work. And neither is Nathaniel."

"Nathaniel, eh? That's Jonesy's full name? Nat is short for Nathaniel?" Fred walked over to Nathaniel and took the boy's chin in his hand. He turned Nathaniel's head left and right as he inspected him. "A gnat is a bug. You don't look like a bug. You look like an apprentice. And someday, hopefully, you will be a full-fledged smith. So no more Nat. You are Nathaniel. Only Nathaniel."

Nathaniel straightened his shoulders. "Nathaniel. Yeah. That's me. Only Nathaniel."

The rest of the week was one of the most confusing times Eden could remember. In the evenings, the smiths in Supperdinner Hall pinged their daily dishes, then cheered Eden as a hero. And all morning long, Fred Tinsmith had her and Nathaniel cleaning soot, scrubbing grease off old tools with a tiny brush, and sweeping up metal shavings, without a word of praise or encouragement.

But in between chores, they slowly began to dabble in tinsmithing. They learned how to solder new tin into a hole to repair pots and pans. They made Revere lanterns out of tin sheeting and formed holes in the side with a hammer and punch, creating outlines of stars and circles that let the light through.

When Eden and Nathaniel arrived at the tinsmithing shop the following Saturday, Fred took off his hat, scratched his head, and looked around. "I guess it's not too filthy in here. Eden, if you can find it in you to keep from whining the whole time, I suppose I could show you two how to tinplate steel cans."

"Tin cans?" said Eden, her ears tingling. "Fred, are you the one who—"

Fred held up a finger and glared at Eden. "Let me stop you right there."

Eden stopped. That glare and that finger looked final.

After tinplating three cans each, Fred left Eden and Nathaniel on their own. Eden said, "I'm glad all the grimy work is over, and I'm glad to know how to plate, but I'm pretty sure tinsmithing is not for me."

"I love it," Nathaniel said, looking at his reflection in a shiny can. "Tin is brilliant. It doesn't rust. It shines as bright as silver. You can eat from it. And it's used in all sorts of alloys."

"Like pewter," spat Eden, "for Pewtersmith."

"Not just pewter. Also bronze. And—and it's mixed with—oh, what's the name of that one weird one? Fred was telling me the other day when I helped him haul out that bin of scraps. Nio…nio…niobium!"

"What the heck is niobium?"

"Niobium-tin. It's an alloy, like I said. It's amazing. It's used to make superconducting magnets."

"Okay, tell me more."

Nathaniel held a steel can in his hands. "You know what an electromagnet is? Fred says some electromagnets are so strong you can pick up whole cars with them. Fred says with niobium-tin, you could make a superconducting magnet ten times that strong. And Fred says it wouldn't be any bigger than this can."

"Fred sure says a lot. You sound awfully impressed by him."

"Who wouldn't be? He's amazing."

After their day in the tinsmith's shop, Eden suggested they go to Records and see what they could find about Burhanu's sabotaged attempt at capturing the steel birds.

"I don't wanna go," said Nathaniel. "We won't be allowed to read anything good. And that dog, Bones. He'll probably eat me."

"We're going anyway," said Eden. She grabbed Nathaniel by the collar and began dragging him along the hallway.

"Fine. I'll come. But it's my choice."

They rode in the elevator with Buzz to Subbasement Two. As they walked along the hallway toward Records, they passed the oiled metal doors again. Eden tried not to look because the battle images carved on them made her mouth go dry.

Sylvia met them at the green door. Today she wore a bright blue scarf with a matching blue fez. Bones stood next to her, the muscles of his huge black neck straining against his shining metal collar. He growled low.

"Back for more criminal history?" Sylvia asked.

"*Family history*," said Eden, "about my great-grandfather Burhanu Tinsmith and the steel birds."

"There is not much to see that is not sealed," said Sylvia, "but follow me and I will get you the public record."

"Sylvia," said Eden. "Before we go inside, can you tell us what's behind those doors back there?"

Sylvia raised one eyebrow. "Those oily doors? Those are the rooms of the gunsmiths, the only smiths who choose to live in the subbasements. I am sure you have heard of them. They play a part in your Tasks."

"I've heard of them," said Eden. "Mrs. Gunsmith's girdle."

Sylvia nodded. "I wish they did not live right next door. They are quite loud. Always, how shall we say, banging and booming. I suppose that is not surprising, considering their line of work. They keep to themselves. But they give me, how shall we say, *the creeps*."

"Me, too," said Eden.

"But those gunsmith men," said Sylvia, "well, I do personally find them to be handsome creatures, with their broad shoulders and their...their..." Her voice trailed off.

"Sylvia?" said Eden, arching her eyebrows.

"What were we talking about? Oh yes. Records of the Five Tasks. Follow me."

Eden followed Sylvia through the sea of gray-green file cabinets. Nathaniel walked behind her, trying to keep Bones' sniffing nose away from him, but Bones kept pushing his huge snout right against Nathaniel's side. "Down, Bones," hissed Nathaniel. "Niiice doggy. Please don't eat me."

"He might," said Sylvia. "I have never seen him act like this with anyone before. Ahh, here we are." Sylvia found the file for Burhanu Tinsmith and, just as she had with Mordan, she pulled out a single sheet of paper. She handed it to Eden and returned to her desk, but Bones stayed behind, staring at Nathaniel with drool dripping from his open mouth.

Eden sat at a table and peered at the document. "Listen. Here are the charges against Burhanu. Says here he made an illegal protest against the Council. With the help of his apprentice, he built a tin automaton that greeted visitors when they entered Humble Gallery."

"A what?"

"An automaton. Kind of like a wind-up robot."

"Awesome," said Nathaniel. "I want to make a robot. Out of tin."

"And the robot greeted visitors? Nathaniel, does the Guildhall have visitors?"

"Yes. Just not that often," said Nathaniel. "I know some of the smiths have family outside—grandkids and nieces and nephews and stuff. Sometimes we cook special luncheons for them. I've seen a few. Robert Blacksmith has a granddaughter. I think Maureen Goldsmith has a grandnephew or something. And I've even heard that Pewtersmith has a grandson."

"Pewtersmith? Probably a horrible kid."

Nathaniel laughed. "Probably. I know the smiths get a few customers that come and see them every now and then. But I think they mostly do their business through the mail. They keep to themselves."

"Why?"

Nathaniel frowned. "I guess that's how the smiths want it. I've heard my mom say it didn't used to be that way. But you know how people are. They get set in their ways."

"Kind of like the birds," said Eden, "staying in their attic cage. Anyway, it says here that the Council didn't like Burhanu's automaton, because it began inviting strangers inside the Guildhall, instead of keeping them out. They made Burhanu put the automaton in storage."

Nathaniel's eyes grew wide. "In storage? Where? We should go find it! Maybe it could help us!"

Eden smirked. "Yeah, then you and I can get imprisoned, too. Anyway, one night, in protest, Burhanu changed the locks on all the councilmember's rooms, locking them inside. At his trial, he said that maybe they were the ones who should be kept out of the Guildhall, not the strangers. His sentence was the same as Grandpa's. Looks like it was three years before he decided to try the Five Impossible Tasks. Oh—here's the part about the steel birds. Just a couple of sentences."

To the surprise of the entire Council, Burhanu Tinsmith did not begin his attempt until two p.m. He garnered immediate progress, but then he was plunged into darkness, powerless to proceed. By sunset, the steel birds were still loose and Burhanu's attempt was deemed a failure. In addition—" Eden stopped reading.

"In addition what?" said Nathaniel. "What's it say?"

Eden gulped. *"In addition, two young apprentice smiths were injured and three bystanders were killed by the birds."*

"Killed?" said Nathaniel. "As in dead?"

Eden nodded. She thought about the injuries of Anit Irenya and of her grandfather. Without speaking, she copied down every word on another piece of paper to take back to Vulcan and the others. While she was writing, Bones snuffed and snorted at Nathaniel, his huge nostrils opening wide as he stepped closer to the boy.

"Niiice doggy," said Nathaniel. "Be a good boy and don't eat me." The dog's giant head disappeared under the table as he smelled Nathaniel's feet and legs.

"What's he doing under there?" said Eden.

"Niiice doggy," stuttered Nathaniel. "There you go. That's all I have."

"What's all you have?"

"Just a treat."

"You brought him a treat?"

"Just some mahguj."

"You brought what?"

"Mahguj. Some people call it Guild jelly. From Kitchens. We always have a lot of it. I figured it couldn't hurt. Bones seems to love it, too."

"I know what mahguj is, Nathaniel. No wonder he can't stop

sniffing you. You're just going to make him hungrier. Then he's going to eat *you*."

"Don't say that," said Nathaniel. "Bones is a good boy, aren't you Bones?"

Bones' black head reappeared. Nathaniel reached out to pet the dog, but Bones growled at him. "Okay. Not friends yet," said Nathaniel, "but we'll get there. Are you through, Eden?"

"I guess so. There's so little here." She turned the paper over. On the back, a piece of yellowed tape held an old black-and-white photograph. Eden studied it. "It's a couple of men at the bottom of some stairs, next to a big crate. Hey! That's the hallway outside the attic door! Look. There are the stairs leading up to the attic. There's the room Mr. Pewtersmith has now. I wonder who lived in it before him. I wonder if that man holding the metal box is Burhanu."

"He kind of looks like you," said Nathaniel. "Like Vulcan."

Eden stared closely at the man—at the darker tone of his skin and his slightly crooked nose. She touched the face with her finger, then pulled the photo from the page and slid it inside her sleeve.

"Put that back!" hissed Nathaniel. "Are you trying to get us eaten?"

"Distract your new best friend," said Eden. "I'm gonna take this picture to Grandpa. Maybe it will spark his memory."

Nathaniel gulped, then let Bones lick his fingers while Eden made a show of returning the file. She hoped the photo stayed in place in her sleeve while they left Records. When they were on the elevator, she let out her breath.

They took the photo, along with their scant notes, back to Vulcan, Eugene, and the sisters.

Vulcan was lying on his bed, staring at the ceiling. Nellie was sitting on the edge of the bed, patting Vulcan on the arm. "He seems to be feeling particularly blue today, the poor dear. It makes me worry so. We've got to get him out of this room before it's too late."

"*Auntie*," said Eden.

"I'm right here, you know," muttered Vulcan.

Eden tried to show her grandfather her notes, but he wouldn't look at them. Eugene took them from her. He moved his lips while he read them silently, then reread them again and again.

"'Started at 2 p.m.,'" Eugene said. "'Immediate progress. Plunged into darkness. Powerless to proceed.' Not much to go on. 'Plunged into darkness.' That sounds like sabotage to me. But, of course, not a mention of who sabotaged Burhanu. I'm sure it was a Pewtersmith."

"We also brought a photo," said Eden.

"You did what?" said Eugene. "Where did you get it?"

"From the file. From Records."

"And you still have all your fingers?" There was a note of respect in his voice. "Let me see it." He stared at the photo, then held it up. "Hey Vulcan, do you recognize that old weasel?"

Vulcan kept staring at the ceiling.

Eugene said, "That's Zephaniah Pewtersmith—the grandfather of Uriah Pewtersmith. And that's Vulcan's father. Burhanu Tinsmith himself."

Vulcan turned on his side. "Show me."

They handed him the picture. He stared at it, then slowly handed it back.

"We were wondering if that was him," Eden said.

"It is," said Eugene. "But what's he got in his hands?"

"You don't know?"

"No idea. Not very big, whatever it is. Hard to tell from an old photo, but the box looks like it's made of brass."

"Does that matter?"

"Sure, it matters. All metals serve different purposes. Brass doesn't rust, for one thing. No iron in it."

Eden read her notes again. "'Started at two p.m.' Grandpa, why did they start at two p.m.?"

Vulcan didn't answer.

"I hope *we* won't start at two p.m," said Nellie, "because two p.m. is nap time. That's when the morning work ends, so us old master smiths can take our naps."

"And apprentices," said Eden.

"It's quiet then," said Nathaniel. "Maybe Burhanu needed it to be quiet."

"It's dark, too," said Eden.

"What are you talking about? It's not dark," snapped Vulcan. "Two o'clock is the middle of the afternoon."

"You don't have to be such a grouch." Eden turned toward Vulcan. "I mean, the lights go off at two o'clock—at least in the rooms. So maybe not dark, but fewer lights are on. You were there. Can't you just tell us?"

Vulcan growled at her. "Don't you think I would if I could? I don't remember. I do not remember. Now get out of my room!"

XXI

In Which Eden Visits the Rooms of Anit Irenya

On Monday morning, when the two children entered Fred's shop, Eden took a deep breath and said, "What do you want us to clean today?"

Fred scratched his left elbow. "Shop hasn't been this clean in years. Not sure I can still find anything. So today, we're making alloys. Pewter for the dishes. And a little solder for fixing stuff. Your friend Eugene Tinker needs some."

"What about that other alloy?" said Eden. "It has a weird name. Nathaniel was talking about it."

Nathaniel said, "Niobium-tin. Fred, you told me about it the other day."

"Not much call for it," said Fred. "And niobium is expensive. Can't use it without an order."

"Why would someone order it?"

"Hardly ever happens around here," said Fred. "Not a lot of old smiths making superconducting magnets."

Eden frowned. "And why would they? Why would a smith make a superconducting magnet?"

"They wouldn't," said Fred, scratching his right elbow. "You don't want to use one around here, where so much ferrous metal is at play—iron and steel. That is, unless you really needed a magnet with massive power.

"*That's what it was!*" said Eden, punching Nathaniel in the arm.

"Ow!" said Nathaniel. "What are you talking about?"

Eden said, "*In the photograph.* Fred, are these magnets small?"

"They can be," said Fred. "They're electromagnets. A coil of wires, not a chunk of metal. The niobium-tin is what the wires are made of. Why are you getting all worked up?"

"Because—oh my gosh. Would you—would you keep one in a brass box?"

"Seems logical. Brass is non-magnetic."

"And—oh my gosh—they need a lot of power?"

"Yes. I said they're electromagnets. So the more power you give them, the stronger they get."

Nathaniel slapped his forehead. "Eden, you and I are thinking the same thing! Fred, if you were to suddenly cut the power—what would happen? Would the magnet still operate?"

"You're a hard worker," said Fred, scratching his ribs, "so I'll try to pretend that wasn't the dumbest question I've ever heard. If you cut the electricity to an electromagnet, then the magnet turns off. Now, no more questions. It's your last day with me, and we've got pewter to make."

The children weren't much help to Fred that final day. They were itching to get back to Vulcan and the sisters with Eden's theory. At five minutes before two p.m., Fred began to yawn. He scratched his belly. "That's enough. You're done."

Nathaniel pouted, "You mean our apprenticeship with you is over."

"You done good enough. Did you want a medal or something? Hit the lights on your way out."

Eden dragged Nathaniel past the elevator and down the stairs to Subbasement Seven, Room K-Minus-One. They found Vulcan inside, just getting ready for his nap. They told him their theory: The brass box next to Burhanu Tinsmith in the photograph contained an electromagnet. The mechanical birds were made of a steel alloy. When Burhanu had turned on the power, the steel birds had been pulled to the magnet so they could be captured. It was such a simple, foolproof plan. So why hadn't it worked?

"Why hadn't what worked?"

"Everything we just told you."

Vulcan blinked at them. "Say it once more."

Eden told him again, but couldn't tell if he was listening. At the end, she repeated her question. Why hadn't Burhanu's plan worked?

"Probably because of a Pewtersmith," said Vulcan. "Everything bad is because of a Pewtersmith."

"A Pewtersmith?" said Eden. "Oh! I bet you're right! I bet a Pewtersmith cut the power somehow. I bet that's what they meant when the record said he'd been *plunged into darkness*," said Eden. "He was powerless to proceed, because someone had cut the power. That was the sabotage."

"Sabotage!" shouted Vulcan. "Pewtersmith!"

"Grandpa, please," said Eden. *His mind is getting worse in this prison,* she thought. *Maybe this is all for nothing. Maybe it's too late.*

"But why'd Burhanu wait until two o'clock to begin the Task?" said Nathaniel.

Eden tapped her fingers on her temple until the answer suddenly hit her. "Because everyone naps then!"

"Huh?"

"All the lights would have been out. That means more power was available for his magnet. At least until they were sabotaged." Eden looked at Vulcan. "Grandpa, could *you* make an electromagnet like that?"

"An electromagnet? Me? Make one?" Vulcan opened one eye. "You don't think I could, do you? I was a master machinist. I was the best that ever was. I was legendary! I was—I—I'm—I'm going to take a nap now." Vulcan rolled toward the wall. "Get Anit Irenya to do it. He's still a free man. And close the door on your way out."

"He drives me nuts," said Eden, as they walked along the hallway of Subbasement Seven. "Come on." She grabbed Nathaniel by the arm and led him up to the first floor, where they found Eugene at his post by the front door.

Eden repeated her theory to Eugene. "But the problem is, we would need an electromagnet to make it work."

Eugene nodded. "And if you had one, you'd still have to prevent some knucklehead from cutting the power. The whole Guildhall is on the same electrical system. If they cut power to the building, then the magnet goes off."

"What about batteries? Or a generator?" said Eden.

"Not near enough electricity," said Eugene.

"Kitchens!" said Nathaniel. "We're on a different system."

"What are you talking about?" said Eugene.

Nathaniel smiled. "Remember when the power went out last year? When Mrs. Fendersmith tried making an electric fireplace—"

"Oh yeah," said Eugene. "She blew the whole breaker board."

"Right. And the entire Guildhall was dark until the next day. But not Kitchens. Mom told me it's on its own electrical system, wired directly into the grid from outside. While you all were in the dark, we had power the whole time."

Eugene nodded. "I do remember that." He paced back and forth, in front of the front door, muttering to himself. "Kitchens is in Subbasement Seven. The birds are all the way up in the attic. That's a lot of distance. And we still need that electromagnet."

"Grandpa said we should ask Anit Irenya for help," said Eden.

"You know where to find him? He had the rooms right next to Vulcan. They were next-door neighbors."

"We'll have to wait until after nap time, won't we?"

"Not for Anit," said Eugene. "He doesn't take naps."

"Great," said Eden. "Let's go."

The door to Anit's room was plain steel, with an unadorned knocker. Eden took a deep breath, then lifted the knocker. She froze. "It's vibrating. The door is vibrating."

Eden let the knocker fall. The door swung open, but no one was there. Instead, they were greeted by a loud hum and the scent of machine oil.

Anit's room was full of machines of all types—lathes, drill presses, table saws, machines that stamped out metal parts, and machines that moved parts along conveyor belts. Machines that sliced, spun, opened, closed, raised, and lowered. Every machine was in full swing, with no workers in sight. Gears and pulleys turned all throughout the room, and shining pistons pumped up and down. Metal tracks ran through the air above the machines, like the tracks of a miniature roller coaster. In the center of the room, a shiny red steam engine puffed away, making a *chug-chug-chug* sound and burping puffy clouds of steam up into a chrome exhaust vent. Eden felt as if she were standing inside the workings of a complicated clock.

"Hello?" said Eden. No one answered. "Hello!"

Nathaniel pointed toward the back of the room. "Look! Here he comes."

Anit Irenya's wheelchair rolled along metal tracks suspended about three feet above their heads. He rode the tracks around the machines, slowing his wheelchair and checking dials and making tiny adjustments along the way. When he was directly over them, Anit reached out and hit a lever. A section of the track dropped down like a ramp. Anit's chair barreled down the ramp right toward them. Eden was about to jump out of the way and drag Nathaniel with her, but at the last second, the chair jerked to a stop. Anit nodded politely.

A large brass box rolled toward them along a conveyor belt. It stopped right next to Anit.

Anit reached out and pushed a black button on a panel that hung next to the tracks. The central steam engine quieted. All the gears, pulleys, and pistons throughout the room began to slow, until the room was humming as quietly as a purring kitten.

"Hello, Eden. Hello, Nat Jones. You like my little machine shop?" Anit smiled broadly.

"I love it," said Eden. "If this is the kind of stuff that machinists get to do, then I want to be a machinist."

"It has been years of work. But it has been years of joy as well. Now then, it is time for afternoon tea."

Anit pushed a green button on the panel near him. The steam

engine chugged back to half speed, while Anit pushed and pulled a series of levers. A whistle blew on top of the steam engine. To her right, Eden saw a machine pour boiling water into a waiting teapot, while another machine sawed a loaf of bread into slices. To her left, another machine peeled, sliced, and salted a cucumber while another spread cream cheese on the sliced bread.

A few seconds later, a steel tray rolled down the conveyor belt and bumped gently into the back of the large brass box. The tray held a teapot, two cups, and a plate of cucumber sandwiches, stacked into a neat pyramid, with a single toothpick flag waving from the top.

Anit pulled more levers and the room grew quiet again. "Help yourselves."

Eden took a sandwich and bit into it. It tasted like machine oil.

"Delicious, isn't it?" said Anit, as he picked one up and took a bite. "I'm assuming you're here for an electromagnet—"

"How did you know that?" Eden took a sip of tea to wash the bitter taste of the sandwich out of her mouth, but the tea was just as oily.

Anit winked, then patted his hand on the large brass box. "I assumed Vulcan would eventually remember."

"He didn't," said Eden. "We had to figure it out on our own."

"And you did? Very impressive. Either way, I just happen to have one niobium-tin electromagnet handy. But it requires an uninterrupted power supply. You do know what happened with this Task the last time, don't you?"

Eden nodded.

"Good. While my machines and I were working on your magnet, I had some time to think about the issue of your power. Your plan is highly susceptible to interference from outside forces. I had an idea that might help. But you're going to need a very long, very heavy extension cord, because the separate power system of Kitchens is far away from the attic."

"You know about that, too?" said Nathaniel.

"I installed both systems. Now then, you will need a lot of help to move the large extension cord precisely when the time is right—not too early, mind you. When you introduce a backup plan too early, it becomes just as susceptible to sabotage. The issue, then, is where to find the necessary help."

"From who then?" asked Eden.

"I was thinking your friend here, little Nat Jones, might be able to provide the solution." Anit turned to Nathaniel. "Little Nat, you know all the other Joneses? You know the Blue Coats?"

"Yes, and all the gardeners and bookkeepers and the maintenance people, too. They're all Joneses, just like me."

"Don't forget Buzz," said Eden. "He's a Jones, too."

Anit nodded. "Do you think you could get them to help? The Blue Coats, I mean?"

"With an Impossible Task? Would they get hurt?"

"They might."

"Would they get in trouble?"

"That might happen, too."

"They work for the Council," said Nathaniel. "We all do. They'd all be putting their jobs at risk. And they take their jobs seriously."

"Of course, they do," said Anit. "I did not mean to suggest anything less. I have always found them to be highly qualified."

Eden jumped to her feet. "What if we could offer them something they've never had? Something that might be enough to risk getting in trouble."

Anit said, "I'm having a hard time imagining what you could offer them."

"It wouldn't be me offering," said Eden. "The offer would have to come from the master smiths. Nellie, Irma, and other smiths who are friends with my grandpa."

"I am not following you, Eden."

"The master smiths could offer to teach them," said Eden. "They could teach the Joneses how to smith."

XXII

Nathaniel

It took three evenings of arguing to convince Nellie and Irma to offer to teach smithing to the Joneses. Nellie kept saying, "It is simply not done." Eden kept saying, "So what?" Nellie said, "It goes against our tradition and our solemn oath."

"Ugh, what is with this oath you all keep talking about?" Eden said. "Aunty Nellie, this is not complicated. I've heard you say you wished you could find trustworthy young people. And I've heard you say that Blue Coats are trustworthy. So there!" By the end of the third night, Eden had twisted six teaspoons into knots with her nervous fingers.

"Stop!" Nellie said. "I'll agree, if only to save the silverware."

Three more days went by as Nellie and Irma reached out to Helena Swordsmith, Fred Tinsmith, Robert Blacksmith and others, slowly convincing them to throw tradition aside in order to help Vulcan.

"I'll do it," Robert finally said. "Partly to help Vulc, but partly because I want my own apprentices. You were right, Nellie. I do want to pass on my skills." He had pounded the floor with his hammer. "If I must pass them on to a Jones or two, then so be it."

"*If* they're willing," Eden reminded him. "All you can do is offer. The Joneses might say no."

On the morning of the fourth day, Eden and Nathaniel stood in the hallway outside the doors of Kitchens.

"I still think you should tell her," said Eden. "There's still time."

"No way!" said Nathaniel. "Have you met my mother? You think she would ever go for this? It's better to beg for your life than ask permission."

"That's not how that saying goes."

"It is with my mom. Look. Here comes the first group for the Gathering of Joneses."

A half dozen young men and women wearing brown overalls came along the hallway. One of the women still carried a shovel in her hand. Eden wondered if these were the same gardeners who had crafted that amazing underground landscape that Buzz had accidentally let her see. "What's this all about, Nathaniel?" said the woman with the shovel.

Nathaniel gulped. "Thanks for coming, Sara. And everyone. You're—you're the first to get here."

"Then you have time to tell us what this Gathering is about."

"Ummm—" Nathaniel was saved from speaking by the appearance of a group of plumbers, carpenters, and electricians. Nathaniel stuttered as he greeted them, then turned to say hi to four people—two men and two women in office clothes and glasses, carrying notebooks. The bookkeepers. A doctor and a small group of nurses came next.

"Nathaniel, where do all these Joneses live?" Eden asked.

"In the lower levels."

"Why can't you take me down there? I really, really, really want to see it again. Are all the levels as amazing as the one I saw?"

"I told you. I can't show you, because only Joneses are allowed down there."

"That's a stupid rule, and more to the point, I *am* a Jones, remember?" hissed Eden.

"Yeah, I'm not sure that argument's going to get you very far at this exact moment, Eden, so don't try to go changing this rule, too, right now. You'll get me in even more trouble."

The hallway was jammed with murmuring, confused Joneses. Then the murmurs quieted. The crowd turned to watch the Blue Coats come down the hall—twenty-two of them, all in their blue jackets and none of them smiling. It was so congested now in the hallway that Eden could barely move.

The Blue Coats were led by a woman with a wide face, brown skin, and black hair pulled back into a bun. She carried a white wooden staff. She pushed her way through the crowd up to Nathaniel. "We are all here for the Gathering, but I see no smiths, other than this girl."

"They'll be here. I promise."

"They had better come soon." The woman looked at her watch. "We have all left our posts for this meeting and will need to return in fifteen—now fourteen—minutes."

The doors of Kitchens burst open. Lillian Jones stood there, glaring out at the crowd, holding her wooden spoon like a cudgel. The rest of the kitchen staff hid behind Lillian, peering around her to see what was happening. Lillian said, "What's all this racket out here then? A Gathering? Why wasn't I told about this?"

The Blue Coat leader parted the crowd with her white staff. "That is an excellent question, Lillian Jones, as it was your boy who called for it."

"Nathaniel?" Lillian's grip tightened on the wooden spoon. "He called for this?" She spotted her son and leveled her eyes at him. "What is this about?"

"I—umm—yes. Yes, I called for it. As is my right as a Jones and a keeper of the oath."

"It may be your right as a Jones, but as my child, you had better tell me what the devil is going on."

Nathaniel gulped and hissed to Eden. "Where are they?"

"They'll be here," said Eden, scanning down the hallway. "I hope."

Lillian said, "Go ahead, Nathaniel. We're all gathered. And I, for one, can't wait to hear the reason for this."

"I—well—so, the reason I called you all here is, umm, because—"

One of the gardeners shouted, "We can't hear you. If you're not going to speak up, we have turnips to plant."

"Sorry!" shouted Nathaniel. "The reason I, umm, called you all here—"

"The reason Nathaniel called you all here," said a loud, gruff voice at the back of the crowd, "is to see if you lot would like to learn how to smith."

With a gasp, the crowd turned. Fred Tinsmith stood there in his old baseball cap and overalls, scratching his ear. Behind him stood Nellie and Irma, Eugene Tinker, Helena Bladesmith, Robert Blacksmith, and a handful of other master smiths. Fred nodded at Nathaniel. "The boy, Nathaniel, he put all this together. See if you might be interested in a bit of a trade. Boy's not an idiot. So let him speak."

Nathaniel cleared his voice. "F-Fred is a tinsmith. He's already teaching me how to smith." A murmur passed through the crowd. Only Buzz smiled.

"It cannot be true," said the Blue Coat woman holding the white staff. "Only Smiths smith."

"It's true." Nathaniel pulled a crooked cheese knife out of a pocket. "I made this knife. It's for cheese. Helena Bladesmith taught me how."

Helena blushed. "It is not a great example of my teaching skills," she said. "Perhaps some of you would be better students."

The crowd began talking and murmuring again. The Blue Coat woman struck the ground with her staff. "We can choose? You are saying we can choose?"

"That's right, Iona," said Fred Tinsmith. "You all can choose. Course, you might not like the work as much as you think. Dirty and hard, sometimes."

"That is the nature of all work. But . . . we can choose?" said Iona.

"Yes," said Nathaniel. "Fred's willing to teach you, too. All of them are. I mean, not *all* the smiths, but these ones, here are. They're looking for apprentices. And they'll take Joneses."

"Then who will do *our* work?" said a plumber.

"Umm, I guess *you* will. This would be on the side."

"So now we have two jobs?" said the plumber. "Ohhh, that sounds lovely. Twice as much work. Do we get twice as much pay?"

"Let my boy say his piece!" Lillian clapped her wooden spoon against her palm. "You don't have to like the idea. Lord knows *I* don't. I'm a cook now and will always be a cook, and have zero interest in being anything else. But this is an official Gathering. And that means you yield the floor to the speaker."

The crowd settled. Nathaniel took a deep breath. "These master smiths here are willing to teach their trade to any Jones who wants to learn. Any Jones who's interested will have to still do their regular duties while they are apprentices, until more help is found and hired. But if they complete their apprenticeships, they become master smiths, with all the skills—and all the rights—of master smiths."

Nathaniel explained that the Guild was getting old and that some of them—at least the ones present—realized they needed young apprentices to carry on their crafts.

Iona tapped her staff on the ground. "We Joneses have been by your side but excluded from smithing for countless generations. Do you assume this change makes up for that?"

"Probably not, dear," said Irma, taking a sip from her cup.

"But—but we'll do our best," said Nellie. "Wouldn't you like to make beautiful things out of metal?"

"I already make beautiful things," said the gardener with the shovel. "From the earth."

"That is true," said Iona. "There is beauty in all work we Joneses do. For my part, I lead these beautiful Joneses in a centuries-old commitment to service. You may not value what we do, but I do."

"I ain't working with *that* one," muttered Fred.

"What is she talking about?" Eden whispered to Nathaniel. "What centuries-old commitment to service?"

"Not now, Eden," Nathaniel whispered back.

"No one is forcing you to accept our offer," said Nellie, waving her cane, "but we are making it available to those of you who may be interested. As the little Nat said, we are giving you the choice."

"My *name* is *Nathaniel*."

"Pardon me?" said Nellie.

Nathaniel stepped toward her. "Ms. Silversmith, my name, it's Nathaniel. Not Nat. I don't want to be called Nat anymore. A gnat is a bug. I'm not a bug. I'm an apprentice of the Guildhall and my name is Nathaniel. Nathaniel Jones."

Nellie eyed Nathaniel, as if she were sizing up an opponent. "Nathaniel Jones, eh?"

"That's right," said Nathaniel.

Fred Tinsmith nodded his approval.

"It is a solid name," said Nellie, stamping her cane on the floor. "Now then, as *Nathaniel* said, we are giving you all a choice."

"Well *I'll* do it!" shouted Buzz, his pillbox hat in his hands. "Because I *want* to do it! I want to learn how to smith. I've spent most of my life bringing smiths and their crafts from floor to floor, wondering how they do what they do. I've always longed to try it. See if I can do it, too. And, well, I want to make a sword." He looked at Helena Bladesmith. "That is, if you'd be willing to teach me, Miss Helena."

Helena started as if she'd just woken up. "What? Me? Well, Buzz. I—I suppose I would. I mean, yes. I would. I will. I will teach you how to make a sword."

Other Joneses began to shout their interest, and the smiths nodded their willingness to teach. Iona shouted for order. "It appears that many of us are interested in your offer. And the rest of us—all of us—appreciate the freedom of choice. But in my experience, there is always a catch."

"Oh!" said Nathaniel. "You're right. There's a catch. There is definitely a catch."

❦ XXIII ❦

Mechanical Creatures That Wind Themselves

"That's the cage?" said Eden. The afternoon following the meeting with the Joneses, she and Nathaniel helped Buzz and Eugene roll a large cube-shaped cage out of the elevator. It was made of copper pipes. "It doesn't seem very strong. Wouldn't steel be better than copper?"

"I made it. It's strong enough," said Eugene. "And we can't use steel. Steel is attracted to magnets. Copper ain't." Eugene smiled. "Besides, it only has to hold them until sunset. That's what the rules say, right?"

"Right." From her pocket, Eden pulled the strip of tin stamped with the official description of the second Task. She scanned it in silence. "Just hold the birds until sunset."

As Buzz pushed the cage along the hallway, he said, "See how I'm helping, Eden? I'm doing my part, so that I can become a bladesmith apprentice."

Eden tried not to laugh. "I see it, Buzz. And you have the Blue Coats positioned, like I asked?"

"Sure do, Eden. Just make sure you note that I helped."

Buzz carried Anit Irenya's large brass box to the bottom of the

193

stairs. "Put it right behind the cage," said Eugene. "Yup. Just like that. Thanks, Buzz. That's all for now."

The sisters came out of one of the nearby doors, along with Robert Blacksmith. "Thank you for a lovely lunch, Robert," said Nellie. "Oh, it looks like the setup has already begun. Such an exciting day. Task number two! Eden, are you finding everything you need?"

"Not much to this," said Eden. "Just plug in the magnet and open the attic door." She unfastened the brass box that Anit had given her. Inside was a silver cylinder about the size of a five-gallon bucket. It lay on its side and had a series of pipes going in and out of one end. An eerie steam rolled off it and settled onto the floor.

"Is that the electromagnet?" said Nellie.

"That thing is called a cryostat. It's full of liquid nitrogen and liquid helium to keep whatever is inside of it supercooled. The electromagnet is inside, made of niobium-tin wires. Anit said that if it isn't supercooled, then the niobium-tin won't work as a superconductor. The magnet's got a kick to it, believe me."

Nellie said, "Nathaniel, where are the Blue Coats with the extension cord from Kitchens?"

"Shhh," said Eden. She looked around the hallway to make sure no one had heard. "They're standing by, but we're not bringing them out until the last possible minute. That way, Pewtersmith won't know we have a backup power source and won't be able to find a way to sabotage it. Nathaniel, just plug it right into that wall socket there."

"This whole plan seems unnecessarily dangerous," said Nellie. "Shouldn't we be wearing protective armor of some sort?"

"Elemo wore armor and it didn't help him," said Eden. "Don't worry, Aunty. This plan is going to work perfectly."

"I certainly hope so. Does your grandfather know about all this?"

"I told him, but it's hard to tell when he understands." Eden folded her arms. "And besides, I'm the one doing the Tasks, so I get to decide how much risk we take. Eugene, how are we doing on time?"

Eugene looked at his watch. "Fifteen minutes until nap time."

"Okay. We should get the rest of the Council, then. Eugene, would you mind fetching them and Vulcan, while I stay with the equipment?"

While they waited for Eugene to return, Nathaniel and Eden double-checked the magnet. On the outside of the silver cylinder—the cryostat—was a large green dial. It was turned to the off position. Next to that was a round gauge about six inches across. It measured electricity in volts. There was a red mark right at the twelve-o'clock position on the gauge. The gauge was connected to a black box, which was connected to a thick, black electrical cord. At Eden's signal, Nathaniel plugged the end of the cord into the wall socket.

In a few minutes, Eugene returned with Vulcan and most of the Council. Vulcan's eyes darted around the hallway. He looked as if he hadn't slept in days.

"It's come at last," he hissed. "My day of reckoning."

"Grandpa!" said Eden, "It's going to be okay. I promise."

"You're going to have to ignore him, Eden," said Eugene, "because you need to stay focused. And I need you to keep your eyes on Pewtersmith."

"I'll watch him," said Eden. "And if I see him causing trouble and shout his name, remember what *you're* supposed to do?"

"Tackle him," said Eugene. "Let's go get the weasel now."

Eugene knocked on the door nearest to the bottom of the attic stairs. No one answered. He knocked again.

The door opened to darkness inside. Mr. Pewtersmith was in his pajamas and hairnet. He had a sleep mask pulled up on his forehead. "Why are you interrupting my nap, you bumbling fool?"

Eugene shrugged toward the small crowd behind him.

"What is this then?" said Mr. Pewtersmith. When he noticed Vulcan, he said, "Ahhh, you're here for the birds, are you? Very well. Give me a few minutes to make myself presentable, so I can watch your failure while properly attired."

It took more than twenty minutes for Mr. Pewtersmith to return. While they waited, Maureen Goldsmith walked over to Eden, hunched under the weight of her gold jewelry. "You've made it to the second Task, dear. If you manage this one today, you'll only have three to go."

Eden nodded.

"Not many of us councilmembers thought you'd make it past number one. Almost none think you'll make it past number two. But I do, Eden. I believe in you."

Eden smiled. "You think I can complete all five?"

"All five?" Maureen stood almost straight up. "Let's not get ahead of ourselves. But I believe in you for number two at least."

Their talk was interrupted when Mr. Pewtersmith stepped out of his rooms in his robes, his hair perfectly combed, with a slight smile on his face. "Now you can begin."

Nellie said, "Took you long enough, Uriah. If you're ready, I want to make sure we're all clear on the Task here. Robert, dear, what is your understanding of it?"

"Just catch the steel birds," said Robert. "All of them. By sunset."

Nellie nodded as she looked around the room. "All in agreement? Good. Now then, you all better remove any steel or iron or any types of ferrous metals from your bodies."

"Why should we do such a thing?" said Robert Blacksmith.

"Because Eden is about to turn on an electromagnet. I am told it has a great deal of force. You don't want anyone to find out the hard way."

"A magnet? You know that I'm a blacksmith, right?" said Robert. "I work in iron and steel."

"It cannot be helped." She waved her cane at the attendees. "Luckily, my cane is silver and therefore is not attracted by magnets."

The councilmembers began inventorying their belongings and clothing. Soon, keychains, watches, bits of jewelry and other steel items, including Eugene's watch, were collected in a wooden box. Robert Blacksmith removed his hammer. "Steel sledge." He removed his shoes. "Steel toes." He removed his belt. "Steel buckle." Then his pants. "Stainless-steel rivets." Then his shirt. "Titanium buttons. You got me standing here in my knickers, Eden. This had better not take long."

Nellie smiled. "You look quite fetching in your knickers, Robert, dear."

Eden walked over to her grandfather. She whispered, "Grandpa—your leg. Won't you have to remove your leg?"

"Why on earth would I do that?"

"Because of the magnet."

Vulcan stomped the metal peg on the floor. "Not magnetic. Pure aluminum."

The cage sat at the bottom of the stairs that led to the attic door. Eugene aimed the opening of the cage toward the attic. The cryostat and the magnet inside it were immediately behind the cage. Eden turned the dial on the magnet's power supply. It hummed. The lights in the hallway dimmed. More cold steam poured off the outside of the cryostat. The gauge glowed with light. The dial on the gauge zoomed up halfway to the red mark.

The wooden box holding all their steel belongings slid across the floor until it clanged against the copper cage. Mr. Pewtersmith made a choking sound and began jerking backward toward the cage. In less than a second, his head was pulled tight against the copper bars and he was grasping at his neck.

Eden's hand covered her smile. "Sorry, Mr. Pewtersmith. You might want to remove that necklace. Looks like the chain has some steel in it." She turned the machine off.

Mr. Pewtersmith fell forward. "You brat! You nearly killed me."

"That's why we told you to—never mind. Take off the necklace and we'll try again." Mr. Pewtersmith cursed as he began to undo the chain at his neck. Eden winked at Nathaniel as she twisted the dial. The chain was jerked from Mr. Pewtersmith's hands, leaving only the U-shaped pendant in his fingers.

Eden nodded at Nellie and Irma. The women each pulled a half dozen candles from their purses and lit them. They set the lit candles up and down the hallway. Eugene climbed the stairs to the attic door. He put his eye up to the peephole, then took a deep breath.

"Ready, Eden?"

"Ready, Eugene. Be sure to get out of the way as fast as you can."

Eugene nodded. He threw back the huge iron bar on the door,

then jerked on the iron door itself. It wouldn't budge. He pulled again, putting all his weight to it, and the door slowly creaked open. Eugene climbed quickly down the stairs and joined the others who were huddled behind the cage.

Thirty seconds passed. Then, a small, strange head poked out of the doorway at the top of the stairs. It looked loosely like a bird's head, but its beak was made from rusty metal and its eyes were old buttons. It hopped out on its one foot and turned its head slowly toward the crowd. It tilted its head to one side.

Eden turned the dial on the magnet. The needle on the gauge leaped forward and cold steam poured off the cryostat. The steel bird zoomed through the air, smacked against the back of the cage and froze there. The bird looked like a bug smashed on a windshield.

"How did you do that?" said Vulcan, reaching out a hand.

"Not now, Grandpa," said Eden.

A few seconds later, two more bizarre birds came out of the doorway. One had wings made of old electrical wire. The other had a beak of broken glass. Eden gave the dial another twist, increasing the power, and the two birds whipped through the air, crashing into the back of the cage. Three more crazy birds flew out and in seconds were caught inside the cage, immobile against the powerful electromagnet.

"It's working," whispered Eden, nervously watching the attic doorway. Three more bird creatures flew out of the doorway and into the cage. Then, all at once, a flurry of small, bizarre birds sailed out and crashed into the cage, until it was half full of crudely made feathers, beaks, and legs. "That must be most of the small ones," said Eden, "but I haven't seen any of the original ones. The ones made by Thợ Tiện. The alpha birds."

"They're smarter than this," said Eugene.

"Smarter?" said Robert Blacksmith. "You act as if they're sentient. They're mechanical creatures. Albeit advanced ones."

"Indeed. Mechanical creatures that wind themselves. And that make their own babies," said Nellie.

Irma nodded. "Whoever said all babies were cute, never saw

these. But what happened to Uriah Pewtersmith? Eden, you said it was your job to keep an eye on him?"

Eden whipped her head around. The councilmember was nowhere to be seen. Eden felt a knot of panic in her stomach. While she had focused on the birds, Mr. Pewtersmith had left and she hadn't even noticed.

"Sabotage," whispered Vulcan. "Doom."

Eugene said, "Just in case, I think we should kick in the backup plan."

Suddenly, they heard a faraway yelp of pain. It sounded as if it came from Mr. Pewtersmith's room. At the same instant, the hallway was plunged into darkness. The gauge dropped to zero. The hum of the electromagnet cut to silence.

"Uriah! That fool!" said Nellie. "He's done something to cut the power. Does he know what he's done? These birds are loose. Quick, Eden, close the cage! Eugene! The attic door!"

"Already on it," said Eugene, running up the stairs.

The only light in the hallway came from the dozen candles scattered around the floor. Eden slammed the cage shut. The birds inside, no longer frozen against the cage, began flapping about, pecking the copper bars with their beaks. Eden looked at the attic door. Eugene had reached the top, but was struggling to push the heavy door closed.

Eden began to run toward the stairs. She had to help Eugene.

"No, child!" shouted Nellie.

Eden could hear Eugene grunting and straining, then he cried out in pain. His thick body tumbled down the stairs and landed at her feet.

From inside the attic door, the head of a steel bird poked into view, its beak wet with Eugene's blood. In a flash, the bird was down the stairs. A sharp steel talon struck at Eden, cutting a gash down her face.

XXIV

In Which Eden Twists the Dial
All the Way to the Right

Vulcan rushed to Eden's side and stepped between her and the birds. "Run!" he shouted.

The left side of Eden's face, including her left eye, felt as if it were on fire. With her right eye, she saw chaos. Every ounce of her wanted to stay with her grandfather and with Eugene's wounded body. And every same ounce wanted to flee the bird that was attacking her. But she knew the plan. She had to make the plan work or more people would be hurt. She ran. She caught up with Nathaniel and sprinted down the hallway. Her face throbbed where the bird had clawed her.

Eden followed Nathaniel to the stairway and pounded after him, each step down the stairs making her think how long it would take and what might happen while she was away. Her vision was blurry, and her feet seemed to struggle to find the stairs.

Only one flight down, she heard voices below her and footsteps coming up. She saw lights. Then Iona and a dozen other Blue Coats came into view wearing headlamps and carrying a huge spool of black electrical cord, unwinding it as they went. "We were ready! As soon as the power went out, we started up," Iona said.

"Hurry!" shouted Eden between breaths. "The birds are loose."

Iona cursed when she saw Eden's face. "Double time, Blue Coats! Life-or-death service!" The Blue Coats powered up the stairs past Eden and Nathaniel. The children followed after them, breathless as they burst out of the stairwell into the hallway. The Blue Coats rolled the spool of cord ahead of them, moving at a full run.

The hallway was chaos. Nellie and Irma, their hair hanging every which way, were fighting off a steel bird with Nellie's cane, Irma's teacup, and what remained of their purses. Over the body of Eugene stood Vulcan, looking surprisingly fierce and holding back another bird by its steel neck. Yet another bird chased Robert Blacksmith and the rest of the Council around the copper cage.

Iona Jones and her Blue Coats rushed forward. Iona ran straight toward the councilmembers, thrusting her body between them and the bird. The steel bird raised up on its legs and spread its wings. Iona rushed forward, striking the bird in the head with her white staff. The bird screamed and dug its beak into Iona's torso. The two of them fell into a tumble on the hallway floor.

The rest of the Blue Coats ran to the electromagnet, unplugging the magnet from the wall and plugging it into the socket on the end of the spooled cord. The magnet hummed to life.

"Eden!" shouted Nellie. "Turn it up! Turn it all the way up!"

Eden rushed to the power supply. She grabbed for the dial, but her hand only found air. She tried again, focusing her one good eye, felt the dial under her fingers, and twisted it all the way to the right. The hum of the magnet turned into a screech. Cold steam poured off it and flooded the floor. The steel birds flew across the room, crashing into the cage, smashing the copper bars. In seconds, all the birds were twisted and frozen against the electromagnet, their beaks and claws still. Only their glass and button eyes twitched back and forth.

Eden heard strains, pops, and loud crashes from deeper in the building—the sound of metal colliding against metal.

"Turn it down!" shouted Robert Blacksmith. "Turn the power down before you tear this whole building apart!"

Eden turned the power of the magnet back to half. The birds still lay frozen inside the twisted cage. More distant crashes followed, shaking the floor they stood upon, then silence.

And then arms reached around Eden and pulled her into a tight embrace. It was Vulcan. Tears ran from his eyes. "I thought I'd lost you."

Eden leaned into his arms and choked back a sob. Nellie and Irma rushed over. "Do not worry about us ladies. We're fine, dearie. We are okay, aren't we, sister?"

Irma held out her teacup. "Didn't even spill my tea. But Eden—your face!"

"I'm all right," she said, even though her left eye throbbed and she thought she might faint. "Eugene—"

They rushed across the room toward Eugene, who lay on the floor, unmoving. Vulcan bent low over his friend. "He's alive, but he has lost a lot of blood." Vulcan called to the Blue Coats, who were gathered together near the remains of the cage. Two ran over with first aid kits and began working on Eugene's bloody figure. The rest of the Blue Coats wrapped Iona in bandages and carried her out of the hall. Nellie handed a lace handkerchief to Eden and told her to apply pressure to the cut on her face. Eden closed her left eye and held the handkerchief there.

"But what about you, Grandpa?" said Eden. "Are you okay?" In the middle of all the chaos, she couldn't help noticing that her grandpa's eyes looked bright and he stood so straight, that he looked taller, younger.

"I am," said Vulcan. "I believe I am. I'm a bit confused about what all happened here. But no one is going to harm my granddaughter while I still have breath left in my body to do something about it. Isn't that right, Eugene?"

Eugene lay still, unable to answer.

Seconds later, Mr. Pewtersmith's door opened. He stepped out, one hand in a pocket and the other hand waving about. "Vulcan and Eden Smith," he said. "Look at what you have caused. My rooms are a total disaster. You may have succeeded with this Task, but at what price? I expect new charges will be levied against you both." He walked across the scene to where his robe lay on the ground. He bent to pick it up, but Robert Blacksmith put his bare foot upon the garment.

"There'll be no need for that," said Blacksmith, still dressed only in his underwear.

"What are you talking about, Robert?" spat Mr. Pewtersmith.

Robert said, "Uriah Pewtersmith, this mess is your doing. I am removing you from the Council."

PART III
Fire

XXV

In Which Promises That Were Easy to Make Are Harder to Keep

Mr. Pewtersmith stood in the corridor, fuming amid the chaos and destruction of the steel birds. "Removing? From the Council? Me? Impossible! It was Vulcan Smith and his brat who are to blame for the mayhem! Vulcan and Eden who are the cause of any injury!"

Robert Blacksmith helped Maureen Goldsmith to her feet. She and the other councilmembers were scattered around the hallway, trying to catch their breath. Robert said, "Pewtersmith, if you say another word, I'll have you charged, the same as Vulcan. If you're found guilty, you'll spend the rest of your life in Subbasement Seven, in a room near Kitchens."

"Guilty?" said Mr. Pewtersmith. "I am guilty of nothing!"

Robert yanked Mr. Pewtersmith's concealed hand out of his pocket. The hand was wrapped in a loose bandage. "Hurt yourself?" Mr. Pewtersmith said nothing, but his eyes grew wide. Robert walked over to Mr. Pewtersmith's door and tried the knob. It was locked. "Open this door," he said.

"I will not!" said Mr. Pewtersmith. "You have no right."

"Someone bring me my hammer!" roared Robert. A few seconds later, a Blue Coat rushed up with Robert's sledge. Robert swung the hammer back and smashed it against the door. The door burst open. Blacksmith marched in. A few seconds later, he returned with a twisted bit of blackened metal and said, "Perhaps you can explain why this was jammed into one of your electrical outlets."

"That proves nothing!" said Mr. Pewtersmith.

"It proves enough," Robert Blacksmith said. "This looks suspiciously like the pendant always worn about your neck. I suspect you jammed the two ends into the outlet to short the electrical system, burning your hand in the process. Pewtersmith, I move that you be removed from the Council. I need someone to second the motion."

"I second it," said Helena Bladesmith, blowing her nose. "You did ask for a second, didn't you?"

Robert nodded. "All in favor of removing Uriah Pewtersmith from the Council?" A round of "Ayes" sounded from the bruised and bloody councilmembers. Mr. Pewtersmith stomped into his room and slammed his door. Robert Blacksmith nodded, then turned on his heel and left the hallway.

"Wait!" shouted Eden toward his departing figure. "We completed the Task. Mr. Blacksmith, can you please count this one as done?"

"And what about the birds?" said Nathaniel. "What are we supposed to do with these things?" But the whole Council was gone by then.

The Blue Coats kneeling by Eugene slid the tinker's large body onto a stretcher and carried him away. Vulcan was taken away on a stretcher as well. "I'm fine!" he protested. "Just a few scratches."

"A few wounds, you mean," said the Blue Coat pulling him along. "I see four that need stitches. You, too, Eden. Your eye is injured and we must tend to your face. Come, please."

"I promise to come as soon as I can," she said, "but shouldn't someone make sure the birds don't get loose again?"

"Yeah, maybe someone could help us," said Nathaniel, his voice breaking. "These things are kind of, you know, deadly."

The Blue Coats left with their other wounded. Nellie and Irma followed after them, clucking at Vulcan along the way. As they left, Nellie shouted, "Children, whatever you do, don't unplug that magnet."

Eden nodded. She and Nathaniel were now alone, standing next to the crushed cage and the tumble of immobilized steel birds.

"They left us," said Nathaniel. "I can't believe they just left us up here. We're just kids! Eden, how's your eye?"

"It'll be fine," she said, but when she tried to open it, she found she could not see out of it.

They decided that Nathaniel should go and get help, so he left to find Fred Tinsmith, hoping the old man could repair the cage and decide what to do with the birds.

A wave of exhaustion rolled over Eden. She sat alone on the floor of the hallway, lit only by candlelight. She still had Nellie's handkerchief. It was wet from her watering eye, and bloody. Her muscles felt rubbery and she wanted to cry. The twitching eyes of the birds kept her alert.

Eden looked back toward the birds with her blurry vision. Even in their motionless state, they were terrifying. Then why did Eden feel pity for them? "Because they were doing what they were made to do," she whispered aloud. They had fought to protect their own, just as she was fighting to help her grandfather. *That's what families do*, she thought. *Families fight with each other or for each other. Or both.*

Fred Tinsmith and Nathaniel returned, carrying toolboxes. Fred scratched his forehead as he studied the tangle of magnetized birds. "Always wondered what these things looked like," he said. "Some fine work. But...now that the Task's over, the responsible thing to do would be to take the birds apart and melt them down. Make sure they never escape. Make sure they never hurt anyone again."

"I guess you're right," said Eden. "But—"

"But what?" said Fred.

"Oh, nothing. They *are* dangerous. It's just that—well, they weren't bothering anyone until *we* bothered *them*. And then they were just defending themselves, like Thợ Tiện designed them to do."

"Their defense skills are too powerful," said Fred. "As you now well know."

Eden gently touched her wounded cheek. She winced. "But no one actually died today. And, well, now that we have the peephole in place, maybe we could keep an eye on them—make sure they don't escape."

"Maybe we should think on it," said Fred. "And while we're thinking, we might as well just put them back into the attic. You two, go way down the hall there."

"What are you going to do, Fred?"

"If anything happens to me," said Fred, "just plug the power back in. That's all you've got to do. Now move down there. Quietly. Slowly."

Without a sound, Fred walked along the power cord until he came to the point where it plugged into the long cord brought up by the Blue Coats. Fred sat down on the floor, then silently watched the birds. With slow, steady hands, he unplugged the cord.

"What is he doing?" hissed Nathaniel.

"Shhh," said Eden.

The instant the power went off, the steel birds tumbled to the ground. They screeched, making sounds like hammers hitting metal springs. They wheeled around the hallway on their feet, their hinged wings flapping and their eyes twitching back and forth between Fred and the children.

"Don't move," whispered Nathaniel.

"I couldn't if I wanted to," hissed Eden.

Other than occasionally scratching himself, Fred sat as still as a statue, holding the plug inches away from the socket. The steel birds continued to screech and whirl, then slowly turned their attention to winding up their babies. One of the large, beautiful birds lifted a broken baby bird in her steel beak and flew it back into the attic, then returned for another. Another of the big birds began to do the same, while the other large birds screeched and flapped their wings at Fred. He sat unmoving.

When the last of the birds had retreated into the attic, Fred slowly climbed the stairs, one step at a time. He strained against the attic door and finally shut it with a clang, sliding the bar in place. The children rushed toward him.

"That's something I'll never forget," Fred said. "Isn't nature wonderful?"

"Nature?" said Eden.

"I'd call it nature. You call it whatever you want. That Thợ Tiện was quite a machinist."

～⌒～

Eden tried to push the elevator button on the Council floor, but her finger kept missing it.

"Your depth perception is off," said Nathaniel.

"My what?"

"Depth perception. I've read that being able to see how far away something is takes two eyes. You only have one. Here, let me do it." He pushed the button.

When Buzz arrived, his pillbox hat was smashed flat and his eyes were bloodshot. "Where to?" Buzz muttered.

"Infirmary," said Nathaniel.

Buzz nodded.

"What happened to you, Buzz?" said Eden.

"I hear I have you to thank," he said. "I was just sitting in my elevator relaxing, a little after two. Usually that's the slowest part of the day for me. Then, all of a sudden, the elevator just took off upward, like a bullet out of a gun. I started screaming, but no one could hear me. Then the elevator stopped. But I didn't. I went flying up and crashed into the ceiling. Smashed my new hat. Got a horrible crook in my neck."

"The electromagnet," whispered Nathaniel. "Eden, that must have been when you turned it to full power."

"Oh Buzz, I'm so sorry!" Eden said.

Buzz nodded. "Ain't just me. Everything made of iron or steel from the third floor up—everything not bolted down, that is—smashed right up to the ceilings. Then I guess when you turned the magnet off, all that stuff smashed back down." Buzz leveled his eyes at Eden. "There are a few dozen master smiths who are pretty mad at you right now. But I reckon they'll forgive you the minute they see your face."

The infirmary was in Subbasement Six. It was clean and white. Doctor Jones—the same doctor Eden had seen at the Gathering of Joneses in the hallway—applied a smelly ointment to the three gashes on Eden's face and covered them with a big bandage. "Those will need stitches," Doctor Jones said. "You might end up with scars, but I hear you'll have a good story."

Eden shrugged.

"Now we'll need to take a look at that eye," said Doctor Jones, "but I'm going to have to give you some anesthesia first."

Before Eden had time to feel nervous, a nurse led her to a bed. A mask was put over her face and the nurse asked her to count backward from one hundred. She fell asleep at ninety-seven.

When she awoke, her face felt better and her vision seemed clearer as well. She smiled slightly, hoping the injury to her eye was almost cured.

She reached up to touch her face and felt something over her eye.

Eden looked around the room until she spotted a mirror on a far wall. She scrambled off the bed to look at her reflection. Her own face stared back at her, with neat stitches handling the cuts on her cheek. But her left eye was covered in an oval-shaped silver patch. Engraved into the silver patch was a simple tree set inside a circle. The same tree she had engraved in her first knife—the knife she had given to her grandfather.

"Doctor said the scars on your face will never disappear completely, but they'll heal," said a voice behind her. In the mirror, Eden saw the reflection of her grandfather and felt him rest a hand on her shoulder. "Guess your eye was not so lucky. Doc said it's damaged beyond repair."

"Beyond repair? So I'll never be able to see with that eye?"

"I'm afraid not," said Vulcan softly. "Doc's coming back in a bit to talk to you about it. But…I'm so sorry, Eden. It's my fault. You wouldn't be here if it wasn't for me."

"That's true," she said. She looked around the room, then back at her grandfather. She wanted to say something that would make them both feel better—something that wasn't a lie. "But…I also wouldn't be *here*. In the Guildhall."

"But your eye."

She touched the silver eye patch as she looked at her reflection. The thought of losing half her vision took a bit of her breath away, and a lump formed at the back of her throat. She didn't know how this might affect her. Would her depth perception come back? Would people treat her differently? She tried to swallow away the lump, but her mouth was dry. After several minutes she heard herself say, "I'll be okay. I think." She hoped it was true. She reached out and touched the silver eye patch again, then tilted her head from side to side, looking at her reflection from different angles.

Vulcan said, "About the patch—"

"You made it," interrupted Eden.

"You knew? Made it from a silver spoon with nothing more than my pair of pliers, while sitting in my hospital bed. First decent thing I've made in some time. Only reason I can even be here visiting you is that I've been recovering in the room next door." He held out a little pewter bowl toward her. "Almost forgot. I also brought you some pudding."

Eden did start crying then. The first tear in six and a half years trickled down her face. But once that first one fell, the rest followed. She let them run. She fell onto the hospital bed and sobbed, her shoulders shaking and strange animal sounds coming out of her mouth. She didn't understand why just the tiniest kindness from her grandfather had broken the dam, but now she felt everything, all at once—the death of her parents, the loss of her home, the loss of her friends, her school, her schedule, and everything else that had once added up to normal life. She cried for the years of being jerked from one foster home to another, for all the years of belonging to no one, of belonging nowhere. And now, her eyesight. She grieved for all of it.

"If you keep this up," said Vulcan, sniffing, "you're going to get me started."

"I...I..." She couldn't get one word out without sobbing again.

"I know," said Vulcan. His voice broke. His shoulders started to shake. "Oh, now here I go." He began sobbing alongside of her.

Finally, the tears slowed. Vulcan said, "Oh, for the love of Saint Dunstan. Here, blow your nose." He handed Eden a tissue.

She took a deep, ragged breath, blew, then said, "What kind of pudding is it?"

"What?"

"You said you brought pudding. What flavor is it?"

"Pudding!" Vulcan laughed. "After all that, the first thing you can manage to say is *What kind of pudding?*"

Eden laughed through her tears. "Well, what kind *is* it?"

"Vanilla."

Eden nodded as she blew her nose again.

"Got a sweet tooth? So do I. And so did your dad." He wiped his eyes and stared at her. "You look like him."

"So I've heard."

"But different. Half him and half your mother, I suppose. The Jones woman."

"Emily. Her name was Emily. And if you say one bad word about her, I'll—I'll throw this pudding right—right—"

"Settle down," said Vulcan. "Didn't mean to offend." He paused, then said, "How did he die?"

"You mean Dad?"

Vulcan nodded.

Eden told him, as much as she could manage without crying again.

"Did he ever mention me?" said Vulcan.

"It was years ago, so it's hard for me to remember, but I don't think he mentioned you much. He might have even said you were dead."

Vulcan groaned. "In a way, I suppose he was right. But I'm alive again, Eden. I'm alive."

Vulcan bid Eden farewell when Dr. Jones and a woman Eden had never seen before came by to talk. The woman introduced herself as Fabergé Jones, the Guildhall's occupational therapist. She would be working with Eden in the months to come, she said, helping her to adjust to her new field of vision. "This will take some getting used to, hon," Fabergé said. "But you'll be okay. Eventually."

The next morning, Dr. Jones reviewed Eden's discharge paperwork and prescriptions with her. Then, she had her first therapy session with Fabergé, who performed all sorts of vision tests and took a lot of notes. When they were finished, Fabergé smiled at Eden. "I know Doctor Jones will be taking those stitches out in a couple weeks, but let's have you back here sooner to get going on therapy. The infirmary will contact you to set it all up. Right now, I think there's someone who wants to see you."

When Nathaniel rushed into the room, he looked at everything except her face. "Hey there," he said, as he stared at the ceiling. "How's it going? You seem, um, good."

"How would you know?" she said. "You haven't even looked at me. By the way, I know that I look like a pirate."

Nathaniel let out his breath in a rush. "Whew. I'm glad you said it first." He smiled. "You look awesome, actually. Arrgghh."

They left Eden's room and wandered around the infirmary until they found Eugene, lying in a bed with tubes connected to his arm. He smiled weakly at them, his eyes half closed. "Hey there, kiddos."

Eden put her hand on Eugene's arm. "You're okay?"

"I'm okay. Takes more than a bird to—well, I guess a bird almost did me in. Ooohh, I'm tired."

Eden kissed him on the tip of his nose. Eugene smiled again, then drifted off to sleep.

They looked for Iona. A nurse told them the Blue Coat would most likely survive and recover, but was not taking visitors. Vulcan had been discharged, so the children made their way to Subbasement Seven and knocked on his door. Vulcan jerked the door open. "Save me!" he said. "These old ladies are worse than the birds!"

"Vulcan, you must sit back down," said Nellie, forcing him onto his bed. "You were attacked. You need your rest."

"And finish your medicine," said Irma, holding out a pewter cup of black goo. "If you drink the whole thing, I'll let you have a cube of sugar."

"Get away from me, you meddlesome quacks!" shouted Vulcan. "Help me, Eden. They'll barely even let me speak. If I can get a word in, it'll be a major victory."

"That is hardly gentlemanly, Vulcan," said Nellie. "But we shall overlook your insults this one time, because you've had such a bad go of it. Won't we, sister?"

"I'm overlooking nothing," replied Irma, pushing the cup in Vulcan's face. "Shush now and drink. It's good for you."

"Then *you* drink it," said Vulcan.

"Not on your life," said Irma. "I try to avoid things that are good for me."

Nellie ushered the children into the room. "Eden, dear girl, we visited you in the infirmary before you woke, so we've already seen your eye. I must say that I find your eye patch quite becoming. It gives you an air of mystery."

"Like a pirate?" asked Eden, smiling.

"Yes, very much like a lady pirate, but hopefully one with excellent manners. Now come here. We have a serving of medicine ready for you as well."

"Thanks Aunty, but I already have antibiotics from Dr. Jones."

"Phooey on your antibiotics. Here." Irma handed her own blue teacup to Eden. It was full of the same black goo. It smelled like tar and dead fish.

Eden wrinkled her nose. "What is this?"

"Tar and dead fish," said Irma. "It will help you heal faster. Drink it in one go, there's a good girl."

Eden pinched her nose and poured the liquid into her mouth. It tasted worse than it smelled and was so thick that she had to chew to get it down her throat. When she finished the cup, she could feel her stomach doing flip-flops.

"There now," said Irma, taking her teacup back and wiping it clean with a rag. "Don't you feel better?"

"No," groaned Eden.

Irma smiled and sat down on the edge of the bed next to her sister. "That's how you know it's working."

Vulcan jumped up out of the bed and began pacing back and forth across the small room.

"Wow, Mr. Smith," Nathaniel said. "You seem more, well, more energetic. You seem better."

"I *am* better!" Vulcan punched the air. "They may have got my old man, but they didn't get me. Gah! What a fight that was! I thought we were all goners there for a minute! Thought Geno was gonna kick it. Didn't know I could still move so fast. I've got aches and pains on every inch of my body! Haven't felt this good in weeks! And look at my granddaughter." He pulled Eden over to his side, stomped his aluminum leg on the floor, and laughed. "A couple of buccaneers! We're like a matched pair, you and me."

"We can talk about that later." Eden smiled. "We have other things we need to discuss."

"That is true, dearie," said Nellie. "We still have three more Impossible Tasks."

"And the Joneses. We have to talk about the Joneses," said Nathaniel.

Nellie ignored him. "I wonder which Task is next?"

"Nothing has come yet?" asked Eden. "From Miss Clara, I mean."

"Nothing yet, dear," said Irma.

"Ummm," said Nathaniel. "Before we get to the next Task, we promised my people—the Joneses—we promised to teach them how to smith."

Vulcan and the sisters grew quiet. Nellie clutched the head of her cane. "Oh dear. It was easy to *make* the promise, wasn't it?"

"Harder to keep it," said Irma. "That's how promises work. That's what I always say."

"Why harder?" said Eden. "You just start training them, same as Helena and Fred have done with Nathaniel and me."

"Perhaps the girl's right, sister," said Irma, taking a sip from her teacup. "No need to complicate it. Think back to when we were young. The master smiths always had apprentices. And we had an Apprentice Master who ran the program. That's what we need. An Apprentice Master. We'll need to find someone to volunteer for that.

Remember back to when we were apprenticed, sister? How many others were apprenticing at the same time?"

"Must have been a dozen," said Nellie. "And wasn't that a lot of fun, all learning together? All in the same class."

"So we start it again," said Irma. "All these Joneses—along with Eden and Nathaniel—they'll be the new class."

"What happened, anyway?" asked Eden.

"To what, dearie?"

"Why did it stop? The very first time we went to Records, we saw a photo of Grandpa, when he started as an apprentice—"

"Oh, I love that photo!" said Nellie. "Irma and I stood on either side of him. Did you see us, too?"

"I thought that was you," said Eden. "Why did you stop having apprentices?"

"Oh, now," said Nellie. "Who knows how these things come about?"

"I'd like to know," said Eden.

Nellie looked at her hands. "There used to be so many smiths. In this Guildhall, we could afford to be—hmmm—selective, I suppose. Doesn't sound very nice when I say it. We only allowed Smiths to become smiths. No Joneses. No Andersons. No Montagues, DeGaulles, Lees, Hansons, Gaos, Prakashes, or anyone whose name does not somehow translate to the work of a smith. And then—well, then we found that many of the young people with the, the Smith name...well, they developed other interests. They wanted to appear on the television, or save lives, or travel to space, or work with money, or—"

"Or do computers!" said Irma. "Dreadful, beeping things."

"Something beeping?" said Vulcan. "I didn't hear anything."

"Nothing is beeping, Vulcan," sighed Irma.

Nellie continued. "Some of the young Smiths even wanted to work in—in *manufacturing*. But by then, well, we were so set in our ways, that we couldn't see...well, we just couldn't see that we needed to *change* our ways." She took a long sip of tea. "It is not easy to change. Yes, our numbers were dwindling. Our Guild was growing thin. But it was—well, we were used to it. We could do things the same old way, same as we always had."

"Even if it wasn't working?" said Eden.

Nellie frowned. "Now—now, that's a bit harsh, dearie. I wouldn't say it wasn't working."

"I would," said Irma. Her mouth was set in a straight line. "It hasn't worked in years. Look at us. We are all so old."

"Just because we are old doesn't mean we are not masters of our crafts," said Nellie.

"And master craftspeople need students," said Irma. "Look how exciting it has been with just the addition of Eden. And she is—well, she is half Jones herself."

"And Nathaniel," said Eden. "Don't forget Nathaniel."

"Yes," said Irma. She held out a hand to the boy. Nathaniel took it. "I'm afraid we owe you an apology, young man. We have been treating you poorly—you and all of your kin. We have been less than hospitable. We have been, well, less than ladylike."

"Sister!" said Nellie.

"It's true," said Irma. "You know it's true, sister. You and I, and so many others, have been guilty. But, now we have a chance to make amends—at least partially. So then, Nellie and I will volunteer to become the new Apprentice Masters."

"We will?" said Nellie.

"Yes, sister," said Irma. "We will."

Nellie nodded. She took Nathaniel's other hand. "Then of course we will."

Eden smiled. "Hey, that reminds me. Nathaniel and I have to figure out who we're apprenticing under next." She sat down gingerly in Vulcan's chair, feeling every sore muscle in her body. "As for the next Task, I hope it holds off for a few days. I think we've earned a break."

XXVI

Muscles and the Memory of Muscles

Miss Clara sulked when she rolled her tea trolley into the sisters' parlor the next morning. "I have nothing for you, Eden. Other than food and drink, I mean." Eden sighed with relief. They already had plenty to think about that day. It was the first day of the new apprenticeship program.

An hour later, the hallway outside of Vulcan's room was turned into a school office, with lines of nervous Joneses filling out questionnaires and huddles of nervous master smiths waiting to have students assigned to them. Nellie and Irma bossed all of them around. Eden and Nathaniel tried to stay out of the way.

"Please stay in line!" shouted Nellie, waving her silver cane. "Behave like ladies and gentlemen. You there, turn off that acetylene torch until you have been properly trained!"

"Eden! Eden!" Buzz shouted. "Guess what kind of smithing I'm going to do first?"

"Let me see," said Eden, smiling. "Bladesmithing?"

"That's right! How'd you guess?" said Buzz.

"Maybe because you've mentioned it a million times," said Eden. "Who's running the elevator while you're in class?"

"I was worried about the same thing," said Buzz. "Then Robert Blacksmith himself said that he would find a smith to cover my shifts. A smith to run the elevator, while I, a Jones, am learning how to make swords. Can you believe it? By the way, I like your eye patch. Makes you look like a pirate."

"Thanks, Buzz."

Eden spotted Kerlin Arrowsmith walking toward her with a group of Jones gardeners in their brown overalls. She smiled. "Kerlin, are these your new arrowsmithing apprentices?"

"Quite the opposite, my dear," said Kerlin. "I am apprenticing under *them*."

"But they're not smiths."

"They are gardeners. *Master* gardeners to be precise! When I heard this hubbub about freedom of choice, I realized that I wanted some of that same freedom, too."

"But Kerlin, you're already a master smith," said Eden.

"Indeed I am. I have been crafting arrows for nearly fifty years. It is said to be my calling, but I confess that I do not find it so. I am supposed to love arrows. But what I really love are, well, petunias!"

Eden laughed. "It's nice to see you so happy, Kerlin. Good luck!"

Within half an hour, the master smiths and their groups of chattering apprentices left the hallway for their various workshops. Nellie called to Eden and Nathaniel. When they approached, she said, "We have the answer! We have found you your next master smith to work with."

"Who?" said Eden.

Irma smiled over the rim of her blue teacup. "Don't tell them, sister," said Irma. "Just give them the room number and let the story reveal itself on its own. There are too few secrets in life."

Eden and Nathaniel headed toward the elevator with the room number written on a slip of paper.

When the elevator doors opened, Mr. Pewtersmith glared at them. He was the smith covering for Buzz.

"What do you idiots want?" he spat. "And what happened to your face? You look like—"

"A pirate?" supplied Eden. She smiled contentedly at him. "I know."

"I was going to say, an absolute *mess*."

Eden shrugged at Mr. Pewtersmith. She knew it was his fault—her injury—but she also knew he was baiting her. Yelling at him would only give him what he wanted.

"You know what happened to my face. And I know you won't believe me—and I don't care if you do or not—but I'm—" It took Eden a moment to find the right words. "I'm at peace with my eye patch." This much, Eden decided, was true. Of course, she wanted her vision to work well and she still wasn't sure how the injury would impact her abilities. It was taking a lot of getting used to, but she wasn't going to give Mr. Pewtersmith the satisfaction of discussing it. But the eye patch was different. She liked that the eye patch made her look tough and, as Nellie had said, mysterious. She liked the design that Vulcan had engraved on it, because it was proof—right there on her face—that he thought of her and cared about her. But most of all, she liked that the patch felt like physical evidence of her commitment to a life as a smith—to life in this Guildhall—forever going forward. It made her feel permanent. It made her feel that she belonged. She smiled when she thought of Vulcan's comments about her patch and his prosthetic leg: *We're like a matched pair, you and I.* She liked having someone to match. She liked matching *him*.

She leveled her gaze at Mr. Pewtersmith. "That's all I have to say about that. And now we need a ride."

"Do you? And precisely where," said Mr. Pewtersmith, stroking his thin moustache, "would you like to go?"

Eden showed him the slip of paper. "Can you take us here?"

"I can"—Mr. Pewtersmith smiled—"but I won't. I assume you know how to use stairs."

❧

Eden and Nathaniel walked the stairs from Subbasement Seven, up flight after flight until they came out on the same floor they had been on with the birds—the Council floor. Breathless and sweaty, they found the door number from the paper. The name on the door read Robert Blacksmith.

"The head of the Council?" asked Nathaniel. "Is this really a good idea?"

"Probably not," said Eden. She knocked.

"You're late," a voice boomed from inside. The door opened. Robert Blacksmith grabbed them both by their collars and pulled them inside his rooms. "Blacksmiths are never late."

The shop was large and hot, with orange light from four glowing furnaces. Robert tossed heavy leather aprons at the children. The aprons were sized for Robert, so when the children put them on, they dragged on the floor. He handed them huge leather gloves and then walked them to a glowing furnace.

Robert used tongs to thrust the end of two long bars of steel into it. "Today we hammer."

"What are we making?" said Eden.

"You must guess before we begin. You must solve my riddle. Blacksmiths are the inventors of riddles. So here is one for you: What does every blacksmith make every time they swing a hammer?"

"Horseshoes?" said Nathaniel.

"No!" roared Robert. "Enough with horseshoes! We make more than that. We make armor and hooks and pots and nearly everything made of steel. But what do we make with every hammer swing?"

Eden and Nathaniel stayed silent, afraid to make Robert any madder.

"I will give you a hint," said Robert. He held up his arm and flexed his massive bicep.

"Muscles?" said Eden.

"Yes! Muscles," said Robert, "and the memory of muscles. And the loud pings of well-hammered steel. Today we make callouses. Today we make sore backs." He gave them each a pair of goggles, a hammer, and a set of tongs. "We start with five-pound hammers today. Your arms are too puny to handle anything heavier. Ready? Begin."

Eden grabbed her tongs and pulled her bar of steel from the

furnace. She placed the glowing end on top of an anvil, and started hammering. At first, she missed the bar more than she hit it. But after a while, she got a little better. She hammered it until it began to cool, then Robert yelled for her to thrust it back into the furnace. When it was hot enough, he yelled for her to remove it again. She pulled it back out and hammered some more. In fifteen minutes, she felt like her arms were going to fall off. She pulled off her goggles and stepped back. Robert noticed right away.

"Are you tired?" he demanded.

Eden hurried to think of an excuse. "It's just that I've done this already," she said.

"That wasn't my question," said Robert. "Are you tired?"

"What I'm saying is, in my very first lessons, I made knives and swords. From steel. I already know how to hammer."

Robert glared at her.

"Fine," said Eden. "I'm tired."

"Good," said Robert. "I'll tell you when you can stop. Pick up that hammer and make some more noise."

Robert Blacksmith didn't tell them to stop until two o'clock. They stumbled to the elevator and hit the button. When the doors opened, Buzz was back. He smiled at them. "You two look whipped," he said. "Not me! The best day of my life. The best! Look at this!" He pulled out a piece of black metal shaped like a crooked butter knife. "What a beauty! Now where can I take you two? Nap time, maybe?"

Eden returned to her room and collapsed on her bed. She gave a quick look at her forlorn orchid. It still looked as dead as her arms now felt. She mumbled good night to the photograph of her parents and fell asleep in less than a minute. At three o'clock, Nellie had to shake her awake. "Nap time is over, dearie. Your grandfather wants to see you."

Eden sat up. "See me? He actually asked to see me?"

"He did. It is a good sign, I think."

It took her fifteen minutes to wake up enough to make it down to Vulcan's room. He opened the door. "Eden! What brings you here?"

"You sent for me, Grandpa."

"I did? Oh! I did. I wanted to tell you something. What was it? Aaah yes—that I'm jealous. I am a master smith in every skill. And I have my kin, right here. My own granddaughter. Yet here you are going from one smith to another. But it should be me. I should be teaching you."

"Do you think you're up for it?" said Eden.

He pulled Eden inside and shut the door. "It's just what I need. So every day, from three until dinnertime, you are *my* apprentice."

Eden rubbed her sore arms. "Does it have to start today?"

Vulcan frowned. "Remind me what you've dabbled in so far."

"Bladesmithing. Tinsmithing. And now hammering."

"Hammering? Ahh, you've got Robert Blacksmith." Vulcan smiled at Eden's half-opened eyes. "Maybe we could wait until tomorrow for any hard work."

"That would be lovely." Eden collapsed onto the guest chair Vulcan had made. Her hand accidentally hit one of the buttons on the arm. The chair legs began to extend, raising Eden up toward the ceiling.

"Watch your head!" shouted Vulcan.

Eden crouched down as low as she could. The top of the chairback crashed into the ceiling, dumping Eden out. She managed to land on Vulcan's bed.

Vulcan squinted. "Still needs a little work."

"Maybe I'll sit on the floor," said Eden.

Vulcan glanced at the tools laid out on his table, then sat next to her on the floor. "Today, how about we just talk?"

"Sounds good," said Eden, yawning. "But can it be about something other than metal?"

"Other than metal? How can a conversation between a master smith and an apprentice be about anything other than metal? I suppose we could talk about the rats."

"You're also my grandpa. So maybe we could talk about... maybe we could talk about that."

"About me being your grandpa?"

"I never even met you until I came here. Don't you think that's a little weird?"

"No point getting into this," groused Vulcan.

"I'd like to talk about it," said Eden.

Vulcan tapped his finger on his leg and said nothing.

Eden said, "You could have come and visited, if you wanted, right? I mean, you could have left here and come to see us. You could have taken me in years ago, when I had no one. You're allowed to leave. The sisters and I—we left for a while."

Vulcan pursed his lips.

Eden continued, "You never did visit, though. I thought you were dead. But you weren't. You were here. Alive. While I was out there alone."

Vulcan said nothing.

"Maybe you could tell me why," said Eden. "You know, so I could at least understand."

Vulcan stood. "Why do you have to bring this up? I was feeling so good."

"I want to know."

"You're just tired. I think that's enough for today."

"I'm not tired anymore."

"I am. Time to go." He held the door open for her until she left.

The following morning, the next Task—and its tin-can container— failed to arrive again.

The rest of the day was more of the same at Robert Blacksmith's. The children arrived a few minutes early, but all it meant was more time to hammer. Their hands, arms, and backs ached.

That afternoon, instead of visiting for a lesson, Eden avoided Vulcan, not sure what she would say to him, and realizing that he didn't know what to say to her. The same happened the next day, although Robert Blacksmith moved her and Nathaniel up to eight-pound hammers. Their arms were just as tired, but their hands and backs hurt less.

The next morning, Miss Clara arrived with their breakfast orders. Eden scanned the tea trolley. "Sorry, Eden," said Miss Clara. "Nothing else for you today."

"Why not?"

"You actually want it to come?" said Nellie, smearing orange marmalade onto a scone. "I thought we were enjoying our little break."

"I did need a break. But now I want to get it all over with," said Eden. "The waiting is driving me nuts. Why is it taking so long?"

Later that day, Eden and Nathaniel were both hammering away on their steel bars, when Robert held up his huge hand. "Wait!" he said. He pointed to Eden. "Hit that again."

She struck the glowing red steel with her hammer. *Ping!*

Robert pointed at Nathaniel. "Now you."

Nathaniel struck. *Ping!*

"Did you hear that?" said Robert. "Now that right there is a lovely sound. That's the sound of well-swung hammers on well-forged steel. I've been waiting for that. Waiting for you to play in tune."

Eden swung her hammer again. *Ping!* She smiled. Robert Blacksmith was right. She did love the sound.

"Now what?" she asked.

"Now you can make something," said Robert. "An order came in just yesterday. From your grandfather, of all people. Not a paying job. Just a favor between old friends. But an order is an order, so now we get to work."

The order was for a large collection of steel rods of various sizes and shapes. Robert showed Eden and Nathaniel how to read the plans and stood shoulder to shoulder with them as they worked. Robert could straighten a bent bar with a single hammer blow, but most of the time, he told Eden and Nathaniel where to strike the metal, or how to pinch it with tongs to get the proper curve.

The scars on Eden's face were getting smaller as her wounds from the birds healed. At the end of each day, Eden considered visiting Vulcan for his offered teaching. But she didn't. What would she say? Every morning, Miss Clara would roll her tea trolley into the sisters' parlor and shrug. Still no tin can. Still no third Task.

Another order came through from Vulcan, this one was for the rods to be welded together into six panels. "What is this crazy man planning to do this time?" said Robert Blacksmith. "You know, Eden, I take it as a compliment that Vulcan sent this work my way."

Eden smiled and said nothing, secretly hoping that Vulcan was sending the work *her* way. It made her feel better about him. It made her hope they could talk again soon, but with every day that she stayed away, it made it that much harder to imagine visiting.

The last day of their session with Robert Blacksmith finally arrived. It had been more than two weeks since Eden had completed the Task of the Steel Birds. At breakfast time that morning, a knock came at the door of the sisters' rooms. Miss Clara rolled in her trolley, smiling and waving a tin can, as if it were a long-expected birthday present. "It's here! It's finally here! Your long wait is over!"

Eden snatched the can. She gave it a shake and heard the familiar rattle from inside. She opened it with her can opener. Nellie was so focused on the can, she forgot to chase Miss Clara from the room. Eden read the curled strip of stamped tin inside the can. "Ugh," she said. "It's the rats."

"I *knew* it would be rats." Miss Clara smiled as she backed out of the room.

"And now the rest of the Guildhall will know as well," said Nellie. "You might as well read it to us, dearie."

Eden read the Task out loud. The Task was to capture all the rats in the Guildhall in a single day, from sunrise to sunset. Like the others, this Task said that failure would result in banishment for the smith and their helper.

Eden wanted to tell her grandfather about the new Task, but the thought of speaking to him still made her nervous. Instead, she visited the infirmary and had her stitches removed by Doctor Jones. When he was finished, he showed her a mirror. Directly below her eye patch, Eden's face now had three thin pink lines down her cheek. She slowly ran her finger along the scars.

"Everything's looking very good," said Doctor Jones. The scars will fade a bit over time. At some point you could choose to cover them with makeup, if they concern you."

"No, it's not that. I'm just…getting used to it all." She doubted she'd use makeup. The scars, like her eye patch, were a part of who she was.

In Robert's shop, they finished the last part of the last order. It was for four small doors, hinged at the top, each fourteen inches square. The doors had springs on them, so they would slam shut. Eden and Nathaniel made the doors themselves, with only a little help from Robert Blacksmith. "You did fine here, both of you." Robert put his huge hand on Nathaniel's bicep again and winked. "Lord, it's as hard as steel, that arm. I'll be watching myself around you, Nathaniel Jones. So then, we began your time with me with a riddle. We'll end with one as well. Listen: Iron is strong. Steel is stronger. The blacksmith can overcome steel. But what is mightier than the blacksmith?"

"I know," said Nathaniel. "The blacksmith's mom."

"Ha ha!" roared Robert. "A good guess and closer than you think. But don't answer now, either of you. Think on it. Now, just one last job and you're all done. Deliver these doors to Vulcan."

✺

When Vulcan opened his door, a sharp, a sour smell poured from his room. Vulcan frowned at the children. "Come on in then."

Eden held her nose with one hand and set the hinged doors on Vulcan's table with the other.

"Smells that bad?" he asked.

Eden nodded, pinching her nose and trying not to breathe.

Vulcan examined the hinged doors, grunting. "Seems solid enough. Your work?"

"Mostly," she said.

"They should do the trick just fine."

"Do what?" said Nathaniel. "What's all this for, Mr. Smith?"

"Nothing fancy." He seemed relieved to have something to talk about as he unrolled a large paper diagram. It covered the table. "Just a big box. For the rats."

"The rats!" said Eden. "How did you know? I just got the Task this morning."

Vulcan frowned. "I didn't know, exactly. But there are only three

229

Tasks left, so I started on the easiest one. It's a cage. The six panels you made are the four sides, plus the top and bottom. These doors go on each of the four sides. They open inward, but then the springs slam them shut. So rats can get in but can't get out."

"You really made these plans, Grandpa?"

"Course I did. But I still have to get the rats to go inside the finished cage. I've been experimenting all this week with various ways to lure them in. Right now, I'm working with cheese. Cheddar, Limburger, and Wensleydale. Some of it fresh... some of it moldy."

"*Some* of it?" said Nathaniel. "Smells like *all* of it."

"Any rats?" asked Eden.

"Just one," said Vulcan. "I call him Willard. He comes. But only at night. Which is another problem. We need to catch the rats in the daytime, but rats are mostly nocturnal."

"We need clues," said Eden.

"No!" said Nathaniel, backing away from Eden.

"What's wrong?"

"I know what you're getting at when you say we need clues," said Nathaniel. "It means research. It means we have to go back to Records. It means Bones."

"Oh, come on, Nathaniel," said Eden. "That dog loves you. I suppose we can wait until tomorrow. After breakfast."

"After breakfast. Great. Then I'll smell even more delicious. I guess I'd better get more mahguj."

Nathaniel left. Eden and Vulcan sat awkwardly next to each other, as Vulcan explained how the trapdoors worked. "But you don't want to hear about this. No talk about smithing, eh?"

"I never said that," said Eden. "It was just that one night. I wanted to talk about family. About *our* family."

"We can talk about it now, if you feel the need, but there's not much to it except an old man's foolishness."

"Only talk if you want to," said Eden.

"If you wait until I want to, you'll be waiting until doomsday." Vulcan cleared his throat. "Like I said, there's not much to it. Your father was smart. Like you. But cheeky like you, too."

"You think I'm cheeky?"

Vulcan squinted at her. "Eric was naturally talented as a smith, but even more than that, he was naturally talented with ideas. Ever since he was a young boy, he figured out better ways to do things, faster ways, easier ways. He would have been the ideal partner on solving these Tasks. His mother, Edna—your grandma and my wife—she encouraged him, of course."

"I wish I'd met her."

"You would have loved her. And she you. The sisters—Nellie and Irma—the two of them and Edna, they were inseparable, those three. Nellie and Irma were like aunts to Eric. They thought he was the smartest boy. They were right. He *was* smart. He liked solving problems more than he liked smithing. He couldn't understand why we all wanted to make everything by hand, when he could build machines to make things so much faster. I think our work drove him crazy."

"I'm not like that, you know." She brushed the tip of her finger on the silver eye patch. "I love smithing."

Vulcan smiled. "We argued about it all the time, he and I. I'd say that he needed to do things the way they'd always been done. He'd say I was just stuck in the old ways. I'd say that the old ways were better. He'd say that if he couldn't do things in his own way, he'd move out. I told him to go ahead."

Vulcan opened and closed one of the trapdoors on the table. "I always thought it was just talk. You know how kids are—always threatening to run away."

Eden nodded. "Kids ran away from the orphanage sometimes."

Vulcan squinted. "They did, eh? I kind of meant this differently. You know, how kids in—in better circumstances—sometimes think the world is out to get them, even when it's not."

"But sometimes the world *is* out to get you. At least sometimes it feels that way."

Vulcan sighed. "Sometimes it does, Eden. As I was saying, one day, your dad did leave. We got in a fight because he showed me a machine he made that could stamp out a pewter bowl, just like that. I told him that it wasn't smithing. It was manufacturing. I think I threw one of his bowls into the trash, if I remember correctly. Anyway, he moved out."

"When? How old was he?"

"He was twenty-nine. I remember because it was exactly one week after his twenty-ninth birthday. He left and started building his machines. He started mass producing metal products—at his factory or foundry or whatever it was called. I should have been proud of him for using his mind and doing so well. But I was embarrassed. I wanted—well, I wanted my son to follow in my footsteps. I wanted him to love what I loved."

"But he didn't?"

"I don't think he did. It's not a requirement. He loved his own work and I—well, I never bothered to figure out what that was or why he cared. But he was a—a manufacturer. A factory man. Eden, I know it sounds like nothing, but we smiths here, in this place, we are craftspeople. Factories are the enemies of artisans. Factories put an end to the Golden Age of Smiths. Almost put an end to us. That's really why there are no young people here. Because we're not needed anymore. We've been replaced by machines. All the smiths here know that. All of them twittered behind my back about my son being one of—of those people."

Eden rested her chin in her hands. "Did you ever think that maybe he loved other stuff, too. I mean, besides his work?"

"Like you?" said Vulcan.

"Like me. And Mom. Like maybe he worked for *us*. Some people work because they love their families."

Vulcan stacked a pile of small gears on the table, then knocked them over. "Eric came to see me. Years ago. Before you were born. It had been months since we'd spoken. It was nice, for a few minutes. Then he asked if I was still doing my hobbies. *Hobbies.* Smithing is not a hobby! I lost my temper and said things about his work. And maybe about him. He said—well, he said he didn't know why he bothered to visit. I told him he never had to come back. And—and, well, you know."

Eden picked up one of the gears. "He never did. He never came back."

"And every day, I thought to myself, *I should go see him. I should go visit.* Edna—your grandma—she did. She'd visit him. Oh, she would have loved you. I think that fight of ours—well, I think maybe it—well, she died before you were born."

"Did you know about me?"

"If I had, I would have come." The words rushed out of Vulcan's mouth, as if he could not hold them back. "Eden, if I'd only known—I'm sorry I didn't know. And I'm sorry I didn't come. I let you down. But I didn't know—about you. Not until the day you arrived here. The day I was sentenced. The day I was shamed." He laughed. "But Eden, that day might have..."

She turned toward Vulcan. "That day might have what?"

"Oh, I guess it just might have been the worst day of my life. When I learned my boy had died. But it might have been the best day, too."

"Because of me?"

"Saint Dunstan's beard! Yes, because of you, you little knucklehead." He brushed her faint scars with the back of his hand. He reached under the table and pulled out a small package wrapped in an oily rag.

"For me?" said Eden.

Vulcan nodded.

She unwrapped a pair of well-worn pliers and a coil of heavy wire. "The pliers are old," said Vulcan. "They're mine, from when I was your age, given to me by *my* grandfather. Grandpa Elemo. So that would be your great-great-grandfather, right? Anyway, your ancestor."

"My ancestor." Eden repeated his words as she opened and closed the pliers. "I love them. Thank you."

"Keep them with you. The wire, too. A smith should always have a pair of pliers and a bit of wire on them. Now, can we talk about something else?"

Eden laughed. "Yes. We can talk about something else. Smithing?"

"Rats," said Vulcan. "Let's talk about rats."

~ XXVII ~

In Which Eden Finds a Stack of Envelopes

The next morning, after breakfast, Eden and Nathaniel headed back to Records. They walked past the oiled metal doors of the gunsmiths and reached Sylvia's green door. They knocked. Sylvia opened the door a crack. She was dressed in a flowered silk robe. She wore a matching flowered fez on her head. The children could hear Bones sniffing on the other side of the door. "It is Sunday," Sylvia said. "Records is closed on Sundays. What is going on today? I have already had to turn someone else away this morning."

"Who else was here?" said Eden.

"That Uriah Pewtersmith woke me up early. I have always imagined him as a late sleeper. And then he wakes me early on a Sunday. I requested that he come back tomorrow during regular hours. If it wasn't for Bones, he would have forced his way in."

"What did he want?" said Eden.

"He did not say," said Sylvia, "but he's a master smith. You're not. If I didn't let him in, I'm sure not letting you. Come back tomorrow."

"Is there any way you could make an exception?" said Eden.

"I cannot," said Sylvia. "Sunday is my bath day. I wait all week for bath day."

"It won't take long," said Eden. "If you could please just let us in, we'll hurry."

Sylvia raised one eyebrow at them. "I'll tell you what," she said. "How about I let you in and give you all the time you need. I am longing for a long hot bath to ease my aching joints, but I have to go down to the Jones bathhouse—"

"Where is that?" asked Eden.

"Subbasement nine, if you must know."

Eden's mouth fell open. She longed to see what all the Jones levels looked like. If the floor Buzz had accidently shown her was so amazing, what might a Jones bathhouse look like? "How many subbasements are there?"

Sylvia smiled but ignored the question. "Now then, if you were to watch Bones while I soaked—he starts barking if I stay in too long. Ruins everything, the bad doggy. But if you watched him here, I could soak longer."

Nathaniel gulped. "You want us to do what?"

"Just watch Bones. I would never ask anyone else. But he likes you."

"How long will you be?" asked Eden.

"Two hours. Three at the most. Definitely no more than four."

"Four hours?" said Nathaniel. "With Bones?"

"Nathaniel, you are the only other person in the Guildhall he seems to like."

"He doesn't like me," said Nathaniel. "He just wants to eat me."

"Ignore Nathaniel," said Eden. "We'll do it."

Nathaniel stared at her in disbelief. "Are you crazy?"

Sylvia smiled and opened the door all the way. Bones growled at them, teeth bared. Sylvia stepped past them and pushed the two children inside. "He won't eat you, as long as you don't make loud noises or sudden movements. And as long as you stay away from Sealed Records." She slammed the door shut. Bones jumped at the noise and barked at the closed door.

"Niiice doggy," said Nathaniel. He slowly reached into his pocket, pulling out a jar. "Come here, Bones. Want some mahguj?" He flicked a glob of the brown jelly into the air. Bones caught it in his mouth and swallowed it whole, then licked his chops.

"Sit," said Nathaniel.

Bones sat so hard the room shook. "Hey, did you see that? Bones knows how to sit." Nathaniel gave him another blob of mahguj.

"Shake," said Nathaniel. Bones held out a massive paw. Nathaniel shook it and gave Bones another glob of brown goo.

"Speak," said Nathaniel. Bones barked and the gray-green cabinets rattled. "Good boy." Nathaniel gave Bones more mahguj.

"Now, Bones," said Eden. "If you want more, you'll have to let us into Sealed Records."

"Into what?" hissed Nathaniel. "Are you crazy? Do you want to die? Because I like being alive."

"We have to, Nathaniel. This is our chance."

"I don't know if I have that much mahguj." Nathaniel's eyes grew wide. "I don't know if there's that much mahguj in the whole world."

"Shh," said Eden. "No loud noises, remember."

Nathaniel gulped. He pulled another jar of mahguj out of his pocket. "I only have one jar left, so if you're really serious about doing this, you'd better hurry. Come on, Bonesy. Want another treat?"

Eden walked over to a red door. The sign on the door read Sealed Records. No Admittance. Bones growled when Eden touched the doorknob.

"Sit," said Nathaniel, holding up a glob of mahguj. Bones sat, but kept growling. Eden opened the door, slowly. Bones growled louder, rising up from the floor.

"I said *sit*," said Nathaniel. Bones sat, still growling, and Nathaniel flicked a glob of mahguj to him. "Now stay, Bones. Eden, go fast."

As quietly as she could, Eden slipped inside Sealed Records. Nathaniel closed her inside, so Bones couldn't see her, saying "Good boy, Bones. Have another bite. Hey, watch the fingers!"

Sealed Records was about ten feet square. It was crowded with cabinets that rose so far above Eden's head that she felt suddenly claustrophobic. All the filing cabinets in the Sealed Records section were painted red, all were covered in a thick layer of dust, and a round seal of wax was stamped across the top of every drawer.

Eden looked closely at one of the wax seals, which read 292. If she opened a drawer, the seal would be broken and anyone who looked—like Sylvia—would know the contents inside had been tampered with. "Saint Dunstan!" whispered Eden.

She took a deep breath, then another, trying to calm her nerves. She began scanning the drawer labels for anything that might mention the Five Impossible Tasks. She saw a sealed drawer labeled Turning Lead into Gold and another labeled Turning Gold into Lead. She saw a sealed drawer for Perpetual Motion Machines next to one for Singing Swords. She saw two cabinets next to each other, both labeled The Automaton Rebellion. In addition to a wax seal, steel chains wrapped around these cabinets. The chains were held together with massive padlocks. Finally, she reached a section labeled Criminal, just like the section in the main files.

I bet they put everything about my ancestors here, she thought, growing angry. Her anger chased away her anxiety and she began to scan the rest of the labels on the file drawers when a particular label caught her eye: Tasks, Five Impossible. She pulled the drawer open as carefully as she could, but the wax seal still broke. Inside was a stack of five red envelopes, each one labeled with the name of a Task: Dishes, Steel Birds, Rats, Mrs. Gunsmith's Girdle. The fifth envelope was labeled The Unknown Task. Eden realized that these were the stories of her family—how they'd been accused, how they'd fought back, and how they'd died. She lifted the envelopes to her nose and smelled them, as if the years of dust would connect her more deeply to her ancestors. She had a sudden urge to sit down on the floor and read the files right there.

Eden grabbed a cardboard box from a corner, dropped the five red envelopes into it, and covered it with the lid, which was lying next to it. She closed the red drawer and gave the wax seal a careful look. If anyone looked closely, they would see that the seal was broken. There was nothing she could do. She tapped her fingertips on the door. "Nathaniel? I'm coming out, okay?"

"O-okay," said Nathaniel. Eden could hear shaking in his voice. "But be quiet. And slow. I'm almost out of mahguj and Bones is looking hungrier than ever."

Eden eased the door open. "I think I found it all," she said, nodding at the box in her hands.

"Then hurry up and get it out of here," said Nathaniel. "Take it to your Grandpa's room before Sylvia gets back. And get more mahguj!"

Eden ran all the way down the stairs to Vulcan's room. She knocked on the door. When he opened, she shoved the box into his arms.

"What's all this?" said Vulcan.

"No time to explain!" shouted Eden. "Gotta get back!" She ran to Kitchens and swiped two more jars of mahguj, running them up the stairs and back to Records.

She found Nathaniel standing on top of a table, with Bones growling up at him. "See," said Eden. "I told you he likes you."

"Likes me?" said Nathaniel. "Look at my pants! He ate them."

The bottom of both of Nathaniel's checkered pant legs were torn away. Eden passed the jars of mahguj to Nathaniel.

Nathaniel fed the mahguj to Bones, bit by bit, but still ran out long before Sylvia returned. By then, both children were standing on the table.

"I think he wants to kill us," Eden said.

"He *wants to*," said Sylvia, scratching Bones behind his huge ears, "but he has not actually done it. Because he's such a good little puppy."

While Sylvia held Bones by his shiny metal collar, the children climbed down and exited Records. They took a few steps toward the elevator when one of the oiled gunsmith doors swung open. A large man stepped out into the hallway, blocking their escape.

"In a hurry?" he said. He was as big around as a barrel and had a smooth, shiny face. He wore a black leather vest and had a huge white mustache. He fingered an empty holster at his waist. "I know why you're here. The Tasks. One of those Tasks involves me." He nodded his head toward the door. "And my wife."

"You must be Mr. Gunsmith," said Eden. She wondered if his face was shiny because of beauty cream.

The man took a step toward them, his fingers itching at the holster, as if searching for the pistol that wasn't there. "I'm Dick Gunsmith. The senior gunsmith in this Guildhall. Now then, you gonna try it?"

"Yes," said Eden. "Not today. But at some point we will. We have to."

"You have to?" Mr. Gunsmith repeated. He took another step forward. "No one touches our historic girdle. If you have to *try* it, then you have to. But mark this: I'll do what *I have to do* to stop you. *Whatever* I have to do."

He stepped back inside his rooms and quietly shut the door.

"I think," said Nathaniel, "that Mr. Gunsmith is only slightly less scary than Bones."

"Maybe. But I see where he's coming from. I mean, *we* just did whatever *we* had to do. You know, to get information. That seems to be how people operate around here, don't you think? Doing what you have to do?"

"Mr. Gunsmith threatening us and you breaking into Sealed Records is not exactly an apples-to-apples comparison."

"Well, the risks are pretty huge in both cases."

Nathaniel sighed. "Whatever. I'm just glad we're not dead. Yet."

They hurried down to Vulcan's room. Vulcan let them in without speaking. "How'd we do?" asked Eden, nodding at the box of envelopes. "Did we get any answers?"

Vulcan nodded, but said nothing.

"Well, did it help?" said Eden.

Vulcan said, "I thought I was a clever smith. But my ancestors—our ancestors, Eden—it's amazing how they solved the Tasks. But it doesn't matter."

"What do you mean it doesn't matter? Is there stuff in there that helps us catch the rats?"

"Of course there is," said Vulcan. "Listen to how Lemerie caught them. So sainted brilliant.

In order to attract the rats, I began working my way through the five senses. Using various cheeses, I tried to lure them with taste. I used pheromones to try to lure them with smell. Then I tried sound and that was when I somehow cracked the code. It took me three months, using all sorts of recordings played back at all sorts of frequencies, but I finally discovered a supersonic frequency that rats cannot resist—a sound that calls them forth.

To achieve this frequency, I recorded the sound of a hammer repeatedly striking a steel bar. The ping of a hammer reads at the frequency of 175 hertz. But rats can hear ultrasonic frequency—up to 90 kilohertz, or 90,000 hertz—so I slowly increased the rate of playback until the frequency was so high that I could no longer hear the sound. I could still measure it, however, with a sound meter. Only by watching the gauge on the meter could I even tell the recording was still making any noise. When it reached the frequency of precisely 76.76 kilohertz, the most amazing thing happened. Dozens of rats squeezed under the bottom of my door. Other rats chewed holes through my wall. They all rushed toward my sound recorder, climbing all over it, trying to get close to the sound—the ping of a hammer played back at precisely 76.76 kilohertz."

"So that's it," said Eden. "That's how we solve the rats."

"That's how," said Vulcan. "If I were to get my cage assembled, we could set it in the center of the Guildhall, with an audio recorder in the middle. We could turn on the sound and all the rats would come running right into the cage. That would be it for the third Task." He tapped his finger on another envelope. "This here tells about the steel birds. It happened just as we expected. Burhanu used an electromagnet, but didn't have a backup power supply. So when Pewtersmith's ancestor cut the power, Burhanu didn't have enough time to find more electricity. He died, of course. According to the story in the envelope, the steel birds avoided recapture for three days. They nearly destroyed an entire floor of the Guildhall before they were returned to the attic."

"Anything about the dishes?" said Nathaniel.

Vulcan pulled out another envelope. "We got that one right, too. The room was indeed lined with steel so it could be superheated and used as a crucible. The pewter dishes were melted and the Task was completed."

"What about the floor?" said Eden. "Is there steel underneath all that melted pewter?"

Vulcan said, "There is. Unfortunately, Mordan failed at the next Task she tried and died in the rooms of Mrs. Gunsmith."

"What does it say about the girdle?" said Eden. "Is there a solution for that Task, too?"

Vulcan nudged an envelope with the tip of his aluminum leg. "There *was* a solution. But it doesn't help us any longer."

"Why not? It worked for one of our ancestors, right?" Eden reached down for the envelope. Vulcan put his foot on it and pressed it to the floor.

"It did," said Vulcan. "Too easily. So one of those damn Pewtersmiths declared that the Task was not impossible enough. They made it harder. More dangerous. No one has solved it since. And no one ever will."

"What do you mean?"

"I mean that I'm at a loss, Eden. If we give up, we'll be banished. We'll have to leave the Guildhall. But if we try this Task, someone will die. What if that someone is you?"

"You worry too much."

"Eden, none of our ancestors even made it this far. And this one—it was solved once, so they made it, well, deadly."

"But that's not fair."

"Not supposed to be fair," said Vulcan. "Supposed to be impossible."

"And what about the last Task—the fifth one? Did you read that?"

"I looked in the envelope, if that's what you mean," said Vulcan.

Eden said, "And?"

"And nothing," said Vulcan. "The envelope for the fifth Task is empty. There's nothing in it."

"Then what is it? You've never even told me what the fifth Task is," said Eden.

"I don't *know* what it is," said Vulcan. "No one does. And no one has ever tried it." He showed Eden the label of the envelope for the fifth Task. It read The Unknown Task.

"How can you complete a Task if you don't know what it is?" said Eden.

Vulcan smiled. "Sounds impossible, doesn't it?"

"But at least we've got one more solution."

"That's true," Vulcan said. He forced a smile. "We do have the answer for number three."

"So let's at least do that one," said Eden. "Maybe we'll figure something out about the next two in the meantime."

Vulcan nodded. "Okay. We'll try one more. We've got all the time we need. But I want us to be careful. I especially want *you* to be careful. If anything happened to you…well…well, let's agree to take it slowly. Safety first, right?"

"Safety first. You all keep saying that. But this is the most dangerous place I've ever been in my life."

XXVIII

Willard and Company

Eugene was still in the infirmary, recovering from his wounds, so Nellie and Irma procured an audio recorder and sound meter for Vulcan. Eden and Nathaniel joined Vulcan in his room for the test. The cage was still in pieces, so Vulcan had the recorder set on his table.

"Before you all arrived, I recorded a loop of an eight-pound hammer hitting a bar of steel, over and over," Vulcan said. "Listen." He played the audio file. *Ping ping ping ping…*

"It really is quite a lovely sound, isn't it?" Nellie waved her cane as if it were a baton and she was conducting an orchestra. "If I were a rat, I believe I'd already find it quite entrancing."

"That's what it sounds like at one hundred and seventy-five hertz," said Vulcan, pointing to the readout of the audio meter. The meter showed two numbers. "This one shows the frequency—one hundred seventy-five hertz. And this other one shows the decibel—how loud it is. Right now, it's just fifty decibels. Not very loud for this test. When we do the actual Task, it will need to be much louder. Then, to increase the frequency, we just play it back at a faster rate. So now, let's see what happens when we speed it up." Eden watched the frequency readout on the audio meter as her grandfather turned a knob on a remote control. The pings grew faster and higher in pitch. The frequency on the meter now showed 5,000 hertz—5 kilohertz. Eden looked around the room, keeping her eyes peeled for any rats. None appeared.

Vulcan turned the dial of the remote control even higher. The pinging was now at 15 kilohertz and Eden could barely hear it at all. It was like a distant ringing in her ears. Still no rats. Her grandfather turned the knob higher and the sound cut out altogether.

"I'm afraid you've turned it too high, dear," said Nellie. "Now we can't hear it at all."

Eden put her hand on Vulcan's shoulder. "Grandpa, this is your first real project since your house arrest. You're still pretty rusty. Maybe you need to get someone to help you."

"I'm fine!" shouted Vulcan, shaking off Eden's hand. "It's working just the way it's supposed to. *We* can't hear it, but rats can." He turned the remote-control dial higher and higher, but the only way Eden could tell the sound was rising in frequency was by the gauge on the meter: 30 kilohertz, 40 kilohertz—finally it reached 75 kilohertz and Vulcan stopped. "We're almost there," he said. "If this is going to work, just a slight turn on the dial and we should see Willard and his friends."

"Who is Willard?" said Nellie.

"The only rat I've found so far," smiled Vulcan. "See that little hole in the corner by the floor. Keep your eye on it." He turned the dial up slightly. It jumped to 77 kilohertz. He turned it down until it landed right on 76.76.

A few seconds later, the nose of a rat poked out of the hole. It twitched its whiskers, then lunged out a few more feet. Its whole body was black, save for one white ear. When it saw the humans in the room, it froze, then backed up a step. With the remote control, Vulcan turned up the volume on the recorder until the decibel meter read 60. Willard took a few more steps forward, his whiskers twitching. Vulcan turned up the volume again, to 70, and Willard rushed across the room and climbed up Nellie's skirts.

"I don't like to use harsh language," said Nellie, "but this is horrible. I'm afraid I shall scream if he doesn't get off of me."

A second later, Willard leaped onto the table, rushed to the recorder, and began rubbing himself against it. "Will you look at that?" said Vulcan. "It works."

"Don't sound so surprised, Grandpa."

"It feels like the old days. I made something that actually works."

"Willard is in love," said Irma, sipping from her teacup. "He wants to marry your audio recorder."

"He does seem to be rather infatuated with it," said Nellie, brushing her skirts down. "Perhaps a bit too infatuated. Vulcan, see what happens when you turn it off."

Vulcan nodded and pushed the stop button on the remote. The numbers on the meter remained steady. "This sainted thing," said Vulcan. "Still got a few bugs, I guess." He gave the remote control a whack and the numbers dropped to zero. Willard stopped rubbing against the recorder. He looked confused and began sniffing around the table, as if he had lost something. Vulcan turned the recorder back on, and Willard rushed back to the recorder and began rubbing against it again.

"Oh, the poor little dear," said Nellie. "He is in love, and we are toying with his heart."

Vulcan was about to turn the sound off again, when they heard a scratching noise. Another nose poked under Vulcan's door. Another rat squeezed through. Then dozens of rats followed. Dozens more came out of Willard's hole in the wall. They rushed toward the table. "Now I believe I shall scream for real," said Nellie. She screamed. More rats climbed and jumped onto the table, pushing toward the audio recorder until the top of the table was a pile of scurrying rats. "Oh, turn it off, Vulcan!" shouted Nellie. "Turn it off!"

Vulcan turned the dials down on the remote control, but nothing happened. He danced around the table, looking for some way into the center of the pile of rats. He grimaced and thrust his hand right into the densest part. He opened a panel on the side of the recorder and flipped a switch. The scurrying stopped. The rats grew still, then sniffed one another. A few bounded off the table and ran back the way they had come. The rest followed, jumping and running, until only Willard remained. Willard sniffed around the table, cocking his head from side to side.

"So many rats," said Nellie. "I had no idea we had *any*, much less dozens and dozens. I do not like them."

Vulcan shrugged. "Guess I better fix this remote."

"Are you sure you don't want me to get you some help, Grandpa? I could ask Anit Irenya to come and look at it with you."

"Just trust me, can't you?" said Vulcan. He pulled a piece of cheese from his pocket and held it out to the white-eared rat. Willard sniffed it, backed away, then finally took the cheese in his teeth. He scurried back to his hole.

"The poor dear seems disappointed," said Nellie.

Irma said, "He came for love, but he left with cheese. A classic story of heartbreak."

Eden told Vulcan that she did trust him, but she still spent her afternoons for the next week and a half helping him run dozens more tests with the audio recorder until it worked every time. To begin attracting rats, they had to hit a frequency of 76.76 megahertz. To attract more, they simply turned up the volume. Finally, they finished assembling the cage as well.

"It seems like we're ready to go," she said.

"As ready as we'll ever be," said Vulcan. "Can't think of anything we might have overlooked."

Eden hurried up to Supperdinner Hall, making it inside just before the last bell. As she was approaching Nellie and Irma's table, she noticed Mr. Pewtersmith sitting at one of the outer-ring tables. She could tell it was a table of locksmiths because the men and women there had keys hanging from their belts. Mr. Pewtersmith had his back to her, so she couldn't hear what he was saying. All she could see were the opened mouths and furrowed brows of the locksmiths listening to him. One of them, a small bald man, looked at Eden, then quickly looked away.

She found her seat. When Nellie and Irma asked about the

preparations of the Task, Eden said it all seemed to be going fine. *So why don't I feel fine? What's Mr. Pewtersmith up to?* She knew it couldn't be good.

They attempted the third Impossible Task two days later, right after breakfast.

The Council was gathered in Humble Gallery, the entryway of the Guildhall. Eden, Nathaniel, the sisters, and about two dozen other smiths stood under the light of a merry-go-round-sized chandelier. Robert Blacksmith was the last councilmember to arrive. Eden watched him stomp down the wide stairway, march across the floor, and rest a hand on the column of Saint Dunstan. He nodded at Eden.

Eugene and two Blue Coats escorted Vulcan into the room. Vulcan frowned when he saw the crowd. "What are all these gawkers doing here?"

"I might have accidentally mentioned a few words about it to one or two very close friends," said Nellie.

"Looks like you sent out invitations," said Vulcan. He checked his equipment. The audio recorder was secured inside a steel box that sat in the middle of the cage he had built. Vulcan held the small remote control in his hands. "Recorder has full batteries. Frequency is already set, so all I have to do is turn it on with the remote. Eden has the audio meter, just to make sure we're getting a signal. I installed a powerful amplifier and turned the volume halfway up, and at that level, every rat in this place should hear it. We won't hear a thing, of course. I tested the trapdoors with Willard and he could get in, but couldn't get out. Have I missed anything? Anything that could hurt Eden?"

"Nothing is guaranteed, my dear," said Nellie.

"I wouldn't be able to live with myself if I hurt her somehow. Maybe we should forget the whole thing."

"Nonsense. We're quite ready." Nellie nodded to Robert Blacksmith.

Robert shouted to the assembly. "I'm glad so many of you came. This is the first time we've had a quorum of councilmembers since our recent tragic incident with the steel birds, and since the removal of Uriah Pewtersmith from the Council. Therefore, I should like to take this time to announce that we have received a nomination for a new councilmember." He pulled out a piece of paper and unfolded it. "We have a nomination for Lawrence Locksmith as the newest member of the Council. Lawrence, are you present?"

A small, bald man stepped forward out of the crowd. Eden recognized him as the same man from the table of locksmiths that Mr. Pewtersmith had spoken to a few evenings before. The man used a walker. Keys of all sizes hung from it. He held onto the walker with shaky fingers. "P-p-present."

Robert Blacksmith smiled and nodded. "Lawrence, I assume your answer will be yes, but do you accept this nomination?"

Lawrence glanced around the room. "I really would—I'd like to, but—"

"But what?" boomed Robert. "Is it a yes, locksmith?"

"Nnn-no," said Lawrence. "I'm afraid not. I can't. At this time."

"You can't?" shouted Robert, fingering the hammer at his waist. "You are refusing a nomination to join the Council?"

"At this time," said Lawrence. His fingers shook so much that all the keys on his walker began to jangle like tiny bells.

"We won't be asking again," said Robert, fighting to control his temper. "You will go down in history as the only smith ever to turn down a Council nomination."

Eden spotted Mr. Pewtersmith leaning against a far wall. He was smiling.

"So be it," said Robert Blacksmith. "We will look to others who recognize the honor. But now to the matter at hand." Robert read the terms and conditions of the Impossible Task. "This is the third of five Tasks. Eden has already proven herself to be a historic smith by completing two. We wish her luck today, and with the two remaining Tasks to come. Today, Eden must capture all the rats in the Guildhall, between sunrise and sunset of the same day."

"Seems like a cheap alternative to hiring an exterminator," said Irma.

"I have lived here seventy-seven years," said Helena Bladesmith, "and I have never seen a single rat. If you catch even one, Eden, I will be surprised."

"Get ready to be surprised, then," said Eden. "You all may want to back away from that cage. And keep the corridors clear." She nodded to her grandfather. Vulcan pushed the button on the remote control.

It appeared to everyone in the room that nothing happened. None of the smiths or Blue Coats could hear the sound. Only Eden, holding the sound meter, could tell that the recorder was working. It was transmitting at precisely 76.76 kilohertz, at a volume of 90 decibels.

Everyone waited. A full minute had passed when Mr. Pewtersmith stepped across Humble Gallery, smiling at Vulcan. "What did you expect from this criminal?" he said. He stopped next to the cage and gestured at it. "This is further proof of the man's ineptitude. Proof that it was Vulcan, and certainly not me, who was to blame for the tragedy with the steel birds."

Just then, Mr. Pewtersmith cocked his head. He turned. All the smiths turned with him. They watched a single rat run from the direction of Supperdinner Hall.

"You see. Everything is working fine," said Vulcan. "And, as Eden said, you may want to back away from that cage."

"For one rat?" Mr. Pewtersmith laughed. "If that's the best these fools can do—" His voice was drowned out by a rising thrum of scratches and squeaks. The doors of Supperdinner Hall burst open as a stampede of rats streamed through.

The crowd screamed and rushed out of the way. But another stampede was skittering down the stairway. From every direction, rats came, running along the walls and across the floor. The smiths had nowhere to escape. They backed around the cage in the center of the room—the exact destination of the rats.

The rats ran through the smiths standing there. They ran under them and over them. Helena Bladesmith fainted as a rat ran up the front of her dress and right over her head. More rats scurried over her prone body. Mr. Pewtersmith gave a high-pitched scream as rats climbed over him. Even Robert Blacksmith roared—in a much lower voice—as rats scurried over his huge frame.

Hundreds of rats forced their way into the cage and surrounded the steel box in the center of it. Those that couldn't reach the box pushed against their neighbors, until the cage was a solid mass of swarming, squirming rats.

Within two minutes, nearly all the rats had entered the cage through the trapdoors. A few dozen stragglers still ran across the floor of Humble Gallery, including a large black rat with one white ear. Willard. He had run all the way up from Subbasement Seven. He pushed through one of the cage's trapdoors and into the swarm of rats.

Nellie knelt down next to Helena Bladesmith, touching the unconscious woman's cheeks with the back of her hand. "Is it over?" said Helena.

Nellie stroked Helena's forehead. "They are captured, Helena dear. All safe and sound inside Vulcan's cage."

"Give it another minute or so, just to make sure," said Vulcan, "but that should be all of them."

"Remarkable," said Robert Blacksmith. "Revolting, but remarkable. How does it work, Vulcan?"

Vulcan smiled. "Ultrahigh-frequency sound. If you get the frequency precisely right, the rats can't resist it. Not sure why."

"It's the frequency of rat love," said Irma.

No more rats appeared. Vulcan pushed a button on the remote control to turn the sound off. Eden watched, expecting the decibel number on the sound meter to drop to zero. Instead, it increased, from ninety decibels to one hundred. The rats swarmed even more.

"That's funny," said Vulcan. "I just turned the sound off, but the rats are still going crazy."

"It didn't go off, Grandpa," said Eden. "Somehow, you just turned up the volume."

"No matter," said Robert Blacksmith. "I declare this Task completed." He slapped Vulcan on the back and the crowd of smiths cheered, even as a few of them looked nervously around the room for more rats.

"Damn this remote," said Vulcan. "Guess it still has a few bugs.

I don't understand why this won't turn off." He pushed the button another time. Again, the numbers on the decibel meter jumped up. The rats squeaked louder and rolled so crazily around the cage that the entire cage began to jerk around the room.

"Now it's twice as loud as when you started, Grandpa," said Eden.

"Saint Dunstan's beard! That's not good!" said Vulcan. "We need to turn that thing off before all those rats hurt themselves."

Eden couldn't help staring at the sound meter. Even though she could hear nothing, the ultrahigh frequency was now set at 140 decibels.

"One-forty—that's as loud as a jet plane," said Nathaniel. "Every rat for a mile around must be able to hear it."

Eden's gaze darted around the room. "But if they can all hear it, and they can't resist it—"

She never finished her thought. Two windows shattered. The front doors of the Guildhall burst inward. Thousands of rats poured into the building.

The crowd of smiths ran for the stairs. Only Vulcan stood his ground, as rats filled the hall, circling around the cage, looking for a way in. Eden shouted at him, "How long until the batteries run out on the recorder?"

"I just changed them!" Vulcan shouted back. "We'll have every rat in Tacoma here by the time they run out. We need to shut the recorder off from inside the cage."

"Smash it with a hammer!" shouted Robert Blacksmith. He pulled his hammer from his belt and surged forward.

"No!" said Eden, jumping in front of Robert. "You'll kill hundreds of rats if you do that. You can't hurt them. Grandpa, can't you open the cage?"

"The only way in is the trapdoor," he said. "And it's fourteen inches wide—too small to fit through."

"Not for me!" shouted Eden.

"No!" shouted Vulcan. "This is just the kind of thing that Pewtersmith is counting on. Something going wrong. Someone getting hurt. We'll just need to wait."

"I wish we *could* wait," said Eden, "because I really hate rats." She took a deep breath, as if she were about to jump in a lake. Then she dove into the swarm of rats.

It was more like swimming than crawling. Rats were under her, over her, in front of her, and behind her. It felt like it took forever just to reach the cage. She pulled herself, bar by bar, to the nearest trapdoor. She felt dozens of rats inside her clothing and all over her hair. As she fought her way through, her grandfather yelled instructions to her: "There's a panel on the right side of the box. Just slide it open and flip off the power switch."

"Which side is the right side?" shouted Eden. Or she tried to shout, but every time she opened her mouth, she tasted rat. She clamped her lips shut.

Eden reached the trapdoor and began pushing her way through. She had to be careful not to crush the rats under her. She just fit, but the inside of the cage was even more crowded with rats. And the closer she came to the black box, the thicker the rats became.

She wanted to scream. Every molecule of her body wanted to rush away from the rats, as she felt their tiny claws and naked tails on her skin. She closed her one good eye and prayed that her eye patch would stay in place. She felt her way along until her hand touched the box. It seemed like it took hours to find the little panel as she felt her way all around the box—she finally touched it on the third side she tried. She pushed it open and flicked off the power.

Eden had imagined that with the flick of that switch, the worst would be over, but the audio recorder had kept all the rats going in one direction. As soon as it turned off, they went every which way. Before, all they had noticed was the sound. Now, they noticed Eden. They squeaked at her, ran toward her and away from her, all at once.

She fought her way back to the trapdoor. Vulcan was holding it open and rats were pouring out of it. Eden poured out of it, too, carried along on a river of escaping rats. As soon as she was out, Vulcan let the door shut, trapping the rest of the rats inside.

There were thousands and thousands of rats outside the cage. With no sound calling to them, they ran all around Humble Gallery, running up the stairs, rushing into Supperdinner Hall, running down into the basement, and running back through the crowds of screaming master smiths.

Above the screams of the smiths and the squeaks of the rats, she could hear the voice of her grandfather. "Don't worry!" Vulcan shouted. "We'll catch them all again! It might take me a few days. But we'll catch them."

XXIX

Mr. Pewtersmith's Voice

Vulcan finally gave in and asked Anit Irenya to help him fix the audio recorder and remote control. In the meantime, rats were everywhere, climbing over tables in Supperdinner Hall, hiding between sheets in people's beds, even scurrying across the floor of Buzz's elevator.

"If this is what comes from smithing," shouted Lillian Jones, "then I want no part of it. Do you know how many rats I found in my kitchen? Seventy-two! I found one swimming in my soup pot. I found one gorging itself on an open jar of mahguj. I have to check the oven before I turn it on, just to make sure I don't cook any of the furry little devils."

Lillian had called Nathaniel back to full-time duties, and he spent all his time catching rats in the kitchen. He named each of them as he returned them to Vulcan's cage. "I wish we could keep them," Nathaniel said. "I'd keep them all if I could. Look how cute they all are. Like this little guy here. See how he looks like a smaller version of Willard? I named him Junior. *Willard* Junior."

By midnight, Vulcan and Anit had fixed the volume control on the audio recorder and recaptured all the rats. Vulcan had already emptied the cage of the original rats and now used it again to trap the rats that had come in from out of doors. Using the volume carefully, he attracted thousands of rats from inside the Guildhall, but didn't bring in any new ones from outside.

"If there are even any *left* outside," said Nellie, as she watched the proceedings from on top of a chair. "Vulcan, what did you do with them all?"

"It's strange," said Vulcan. "Those little creatures grow on you. I'll keep Willard with me, if he'll have me. And all those other rats—who knows how many were related to Willard? So...let's just say that Nathaniel and I found a place to release them where they won't bother anyone—at least not anyone I like."

"Where?" said Nellie.

"Safe and sound," said Vulcan. "That's all you need to know. Isn't that right, Nathaniel?"

"Safe and sound," Nathaniel said.

"Nathaniel!" said Eden. "Where are they?"

"I can't tell you," Nathaniel said. "Vulcan swore me to secrecy,"

At dinner the next night, Eden sat between Nellie and Irma. Nellie said, "Dearie, I just wish all this were over. It is too much. And watching you climb into that cage, well—I began to wonder if perhaps Vulcan was right. You've already lost an eye. Perhaps we should quit before you get even more seriously hurt."

"No!" said Eden. "The rats weren't that bad. I mean, they were horrible, but—" She stopped talking.

"But what, dearie?"

"Shhh," said Eden. "Listen." She turned around. Mr. Pewtersmith was at the table closest to them, on the outer ring. It was a table of tinsmiths and coppersmiths. With her good eye, Eden spotted Fred Tinsmith sitting across from Mr. Pewtersmith. Fred's arms were folded across his chest.

The room was loud, but Mr. Pewtersmith's voice boomed and Eden could hear most of what he was saying: "Mark my words, those rats were not the end of the trouble that man and his meddlesome granddaughter have caused. Remember the first Task, how he almost burned the whole Guildhall down?"

"Didn't burn anything down," said Fred.

"I said *almost*," said Mr. Pewtersmith. "One old door was all that kept us from dying in a blazing inferno. Not exactly *safety first*. And then look at what happened with those horrid birds. His own grandchild lost an eye. Our beloved Eugene nearly killed—"

"Never knew you cared much for Eugene," interrupted Fred.

"Certainly I care for him," said Mr. Pewtersmith, looking shocked. "And poor, dear Iona, the best of the Blue Coats, nearly cut down in her prime."

"That was your fault," said Fred. "If it wasn't, you'd still be on the Council."

"Speculation! Unproven rumors. Nothing more." Mr. Pewtersmith drummed his long fingers together. "And, Fred Tinsmith, let me ask you a simple yes or no question. If Vulcan hadn't partaken in such a dangerous enterprise in the first place, would Iona have even been attacked?"

"Like you give two bits about—"

"*Yes or no*, Fred. And the answer, by the way, is yes. She would still be unhurt. But she's not. And there are two Tasks yet to go." Mr. Pewtersmith rose to his feet. "So let me leave you with this warning. Beware of Vulcan and his granddaughter. If anyone gets involved with these...these deathmongers, then they are asking for the worst kind of trouble. They might as well invite the grim reaper to watch over them while they sleep."

Eden's face flushed with rage.

The next morning, Miss Clara delivered nothing more than breakfast. Eden was half relieved and half maddened with anticipation. That evening, the meal was sardines and toast, and the entire Supperdinner Hall smelled like fish. Eden felt a little sick and excused herself. As she was walking toward the exit, she heard Mr. Pewtersmith's voice again. She spotted him at a table of gunsmiths, so she quietly took an empty seat at a table behind him, where he couldn't see her, but where she could just hear the conversation.

Since the completion of the third Task, she'd thought constantly about whatever was in the envelope that Vulcan had hidden from her. He'd said that it had the solution to the Task of Mrs. Gunsmith's Girdle. But he'd also said it didn't matter anymore, because the Task had changed and it was now too dangerous to even consider.

Were the gunsmiths really that dangerous? She kept imagining the horrid battle images on their oiled metal doors. They kept to themselves. Even if everyone else in Supperdinner Hall was laughing at a joke or singing a song, the gunsmiths often looked grim. They all dressed in black, all the time.

She thought back to a dinner weeks earlier. She had asked Nellie about the gunsmiths. Nellie had said, "They're very serious about everything they do. Smithing, eating, facial creams—they never shirk. But they rarely smile, either. Still…" Her voice trailed off.

Kerlin Arrowsmith, sitting with a potted pink flower in front of him, had interrupted. "Still, indeed. With all due respect to the late Mrs. Arrowsmith, there is something, *ahem*, appealing about them. Yes, sir."

"They are all undeniably beautiful." Nellie had said as she touched the wrinkles at the corners of her eyes. "I must remember to ask Mrs. Gunsmith for another jar of her skin cream."

"They really hardly ever smile? *Ever?*" Eden had asked.

"Not that I have noticed," Nellie'd answered. "The Gunsmiths are a jealous lot. You are seeing them at their happiest, dearie. In this Supperdinner Hall, I mean. Other than smithing, they have a great passion for food. They are constantly giving menu suggestions to Kitchens."

"The one thing they never complain about is mahguj," Irma had said. "They put it on everything. They go through jars and jars of it."

Back in the present, Eden leaned her head toward the gunsmith table. She heard Mr. Pewtersmith speaking. "Of course, Vulcan has every right to attempt the Tasks," he said, "but does he also have a right to put the rest of us in danger? So far, he almost burned down the Guildhall, he released deadly birds that resulted in serious injuries, and he brought in who knows how many diseases into the building, with all those vermin. How much more are we willing to put up with?"

"How much more is there?" asked the large mustached man Eden had seen outside the Gunsmith rooms. He stabbed a sardine with his knife and shoved the whole fish into his mouth.

"You should know the answer to that, Dick," said Mr. Pewtersmith. "Two more Tasks. One has to do with your very own Guild." Mr. Pewtersmith leaned in close. "The dangerous eye of Vulcan Smith is turning toward you."

The large, smooth-skinned woman next to Dick Gunsmith nodded. "Toward the girdle, you mean. I've thought about that, Mr. Pewtersmith. If we were to just *give* the girdle to Vulcan, then all this trouble could be avoided. After all, the girdle was already altered once, long ago."

Eden wondered what Mrs. Gunsmith meant—about the girdle being altered—but her thoughts were interrupted by Mr. Pewtersmith. "Is that what you want, Dick? For this strange little man to be in possession of your historic girdle. Of your own legendary artifact?"

Dick Gunsmith turned the knife slowly over in his hands. "You think Vulcan's a dangerous man, eh? You want to see a dangerous man? Anyone comes near that girdle, and you'll see real danger." He stabbed the knife through the head of the last sardine on his plate. "Where's the mahguj? Someone pass me more mahguj."

The next morning, no fourth Task arrived. Eden and Nathaniel should have begun their next round of apprentice training, but they had not been assigned to a new master smith. The master smiths who were friendly toward Vulcan were already busy with the many Blue Coats and other Joneses who were waiting to learn smithing. Nellie and Irma were consumed with their jobs as Apprentice Masters. Everyone else who Nellie asked had refused to take on Eden and Nathaniel.

"It's that horrible Uriah Pewtersmith," Nellie said to the children. "He has this whole Guildhall scared of you poor young innocents."

"What could possibly be scary about us?" demanded Eden.

"It's not you, particularly," said Nellie. "It's the devastation that follows you around. Birds and rats and such."

Lillian demanded that Nathaniel work in Kitchens if he had nothing else to do. He grumbled as he left. Eden decided to go to the infirmary and visit Eugene.

"He is almost ready to be discharged," said Dr. Jones, when Eden arrived. "Even so, don't get him too excited. He still needs to take it easy for the next few weeks."

"Oh, come on, Doc," said Eugene. "I've never felt better. At least not in the last ten years. I've never had more than one day off before. Laying around like this has been good for me."

Dr. Jones demanded that Eden submit to a brief examination of her face and eye. When he finished, he smiled and gave her shoulder a squeeze. "You're coming right along. And Fabergé tells me you're progressing very well in OT." By now Eden had had numerous consultations with Fabergé Jones, the occupational therapist. Eden smiled, too.

After the doctor left, Eden pulled a chair next to Eugene's bed and told him about the conversation she'd overheard at the gunsmith's table. Eugene listened, then said, "That Dick Gunsmith—he gives even me the creeps. Getting *anything* from them, much less getting the girdle, is gonna be tough. But I thought Vulcan already had this one figured out."

"I've already told you that there was a solution—from Sealed Records—if that's what you mean. And I've told you that Grandpa would not share it with me and that he said it doesn't matter anymore. The Task has changed. I don't know anything else, except that the new Task scares him."

"I can't imagine much that would scare Vulc," said Eugene. "It must be pretty bad." His frown turned to a smile. "Hey, how's it going with the new recruits—with all the Joneses?"

Eden gave him an update. Eugene laughed when she told him how proud Buzz was of the crude, misshapen knives he made with Helena Bladesmith. He laughed even louder when she told how Mr. Pewtersmith had been forced to cover Buzz's shifts operating the elevator.

"It's a good thing you're doing, Eden," said Eugene. "One I wish someone would have done for me."

"What do you mean?" said Eden. "You're already a smith. Aren't you?"

Eugene shook his head no. "Not a smith. I'm a tinker." He held out his left hand. "See the tinker ring on my little finger? Has our tinker symbol on it."

Eden bent close to Eugene's rough hand. Etched into the surface of the pinkie ring was an image of a hammer and a knife. "All tinkers wear a ring just like this. Tinkers don't usually make things. They usually only fix things. Most tinkers are travelers, going from town to town. That's what my old dad did. What I used to do." Eugene twisted his pinkie ring. "Other than Tacoma, I like France best. Some nice metal work, especially in Marseilles. Paris is nice, too. Old Gustave Eiffel hired some of the world's best smiths to make his tower. Paris used to have one of the best Guildhalls, back when I was younger, but it shut down years ago. The Marseilles Hall is still surviving, though, last I checked."

"There are other places like this?"

"Used to be hundreds." Eugene smiled. "In the Golden Age of Smiths, there were three hundred and fifty-six Guildhalls. This one here is one of the later ones—number two hundred ninety-two."

"Where is the first one?"

"Glastonbury, of course. In England."

"Is that something I should know?"

"It is, especially since you have so much interest in the Joneses, too."

"Can you tell me about it?"

"Help me sit up a bit, and I'll give it a try."

Eden propped another pillow behind Eugene's head. He took a deep breath and began. "Saint Dunstan was born in Glastonbury, in what is now England, in the year nine-oh-nine."

"Before he was a saint?" asked Eden.

"Yeah. Before he was a saint. Not many baby saints. Anyway, as a young boy, Dunstan, an orphan—"

"Like me," said Eden. "I was an orphan before I came here."

"But you ain't one now," said Eugene. "Now you're a smith. As I was saying, Dunstan studied under the Irish monks who occupied the ruins of Glastonbury Abbey. Even as a child, Dunstan was known for his devotion to learning. He worked harder than anyone. When he was still in his teens, he was already a master of many kinds of crafts, but mostly was a master of smithing silver and steel. He became so well known that he was appointed as smith to the court of King Athelstan—the first king to rule the whole of England.

"Dunstan's amazing artistry in metalworking made him a favorite of the king. The two were more like father and son—the high king and the humble smith. This also made Dunstan the envy of other members of the court. So a plot was hatched to disgrace him."

"A plot," said Eden. "Sounds like something a Pewtersmith would do."

Eugene nodded. "Anyway, Dunstan's enemies accused him of witchcraft and black magic. How else could he turn raw metal into swords and crowns? Of course, we know that smithing ain't magic. It's craft. But King Athelstan was deceived into believing these lies and he banished Dunstan from the court."

Eden gulped.

"As Dunstan was leaving the palace, his enemies tied him up, beat him almost to death, and threw him into the sewer."

"Gross."

"No kidding. Dunstan barely survived. He wandered the countryside, working at his craft wherever he could and eventually settled back in the town of Glastonbury as the village smith. Again, he became renowned for his mastery. Glastonbury was ruled by Lady Athelflaed, who just happened to be King Athelstan's niece. Lady Athelflaed made Dunstan her trusted adviser and, on her death, she left all her money to him. He used her money to build the first Guildhall. In fact, Guildhall number one is still in Glastonbury today. But Dustan, innocent Dunstan, was still banished from the presence of the king.

"One day, King Athelstan rode out to hunt a stag in Mendip Forest. He followed the stag at a full gallop, right toward the Cheddar cliffs. The poor stag rushed right over the cliff edge, followed by the king's hounds. Athelstan was sure that he, too, was going to plunge over the cliffs and die. As he heaved back on the reigns of his horse, his mind went to Dunstan, how unfair he, Athelstan, had been to the smith and how much he missed him. If somehow his life was spared, Athelstan promised to make it right.

"Miraculously, his horse somehow stopped on the very edge of the cliff. The king turned his horse and rode straight to the Glaston-bury Guildhall. He knelt down and took Dunstan by the hand, gave him the kiss of peace, and promised, right on the floor of the first Guildhall, that he and all his descendants would serve Dunstan and all his descendants, always." Eugene took a deep breath. "That's the end."

"Cool story," said Eden, "but what's it have to do with the Joneses?"

Eugene smiled. "Dunstan was the founder of our Guild and the father of all smiths who came after him. King Athelstan had no sons, but had one daughter, Matilda. Matilda was wed to a Welsh lord named Iowan. Iowan is the ancient Welsh form of Jon. So Iowan's—and King Athelstan's—descendants ended up with the surname *Jones*, which literally means *the offspring of Jon*. In other words, all Joneses are pledged to serve the offspring of Dunstan. Dunstan had no children, but, like I said, he was the father of all modern smiths. All of the Guild-halls trace themselves back to Dunstan. And all the descendants of Athelstan—the Joneses—consider it a great honor to fulfill their oath and to serve smiths. Well, most of them do. Nowadays, the smiths don't do quite as good a job respecting that honor, but in the smiths' defense, the Joneses *are* paid very well, and always in gold and silver coins." He smiled. "Come to think of it, them coins may be the real reason they stick around. I've heard some of them are quite rich. And I've heard that their floors—way down in the subbasements—ain't too bad, either."

Eden pictured the rolling green grass of the Jones floor she had accidentally visited. "You've never seen them?"

"Not allowed. Jones-only access."

"I know, but still, haven't you seen them at least once? Just a peek?"

Eugene shook his head.

Eden said, "Well, if you ever decide to go see them, please take me with you." Then she smirked. "So if I understand this correctly, the smiths are descendants of plain old smiths, while the Joneses are descended from an actual *king*."

Eugene smiled. "The smiths try not to hold it against them."

Eden laughed. "How many Guildhalls are left?"

"Last time I made a tour, there were only eleven. That's why I decided to stop traveling. It was too sad to visit the old Halls and see them closing down. This one, here in Tacoma, is one of the best." Eugene twisted his pinky ring again. "As far as my place here within the order of things, I take pride in being a tinker. We're as ancient a Guild as any. But being a tinker in this place does not give me the same rights as a smith."

"That's the *old* order," said Eden. "That's all changed now. Eugene, if you want to be a smith, you can. Just like the Joneses. I'll make sure of that."

"A smith," said Eugene. He looked up to the ceiling. "Wonder if I could do it."

"Of course, you could," said Eden, patting Eugene's rough hand.

"Kid, when you're as old as I am, a change like that don't exactly come easy."

Eden thought back to how she had often seen Eugene standing outside Supperdinner Hall when she had gone in with the sisters. "Is that why you don't eat with us?"

Eugene shrugged. "No tinkers allowed in Supperdinner Hall. Only smiths."

"That's horrible."

Eugene sighed. "I still get to eat. I socialize with everyone here, just not during smiths' mealtimes. Eden, my life ain't been that bad. I got a home here. I mean, I kept thinking that I could someday, somehow become a smith. I kept waiting for someone to make an exception. But hey, now here you are, making things happen." He reached for a tissue on the table near his bed and blew his nose, as loud as a saxophone. "You're good people, Eden Smith. That Nathaniel—he's pretty good, too."

⁓

The next morning, Miss Clara snapped, "No need to ask me, Eden. When I have a tin can for you, I'll let you know." Eden took the breakfast tray from her without speaking. Fifteen minutes later, Nathaniel met Eden to see if there was any news about their apprentice training.

"I do indeed have news," said Nellie, as she collected the breakfast dishes onto a silver tray.

Eden was still holding onto her breakfast spoon. She began to bend it. "You found a master smith for us?"

"A master smith?" Nellie shook her head. "I'm afraid not."

"No one likes you anymore," said Irma with a smile.

"Now, that's not true, sister," said Nellie, as she put the last pewter teacup on the tray. "Give me that spoon, Eden, before you destroy it completely. Thank you, dear. My suspicions were correct that Uriah Pewtersmith has been spreading lies about you. Dearies, I just spoke to Lawrence Locksmith. I thought for sure he would take you on. But he said he was too afraid. 'Afraid of what?' I asked him. 'Of the danger,' he said. He explained that Uriah had convinced him that anyone involved with you or Vulcan was just asking for trouble. Uriah Pewtersmith has reminded them all of one of the remaining Tasks—Mrs. Gunsmith's Girdle."

"What about our apprenticeship?" said Nathaniel. "If we can't find a new teacher, can't we just go work with an old one some more? Like Fred Tinsmith?"

"I'm afraid Fred is busy, dearies," said Nellie. "He has four Blue Coats working with him already. But then an unexpected person came forward and offered to train you for the next two weeks. At first, I rejected the offer, as it's a bit of an unorthodox idea, but I must say, after giving it thought, I like it more and more. It seems both reasonable and just. So I agreed."

"It's not Pewtersmith, is it?"

"Uriah? Heavens, no!"

"Then who?"

A sharp knock sounded on the door. "That should be your new teacher now," said Nellie.

"I'm here," said a woman's voice outside.

Nathaniel's face turned white. "No!" he said. "No no no!"

Nellie opened the door and let in Lillian Jones.

XXX

Kitchens

Mom!" said Nathaniel. "What are you doing here?"

Lillian smiled. "I'm to be your teacher. Six days a week for the next two weeks."

"But you're not a smith!" said Nathaniel.

"Of course I'm not. I'm a Jones. What difference does that make? The two of you keep reminding us that names don't matter. That a Jones can be a smith. Well then, as people are now pointing out, why can't a smith learn the work of a Jones? Why can't a smith learn to be a doctor? Or an astrophysicist? Or a cook?"

"Why would they want to cook?" shouted Nathaniel.

"Nathaniel Jones! Don't you dare say another word against the work I do—against the work we've always done."

"Fine," said Nathaniel. "I won't say another word about it. But I already know how to work in a kitchen. I'm not going."

"Oh, yes you are. Nellie already agreed. So did Vulcan. For the next two weeks, you two are the students and I—well—I am the teacher."

"And you have to do what she says," said Nellie. "If you want to continue in your apprenticeship, you have to do what Lillian says."

"Sounds okay to me," said Eden. "I've always wanted to learn how to really cook."

Nathaniel glared at his mother. Lillian tapped Eden on the head with her wooden spoon. "Thank you, Eden. Now then, you two are already late for your first day. Nathaniel, I assume you know the way."

Eden giggled as she followed Nathaniel to Kitchens.

Eden had been inside Kitchens many times before, but never as an apprentice. She saw it differently now, as a place of work—as a workshop. Like the shops of smiths she'd apprenticed in, the walls and shelves were covered with tools. But instead of hammers and tongs, the tools were knives, spoons, ladles, colanders, and pots of all sizes. The worktables—Lillian called them *stations*—were made of stainless steel. There were even fires of sorts: stoves, ovens, and small propane torches.

Lillian handed Eden a chef's knife. Eden wondered who had made it. The maker's mark on the base of the blade read HB. Before she could think about it, Lillian pointed to a huge pile of red and green bell peppers. "Dice all these and put them into that big pot over there. I'll give you a quick example and then you can do the rest."

Lillian picked up a big green pepper and tossed it into the air. A knife in her hand zipped twice through the air—so fast that Eden couldn't see it move. Four perfectly quartered sections of bell pepper landed on a nearby cutting board.

"Wow," whispered Eden as Nathaniel rolled his eyes.

Lillian turned on the pepper. Her knife began chopping up and down on the board—*chungchungchungchungchung*. The sound reminded Eden more of a machine than a human. In just a few seconds, the pepper was turned into a neat pile of identical jewel-sized cubes.

Eden watched as Lillian reduced another pepper to a pile of diced cubes and then tried to copy her technique.

"Good work, Eden," said Lillian, "but cut the pepper in half first. Less likely to slip that way. And you're holding the knife wrong. Hold it less like a club and more like a paintbrush. Like this."

Slowly, Eden's pepper turned into a neat, diced pile while Lillian watched. She heard a grunt behind her and saw Nathaniel picking his pepper up off the ground."

"Now you have to wash your hands again, Nathaniel," said Lillian. "And wash the pepper again, too." Eden could hear the strain in Lillian's voice. It matched the strained smile on the woman's face.

Eden kept working. Nathaniel came back to his station with the freshly washed pepper, set it down, and promptly cut his finger. "Ow!"

"Pull in your fingers, son," said Lillian. "And now you'll need a bandage. And then you'll have to wash your hands again."

"I *know*, Mom. You don't have to tell me. I've done this a million times."

"Oh. *You know.* Well, I will leave you to it, then. Come and get me when you're done." Lillian left.

Eden dumped another fully diced pepper into the pot. Nathaniel slumped down onto the kitchen floor, then curled into the fetal position. Eden hissed at him. "What are you doing down there?"

Nathaniel moaned. "I do not want to be here."

Eden's knife chopped another pepper into tiny cubes. "Why? This is fun."

"Fun? You call this fun? This is what I'm trying to escape."

"Just get up here and help, would you?"

Nathaniel moaned as he rose from the floor in slow motion. He picked up a pepper and stared at it. "I don't even like peppers. They're too...peppery." He stabbed the vegetable with his knife and then slowly sawed at it. For every single pepper Nathaniel cut, Eden cut four. "Darn it, Eden!" he said. "Why are you so good at this?"

"I'm not trying to be," said Eden. She wanted to say, *How can you be so bad at this?* but she managed to keep her mouth shut.

"You've never even cooked before."

Eden smirked, thinking back to all the meals she'd made for herself to keep from going hungry. "What makes you think that? I've been cooking for myself for years."

By the time they finished the peppers, two more of Nathaniel's fingers were wrapped in bandages. Lillian came to inspect their work. "Oh, now most of these are lovely. Like little rubies and emeralds. But what happened to the rest of these pieces? They look like they were chewed on by a beaver."

Nathaniel growled.

"You'll have to do these ones over. I can't make soup out of ingredients looking like this. Pick out these wretched pieces and cut them more neatly. When you're done, we've still got onions and celery to cut."

Eden helped Nathaniel pick out his poorly cut pieces and reshape them. Then they cut all the other vegetables. Eden stopped Nathaniel whenever he began to get sloppy. "You need to slow down and do it right," she said.

Nathaniel groaned. "Why? What difference does it make? It's all gonna get chewed up anyway."

"It matters," said Lillian, who had reentered the space without their hearing her. "Even the most basic of tasks must be done well. We eat first with our eyes, and then with our mouths. Food must look good for it to taste good."

Lillian instructed Eden to add four huge scoops of butter and two large bottles of white wine to the pot. They put the pot on the stove and turned on the burner.

"It's Monday," said Lillian. "Vegetable gumbo day."

Nathaniel groaned again. "The same food, over and over. Week after week."

Lillian clapped a wooden spoon against her hand. "Precisely. It is within those constraints—the constraints of a menu and of recipes—that we find excellence." She placed a recipe sheet down on Eden's station and instructed them to follow it.

As soon as Lillian left, Nathaniel groaned and slumped to the floor again.

"*Now* what's wrong with you?" said Eden, as she measured water and poured it into the pot.

"So boring."

"It's only boring if you let it be," said Eden.

"We make it. They eat it. We make it. They eat it. It never stops. What's the point?"

"You are very annoying right now." Eden carefully measured out

268

the herbs, salt and pepper, black-eyed peas, mustard greens, a large bag of rice, and a few other things. She turned up the burner. When it was hot, she fetched Lillian. Lillian dipped her wooden spoon into the pot and took a sip. "Very nice," she said.

"Can I taste it?" asked Eden.

"You must. A cook must taste their food." She handed Eden a clean spoon. Eden dipped it in the pot, blew on the steamy broth to cool it, then slurped it into her mouth. She could feel the butter on her lips and taste the sweetness of the peppers mixed with the sharp onions and aromatic celery. It was delicious. Tasting her work, she had the same feeling as when she completed a sword or helped her grandfather survive another Task. It felt good.

At the end of the first day, at two o'clock, Eden wiped her hands on her apron and hung it on a hook by the doors of Kitchens. "That was fun," she said to Nathaniel.

Nathaniel yanked his apron off his head and threw it at the hooks. "Fun? That wasn't fun. All we did was cut vegetables and mix ingredients. For six hours!"

"For gumbo." Eden smiled as they walked outside. "When we got here, there was no gumbo. When we left, gumbo existed. Like magic. Tonight, every smith in this Guildhall will eat that gumbo. And we made it."

"You mean *you* made it."

"Well, you helped. Sort of. Hey, have you ever noticed how similar cooking is to smithing?"

"You're crazy," said Nathaniel, wiping his soapy hands on his pants.

"It is, though. You gather your materials. You do prep work. You put it all together. You use fire to heat it. And then, right before the end, you put on the little finishing touches that make the work special. Like an engraving on a knife blade. Or a scoop of sour cream in a bowl of soup."

Nathaniel cocked his head at her. "I still say you're crazy. I'll see you at Vulcan's, after nap time. I'm tired. Kitchen work makes me tired."

"Because it's hard," said Eden.

"Because it's *boring.*"

Eden and Nathaniel spent six-hour days in Kitchens. The work helped keep Eden's mind off the fact that the next assigned Task had still not arrived. She learned how to keep her knife sharp, how to knead bread dough without getting flour everywhere, and how to make vanilla pudding from scratch—without lumps. Even Nathaniel, who had spent his entire life around Kitchens, improved.

Eden asked Lillian about making chocolate cake with chocolate frosting, but Lillian just frowned at her. "Here we make pudding. Not cake."

"Even if it's my favorite?"

"Pudding."

The fourth Task arrived on the Wednesday morning of the second week in Kitchens. Miss Clara rattled the tin can as she handed it to Eden. "Here I am, with a present for you! Fourth one is here, Eden. Only one to go after this."

Eden waited for Miss Clara to leave, then opened the can and pulled out the stamped coil of tin.

WITHIN ONE DAY, DEFINED AS SUNRISE TO SUNSET, THE TASK OF MRS. GUNSMITH'S GIRDLE MUST BE COMPLETED, ACCORDING TO THE OFFICIAL HISTORIC CONDITIONS. IF THE REQUIREMENTS ARE NOT MET, OR IF THIS OR ANY OTHER TASK IS ABANDONED, THEN THE SMITH AND THE DESIGNATED HELPER WILL BE BANISHED FROM ALL GUILDHALLS FOREVER.

Eden shook her head, "'According to the official historical conditions'? What's that supposed to mean? They don't even spell out what we need to do." She thought back to the envelopes she'd stolen from Sealed Records and given to her grandfather. He'd said that the Task of Mrs. Gunsmith's Girdle had been solved once. He'd said that it had been made even harder, even deadlier. But how?

"We'll talk about it with Vulcan this afternoon, dearie," said

Nellie. "I'm sure he has a better understanding of what needs to be done. Try not to worry about it until then."

Eden worried about it all day. She finally finished her work in Kitchens and was lying awake on her bed in the sisters' rooms when she was startled by someone pounding on the door.

Nathaniel stood in the hallway, out of breath. "You all need to come," he gasped. "Vulcan's room. Hurry."

As they all rode down in the elevator, Nellie asked, "What is going on, Nathaniel?"

"Pewtersmith," was all Nathaniel said.

The four of them hurried down the hall of Subbasement Seven. When they reached Vulcan's room, Vulcan, the Council, and a crowd of smiths stood outside his door. Vulcan was cradling Willard the rat. Uriah Pewtersmith was there, too, explaining something that Eden couldn't quite hear. As she drew near, Eden heard Helena Bladesmith shout, "Oh, this is preposterous. Completely preposterous."

"It is in the rules," said Mr. Pewtersmith, scowling. "And if it is in the rules, then it is required, according to the original terms and conditions."

"But it's never been required before," said Helena. "I've certainly never heard of it."

"There's a lot you haven't heard," said Mr. Pewtersmith. "And I suppose you're an expert on the Impossible Tasks."

"Are *you?*" asked Helena.

"I am certainly not. None of us are. Therefore, all of us, including Vulcan and Eden, must adhere to the original terms and conditions, as they were written."

"But this condition makes the whole thing *impossible,*" said Maureen Goldsmith. She pulled a gold handkerchief out of her purse and dabbed her eyes with it.

Robert Blacksmith stepped forward and put his huge hand on Vulcan's shoulder. "I'm afraid there's nothing we can do about it, Vulc. The wording is clear."

"What wording?" said Eden. "What are we talking about?"

Mr. Pewtersmith smiled sadly at Eden. "Unfortunately, the news is not good for your grandfather. Or you either, I fear. You see, I took it upon myself to read every word of the original documentation of the Five Impossible Tasks, as written by my ancestor, Malachi Pewtersmith, and as approved by the Council of that era. I just wanted to make certain that we understood the rules correctly."

"And?" said Eden. "I know it's something bad. Just say it already."

"Dear child," said Mr. Pewtersmith, "it pains me to say so. It truly does. But the rules clearly state that all Five Tasks must be completed in *threescore days*. A score is twenty, so three score, of course, means sixty."

"Sixty days?" said Eden. "No one's ever said anything about any kind of deadline. It's not fair!"

"Fair or not, that is the condition," said Mr. Pewtersmith. "I thought it my duty to bring it up immediately, to be merciful. To give Eden and Vulcan a fighting chance."

Eden's mind raced back to the day when they first attempted the Tasks, when they melted down all the pewter dishes. She couldn't remember the exact date. "How many days to go then?" she said.

"Three," said Mr. Pewtersmith, "counting today."

"Three?" shouted Eden. "But we just got the fourth Task this morning. We've just been sitting around waiting. We could have completed them by now."

"Nevertheless," shrugged Mr. Pewtersmith, "rules are rules."

"You've set us up," said Vulcan.

"Oh, come now, Uriah! Three days is not enough, even for Vulcan," said Nellie, shaking her cane. "We'll appeal to the Council to reconsider."

"There's no point appealing, I'm afraid," said Robert Blacksmith. "The wording is clear."

"It's not clear to me," said Helena Bladesmith.

Robert said, "Today is Wednesday. By sundown Friday, Eden must successfully complete the remaining two Tasks. If she fails, she and Vulcan will be banished from all Guildhalls forever."

"Banished," whispered Vulcan, as he stroked Willard's fur. "A fate worse than death."

XXXI

The Helper

Inside Vulcan's room, Eden's mind spun. She and her grandfather would be banished. The Guildhall had come to feel home to her—the first real home she had known in years—and now she was three days away from being kicked out. Where would they go—a young girl and an old man who seemed terrified of the outside world? She wondered if there might be some way she could get any money out of her father's foundry. She wondered if Vulcan had any money of his own, or if that had become *property of the Guild*, like all of Vulcan's other possessions.

Vulcan paced back and forth in his tiny room, petting Willard so hard that the rat squeaked. "I hate being rushed. Bad things happen when a smith is rushed."

"We don't have time to talk about this," said Eden. "We have two Tasks to go: Get Mrs. Gunsmith's girdle, and whatever the fifth Task is."

"In three days? Three days means rushed. We're done," said Vulcan, as he spun around on his peg-shaped prosthetic. "It's over. We need to start packing. And thinking about what we'll do when we leave."

"No!" said Eden. "You can't give up now. We still have time."

"Not enough. Pewtersmith knows it. You think he just found out about this new rule today? He waited until now to tell us. He stalled us. Just like you said."

"He could have waited until there was no time left at all," said Eden. "At least now we still have a chance."

Vulcan nodded, his mouth in a straight line. "He chose today on purpose. Just enough of a chance to tempt us to try it. That's why the fourth Task took so long to get here. And that's why he told us today. Because it's still possible. But now, if we try it, it'll be rushed. Safety becomes impossible. So I'm not playing anymore. Pewtersmith can go hang. I quit."

"You're giving up?" said Eden, stepping in front of Vulcan.

"Damn right. I quit."

"I thought you were brave," said Eden. "Everyone says what an amazing smith you were. The smartest and most talented. And the bravest, too. That's what they say. But now you're just afraid."

Vulcan nodded. "Fine. I'm afraid. Now leave Willard and me alone." He pushed them all out into the hallway and slammed his door.

"At least tell me how the Task has changed! You coward!" Eden yelled at the closed door.

"Hush now, dearie," said Nellie. "Vulcan is not a coward. Are you such a little fool that you don't see what he is doing?"

"I see it," said Eden. "He's quitting. He's giving up."

"Oh, you are such a bullheaded little idiot," said Nellie, gripping her cane in both hands. "Eugene, I am too angry to speak. Can you explain to this girl what just happened?"

Eugene said, "He quit to save you, Eden. To keep you alive."

"He's not saving me. He's saving himself."

"If it was just him—if you hadn't come—he'd still make the attempt at the last two Tasks," said Eugene. "But you're here now, Eden. He doesn't want to put you in more danger. He's not willing to risk your life."

"But *I* am!" said Eden. "I want to do it."

"That's exactly why he's quitting."

"But then what? They'll kick us out."

"They will," said Eugene. "He knows that. It's the worst thing you could do to a smith, especially one like Vulcan. But you'll still be alive. He knows that, too. So no one gets to call him a coward. Not even you."

The sisters followed Eugene to the elevator, leaving Eden and Nathaniel alone in the hallway.

"Sorry," said Nathaniel.

"Don't be," Eden said. She grabbed Nathaniel by the arm and dragged him down the hall.

"Where are we going?" said Nathaniel.

"Back to Records," said Eden. "We need to hurry. We only have until Friday."

"Didn't you just hear? It's over. Vulcan quit."

"*He* might have," said Eden, "but *I* didn't. And I need your help."

"*My help?*" said Nathaniel. "But Eugene just said that it's too dangerous to continue. That's why Vulcan stopped."

"Vulcan's nicer than I am," said Eden. "Unless you want me to get kicked out."

Nathaniel laughed grimly. "If I'm coming with you, then I have to go to Kitchens first for some mahguj."

"Well, hurry then," said Eden. "I'll meet you outside of Records."

Ten minutes later, when Nathaniel finally arrived at the door of Records, his pockets were bulging. "You think you brought enough?" said Eden.

"Probably not," said Nathaniel. "You can't have too much mahguj when it comes to Bones."

Eden knocked on the door. After half a minute, Sylvia's voice came through. "Go away. We are closed."

"It's us—Eden and Nathaniel," Eden said. "It's an emergency."

Sylvia opened the door a crack. "I'm sorry," she said. "I still cannot let you in. Records is closed."

"What? Why?" said Eden.

"There has been a theft," she said. "Somehow, someone got past Bones and stole files from Sealed Records."

"But we have to get in," said Eden. "It's life or death."

"What did they take?" asked Nathaniel.

"The thieves stole the histories of all five Impossible Tasks. The wax seal on the drawer was broken." Bones pushed his nose through the door and began sniffing the air. Sylvia scratched him on the head. "It was your fault, you slobbering beast. You are getting soft in your old age."

"We have to get in, Sylvia. We need to look something up."

Sylvia raised one eyebrow. "Eden, you are the last person I can let in. You are my lead suspect. I like you, but there is no way you're coming inside. Bones! Down! What is the matter with you? And even if you did come in, it would not help you. The records are gone. I told you. Down, Bones!"

"There's nothing else?"

"Nothing. Whomever has those envelopes has every bit of information there is. Everything known about the Impossible Tasks is in those envelopes. In them or on them."

"On them?" said Eden. "What's that mean?"

Just then, Bones shoved his way through the door, lunging at Nathaniel. Nathaniel jumped out of the way. Sylvia reached out with her skinny fingers and tried to grab Bones by his silver-colored collar. "I do not know what has gotten into this beast, but you had better run, children."

"What?" said Eden.

"Run!" shouted Sylvia.

Nathaniel grabbed Eden by the sleeve and pulled her down the hallway. They sprinted toward the stairwell door. Bones jerked away from Sylvia and pounded after them.

"Hurry, children!" Sylvia shouted. "Bones is loose!"

Nathaniel reached the door to the stairwell and yanked it open. They leaped through, slamming the door behind them, just as Bones crashed into it.

The door held. Bones barked on the other side, so loudly that it shook the door on its hinges.

They stomped down the stairs, putting as much distance as they could between themselves and the dog. Eden said, "Do you think, just maybe, that you brought too much mahguj?"

They continued all the way down to Subbasement Seven and knocked on Vulcan's door.

"Don't ask me anything about the Impossible Tasks," he said, as he let them in. "In fact, if that's why you're here, you might as well just leave."

"Fine," said Eden. "We won't ask you. Just let us look at the envelopes."

Vulcan cradled Willard the rat in one arm. He nodded toward the stack of envelopes on the table. "Help yourself."

Eden thumbed through them. "There are only four here." She looked through the labels. "Where is the fourth Task? Mrs. Gunsmith's Girdle?"

"You don't need to worry about it," Vulcan said, "because we're not doing it. But you can look at those other ones to your heart's delight."

She glared at her grandfather, then found the envelope labeled The Unknown Task and looked inside.

"Still empty," Vulcan said.

She examined the front of the envelope, remembering Sylvia's words—that everything known about the Tasks was in the envelopes, or on them. The only thing on the front of the envelope was the very plain label. She turned it over. Her eyes scanned the back. Down in one corner, she saw a handful of words, scrawled in pencil.

"Look at this," she said. "Something is written here."

"I saw that," said Vulcan, "but the words make no sense. Probably just some scribbled notes by an old Records keeper."

"What's it say?" said Nathaniel.

"It says, 'Begin at black metal, and read me a riddle. Bring me the answer back to black metal.'"

"What's that supposed to mean?" said Nathaniel.

"Who knows?" said Vulcan. He scratched Willard behind the ears. "Like I said, nonsense."

"Is there anything else?" said Nathaniel.

Eden shook her head no.

Nathaniel said, "'Begin at black metal, and read me a riddle. Bring me the answer back to black metal.' Is that right?"

Eden nodded.

"I have an idea," said Nathaniel. "I'm probably wrong, but let's go check it out."

As they left, Vulcan said, "Don't do anything stupid, Eden. That's what Pewtersmith is counting on—for either you or me to do something stupid. That's our longest-held family tradition."

Buzz was working the elevator. He smiled. "Hello, fellow apprentices. Where can I take you?"

"Yeah," said Eden to Nathaniel, "where can Buzz take us?"

Nathaniel smiled. "Buzz, we need to do some work in black metal. Take us there."

Buzz nodded. "To a blacksmith, eh? Which one?"

"Umm, Robert Blacksmith, I guess." said Nathaniel.

"Council floor it is," said Buzz. He tightened his bow tie, straightened his hat, unlocked the panel, and pushed the gold button.

At the top floor, the children found Robert Blacksmith's door. They could hear pounding and pinging inside.

"What are we doing here?" said Eden.

"Trying to get someone to give us a riddle," said Nathaniel as he knocked.

The pounding stopped. After a few seconds, Robert Blacksmith opened the door. He was wearing his heavy leather apron and held his hammer in his hand. "You're interrupting my hammering," he said, "so make it quick. Oh, Eden. Didn't realize it was you." His hard face softened all the way to sadness. "How can I help you?"

"We need a riddle," said Eden. She told Robert about their latest clue.

Eden held her breath. Robert stroked his thick beard. "A riddle, eh? You're on the right track. And as a blacksmith, I come from a long line of riddlers. But I'm truly sorry to say I don't have any riddles I can tell you."

"But you have to!" said Nathaniel. "*Black metal* means blacksmithing, doesn't it?"

Robert Blacksmith nodded. "It does, but I still can give you no riddle. I wish I could do more, but all I can offer you is the vaguest of hints: The best riddles are the oldest. So go back to the beginning. The very beginning."

"The beginning of what?" asked Eden.

Robert set a huge hand on Eden's shoulder. "Good luck to you. I will hate to see you go."

They returned to Subbasement Seven, but Vulcan wouldn't answer when they knocked on his door. The children sat down in the hallway.

"'Back to the beginning,'" said Nathaniel. "That's what Robert Blacksmith said. The beginning of what?"

Eden said, "If we can't figure out this riddle, then we're stuck. And we're just as stuck when it comes to this girdle of Mrs. Gunsmith's. You heard what Mr. Gunsmith said. He'll kill us."

"But someone solved that one already. You said so yourself."

"They solved it, but then it was changed."

"Changed how?"

"How should I know? Grandpa won't show me the envelope for that Task."

"Well, you need to get that envelope and look at it soon. After tonight, there are only two days left."

Eden slumped lower on the floor. "We need to get in Grandpa's room. But he never leaves."

"Of course he doesn't leave," said Nathaniel. "He's not allowed to. *House arrest* means *in his room*."

They sat talking in the hallway late into the night, but no ideas came.

XXXII

In Which a Door Is Opened

The next morning, Eden brought a bowl of oatmeal to Vulcan for his breakfast. Eden noticed that Vulcan's few clothes and tools were stacked in a neat pile on his table. He'd already started preparing to leave. He spooned some of the oatmeal onto a plate for Willard, who gnawed at it silently. While Vulcan and the rat ate, Eden scanned the room, looking for the missing envelope.

"It's under my bed," Vulcan said, as he spooned sugar onto his oatmeal. "But you can't see it. Only today and tomorrow, then all this nonsense will be over. You and I will leave and then Pewtersmith can forget about me forever."

"If we had to leave," said Eden, the words nearly sticking in her throat, "I might eventually be able to get some money, if I could figure out how to get at it. It might take lawyers or something, but it seems like I should have some kind of part ownership of—"

"Of what?" interrupted Vulcan. "Of a f-f-factory? I'd work for Pewtersmith before I took a penny from such a place."

Eden sighed. "Then I don't know what we'll do. Grandpa, just let me look at the envelope. You said yourself that I have good ideas."

"You've got both good and bad," Vulcan said. "Like your father.

But I'm not losing another." He pushed Eden from the room and locked his door.

Eden found Nathaniel. "Any luck?" he asked.

"He told me where it was. Under his bed. But he still won't let me see it," said Eden. "I feel lost."

"If we can't work on that Task, then maybe we can figure out the last one. The Unknown Task. The words on the envelope said, 'Begin at black metal, and read me a riddle. Bring me the answer back to black metal.'"

"I have zero idea what that means," said Eden, "and I have no idea where to even look."

"Then let's look everywhere," said Nathaniel.

"*Everywhere*?" asked Eden. "Even on the Jones floors?"

"Everywhere except there."

They took the elevator to the Council floor, the top of the Guildhall. They looked at the images carved into the metal panels on the wall. "This whole Guildhall is covered in weird pictures," said Eden. "Any of them could be a riddle."

"Then we have to look at all of it."

They took the stairs down to the next floor and started again, scanning the hallways, looking for clues.

As they looked, two Blue Coats came around a corner carrying cardboard boxes. A tall, thin woman with jet-black hair followed behind them, waving her hands. "Just throw it away," she said. "I don't care what you do with it, as long as you get rid of it."

"Who is that?" whispered Eden. "She looks familiar."

"That's because she's a Pewtersmith," Nathaniel said. "That's Uriah Pewtersmith's sister. Her name is Morgana."

"I wonder what she's throwing out," said Eden. "And I wonder if she's as nasty as her brother."

"I heard that," said Morgana, pointing a bony finger at them. "You two brats. What are you doing here?" She scowled down her thin nose. "I know who you are. You're Vulcan's granddaughter. I've seen you in Supperdinner Hall with those senile little sisters. Are you spying on me? Trying to see what I've done with the place? With Vulcan's old rooms?"

"Do you—do you live there?"

"I'm moving in as we speak," said Morgana with a sneer. "Or trying to. These rooms are so full of junk, it's taken me weeks and weeks just to get them cleared out."

"What—what are you doing? With his things? What are you doing with Grandpa's tools?"

"Throwing it all away, of course," spat Morgana. "That's what you do with junk." She spun on a heel and stepped back into Vulcan's old rooms. As she ordered around the Blue Coats inside, Eden grabbed Nathaniel by the arm and dragged him down the hallway, after the other Blue Coats carrying the boxes.

"Wait!" she yelled, just as they were entering the elevator. "Where are you taking all that?"

"To the trash," said the Blue Coat, "as instructed."

"You can't!" said Eden. "That belongs to Vulcan Smith."

"It belongs to the Guild," said the Blue Coat.

"Please," said Eden. "Those are his tools. If he gets out of his—if he ever becomes a smith again, he'll want those back."

The Blue Coat smiled. "Eden Smith, we know what you have done for the Joneses in this Guildhall. We are grateful. But you and your grandfather are about to be banished, without these tools."

"There's still time," said Eden.

"Not enough," said the Blue Coat. He left.

Eden sat on the floor of the hallway. The Blue Coat was almost surely right. Vulcan would never leave his room. They had two Tasks to go and didn't even know what one of them was.

"Come on," said Nathaniel. "Let's keep looking."

"What's the point?" said Eden. She slumped lower. "We'll never find anything."

Nathaniel tried to pull her up off the floor. "Come on! You can't quit now."

"I'm gonna take a nap," said Eden. "It's almost two o'clock. I'm tired."

"We can't," said Nathaniel. "We need to keep looking."

"You do that." Eden stood up and pushed the button for the

elevator. Nathaniel stared at her, then turned away and marched down the hall, alone.

Eden didn't sleep during nap time. She didn't eat during teatime or bother to visit her grandfather in the afternoon. At dinner, she followed the sisters silently to Supperdinner Hall. Instead of eating, she sat bending a silver spoon. Nellie didn't stop her.

"Dearie, you must eat something," said Nellie. "How about a little pudding, at least. Oh sister, the poor dear must be a ball of nerves."

"It will all be over soon," said Irma, setting down her teacup. "Why give up hope tomorrow when you can give up hope today? That's what I always say."

After dinner, Eden went to her room and lay on her bed. She didn't want to see anyone. She thought she might just lie there until sunset the next day. If she was going to fail, she wished she could just get it over with and leave.

She checked on the orchid on her bedside table. It looked deader than ever. Next to the orchid, she saw the photograph, her mother and father smiling out at her. She whispered, "Unless you have some ideas you'd like to share, stop looking at me like that." From habit, she kissed the tip of her finger and was going to press it against the photo, but before she could, her eyes closed. She slept.

She was still asleep just after midnight when a hand clamped over her mouth. Her eyes opened and she saw a figure kneeling by her bed in the dim light. It was Nathaniel. With one finger to his lips, he motioned for her to be quiet, then took his hand away.

"How did you get in here?" whispered Eden.

"I'll show you," hissed Nathaniel. "Come on. But be quiet."

She climbed out of bed and snuck behind Nathaniel, past the sisters' rooms and out into the hallway. A small, bald man stood there with the help of a walker. The walker was hung with dozens of keys. Eden recognized him: Lawrence Locksmith.

"I understand there is a door you need opened," Lawrence whispered. "I'd like to help."

Eden's mind was still groggy with sleep. "What is he talking about?"

"Vulcan's door," whispered Nathaniel. "He just let me into the sisters' rooms. Now he's going to let us into Vulcan's, so you can get that envelope and see how the fourth Task was changed."

Eden rubbed her eyes. "Now? Serious?"

Nathaniel glared at her. "Am I serious? I just snuck out of my room, snuck past my mom, snuck all the way up to the second floor, and woke up Lawrence. I talked him into this. Then we broke into your room. So yes. I'm serious."

"But Grandpa hid the envelope under his bed."

"Then you'll have to be very careful when you steal it," said Nathaniel.

Eden sucked in her breath, then nodded. Nathaniel told her the elevator was turned off after midnight, so the three of them took the stairs down to Subbasement Seven. It was slow going, as Lawrence and his walker had to navigate each step. As they descended, Nathaniel said, "It came to me, in the middle of the night. We needed to get inside Vulcan's room. So we needed a locksmith."

"I'm not a brave man," said Lawrence, the keys on his walker jangling, "but I would like to help Vulcan, if I can."

Eden nodded. "Thank you, Lawrence." She paused, then said, "Why did you refuse to join the Council?"

"Ohh," he said, "I don't think I should tell you."

"We're good at keeping secrets," said Eden.

"I'm not a brave man."

"So you've said. Why didn't you join?"

"Well…well you see, Mr. Pewtersmith—"

"I knew it!" said Eden.

"Yes. Well, as I was saying, Mr. Pewtersmith, he came to visit me. The day before the nomination. He had an old key he needed a copy of, he said. Although, come to think of it, I never did see the key. But he told me how lucky he was to have escaped the Council with his life. He said that Vulcan's obsession with the Five Tasks was putting us all in great danger—fires and birds and eye patches and rats and such—and none more in danger than the Council. He said that accepting a nomination would be like accepting a nomination to, well, to die."

"And you believed him?"

"I suppose I did. But—"

"So when Robert nominated you—"

"As I said, I'm not brave. I wish I was. I've always dreamed of being on the Council. But I—I like Vulcan. He's a good man. Well, perhaps not a good man, but he is quite an excellent locksmith. So, if I can help—in secret, of course—well then, I'd like to."

They finally reached Vulcan's door. "All you have to do is open it," said Eden, "without making any noise. Then you can leave. And we promise not to tell anyone."

Lawrence ran his fingers over the flowers that covered the door. "Oh, I do like this silverwork. Looks like it was done by the sisters. I especially like the snake."

"Lawrence, please hurry," whispered Eden.

"Quite right," Lawrence said. "Not much to this lock. Old Hammersmith model. I could open it with my eyes closed."

"Then do it," said Eden. "Quietly."

Lawrence nodded. He pulled a skeleton key from his walker and stuck it into the lock. He turned the key back and forth, tilting his head as he did so. He tried a different key, repeating his actions. He nodded, then used a pair of pliers to bend a piece of heavy wire. He stuck the end of the wire into the lock and turned it with a jerk. The lock snapped open. Lawrence pulled out the wire and pointed it at Eden. "All done. I hope it helps." He took a few steps toward the stairway with his walker, then said, "I wonder how long it's going to take me to get back to my floor." He left.

Eden looked at Nathaniel and put her fingers to her lips. "Shhh." She grabbed the handle and slowly opened the door, just half an inch. The room inside was dark. She could just make out Vulcan lying on his bed, snoring. "Here goes nothing," whispered Eden. She slipped inside the room.

The only light in the room came through the crack under the

door. Eden waited for her eyes to adjust to the shadows, then felt her way across the floor, her hands held out in front of her. She followed the sounds of the snores. When she was close to Vulcan's bed, she dropped down onto her belly and peered underneath.

A set of small, shiny eyes peered out at her. Eden had to bite her lip to keep from screaming. Then she recognized Willard, the black rat with one white ear. Willard squeaked at her and Vulcan's snoring stopped.

"Hush up, Willard," mumbled Vulcan. Eden held her breath. After what seemed like hours, the snoring began again.

Eden slowly reached under the bed, hoping the rat wouldn't bite her or climb on her fingers. She finally felt the envelope and slid it out, inch by inch. Then she tiptoed to the door and eased out into the hall. When the door was closed, she finally let out her breath.

The envelope was labeled Mrs. Gunsmith's Girdle. "Let's see," said Eden to Nathaniel, as she scanned the pages. "Here's the original Task: 'Obtain the girdle of the first Mrs. Gunsmith and deliver it to the Council by sunset of the same day.' Oh, and here's where it was solved. By—by Eden. Same name as me." She read silently, then burst out laughing.

"What's it say?" said Nathaniel.

"So brilliant. So very brilliant."

"What? Read it."

"Okay, okay. Hold on. It says that the original Eden realized that Mrs. Gunsmith only removed the girdle at night, but the rules of the Task determined that Eden must recover the girdle during the daytime. So she worked with a woman named MaryHarris Jones to—"

"Wait," interrupted Nathaniel. "Say that name again."

"MaryHarris Jones. Why?"

"Because I know that name. That's the same name as my great-great-grandmother. That's *my* ancestor. Keep reading."

"Okay. It says Eden worked with MarryHarris Jones to create a huge vat of the richest, most delicious jelly—"

"I *knew* it was jelly."

"What do you mean, *you knew?* You can't have known that. Now quit interrupting. They combined bacon, brown sugar, fresh raspberries, maple syrup, and one secret ingredient to create a huge vat of the most delicious jelly. They brought it to Supperdinner Hall at a luncheon. They set it on a table, right near the gunsmith's section, and then they served the jelly—as much as anyone wanted. So brilliant."

"What's so brilliant? What happened?"

"Don't you get it?" said Eden. "You know how much the gunsmiths appreciate a good meal? This Eden knew that Mrs. Gunsmith wouldn't be able to resist this jelly. She was right. Mrs. Gunsmith enjoyed it so much that, well, you know how your pants get too tight when you eat too much? Her girdle—her gun belt—it got too tight. She ran to her room and took it off, then came back for more jelly. As soon as this Eden saw her return, she broke into Mrs. Gunsmith's room, grabbed the girdle and ran. Mr. Gunsmith chased her. Shot at her, even. But Eden escaped and brought the girdle to the Council."

"By cooking," said Nathaniel, smiling. "They solved it by cooking. Cooking jelly. MaryHarris Guild Jelly. Mah-Guj. No wonder it's so good. Because lives depended on it."

"Oh, here's where it says how the Task was changed. Haggai Pewtersmith said that Eden's solution shouldn't count. Said it was too easy to solve, so it shouldn't be considered *impossible*. The Council agreed—I hate the stupid Council! Oh, and here's the part about what they transformed it to. The Task was rewritten by George Henry Blacksmith. Wonder if he's a relative of Robert Blacksmith..." Eden's voice trailed off as she read silently to herself.

"What's it say?" said Nathaniel.

"Shh!" Eden kept reading. She jumped to her feet. "We can do this."

"Do what?" said Nathaniel.

"We can do this! They thought—oh my goodness. I bet they thought they were making it so hard. And they did. For almost everyone. Even for that first Eden. It seemed so hard she never even tried solving it the second time. Vulcan thought it was too dangerous to even try. But it's not impossible for us! We can do this. Or *you* can! Nathaniel, you are the only one who can complete this Task. You can do it tomorrow."

"Me? What are you talking about? What was the girdle Task transformed into?"

"Listen: 'A portion of the original titanium girdle was shaped into a collar.'" Eden remembered what she'd heard Mrs. Gunsmith say, that night in Supperdinner Hall, when she'd spoken about the girdle being altered once, long ago. Eden continued reading. "'The titanium collar was placed around the neck of the fiercest beast in all smithdom. To complete the Task, the collar must be returned, intact, to the Council, by sunset of the same day.'"

"The fiercest beast?" said Nathaniel. "You're talking about Bones, aren't you?"

"He's the fiercest, isn't he?" said Eden. "Sylvia said he was the forty-somethingth of his line and his name. His collar—do you remember? It's silvery. So I bet it is titanium. And they don't know. Vulcan doesn't know. Pewtersmith doesn't know. None of them know that there's only one person who could ever get something from Bones."

"Me?"

"Of course, you! Bones loves you. Or at least he loves your great-great-grandma's jelly. We'll do this Task first thing in the morning, according to the historic conditions, just like the Task requires. We can probably have it done before lunch. Then all we have to do..." Her voice trailed off. "Then all we have to do is figure out what the last Task is all about, and then solve it."

"Before sunset," said Nathaniel, "assuming I don't get eaten first."

XXXIII

The Gunsmiths

The next morning at breakfast, Eden asked Eugene and the sisters to gather Vulcan and the Council. At first they refused.

"We couldn't live with ourselves if anything happened to you, dearie," said Nellie. She poked her fork at an uneaten scone.

"Nothing will happen," said Eden. "Bones really does love Nathaniel, because Nathaniel feeds him mahguj every time we visit."

"He does what?"

"Feeds him mahguj. MarryHarris Guild Jelly. Bones loves it."

"Nathaniel?" said Nellie. "You do that?"

Nathaniel gulped. "Am I in trouble?"

Nellie pointed at Nathaniel with her fork. "You are not in trouble, young man. You are slowly revealing yourself to be remarkable."

With that, Nellie and Irma gave in. Eugene said he would gather everyone in Humble Gallery at ten o'clock. "You think you'll be done by then?"

"I hope so," said Eden. "It shouldn't take very long. But if it does, just keep them there. No matter what, keep them there, Eugene."

"I'll keep them," he said. "All day if I have to. After sunset it will all be over, anyway."

Eden and Nathaniel ran to the elevator and rode down to Sub-basement Seven, where Nathaniel disappeared into Kitchens. A few minutes later, he returned with a bulging school backpack slung over one shoulder.

"What's in there?" said Eden.

"Nothing but mahguj. Ten pounds of it. I don't want to run out."

The elevator door opened. Mr. Pewtersmith stood inside. He scowled at them. "Well?"

"We need to go to Subbasement Two," Eden said.

Mr. Pewtersmith sneered. "The stairs are to your left."

Eden turned away from Mr. Pewtersmith and began pulling Nathaniel toward the stairs, then stopped. "Look," she said, pointing at the dial on the wall above the closed elevator door. It showed that Mr. Pewtersmith's elevator was going up. They watched it stop at Subbasement Two.

"That jerk," said Nathaniel "If he was going there anyway, then why didn't he take us?"

Eden swallowed. "Maybe he wasn't going there until we mentioned it."

They took the stairs five stories up and exited into the hallway of Subbasement Two. Eden felt the hair on the back of her neck tingle. "Something's wrong," she said.

"What are you talking about?" said Nathaniel, as they walked along the hallway. "Let's just go to Records and get this over with."

Right then, the gunsmith's oiled metal doors burst open. Two barrel-chested gunsmiths charged into the hallway and grabbed Eden and Nathaniel by the arms.

"What are you doing?" shouted Eden. "Let us go!"

Mr. Gunsmith stepped into view. Mr. Pewtersmith stood behind him. "Just as I told you," Mr. Pewtersmith said. "Here to steal the girdle." Without a word, Mr. Gunsmith motioned with his head toward the open doors. The children were dragged inside and the doors were slammed shut. The gunsmiths pulled them to the back of the rooms to a small, empty workshop. Eden and Nathaniel were shoved inside. The workshop doors were shut from the outside. They heard a key turning in the lock.

"You can't keep us here!" said Eden. "This is—this is kidnapping."

"Only until sunset," said Mr. Gunsmith, from the other side of the doors. "Then this will all be over."

"But we're not here for you. Or for Mrs. Gunsmith. The Task has changed!"

"That's just what a girdle thief would say," sneered Mr. Pewtersmith.

"Let us out!" shouted Eden. "You have to let us out."

No one responded. The only sound from the other side of the doors were footsteps fading into the distance.

"Now what?" said Eden. "Now we're trapped here? This is how it ends?"

Eden and Nathaniel banged on the doors, but no one came. The only neighbor of the gunsmiths was Sylvia. Eden recalled her words, about how the gunsmiths were loud neighbors. "Probably sounds like just another ordinary day to her."

Eden and Nathaniel quickly explored the small shop, but it was empty, other than an old clock that hung from the wall, showing the time.

Ten o'clock passed.

Eden imagined how Eugene, Vulcan, and the Council were gathered in Humble Gallery waiting for them. She wondered what her grandfather thought when she hadn't arrived. She wondered if anyone was looking for them and if they would find them in time.

They paced the floor. Nathaniel asked if Eden knew when sunset was on that day.

"Seven twenty-one."

"Then there's still time. If we get out soon, there's still time."

Hours went by. With each click of the clock, Eden felt hope slipping away. She kept praying that someone would come. She strained her ears to listen. But no one came.

"If you get banished, how soon will they make you leave?" asked Nathaniel.

"I don't know," said Eden, as her throat tightened. She wondered if she and her grandpa would at least be able to spend another night in the Guildhall, or if they would be shut outside in the dark, tonight. She was really afraid now—so afraid that it felt like long, cold fingers were closing around her neck. The fear was so real that it was hard to breath. It had felt so distant before—like some future that may never come about. Now she was hours away from leaving the Guildhall behind.

She looked across the room at Nathaniel. She would have to say goodbye to him, and to Nellie and Irma, too. They were family to her now. She didn't know if she could stand another loss. But she didn't know what she could do to prevent it.

At four o'clock, Nathaniel said, "How long do you think it will take? To get the collar, I mean?"

"Too long," said Eden. "We have so little time left."

The clock struck six. Then six thirty. At fifteen minutes to seven, Nathaniel said, "It doesn't even matter now. If we get out, we might just get the collar down to Humble Gallery. But we're out of time on the last Task. We still don't even know what it is."

"You're right," said Eden. Her empty stomach gurgled. "I know you're right. But—oh, I'd just like to finish one more. Just to show Grandpa that I was trying. But we're stuck in here with nothing."

As she sat down on the cold floor of the workshop, she felt a familiar bulge in her back pocket. She'd felt it countless times before, but, at this moment, it got her attention. "Wait! We do have something. I can't believe I forgot!" She reached into her back pocket and pulled out her pair of pliers and the coil of heavy wire her grandfather had given her. She stared at them. Her grandpa had said that a smith should always have a pair of pliers and a bit of wire.

"What are you going to do with that?" said Nathaniel.

"Try to open that door," said Eden. She tried to remember how she'd seen Vulcan do it, when he opened the doors to his old rooms, back on the first day she'd come. And she'd seen Lawrence Locksmith do it as well, on Vulcan's door down on Subbasement Seven.

She bent the wire into what looked like a key shape and then stuck it into the lock. When she turned the wire, she could feel it hitting something, but the door remained closed.

"Do you know what you're doing?" said Nathaniel.

"Of course I don't know. I'm trying to figure it out. Now be quiet and let me focus." She pulled out the wire and adjusted the shape, then tried again. This time, when she turned the key, whatever it was hitting made a slight movement.

"I think I'm getting somewhere," said Eden. She tried again. Then again.

"Get there faster," said Nathaniel.

At five minutes to seven, Eden put the wire into the keyhole one more time. She felt resistance, and turned the wire with a snap of her wrist. The lock popped open. "Yes!" shouted Eden.

They stepped out of the workshop into the gunsmith's rooms. They rushed to the outer doors. Eden reached for the latch just as she heard the sound of someone walking outside. She froze. A woman's voice said, "Now where did I put that extra jar?"

Eden said, "I know that voice. That's Mrs. Gunsmith." Eden turned the latch and jerked open the door.

Mrs. Gunsmith stared at them, her mouth hanging open. "What on earth are you two doing in here?"

Eden yelled, "We've been trapped in here! Now we need to go!"

"But how did you get in? Wait. You're Vulcan's granddaughter. Did my husband do this? Did he lock you up in here?" Mrs. Gunsmith's smooth face began to grow red. "Because if he did—"

"He did," said Eden, "but right now, we have to leave."

"Wait," said Mrs. Gunsmith. "If you are after the girdle, you can have it, with my compliments."

"We don't need it, but thank you."

"Hold on. Are you going to see Nellie Silversmith?"

"Yes," said Eden, "but hurry. We're almost out of time!"

"Then take her this," said Mrs. Gunsmith, handing Eden a jar of her beauty cream.

Eden snatched the jar out of Mrs. Gunsmith's hand and pushed Nathaniel ahead of her as they ran out the door.

XXXIV

Sunset

They reached Records at one minute after seven. They had twenty minutes left. Eden pounded on the door.

"We are closed for the day," said Sylvia, from inside. "Come back tomorrow."

Eden shouted, "It's us. It's Eden and Nathaniel. You have to let us in."

"Not so loud," said Nathaniel. "You don't want to get Bones too excited."

They heard barking inside and Sylvia shouting at Bones. Sylvia opened the door a crack and peeked out. "You two again? It is after hours. What do you want?"

"We want Bones," said Eden. "Please!"

Hearing his name, Bones shoved his huge black head through the opening. He sniffed.

Nathaniel had his backpack open. He tossed a huge glob of mahguj into the air. Bones snapped it between his jaws.

"What do you think you're doing?" said Sylvia, raising both eyebrows. "You will get him riled up."

"Sit!" said Nathaniel. Bones sat. Sylvia's mouth dropped open.

Nathaniel stuck his hand into the tub of mahguj and pulled out a huge wad. Bones stared at it, drooling, licking his chops, and paying no attention to Sylvia. Or to Eden as she grabbed his titanium collar to undo it.

"Eden, you take your hands off of him," said Sylvia. "He does not like being touched."

"Sorry," said Eden, "but I need this collar. How does this thing come off?" The titanium collar was tight against Bones' massive neck. As Eden traced its shape all the way around, a sick feeling grew in her stomach.

"It does not come off," said Sylvia. "There is no buckle. No clasp. It is all one piece. It was formed that way. Bones grew into it. So you cannot take it."

"What do you mean?"

"It will not come off. There is no way to get it off. Now please, children, leave us in peace before something horrible happens."

Bones growled. Nathaniel held out the giant blob of mahguj, but before he could throw it, Bones snapped it out of his hand. "Ow!" yelled Nathaniel. "I almost lost a finger. Eden, what are we going to do?"

Bones growled lower and stepped toward Nathaniel. He sniffed and lunged toward the backpack. "Sit, Bones!" said Nathaniel. Bones sat for half a second, then bounced back to his feet and lunged toward Nathaniel again.

"I warned you," said Sylvia. "Oh, this is not going to end well."

Eden said, "Nathaniel, I have an idea, but—"

"But what?"

"But you're not going to like it."

"Just hurry. Down, Bones!"

"The Task is just to bring the collar to the Council. It didn't say it needed to be off the dog."

Bones pushed toward Nathaniel, the black hair on his neck raised. He growled low as drool dripped from his bared teeth. Nathaniel took another step back. "What are you saying?"

"I'm saying, *run!*"

Nathaniel looked at her, terror in his eyes. Bones growled and lunged at Nathaniel. With a spin, Nathaniel turned and sprinted down the hallway. Bones lunged after him, his barks shaking the walls.

Nathaniel raced for the elevator. He reached it and pushed the button, but before the elevator came, Bones was at his heels, snapping at the backpack with his huge jaws. Nathaniel darted to the side. "Help!" he shouted.

"This way!" yelled Eden. She had reached the door to the stairwell and jerked it open. Nathaniel jumped inside. Eden followed him and slammed the door shut. Bones barked and growled outside, slamming his huge weight against the door.

"We're not going to be able to hold it," said Nathaniel.

"I don't plan on holding it," she said. "Run to Humble Gallery. To the Council. I'll give you a five-second head start."

"What?! If he catches me, he'll eat me!"

"Then don't let him catch you. Ready?"

Nathaniel screamed and ran up the stairs. Eden counted to five, then yanked open the door. Bones burst through it. With a thunderous bark, he chased after Nathaniel.

It was all Eden could do to keep up with the huge dog. The three of them pounded up the stairs. The noise of Bones' barks echoed through the stairwell. On the next floor, a door opened right in front of Eden. As she ran past it, she saw a group of Blue Coats staring at her. They gave chase, shouting at them all to stop.

Bones was close now. He snapped at Nathaniel's backpack, tearing a piece of the fabric with his slobbery teeth. Nathaniel yelped and leaped up the last six stairs, jerking open the door on the main floor.

Bones crashed through the door behind the boy. Eden sprinted after them. She shouted, "Here we come! With the collar!"

Nathaniel ran across the floor of Humble Gallery toward the huddle of bewildered councilmembers, Vulcan, the sisters, and the other smiths who had gathered with Eugene near the Pillar of Saint Dunstan. Nathaniel dashed right into the heart of the crowd. Bones plowed after him, sending dozens of elderly smiths tumbling to the ground. Nathaniel ducked behind the pillar. Bones lunged at him, cracking his huge black head on the pillar. The pillar tilted, then crashed to the ground.

Bones sat back on his haunches, dazed by his collision. He shook his head. A host of Blue Coats circled around the dog. More Blue Coats rushed into the room with ropes in their hands.

"Don't hurt him!" yelled Nathaniel. "He's a good dog."

"A good dog?" said Mr. Pewtersmith from where he lay sprawled on the ground. "That monster nearly killed us all."

"He's not a monster," said Nathaniel. "He just wants a treat." Nathaniel yanked the backpack off his back and set the tub of Guild jelly in front of Bones. Bones wobbled forward, sniffed the jelly, and began licking. As he did so, his muscles relaxed. Bones licked the tub clean. Nathaniel rubbed him on the top of his head. "Good boy, Bonesy. Nice doggy. Sit."

Bones sat.

Mr. Pewtersmith rose unsteadily to his feet. "You and your *nice doggy* nearly got us all killed. And look what you've done. You've overturned the sacred Pillar of Saint Dunstan."

"And *you* had us kidnapped. But we got out and brought the collar, anyway. All that remains of the original girdle of Mrs. Gunsmith." She pointed to the shiny band around Bones' enormous neck.

Vulcan smiled at her. "You did it, Eden. It doesn't matter, but you did it."

Eden nodded, feeling out of breath, victorious, and heartbroken all at once.

"It was a valiant effort," said Nellie, sitting on the floor and dabbing at her eyes with her lace handkerchief. "Only five minutes until sunset. And today is the final day. Oh, dearie."

Mr. Pewtersmith said, "It's over. You and your runt of a grandfather are getting what you deserve—banished for the rest of your lives."

Robert Blacksmith rolled onto his belly and forced himself up with a groan. He shook his head. "Is anyone hurt? Other than bruises, I mean?" He and Eugene helped the sisters and the councilmembers to their feet. Robert glanced at his watch. "One minute to go, Eden. One minute left on the final day. And here you are. You really are a remarkable girl."

"A remarkable failure," Eden said.

"No," said Vulcan. "Robert is right. You are a remarkable girl. And you are my granddaughter. And you are alive. And so am I. What else do I need?"

"We need a place to live," said Eden.

Vulcan smiled from his seat on the ground. "We'll figure it out. And wherever we end up, you and I, we'll be together."

"We still failed," said Eden. "I failed."

Robert looked up from his pocket watch. "Time's up," he said. "Congratulations."

Nellie stomped her cane on the floor of Humble Gallery. "Robert Blacksmith, what a horrible thing to say. Don't mock the poor girl."

"I'm mocking no one," said Robert. "I am congratulating Eden on completing all five of the Impossible Tasks."

Mr. Pewtersmith stepped forward. "She didn't complete them. She failed. They failed."

"They did not," said Robert. He walked to the fallen Pillar of Saint Dunstan. With a mighty heave, he set the pillar upright again. "What did the riddle on the Task say, Eden?"

"The what?"

"The Unknown Task. What was the riddle? On the envelope? Tell it to me again."

Eden cleared her throat. "Let me see. I think it said, 'Begin at black metal, and read me a riddle. Bring me the answer back to black metal.'"

"That's right," said Robert. He nodded at the pillar. "And I told you that you should go back to the beginning. The beginning is Saint Dunstan, the founder of our Guild, who began it all for us. So then, Eden, begin at black metal. And read me a riddle."

"The time—is up!" shouted Mr. Pewtersmith. "The brat has lost and must be banished!" Bones growled at him.

"Shut up, Pewtersmith," said Robert. "Go ahead, Eden."

Eden frowned at the pillar. "Well, you're a blacksmith. So if I begin at black metal, it would be this part here, where it says, 'Best of friend to fight your foe.' That's for blacksmiths."

"This is nonsense," said Mr. Pewtersmith. "Why torture the girl? It's over! I demand that you declare it over!"

"I said, shut up, Pewtersmith," said Robert Blacksmith. "Need I remind you that you are no longer on the Council?" He nodded at Eden. "Keep going."

Eden took a deep breath. "'Best of friend to fight your foe, Guarding treasure, causing woe. Unsmith, unstill, unbroken, untame. Slay the wolf and eat the name.'"

"That's right," said Robert. "So what is the answer?"

"You can't help her!" said Mr. Pewtersmith. "She's failed."

"Not another word," said Robert. "I won't warn you again. Eden, you haven't failed. You've already delivered the answer. You just don't know it."

Eden stared at the words on the pillar. "But all I've brought you is the collar."

Vulcan laughed as he struggled to stand up. "That is not all! That is not all at all! O my dear girl! O my granddaughter! O the snowy white beard of Saint Dunstan!"

"I don't understand," said Eden.

"Who cares?" said Vulcan. He spun around on his aluminum leg. "You've done it! We get to stay! Pewtersmith, you nincompoop, you rat bastard, she's done it!"

"The only other thing we brought was Bones," Eden gasped. "Oh, I think I see! 'Best of friend to fight your foe.' That could be Bones. Because a dog—a dog is a human's best friend. 'Guarding treasure, causing woe.' That's Bones, for sure. He's a guard dog."

"And he's an unsmith!" shouted Nathaniel. "Because he's a Jones. And he sure is untame!"

"'Slay the wolf and eat the name.' Dogs fight wolves, like Sylvia said. When they're protecting sheep," said Eden. "But how does he eat the name? Oh! Because Bones' name is Bones! He eats bones! The answer to the riddle is *Bones*!"

Vulcan shouted. "Hell yes, it is! And you brought the answer. You brought Bones. You brought that big, slobbering dog. And you brought him in time!"

Robert nodded. "Whether you knew it or not."

"Then we don't have to leave? It's done?" said Eden, wiping her one good eye.

"Council, is it done?" said Robert Blacksmith. "I need a motion."

"So moved!" shouted Helen Bladesmith.

"I second the motion," said Maureen Goldsmith.

Robert Blacksmith smiled. "All in favor of declaring the Five Impossible Tasks complete?"

A round of *ayes* rose from the bruised members of the Council. It was done.

"It's not fair!" said Mr. Pewtersmith, his voice high and squeaking. "This is not fair at all. Not one little bit fair."

"I warned you not to speak," said Robert Blacksmith. "Nathaniel, release the hound!"

XXXV

In Which Eden and Nathaniel
Make Their Final Choices

They gathered in Vulcan's room for a celebration.

Nellie sat on the edge of Vulcan's bed. "I am both relieved and delighted that you both will remain in the Guildhall, but I am glad you will not be staying in this particular room. I will not miss this jail cell. I cannot believe we spent so much time in this uncivilized location."

"I might miss it," said Vulcan. He held Willard with one hand and petted him with the other. "You all did a nice job on the door. It's where I met Willard. And I'll miss the smell of Kitchens."

Irma sniffed. "Smells like chicken noodle. I do love noodles in my soup."

Eden laughed. Then she realized she was still holding the jar of Mrs. Gunsmith's Beauty Cream. "This is for you, Aunty," she said, handing it to Nellie.

Nellie examined the jar. "Oh, thank you for bringing it to me. Did it actually work?"

"What do you mean?"

"She means," said Eugene, "that she sent Mrs. Gunsmith to fetch her a jar, because she thought you just might be trapped inside the gunsmith's rooms."

"When you didn't show up at ten o'clock, we thought something might have happened," said Nellie. "We searched everywhere we could, all day long. But Mr. Gunsmith thought you were still after his wife's girdle—like us, he did not know the Task had changed—so he wouldn't let us in his rooms. He would barely let us on his floor."

"I assumed you were dead," said Irma.

"Of course she wasn't dead, sister. There were only a handful of places we couldn't get into—Uriah Pewtersmith's rooms, the gunsmiths' rooms, a few others. Mr. Gunsmith was being very disagreeable, so I knew he would never let us in. But Mrs. Gunsmith—well, I am one of her best customers." Nellie held up the jar. "So I called in an order for her beauty cream, hoping she might find you there and let you out."

"She did," said Eden, "just as we escaped. She didn't seem very happy with her husband."

Vulcan said, "I'm sure she'll deal with him directly. What I want to know is how you managed to get under my bed and steal the envelope for the fourth Task."

"Lawrence Locksmith helped us," said Eden. "Nathaniel woke him up in the middle of the night."

"Oh, Nathaniel," said Nellie holding out her hands, "such a wise and courageous thing to do. Come here dear boy, so I can give you a kiss."

Nathaniel blushed and stayed where he was. "Lawrence is a nice guy. And I think it was brave of him to do it, what with Pewtersmith telling him how dangerous it was."

"It *was* brave," said Vulcan. "We need to let Robert Blacksmith know. See if we can still get Lawrence a spot on the Council."

"He certainly couldn't be any worse than Uriah Pewtersmith," said Nellie. "I've never seen someone run as fast as that man did, once Robert Blacksmith sicced that dog on him. He barely made it to the stairwell."

"Lucky for Bones." Irma stared into her empty teacup. "I'm sure Pewtersmith would have left a bad taste in his mouth."

"Speaking of locksmiths," said Nathaniel, "did Eden tell you how she picked a lock herself? With nothing but wire and a pair of old pliers." Nathaniel explained how Eden's lock-picking skills had gotten them out of the storeroom.

"With my old pliers?" said Vulcan. He sniffed. "You really are a remarkable girl."

Eden smiled. "None of this would have mattered without Nathaniel."

"I know that," said Vulcan. "Nathaniel, we have many reasons to be grateful to you. You, a Jones, were the only possible solution to the final two Tasks. What was impossible for a smith was possible, but only for a Jones."

Nathaniel blushed even deeper. "Eden's the one who figured it out."

Nellie dabbed her eyes with her lace handkerchief. "We are slow learners, and I am the slowest of all. But I hate to think how this all would have ended without the help of so many Joneses. We are not just grateful to you. We are dependent on you. I hope that someday, we can find a way to make things right."

"I know one thing you could do," said Eden. "Make Eugene a smith."

"Geno? Why would he want it?" said Vulcan. "Nothing but trouble. A bunch of rules you have to follow. And access to a dining room you don't want to go to."

Eugene shrugged. "I'd kinda like to go to the dining room. Or at least, I'd like to *choose* not to go."

"Then we'll do it," said Vulcan. "I'll bring you tomorrow night myself. Eugene Tinker, you'll be my guest to Supperdinner Hall. Nathaniel? Wanna come? As an apprentice, Supperdinner Hall is open to you, too."

"Of course I want to come!" said Nathaniel. "I've been washing those pots and pans my whole life! Now I'll finally get a meal cooked in them!"

"Then it's a plan," said Vulcan. "And if it breaks a rule, who cares? I'm not gonna follow another stupid rule for the rest of my life!"

"Grandpa!" said Eden. "Ignoring rules is what got you into this mess in the first place."

Vulcan smiled "Who cares? What can they do to us now? We've solved the Five. We're not going anywhere. Together, we're the greatest smiths who've ever lived."

"And an above-average Jones," said Irma. "Now then, someone pour something in my teacup. Because this calls for a celebration."

At the end of the night, Eden was preparing to leave for bed with the sisters. Vulcan stopped her. "Eden, after tonight, I should have space in my rooms for you, if you'd like to live with an old coot like me."

"I'd like to," Eden said.

"You would? I was afraid you might say no. I'd understand it if you did. I'm a bit of a grump."

"I've heard I'm kind of cheeky," said Eden.

"I guess it proves we're related," said Vulcan. "Hope you're okay living with a rat. Not me. I mean Willard. He'll be there, too."

Eden gave him a hug. He let her. She kept hugging until Vulcan said, "That's long enough. Get out of here and go to bed."

The next morning, Miss Clara arrived with breakfast on her tea trolley. Sitting on the trolley was the fifth tin can. Miss Clara handed it to Eden with a shrug. "This one seems a little late, Eden. But better late than never!"

Eden took the can and shook it. Nothing rattled inside. Eden set the can on one of the sisters' crowded shelves. The tin shone like silver.

Miss Clara leaned toward her. "You're not going to open it?"

"I kind of like having one in perfect condition," said Eden. "A nice memento, don't you agree?"

Miss Clara shook her trolley. "No, I don't agree. Open it. Please?"

Nellie pushed Clara out the door.

After breakfast, Eden went to see Vulcan in his new-old rooms on the third floor. She found him outside his door, standing toe-to-toe with Morgana Pewtersmith. "But I am settled in here!" shouted Morgana. "I just finished decorating! Why should I have to suffer because of some decision of the Council. Possession is nine-tenths of the law and I am in possession of these rooms. Besides, where will I go?"

"Go to blazes for all I care," said Vulcan. "Just get out."

It took a full company of Blue Coats to remove Morgana. Iona, with her white staff, walked at the front of the company. "Morgana Pewtersmith, until further arrangements can be made, you will be staying with your brother, Uriah Pewtersmith."

"Ohh, no," said Morgana. "Have you met him? He's not a nice man. I am not staying there. Show me what else you've got."

Iona showed Morgana Vulcan's room on Subbasement Seven. She moved in with her brother.

Vulcan, meanwhile, was informed that his rooms would be ready by bedtime.

That evening, Vulcan, Nellie, Irma, Eden, and Nathaniel stood next to Eugene, just outside of Supperdinner Hall. Eden was wearing another new dress, along with her eye patch and her silver bracelet and necklace.

Vulcan shook his head. "Geno, I'm still not sure why you want to go in there. Bunch of stuffy old people sitting around, eating the same food you can get in the privacy of your own room."

Eugene shrugged, then ran his calloused hand over his hair. "How do I look?"

"You look very handsome, dear," said Nellie. "I have always thought so. Now then, take my arm. Irma, get on his other side. We shall make this a procession."

That's how they went in: Vulcan, Eden, and Nathaniel took the lead, arm in arm. Eugene, with the sisters holding onto his elbows, followed. They marched across Supperdinner Hall to the sisters' regular table, with all eyes on them.

"Smells good in here," said Eugene. "Too bad I'm trying to watch my weight."

"Chicken noodle tonight," said Irma. "My favorite."

While they were sitting down, a voice said, "Mind if I join you?" They turned to see Mrs. Gunsmith standing behind them. Vulcan gulped, then made room at the table. Mrs. Gunsmith sat down next to him, saying that she refused to sit with her husband until he apologized to Eden and Nathaniel for kidnapping them. "Besides," she said, "it's not every day a simple woman like me has the opportunity to break bread with the greatest of all smiths."

"Who's that?" said Vulcan.

"She means you, Grandpa," said Eden.

Vulcan blushed. "Dear lady. A woman of your charm and talent is always welcome here."

Nellie shook her head. "Oh, good grief. Mrs. Gunsmith, I'll make sure your husband apologizes soon, for the sake of all of us."

"There is no hurry," said Mrs. Gunsmith. "Both he and I would benefit from a temporary change in company. I am tired of his nonsense. And I am tired of guns. I just want to make my beauty cream. I'd rather make people more beautiful than make people more fearful. By the way, did you hear what our Mr. Pewtersmith is bragging about these days? Recycling. He says it's high time this Guildhall becomes better at reuse. He said that he will start it himself, by reclaiming old pewter."

"That is the first decent idea that old weasel has had in years," said Nellie. "What precisely is he suggesting?"

"Dishes," Mrs. Gunsmith said. "He said that there's enough old pewter in there for each of us to make our daily dish for the next hundred years."

Vulcan dropped his fork. "Has he—has he gone in there yet?"

"I don't believe so," said Mrs. Gunsmith. "You know how Uriah is. He likes to talk a great deal before he actually does anything. I believe he said he planned to start tomorrow. Why?"

"Oh, no reason," said Vulcan. "It's just that I've already put Dishes to use. Nathaniel and I are storing some things in there."

"Nathaniel and you? What kind of things?" said Mrs. Gunsmith.

"Just a few thousand rats." Vulcan squinted. "Nathaniel feeds them when he drops off the daily dishes."

"That's where you put them?" asked Eden. "That's what you were sworn to secrecy about?"

"They're so cute," said Nathaniel with a giggle, "but I think they've been multiplying."

Vulcan squinted. "I wonder if I should warn Pewtersmith."

Robert Blacksmith rose to his feet at the center table. He lifted his pewter dish and his spoon. But instead of pinging the dish, he laughed. "The daily dish can go to blazes. Let's eat." A cheer rose from every table.

At the end of the meal, while vanilla pudding was being served for dessert, a Blue Coat approached Eden's chair. "A special delivery for you from Kitchens," said the Blue Coat. She set a chocolate cake on the table. "Lillian said to mention that she made it herself. Chocolate cake with chocolate frosting. She thought it might be your favorite." Eden smiled with delight as she thanked the Blue Coat, then cut the cake and passed slices around the table.

While Eden was eating her second slice of cake, Robert Blacksmith came over and knelt by her. She thanked him again for his help. He said, "I'm not here for thanks. I want to know if you've solved the riddle I gave you, when you were my apprentice."

"I'm afraid I've forgotten it," said Eden. "What was it again?"

Robert frowned. "Forgotten it? How could anyone forget one of my riddles?"

"Sorry," said Eden. "We had a lot of other things to think about."

"Well, I suppose that's true. Very well. I'll say it again." Robert cleared his throat and said, "'Iron is strong. Steel is stronger. The blacksmith can overcome steel. But what is mightier than the blacksmith?'"

The answer popped into Eden's head immediately. She knew how she'd solved the Tasks. She hadn't done it alone. She'd done it with the strength and wisdom of her ancestors—the long line of Smiths reaching out to her from the distant past, through her grandfather, through her mom and dad, and straight into her own blood and bones. Then she thought of Eugene, Nellie and Irma, and a faint image of Nathaniel with his hair sticking up every which way. Eden smiled. She knew the answer to the riddle. "I can't think of much of anything stronger than you, Robert. Except maybe family."

Robert laughed so loudly he shook the dishes. "You are both lucky and wise, Eden Smith. A rare combination."

After dinner, Iona escorted the six of them to Vulcan's old rooms. "We have succeeded in getting Morgana Pewtersmith completely moved out. Therefore, we have moved all of your belongings up from Subbasement Seven, Room K-Minus-One." She opened the door.

The rooms still had thick carpet underfoot and burnished bronze panels on the walls. The guest chair Vulcan had built in Sub-basement Seven sat in the middle. On the seat of the chair lay Willard. He snored gently. Otherwise, the rooms were bare.

"Where are my tools?" said Vulcan. "Where's my good hammer? Where are my books? Where's all my sainted stuff?"

When Iona explained that Morgana had thrown away all of Vulcan's things, he exploded in a long string of curses, while he marched back and forth in his rooms. "Those Pewtersmiths! What have they done to me? Years! Decades! It took me a lifetime to accumulate those things! Saint Dunstan!"

"Dearie, let's leave him be for a while," said Nellie. She used her cane to shepherd Eden away from Vulcan's door. "He'll need some time to stomp around, until he remembers how lucky he is just to be here. Don't worry. His rooms are quite nice and he has plenty of space for you. But Eden, dearie, dearest girl, are you sure you want to live with that old rascal?"

"I'm sure," said Eden. "I'm going to miss living with you both, but he is my grandfather."

Nellie nodded, then pulled a handkerchief from her sleeve and dabbed her eyes. "Of course you're right, dearie. It's just that we'll miss you so. But you'll certainly be a good influence on him."

"And he'll be a horrible influence on you," said Irma, sipping from her teacup. "That's what family is for."

"Now, Eden, let's go back to our rooms for one last time. If we hurry, we might be able to catch Miss Clara for a late-night snack and get some of those delightful cucumber sandwiches."

"I'll catch up to you," said Eden. "I'm just going to say goodnight to Nathaniel."

The sisters tottered off while Eden and Nathaniel rode with Buzz down to the first floor.

"I can't believe it's all over," said Nathaniel, as they stepped off the elevator into Humble Gallery. "And I can't believe we actually survived."

"I know," said Eden. She looked around the room, with its huge silver chandelier, massive staircase, and intricate mosaics. She remembered the first time she had stepped into Humble Gallery. It was hard to believe so much had happened since then. It was hard to believe she was almost forced to leave it forever. "Now I guess we just go back to ordinary life. Come to think of it, I've never really experienced ordinary life in the Guildhall. I guess it starts tomorrow. Hey, I wonder what master smith they'll put us with next."

Nathaniel squirmed. "Umm, I won't be joining you, Eden. I've made my decision. I've chosen to become a tinsmith."

"A tinsmith! I knew it. Congratulations. Fred will be lucky to teach you."

"I didn't mean to abandon you," said Nathaniel, "and I should have told you sooner. But what about you? You need to make your decision, too. What are you going to choose?"

Eden's stomach turned. "I have no idea. How am I supposed to decide?" She smiled at Nathaniel. "If I decide right now, will you take me to the Jones floors?"

"No! And you need to stop asking. What if someone heard you?"

"Someday, Nathaniel. Someday, I'm going to go to every single part of this Guildhall. And you're going to go with me."

Nathaniel gulped as he stepped into the stairwell. "That's what I'm afraid of, Eden Smith. Goodnight."

Eden followed Nathaniel into the stairwell, but went up instead of down. When she had settled onto the couches with the sisters, sandwiches in hand, Nellie said, "Eden, now that all this commotion has ended, you have a decision to make. Have you chosen the type of smith you want to be?"

"Nathaniel just asked me the same thing. Do I have to choose tonight?" Eden picked a silver spoon off the low table. Nellie watched the spoon suspiciously. "I want to work with both of you," said Eden, "but I also want to work with Grandpa."

"It is decision time, dearie," said Nellie.

"But Grandpa didn't choose. He's a master of all the types of smiths."

"He is," said Nellie, "and a master machinist, too."

"I still haven't spent time with the machinists," said Eden. "They kind of scare me, but I'd still like to do it. Because some day, I want to play bingo."

"You will, Eden. I'm almost certain of it. Your grandfather did the same. But before becoming a machinist, he had to be a regular smith. So he still had to choose. At the beginning, he had to choose."

"I didn't know that," said Eden, bending the handle of the spoon she was holding. "What was he? At the beginning, I mean?"

"Why, a silversmith, of course," said Nellie. "That's why we are such fast friends. We came up together, as apprentices."

Eden smiled. "I didn't know that, either. Then silversmith it is." She straightened the silver spoon and set it down on the table.

Nellie nodded. "An excellent choice, dearie. Right after breakfast, you shall begin your official apprenticeship as a silversmith—with us!" She ate the last bite of her cucumber sandwich and dabbed the corners of her mouth with a napkin. "Now then, that's quite enough for tonight. Time for bed, I think. Don't you agree, sister?"

"Of course I do, sister." Irma drained her teacup. "No matter the time of day, I'm always ready for a lie-down, that's what I always say. Sweet dreams, Eden dear."

"Sweet dreams, Aunties."

Eden was wide awake, so she sat on the edge of her bed. She kissed the tip of her finger and pressed it onto the faces of her mother and father, in the photograph by her bedside table. "G'night, you two," she said.

She checked on the orchid next to the photograph. At first, it looked like nothing more than the same broken stick in its pot of dirt. Then she noticed a tiny green bulge, halfway up the stem. Could it be a bud? It was hard to tell for sure, but she thought it just might be.

She stared around the room at the silver decorations on the walls. In the morning, her new apprenticeship would begin. Her thoughts ran to hammers, to tongs, and to fire. There was still so much to learn, so much to do.

She sat there for a long time.

Just smiling.